W9-ACV-905

"The best Canadian book I've read this year is Guy Vanderhaeghe's *The Last Crossing*. . . . If 'excellence' means anything, this novel is excellent." — Martin Levin, *Globe and Mail*

"A feast of a book. . . . Guy Vanderhaeghe, one of North America's best writers, is at the top of his form." — Annie Proulx, *Globe and Mail*

"A tour de force. Wonderfully written, suspenseful and totally absorbing. . . . This book is a remarkable achievement, a page-turner not only of epic proportions but of exceptional literary merit." — *London Free Press*

"An absolutely wonderful book. . . . It is a joy to read, to go through this wild world with a writer who has fully stretched out over a landscape big enough to accommodate his stride." — *National Post*

"*The Last Crossing*'s epic sweep, historical scope, unforgettable characters, thematic complexity, compelling narrative and mythic underpinnings make it a hugely satisfying read. It is a novel of staggering literary achievement and immense emotional power that brings Canadian history to life." — Kitchener-Waterloo *Record*

"*The Last Crossing* is truly Vanderhaeghe's masterpiece. . . . His ability to hold in his imagination all of these characters and all of this vast narrative with its complexity of tensions and intensity of meaning, is testament to the creative genius of this writer and his passionate commitment to his craft." — *Books in Canada*

"An enormously rich and complex work, spanning time and place. It is an amazingly good story, and it both creates and satisfies a profound emotional need in readers. Thank you, Guy Vanderhaeghe." — *Edmonton Journal*

"There's no putting the book down. . . . Masterful." — Montreal *Gazette*

BOOKS BY GUY VANDERHAEGHE

FICTION
Man Descending (1982)
The Trouble With Heroes (1983)
My Present Age (1984)
Homesick (1989)
Things As They Are (1992)
The Englishman's Boy (1996)
The Last Crossing (2002)
A Good Man (2011)

PLAYS
I Had a Job I Liked. Once. (1991)
Dancock's Dance (1995)

GUY VANDERHAEGHE

THE

LAST

CROSSING

EMBLEM
McClelland & Stewart

Cloth edition published in 2002
First Emblem edition published in 2003
This Emblem edition published in 2012

Emblem is an imprint of McClelland & Stewart Ltd.
Emblem and colophon are registered trademarks of McClelland & Stewart Ltd.

Library and Archives Canada Cataloguing in Publication

Vanderhaeghe, Guy, 1951-
The last crossing / Guy Vanderhaeghe.

ISBN 978-0-7710-8784-4

I. Title.

PS8593.A5386L38 2012   C813'.54   C2011-907969-0

We acknowledge the financial support of the Government of Canada through the
Canada Book Fund and that of the Government of Ontario through the Ontario
Media Development Corporation's Ontario Book Initiative. We further acknowledge
the support of the Canada Council for the Arts and the Ontario Arts Council for
our publishing program.

Jerry Potts was a real historical figure. Some of the incidents in the novel are based on
actual events and people in his life. Other events and characters are entirely fictitious.

Typeset in Sabon
Printed and bound in Canada

McClelland & Stewart Ltd.
75 Sherbourne Street
Toronto, Ontario
M5A 2P9
www.mcclelland.com

1   2   3   4   5   16   15   14   13   12

This book is dedicated to all those local historians who keep the particulars of our past alive.

1

CHARLES GAUNT I let myself into the house, stand looking up the stairs, turn, go into the study, pour a whisky and soda. Today's mail is waiting, envelopes on a salver. My man, Harding, has laid a fire, but I don't trouble to light it. I leave my ulster on, stand sipping from the tumbler with a gloved hand, staring at the day's letters.

I know what they are. Invitations. Invitations for a weekend in the country. Invitations to dine. More invitations than I am accustomed to receiving. Now people court me. Queer old Charlie Gaunt has become a minor, middle-aged bachelor celebrity. Even Richards and Merton, long-time acquaintances with whom I dined tonight in the Athenaeum, did not allow my new eminence to pass unremarked. For years, I was never anyone's first choice as a portrait painter, never admitted as a full member of the Royal Academy, only very lately handed the privilege of sporting the initials A.R.A. after my name. Merely an *Associate*. Tardy laurels finally pressed upon an indifferent brow.

The highest praise ever bestowed by my fellow artists was to say I ought to have been a history painter, my rendering of marble in oil paint was as exquisite as Alma-Tadema's. Cosgrave, with a picture dealer's disdain for the truth, once described me to a dewlapped matron as a "court painter." By that he meant I had doodled up a portrait of a demented claimant to the throne of Spain (of which there are legion), a sallow-complexioned fellow who sat in my studio morosely munching walnuts and strewing the floor with their shells. I cannot recall his name, only that he wore a wig, but never the same wig twice. This led to an indistinct element to the portrayal of His Catholic Majesty's coiffure which mightily displeased him.

But now, the mountain comes to Mohammed. Artistic success won in an unexpected quarter. The dry old stick Charlie Gaunt publishes a volume of verse. Love poems, no less. For months, much of London society has been mildly engrossed in tea-time speculation about the identity of the lady of whom I wrote. A small assist to sales. Of course, it didn't hurt that the *Times* was laudatory and the *Edinburgh Review* kind in a niggling, parsimonious Scottish way.

Yesterday, I ran into Machar, the Glasgow refugee, outside Piccadilly Station. He was arch, and I was short with him.

"We hadn't guessed, Gaunt," he cooed. "I mean the book – that's a side of you we hadn't suspected."

I challenged him. "You've read it, have you?"

"Haven't had time to read it yet. But I bought it."

He was lying. If he had it at all, it was borrowed from a lending library. "Well," I said, brandishing my stick to hail a passing cab, "then you don't know what you're talking about, do you, Machar?" I showed him my coattails, spun off without another word.

One of the envelopes on the tray attracts my eye, addressed by an unfamiliar hand and bearing a Canadian stamp. Inside, I discover a newspaper clipping already a month old.

The Macleod Gazette   July 17, 1896

JERRY POTTS DEAD

AN HISTORICAL LANDMARK GONE

Jerry Potts is dead. Through the whole North West, in many parts of eastern Canada, and in England itself, this announcement will excite sorrow, in many cases sympathy, and in all, interest. Jerry was a type, and a type that is fast disappearing. A half-breed, with all that name implies, he had the proud distinction of being a very potent factor in the discovery (if it might be so called) and settlement of the western part of the North West Territories. When Colonels French and Macleod left their worried, and almost helpless column at Sweet Grass in '74, after a march of 900 miles and a vain search for the much vaunted "Whoop-Up" it was the veriative accident of fortune that in Benton they found Jerry Potts . . .

My eyes skim the remainder of the obituary, settle on the last paragraph.

Jerry Potts is dead, but his name lives, and will live. His memory will long be green in the hearts of those who knew him best, and "faithful and true" is the character he leaves behind him – the best monument of a valuable life.

The indestructible Potts dead. The news excites a pang of melancholy despite the fact that I have not laid eyes on him for a quarter-century. Yes, faithful and true he certainly was. And now, apparently famous too, after a fashion. Jerry Potts, how unlikely a candidate for renown.

Wondering who could have sent me such a notice, I peek into the envelope and dislodge a small piece of notepaper, a few words scrawled on it in pencil. *There is something you must know. I can only tell it to you in person. I beg you to come soon. Signed, Custis Straw.*

The shock of the name turns me to the window. In the square below, street lamps are shedding an eerie jade light which trembles in the weft of the fog.

It seems I am asked to perform at another's bidding, just as I did more than two decades ago when my father set my feet on the *Pasha*, 1,790 tons of iron steamship breaching the Irish Sea, bound for New York.

Twilight, the ship trailing scarves of mist, the air wet on my face. Standing at the stern, damp railing gripped in my gloves, sniffing the fishy salt of the ocean, gazing back to the blurred lights of the river traffic plying the mouth of the Mersey.

The land slowly vanishing from sight, retiring at ten knots per hour, as the screw boiled water and I stood, one hand clamped to my top hat to hold it in place, and peered down. Alone. The other passengers had gone to dress for dinner. The propeller frothed the water, beat it white, the ship's wake a metalled road pointing back to England. The breeze freshened, the skirts of my frock coat fluttered. Sailors cried out, preparing to raise auxiliary sail. Chop clapped the sides of the vessel, pale veins of turbulence in the dark granite sea. A first glimpse of stars, their salmon-pink coronas.

Deferential footsteps behind me, a smiling steward had come to announce dinner was served. I shook my head, "Thank you, I shall not dine tonight." The puzzled steward's face. Thirty guineas passage, meals, wine included, and the gentleman does not wish to dine tonight?

Not when I preferred to gaze upon what I was leaving, to recall those figures in the Ford Madox Brown painting, *The Last of England*. A young couple in the stern of a boat, holding hands, faces sombre, the white cliffs of Dover sentimental in the distance, the ties of the woman's bonnet whipping in the wind. A lady flying from England just as Simon, my twin brother, had fled it.

Beneath my feet, the deck of the *Pasha* lurched, grew more and more tipsy with every minute that passed. Yet that unsteadiness was nothing to how unbalanced I feel now, staring down into Grosvenor Square, wondering what has prompted Custis Straw's blunt and peremptory summons, what it means.

2

Out of the black inkwell of the night sky, incongruously, a white flood poured. Fat flakes of lazy snow eddying, sticking like wet feathers to whatever they touched. Simon Gaunt, waking with a start, discovered himself seated on an inert horse, becalmed in a storm. For the briefest of moments, mind a blur of white, he searched for a name. Seized it. "Reverend Witherspoon!" he shouted. "Reverend!"

Nothing answered, nothing moved except for the palsied snow.

Since dawn, Witherspoon had been driving them to the brink of collapse. In London, Simon Gaunt had not recognized the danger of that side of Witherspoon, the reliance on iron rules. Cited like Holy Scripture. *When journeying one must never halt until wood and shelter are obtained.*

But here, on a barren tabletop plain, wood and shelter were a figment of the imagination.

Press on, my boy.

As the October dusk drew down, Simon had argued desperately for making camp. But Witherspoon would not hear of it; the imposing face that ecstatic love could render soft as soap in London was now cast as hard as an Old Testament prophet's certainty. *We shall not yield to adversity.*

So on they went, deeper and deeper into bewildering nightfall, Witherspoon flogging his mare until he opened a safe ten yards, a cordon sanitaire between himself and the weak-kneed naysayer. Ten yards to symbolize the moral gulf separating master and disciple.

The last thing Simon could remember before falling asleep was the Reverend's broad shoulders rocking side to side like a wagging forefinger, reproving his feebleness, admonishing his sloth.

How long had he slept?

"Reverend Witherspoon! Reverend Witherspoon!" The snow drowned his cry. Knowingly or unknowingly, Witherspoon had ridden on and Simon was alone. A cold clinker of fear settled in the grate of his belly. Lost. He lashed his horse into a trot; the gelding submitted for a hundred reluctant yards, then faltered, came to a complete standstill.

How dreadfully cold it was. A breeze sprang to sudden life and his cheeks, wet with melting snow, stiffened at the icy touch. The wind panted, flakes swirled, thickened. Twisting in his saddle, Simon strained for a glimpse of Witherspoon hastening to gather the lost lamb, some darker blot in the darkness of night. The blizzard was strengthening, slapping at horse and rider; he could feel the gelding's mane fluttering against his hands clamped to the reins.

Bouncing his heels on the gelding's ribs, he urged it to resume an unwilling shamble. The gusts were growing fiercer, snow was biting at his face like flying sand. He ducked his head and watched the drifts unroll beneath him, a white scroll of vellum, luminous in the dim light.

The scroll stopped. His hat sailed off. Dismounting, Simon rifled the saddlebag, found his old Oxford scarf, bandaged his burning ears with it, knotted it under his chin. Wind keened through the weave of the wool. Never had he known such cold; it drew heat out of the body like a leech draws blood. Forehead, eyes, cheeks ached from the frigid, sucking mouth.

Weariness overwhelmed him, dropped his forehead heavily against the horse's flank. He let it rest there. Just a minute. Only a minute. Then he would move. Go on. The gelding's rump was crusted with ice and snow, so was Simon's beard. Raking his fingers through it, he plucked away clots of ice, trying to pray. "Lord God of Hosts," he began, but his thoughts were lost in the roar of the storm, brain nothing but a puddle of numb slush. Falling back on memory, he recited from the Book of Common Prayer. " 'O most glorious and gracious Lord God, who dwellest in heaven, but beholdest all things below,' " he mumbled. " 'Look down, we beseech thee, and hear us, calling out of the depth of misery, and out of the jaws of this death, which is now ready to swallow us up: Save, Lord, or else we perish. The living, the living shall praise thee. O send thy word of command to rebuke the raging winds and the roaring . . .' " His voice ebbed away.

It was no good. He dove back into the saddlebag, fingers turned to pincers by the cold, and grappled a tin, pried away the top. The wind caught the lid, tore it from his hand, kited it off into the howling night. He patted, crooned and clucked, feeding the exhausted horse his shortbread, trying to kindle in it a little strength to continue on.

The gelding shied when he tried to remount. Somehow Simon snagged the stirrup with his boot and clambered aboard, weeping when the horse once more stubbornly stalled, beating its neck with a fist. But then it swung its head, put the wind to their backs, moved off hesitantly. With the blizzard whipping its hindquarters, the gelding broke into a lope, then a wild staggering gallop, heaving like a storm-driven ship. Simon tasted long white streaks of snow, smears on the chalkboard of night, as his brain jerked from spot to spot on his body, probing. Face dead, a slab of wood. Fingers dead. Twigs.

Latimer, bound to the stake, had said to the chained and sobbing Nicholas Ridley beside him, "Play the man, master Ridley; we shall this day light such a candle, by God's grace, in England, as I trust shall never be put out."

He would have welcomed to burn like Latimer now.

The horse gave a grunt, stumbled, fell in slow, dreamy increments. Simon became a boy again. His father had bought him a ticket at the London zoo for a ride on the camel. The dromedary was lowering itself to earth, in stages, a complicated, groaning piece of machinery, settling to its knees, sinking.

Pitched headlong, Simon lay in a pillow of snow, listening to Ridley screaming in the flames.

No, not Ridley screaming, the horse. He staggered to the fallen gelding. It was trying to rise on three legs, the fourth was horribly

7

broken. Lurching up and falling back, lurching up and falling back. Simon caught the head stall, pulled the beast down and squatted on its neck, bringing to an end the terrible struggle. The horse stared up at him. Its eye a coal-yoked egg.

He placed his hand over the eye. His brother Addington had smashed a lot of hunters' legs. Addington, merciless rider. Long ago, a boy of ten, he'd seen one of the victims of Addington's recklessness destroyed. The gamekeeper delivered the coup de grâce while Addington and his fox-hunting friends drank whisky in the house. The callous cruelty of it had made him sob miserably, displeasing his father. "Buck up," Father had commanded him.

Left hand blinkering the eye of the horse, Simon reached for the knife sheathed on his belt. Less a knife than a small, bone-handled sword bought in Fort Benton, a bowie knife the Americans called it.

He told himself, "The Holy Ghost reads hearts."

When he sliced the throat, a tremor ran down the horse's neck, hot blood scalded his hand. The weary horse did not take long to die.

Whimpering, Simon huddled against its belly, cringing from the wind. His hands were alive with needles of agony; when he slipped them down the front of his pants to warm them, he felt the gluey blood on his privates.

There was a hymn – it skipped about his brain before he heard himself singing. " 'How mighty is the Blood that ran for sinful nature's needs! It broke the ban, it rescued man; it lives, and speaks, and pleads!' " Blood running for sinful nature's needs. Living, speaking, pleading. To rescue man.

Simon scrambled to his knees, knife upraised. Drove the sixteen-inch blade into the horse's chest, sawed the belly down to the legs. Guts spilling, a thin steam sifting out of the lips of the incision. Plunged his hands into the mess of entrails. Tore away, scooping offal behind him, hacking with the knife at whatever resisted, whatever clung. Moaning, hunching his shoulders, drawing his knees up to his chest, wriggling away at the mouth of the wound, he burrowed into the balmy pocket.

O precious Side-hole's cavity
I want to spend my life in thee . . .
There in one Side-hole's joy divine,
I'll spend all future Days of mine.
Yes, yes, I will for ever sit
There, where Thy Side was split.

Safe in the slick, rich animal heat, out of the cruel wind. Not all of him, but enough. An embryo, curled in the belly of the dead horse.

The little bells sewn to the hem of Talks Different's caped buffalo robe jingled crisply as she strode along, towing an old buffalo bull hide piled with sticks rooted out of a coulee bottom. The sharp cold that had greeted her at dawn was lifting; Sun was climbing higher and higher, softening the snow, making it stick to the parfleche soles of her moccasins.

The passing of last night's blizzard had left the air perfectly still. Talks Different sweated in her robe, eyes squinted against Sun's dazzling dance on the white plain. All at once, she stopped and stared. Off in the distance, something was moving, most likely a prairie wolf gorging on a kill. She gave a tug to the hide-tail, briskly covered another hundred yards, but still could not give a name to what it was she saw. Something crouched above a carcass, something forbidding and black. The bells of her robe pealed a thin warning, but the creature did not run from the ringing like a coyote or wolf would. And it was too small to be a grizzly.

The glaring light stabbed thorns in her eyes; they streamed with tears. What she was straining to see could not be a vision, visions were given freely to her. This seemed to be a thing of the earth, but very strange. She hurried on.

Now she could recognize the body of a horse, one hoofed leg jutting up. But the black thing that had moved before now stayed absolutely still, wrapped up in a ball. She called out to it, identifying

9

herself as a holy being, asking it if it were a holy being too. At the sound of her voice, it stirred, twitched.

Talks Different was not afraid to meet anything strange because she had been made an unusual being herself, a *bote* granted the blessing of Two Spirit. Confident in her sacred power she came forward, ready to face whatever waited there.

Slowly, unsteadily, it rose up on its hind legs and became a Hairy Face dressed in black pants and black coat. He said nothing. His clothes, his hands, the hair of his head, even his beard, downy as a fledgling duck, were smeared with dried blood.

Now he worked his lips, trying to make words, but nothing came from his mouth except the sounds of a baby wanting to nurse. He took a step and his legs gave way, dropping him on his bottom like a toddler. And like such a child, he stretched out his arms to Talks Different, begging to be picked up, carried and comforted.

3

In the spring of 1871, Henry Gaunt stood at a window looking down on the splendid grounds of his country estate, Sythe Grange. Earlier that morning, his son Addington had conducted preparations for the day with his customary military exactitude. Now they had the gift of a lovely afternoon, a few mares' tails whisking a soft-blue sky, bright-green turf spread like billiard-table cloth. Red-and-white-striped marquees were wrinkling in a gentle breeze while, in the tidal shade cast by the flopping canvas, reefs of children clamoured for ginger beer and lemonade as their elders sampled claret cup and champagne.

More guests were streaming in, the gravel of the long, sweeping drive crunching under the wheels of a procession of traps, dogcarts, and carriages conveying his neighbours to the Annual Meeting of the Society of Toxophilites. Their host knew he ought to go down, ought to greet them, but found he couldn't bring himself to.

Was he losing his grip? Grip was what had always distinguished him from other men of business. Unscrupulous was what they had called him – those crabbed, anxious, whining clerks; the idle rich and their pettifogging lawyers.

No one had ever given him a hand over the stile, he had clambered over himself. No advantages. His father nothing more than a mid-dling builder of gimcrack little houses and stucco villas. But after Father had gone to his reward, Henry Gaunt seized his chance, knew what would be the going thing. Railways. Contracting work at first.

Using profits from contracting to build and operate his own railways. Short lines at the start, but ones that paid handsomely. Nothing grandiose like the Enfield and Edmonton Railway, three miles of track and at the end of it a station house like a maharaja's palace, pounds poured into the restoration of a Stuart house by fools. A dream of grandeur resulting in bankruptcy.

He had always been one step ahead of the competition. When Railway Mania struck, the greedy had all come to him wheedling for advice, those stupid men of property, the proud county grandees, gentlemen who looked down on Henry Gaunt because he had no Latin and Greek, and them not able to reckon the simplest sum on the back of an envelope. All burning with speculation fever, falling over themselves to buy railway shares, licking their lips at the promise of premiums of two thousand per cent. October of 1845 and three hundred and fifty-seven new railway schemes announced in the press, three hundred and thirty-two million pounds of shares subscribed to. But he had been able to tell fool's gold from the real article. Indeed he had.

Rats swimming to scramble up on the sinking ship. He had sold all his leaky vessels, saved a few solid timbers to keep him afloat while the speculators drowned. Land doesn't sink, not with farm labour bought at nine shillings a week. This estate bought cheap by any reckoning, four thousand acres, the fine house he stood in. Put the bulk of his capital in British Consols, kept his famous grip still clamped tight on the railways that could make a return on traffic and didn't need to depend on an artificial rise in share prices. George Hudson, the Railway King, who had had the Queen and Prince Albert to dine, had gone to the bottom like a stone while Henry Gaunt bobbed about merrily, light as a cork as the typhoon raged.

He smiled to himself. No gainsaying who had been the man of the hour then. It was he, not Hudson, who got the special invitation to the Great Exhibition of 1851, a tour of the facilities in the Prince Consort's party. His hand shaken by the Queen's husband. The fingers Prince Albert had favoured with his royal touch abruptly doubled into a fist. Seventy-five, but he still had the handshake of a navvy.

The Crystal Palace. What a glory of glass. There was engineering for you, a palace of iron and shimmer. The glass fountain too. Twenty-seven-foot high of the most cunning work, water gushing from three tiers of basins, the whole edifice clothed in glimmering, liquid raiment. Shining glass and shining water.

But none of it a match for the delight of taking his supper in Soyer's Symposium. The most extraordinary of restaurants, each dining room designed, decorated, and furnished so that it mirrored some exotic portion of the globe. His favourite was Polar Latitudes.

What a strange feeling it had evoked in him, the painted iceberg of vast extent looming above him all bluey white, the infinite plain of eternal snow, the polar bear shambling off the wall towards him. The titillation of threatening, jagged cakes of ice, of blinding sky, of a menacing predator. Why, it had been the living heart of another world. Polar Latitudes had entered into him, and he into it. The worries of business, the clatter of plates and knives, the penetrating smells of roast beef, pudding, all simply evaporated in a flash.

Nothing but Henry Gaunt alone in a snowy waste. He wanted to seize that feeling again, or be seized by it, to stand in the midst of a world that bore no reference to him, a world so strange it banished anxiety.

He turned away from the window, crossed to the rosewood table where port and a tray of biscuits rested, poured himself a glass, snatched a biscuit, and began to circle the room in a panicky shuffle. Around and around he went, gnawing and slurping, leaving a trail of biscuit crumbs, raining drops of port on the parquet floor.

Oh God, he thought, what was happening to him? Who was there for him to lean on? Certainly not his sons. Charles had departed England on March 27. As yet, no letters had arrived from Fort Benton to explain the steps he had taken to learn of his brother's possible whereabouts. Charles would blame the tardiness of the American post. Dodgy fellow, that Charles.

The twins, Charles and Simon, had always been so close, so loving that he had expected Charles to show more fire in this matter.

But then Charles had never had any push, any go to him. All he was interested in was splashing about in his paint puddles. He should never have indulged him at such an early age in his artist nonsense. As the sapling is bent, so shall it grow. Besides, that Italian drawing master had cost him a packet and what had been his thanks for it? It was Simon, not Charles, who had warmly expressed gratitude to his father. Kissed his cheek. Charles, on the other hand, was a chilly chap, standoffish even as a boy. Too old for his years. How could twins treat their father so differently? Simon so affectionate, Charles so distant.

What a fool to agree to let Addington stay behind to mind the business of supplying the expedition while Charles went ahead to prepare a "base camp," to "scout the terrain." Army jabber. Several days in London would have been sufficient for Addington to carry out his task. But on and on it dragged, Addington reporting he'd had to ransack shops for gear, arguing that such an expedition succeeded or failed on its *matériel*. The man must be suffering from the delusion he was off to fight Napoleon. He was beginning to believe Addington had no hope of finding his younger brother, beginning to suspect that for Addington this venture in America was simply an opportunity to add to his trophies, his collection of animal skins and heads. In the end, he had had to bring him up short, order him home from London, and hand him his marching papers.

Had Addington and Charles no pity? Had they not seen his worry and longing for Simon? One disaster after another piling up on him. First, his darling boy's disappearance and then the attacks on his deer. Could his sons not fathom the concerns that weighed upon him?

Henry Gaunt's face purpled with rage. Poachers daring to lay hands on his deer! He'd lashed Walker with his tongue yesterday about that. Made it clear the poaching must be stopped at all costs. Load the guns with swan shot! he'd roared. Break out the mantraps! See to those poachers, do for them proper! The bloody cheek, killing his deer, selling his venison in London game shops!

His rage burned away and left him suddenly cold. Who or what was turning against him, now that he was old?

He was afraid. Lord, it left him choked and breathless. He had never been afraid before.

Since Simon had been lost last autumn, how he had yearned for a room like one of those in the Symposium, a room to help him forget, push back his fear. When he had hinted at what he wanted to Charles, Charles had remarked in that dry, infuriating way of his, "And what am I to paint, sir?"

What he had wanted to do was cry out, "Paint me a room into which my terror will not follow me! That is what I want!" But one could not say such a thing to Charles. Instead he had given him three choices of subject: The Siege of Sebastapol, Merry Old England, Ancient Rome. To ask him to paint the Arctic was impossible. The boy would never come up to the mark set by Polar Latitudes.

When he stood in the conservatory, gazing up at the ripening fruit, struggling to think of orchards in France where pears glowed in the sun – why then suddenly Simon's dear, gentle face peeped out at him from between the branches, the leaves, the dusky golden pears. Warm and smiling. Not dead, not frozen. That was all that he required, to know Simon was still alive.

Those early letters from Montana sent by the firm of I. G. Baker were mistaken. It was dreadful of them to say Simon was likely dead. What right had they to suggest such a thing?

❖ ❖ ❖

Addington was loitering in the vicinity of the marquees, seeking a chance to purloin a pair of gloves, a handkerchief, a reticule from the young misses gathered to take refreshment. He couldn't help himself pinching dainty articles, at balls, in the crowded porches of churches, in the first-class carriages of trains, wherever and whenever an opportunity presented itself. Last year during the Annual Meeting of the Toxophilites, amid the press of spectators, he had tugged Miss Crawford's cambric handkerchief out of her sleeve. But the spoor of the cologne that had clung to the cloth had grown so faint it was no longer any use to him.

It is curious, he thought, when he noticed the servant girl Alice passing, how very unsatisfactory coarse women are.

In the bustle of fetching the guests their drinks, Alice's hair had come unpinned and was straggling down her neck. Heat and busyness had daubed two hectic spots of red on her cheeks, working-class rouge.

Servant girls ought to be eager, but when he last rogered her, she lay like a drowned woman, pale and lifeless. And there was her smell. He was always catching faint whiffs of musty fustian, toasted herring. Still, no faulting her figure. And her soft, milky skin – all but the heels, yellow and rough with callouses. He hated the feel of them on the backs of his legs.

His mind shifted to the angelic Miss Venables, a more obliging thought. What a thrill it would be to possess some trifle of hers. Lounging about the refreshment tent had won him no plunder. Better to stalk new hunting grounds. Miss Venables's father, the portly vicar of Kingsmere St. George's Church, was hovering about in a badly cut black suit and preposterous shovel hat near the umpire of the ladies' archery competition. The father was never far from the daughter.

Just as Addington sauntered up, applause rippled through the crowd as a "gold" was scored. He ran a discriminating horse dealer's eye over the women. Most of the female toxophilites had selected conventional Lincoln green for their wardrobes. Green velvet jackets and long green skirts, soft leather quivers embroidered with leaves of green thread, green archers' hats adorned with the same grey goose feathers that fletched their arrows. All except for Miss Venables, whom he spied drawing her bow at the target. No Lincoln green for her. Amply bustled, waist looped with a large, rosetted pink ribbon that made an appealing contrast with the dove-grey lower skirt and the dark-blue bodice of her dress. What's more, the bold little minx had decorated her hat with an ostrich plume that swayed and drooped alarmingly. The plump, lustrous chignon riding the nape of her neck quivered with exasperation at this impediment to her marksmanship.

Addington glanced over to Papa noisily offering encouragement and advice to his pet. It was a mystery how the voluptuous, comely Miss

Venables could have been generated by the seedy divine. A most vexing individual, who was continually button-holing Addington for contributions to foreign missions, extending invitations to him to teach Sunday school, or to accompany the parson on visits to the sick and the deserving poor. What the insufferable fool took him for, Addington didn't know, unless he confused him with Simon, little, pecksniffing, pious ass.

A burst of cheering broke out as Miss Venables completed her round, Reverend Venables attempting to outdo everyone else, bawling like a lunatic, waving his shiny, dented hat in the air with crazed abandon. Miss Venables, mouth composed in a mysterious half-smile, paid her father not the slightest bit of attention.

Addington waited for the daughter to join her father before hazarding an approach. The Reverend pumped his hand enthusiastically. "See how all come to pay homage to the huntress Diana! How d'you do, my dear Gaunt! How d'you do!"

Addington bobbed his head curtly to Venables, bowed deeply to the daughter. "Miss Venables, I cannot say which exceeds the other – your beauty or your skill."

Miss Venables received the compliment by remarking, "To draw the comparison mocks the compliment, sir. Since I am such a poor hand with the bow."

Addington smoothed his moustache with his thumb. Miss Venables's polish was amazing. How she came by it, whetting her wit on her dull Papa, he couldn't guess. "On the contrary, Miss Venables –" he began.

The vicar broke in excitedly. "The hat, the hat," he said, tapping the crown of his own to illustrate his point. "I warned Ellie she ought to remove *le chapeau*. It interfered."

"I disagree entirely," said Addington coolly, readying to launch another salvo of compliments at the daughter. He got no further. Reverend Venables contorted his body into a grotesque pantomime of an archer, absurdly struck the brim of his shovel hat, knocking it to the grass. "You see! You see!" he crowed triumphantly, bending over to recover it, presenting them with his fat arse. "D'you take my meaning!"

Miss Venables serenely ignored her father and addressed Addington. "Mrs. Colefax has shot a round of five hundred and outdistanced the field."

"No, never outdistanced the field," murmured Addington.

Miss Venables might feign innocence, but she did not mistake a gentleman's tribute. The corners of her lips turned up in appreciation.

"Reverend Venables," said Addington, pointing to the claret cup clutched in the divine's hand, "you are empty. Won't you have another?" He gestured towards the marquees.

"Very good of you. Very good indeed," Venables mumbled, but stayed planted to the spot.

Mr. Barlow approached, a hearty, stout, middle-aged fellow. "A splendid meeting, Captain," he said. "Organized to satisfy in every way. What would the Society of Toxophilites do without the patronage of the Gaunt family? Everything first-rate, as usual."

"I am obliged to be of service," replied Addington.

Barlow turned to Miss Venables. "The rest of we poor chaps bend our bows in vain when the Captain competes."

Addington did not deign to reply. He was gazing off above Barlow's straw hat to the horizon where the heat of the day was drawing a finger of haze. There were deer emerging from it.

Barlow, who expected the Captain to exchange flattering comments on their respective prowess and so elevate him in Miss Venables's eyes, was forced to continue solo. "Captain Gaunt always gets the better of me," he said to her. "But all winter I studied Mr. Horace Alfred Ford's scientific treatise on archery in the hope it will give me a leg up."

Addington was still fixated on the progress of the deer. They were edging over the meadow, towards the house, moving cautiously, timorously. Walker, on Father's orders, must be up in the woods, stalking the deer out of the copses, where they were vulnerable to depredations by the poachers.

"Mr. Ford, Mr. Ford . . ." mused the vicar, searching for the significance of the name. Suddenly his face brightened alarmingly. "Yes, of course. Mr. Ford. He renounced the archery championship of England because of the nicety of his religious principles. Admirable fellow! And I seem to recall another sportsman who did likewise. The prizefighter who left the ring to preach Christ. Who was that chap? What was his name?"

Addington, a ring fanatic, could stand no more of this bumble and blather. "Bendigo," he said curtly.

"Bendigo, yes, Bendigo!" cried Venables. "There you have it! Two worldly champions become champions of Christ!"

"Like knights of old," Miss Venables murmured. During the past months she had been reading and rereading Tennyson's "The Last Tournament" in a back issue of her father's *Contemporary Review*. The dolorous music had got into her blood, investing it with a pleasurable melancholia as she contemplated the decay of high ideals and chivalry. Reading Sir Tristram's challenge to the other knights and finding that "so many of those / That ware their ladies' colours on the casque / Drew from before Sir Tristram to the bounds," Ellie Venables had fairly sickened with indignation at their pusillanimity. How would she feel if her champion, carrying her favour, chose to withdraw from the field? Fiendishly humiliated.

How delicious it was to wander in her father's garden, pretending the chill of early spring was really winter's onset. Mr. Tennyson's verses stirred her romantic depths. "And ever the wind blew, and yellowing leaf, / And gloom and gleam, and shower and shorn plume / Went down it." Wonderful.

"The knights of old," said Barlow, who liked to play iconoclast, "were apt to champion their own interests and pay precious little attention to anyone else's. Brigands they were, at heart." To emphasize his point, he went briskly up on his toes, once, twice, smirking at his own dash.

"Nonsense!" Miss Venables chided him. Mr. Barlow had spoiled her contemplation of Sir Tristram. On the cold field of his armour a hundred silver deer were engraved. The berries of a holly spray fastened to his helmet were as bright as drops of blood. Of course, she could not see his face. It was hidden by his visor.

Barlow hurried to correct himself. "My dear Miss Venables, my remark was not meant to give offence. I beg your forgiveness." It was well-known Miss Venables brooked no contradiction, not even from her father.

"Forgiven," she said sharply. Addington found her spirit, her indignation exciting. Especially when it was directed at Barlow. With a rosy flush climbing her throat, she said, "It may be silly of me to believe that in some distant time men wore their ladies' favours upon their sleeves, as a pledge of love and protection. But that, sir, is a belief in *ideals*."

Barlow was humbled, struck to the dust. "How right you are. How very right."

"Froissart?" chirped Reverend Venables. "Did you have in mind Froissart, Mr. Barlow? Knights and such. Froissart's *Chronicles* perhaps? Was that it, my good man?"

Addington lowered his eyes from the timid deer. "Miss Venables," he said, "would you do me the honour of allowing me to wear your colours in the contest?" Smiling persuasively, he gently drew the glove from her compliant fingers. "I would be honoured to sport your favour."

Slowly, as the glove slipped free from her grasp, Miss Venables saw Sir Tristram's visor lift, saw the bones of his face knit themselves into a shape.

Addington was gazing intently into her eyes, as intently as he had gazed at the deer.

4

The match crackled, stuttered fire, flared into life in the darkness of Addington Gaunt's bedroom. Addington groped his way to the dressing table, lit two candles resting there, and stared into their flames reflected in the glass, an unsteady brilliance that waxed and waned like the beating of a weakened heart. When wakened by his Dunvargan dream, he needed a fiery mirror in which to see his face. It was the only way to banish the grey horse from his mind. No matter how early the night-frights came, he never returned to bed, but remained alert and wakeful, a sentry at his post. It was well past midnight, the last of the guests having waved their goodbyes long ago.

At the beginning of it, the dream never diverged from what actually occurred that day in 1865 in the Irish town on the borders of Cork and Wexford. A troop of horse drawn up at one end of the narrow, cobbled street, a Fenian mob at the other.

His regiment, the 12th Royal Lancers, had been sent from Leeds to deal with discontent in Ireland, to put an end to years of outrage at the hands of dirty Irish potboys who flung stones at officers, intimidated magistrates into dismissals of charges or derisively lenient sentences. With the legal authorities so craven, regimental tempers had been on edge.

That afternoon in Dunvargan, he was determined to teach the rebels a lesson. So he held his troops steady in the face of a barrage of cobbles clattering down in the mean little street, allowed the rioters to creep closer and closer, emboldened them to howl and jeer. Bloody savages. On they came, their missiles falling nearer and nearer, the Lancers' mounts growing restive, tossing their heads, champing their bits, making the roadway ring with the stamp of iron-shod hooves.

Until this moment of testing, he had not understood how much he despised the Irish, their cowardice, their unmanliness. Starved, dark peasant gnomes who arrayed their women in front of them, a blowsy barricade behind which they felt safe to hurl stones and curses. Men cowering behind the skirts of red-faced bitches; it was enough to make you sick. See if it did them any good. He did not care a fig for a packet of skirts.

The Irish had drawn within range. Stones began to strike the ranks. A horse reared. Behind him, a man cried out in pain, tumbled from the saddle. He paid it no mind. What was required was coolness, and that he possessed in full measure. A few men done an injury would heat the blood of their fellow Lancers to pay the Irish skulkers back. Hold the men in check until they were seething, brimful of wrath.

"Steady, lads!" he called out, as the cobbles rained down around him. "Steady!" The Irish sluts were stooping to gather up the ammunition that had fallen short, cradling it in skirts and aprons, passing it back to their men.

Another soldier groaned, reeled in the saddle. Addington fastened a taunting smile to his face. Let the Irish bastards see him smile; they were close enough now. What did the trulls make of him? A fine figure of a man, tall, straight, well-knit, with a cavalryman's narrow hips, his long legs booted in soft leather. Let the muck hate him, hate his blue double-breasted tunic with scarlet lapels, hate the double gold stripe on his trousers, hate his lance cap with scarlet top and cock-feather plume. Hate him, because those below always hate the one above them, the man on the horse.

A bit of pale sun broke through the clouds and rinsed the Lancers with light. His sorrel quivered, anticipating the spurs. Addington caressed its neck, choked with instinct, with blind, passionate eagerness for the fight.

It was at this moment, with this caress, that his dream always departed from the reality of that day in Dunvargan. Because in Dunvargan he had torn his sabre from its scabbard, held it at the ready, and all about him had heard the men's answer, a slithering of steel unsheathed. Forward they went at a trot, then a canter, the narrow street beginning to fill with screams. Women scrambled away from sabres; shrieking, they stumbled under the hooves of horses. Mouths gaped terror, the hands of the men clutched shapeless hats tight to heads, the mob splintered like a rotten fence with the impact of maddened horses, bodies skittered across the street. Fingers clawed at his thighs, scrabbled at his boots. Standing in his stirrups, he wielded the bright blade, scythed uplifted hands, ducking heads.

Then he was clear of it, had chopped clean through the clinging rottenness of fetid breath and stinking clothes. His horse galloped crazily down the street, iron shoes clacking on the cobblestones as he sawed and jerked the bit, foam spattering his sleeves. Bringing the sorrel to a wild stop in front of a tobacconist's, he shattered the window glass with a triumphant kick of his boot, wheeled about to have a go at the rioters again.

Others had broken free of the mob. Sergeant Tompkins and four Lancers cantered towards him. A blond-haired boy had lost his cap in the melee; another lad streamed blood from his nose. Back up the street, the rest of the Lancers bobbed about on milling horses, hacked at a swarm of Irish.

"Again!" he screamed to his men, pointing to the Irish with his sword. The five of them charged back up the street, heels braced in the stirrups, ready to meet the shock of collision. A whirl of hands below, straining fingers spiking the air, horrible cries, cowardly begging as the blades descended.

How quickly it was over. Bodies splayed on the cobblestones, wives clutching their dead and injured husbands to their breasts, wailing like banshees, calling on Christ and Mary, a few with faces buried in shawls or hugging the planks of barred doors.

But in the dream, when his hand touches the arched neck of the sorrel, the past alters. He feels himself astride a skeleton horse, bony ribs bulging between his legs. He looks down and finds the glossy, muscular red horse transformed into an ashy-grey beast, a nag only fit for the knacker. He snatches back his hand in terror and disgust; the neck he has caressed is crusted with scabs and running sores. This is when he wakes, filled with horror.

Addington pads silently across the room. The white, muscular body glides over the windowpanes, over the burning mirror, as he goes to a large walnut armoire. Here he rummages among the clothes, retrieves a long tubular bundle wrapped in chamois that he carries to the dressing table. Seated, flanked on either side by a burning taper, surrounded by the hot scent of melting beeswax, he remains motionless, shallow blue eyes intent on his own image in the glass.

Finally, he moves, nervous fingers touching the ends of his moustache. What would a stranger make of such a face? What words would apply? Calm and severe, perhaps. He is thankful to see no resemblance there to his brothers. Strange, how very different in appearance they all are. Even Charles and Simon, despite being twins, do not look alike.

But Addington has inherited his father's features. He wishes it wasn't so, wishes he could find something of his beloved mother there, but fails. Instead, he is stuck with the face of the man who ruined her, the man who poisoned his life.

He passes a hand over the flat, hard muscles of his breast, a lingering gesture, then drops it to the bundle, shakes out six clothyard arrows onto the dresser top, their barbs gleaming. He begins a thorough, deliberate examination of the arrows, sighting down the shafts to ensure they are true, checking the fletcher's work, delicately smoothing the vanes with gentle fingertips. At last satisfied, he opens a drawer, removes a small whetstone.

Thinking of Walker, a smile parts his lips. Father has ordered the gamekeeper to muster the tenants, to arm them with guns loaded with swan shot, to command them to fire upon any trespasser. He knows Walker is mystified. Never the report of a poacher's gun heard while they lie in wait, only a single haunch taken from a slain deer, the rest of the carcass left to spoil.

Addington spits on the whetstone, works his saliva into the gritty surface with the ball of his thumb, sets to sharpening an arrowhead. The spittle grows dark, thick, soapy as it polishes the steel to a cruel, razor brightness. Demand the best and get it. Sabre steel. The archer's muscles beneath the shoulder blades twitch as he lovingly draws the stone back and forth over the three-inch cutting edge.

"I want heads," he had told the London cutler, "that'll spring a fountain of blood. Go deep, bite, hold."

As he works, anticipation builds. He thinks of tonight's hunt, the last before he leaves for America. He imagines the pearl-grey light he is about to go into, pictures the mist rising out of the hollows of the drenched earth, threading through the beeches, tumbling over hedges like smoke from a serene, soundless battle. Swaddled in a shroud of vapour, a spectre wrapped in dank, grave clothes, the marrow of his bones ice, the drear mist distilling on cold arrowheads, every sound lost to him except the ponderous thudding of his own heart, he runs the risk of capture and discovery by Walker and Father's minions. So arousing in every way.

Addington dresses himself in nothing but a pair of trousers, takes his belt from a drawer, cinches it around his waist.

Then he scrapes an arrowhead lingeringly along his jawline. Fragments of his dark beard, fine as cat dander, sprinkle his bare chest.

Creeping back into the house shortly before dawn, he is well pleased. He sniffs his hand, the salty blood that bathed it when he cut the deer haunch to pieces and scattered it in the wood, his gift for the foxes, the ravens. Somehow the blood reminds him of the smell of a woman on his fingers. Sexual congress. He holds his fingers beneath his nose and breathes it in, drinks in the memory of sweet Pearl, his best girl.

What a discovery she had been, found among the gay freelances of the Burlington Arcade, haunt of his days as a young subaltern, strolling arm in arm with brother officers, bellowing out their favourite tune when in their cups.

"Bazaars have long since had their day,
Are common grown and low,
And now, at powerful fashion's sway,
Arcades are all the go.
Then let's to Piccadilly haste,
And wander through the shade,
And half an hour of pleasure taste
In Burlington Arcade."

On a winter afternoon, chin buried in his collar against the nipping air, he would catch a cab to the arcade, sometimes accompanied by Macdonald, or Cheek, or Reynolds, but more frequently for a prowl on his own. Burlington Arcade, with its smart shops and throngs of military men in scarlet, blue, or plum, made him feel as at home as in the regimental mess.

Garish gaslights and garish strumpets making coy pauses to allow gentlemen eyeing their reflections in the shop windows to approach them. Heartbreakingly beautiful girls, disarmingly beautiful girls whose unaffected laughter was enough to stir the blood of a eunuch. And once they caught the eye of a gentleman, they were apt to take the initiative. "May I have the pleasure of paying my addresses to you?" and when you said, "Delighted," off they would tow you to a convenient nearby apartment.

This was where Pearl had snared him, dropped her net on him in the Burlington Arcade, deft little fisher of men. He knew her only by her first name, sufficient for their purposes. Pearl, a young woman with pale skin and swirling, wickedly raven hair piled high on her head.

He had been a regular of Pearl's. She made him feel easy. If his father had provided him with a decent allowance, he could have kept her to himself in a villa in St. John's Wood, but Father was a miserly skinflint, so an exclusive, proprietorial interest was out of the question.

It had never been necessary to explain to Pearl what he wanted, a mere hint was enough for the clever thing. When in London, he had her as frequently as his pocketbook permitted, feverishly pined for her when he was away.

Then Pearl vanished. He patrolled the arcade, accosting whores, cross-examining them as to her whereabouts. Several different tales were related. She had left for the Continent, contracted to serve in a brothel in Brussels catering to the English trade. It was well-known that English men of business preferred a touch of home when abroad. Another girl swore Pearl had married a Nottingham stocking manufacturer and retired to a life of respectability. Whatever the truth, she was lost to him.

Even now, thoughts of Pearl turn him a trifle sad and sentimental. She was a good, kind-hearted girl, soft-spoken, very satisfactory.

Once he had even believed she cared for him.

Tonight he would enjoy Alice the servant girl as he had enjoyed saucy Pearl. Shove his finger in her mouth, hook it in her cheek, reel her about the room, murmuring, "Little fish. Dearest trout." Fling her on the bed, gasping for air, darling minnow.

Of course, Alice was not the charming actress Pearl had been. If you laid five gold guineas on Pearl's bureau, she would play any part, perform like Fanny Kemble. The very picture of outraged modesty, of struggling virtue, a chaste Sabine woman shrinking from the Roman conqueror. How movingly, pathetically she would feign tears and plead for her maidenhead. Beg him to be gentle. And why shouldn't she act the part required? If she bruised, hadn't he paid her handsomely for each and every one? Kissed them too?

Pearl, the only girl whom he had ever permitted to see him hold some stolen gentlelady's article to his nose at the moment of climax, of spending.

How many lace handkerchiefs, embroidered gloves, muffs, had he posted anonymously to their virgin owners after using them to sop up the juices from Pearl's mott, after giving that curly black bush a thorough wiping after love?

But there was no Pearl at Sythe Grange. Tonight, he would inhale Miss Venables's fragrance, imagine her under him, perform the old rituals and ceremonies with Alice. Her protests be damned. Afterwards, he would make it right with her.

But Miss Venables's glove must not be posted, however great the temptation. Miss Venables had exacted his promise to treasure it, to keep it close, so she might live in the knowledge that chivalry was not dead. It seemed he had given her a great moment in her young life.

Addington found himself at the foot of the stairs leading up to the servants' quarters. He was not sure how he had got there. He looked up to where Alice lay abed. "Pearl," he whispered, "dear girl. Best of girls." Then he began a climb he knew would end in nothing but disappointment.

5

CHARLES Until Addington attempted to requisition this room for his own use, I was disgusted by the state of it, the very room which the proprietor boasts is the finest the Overland Hotel has to offer. Pure luxury, a maple commode, a dresser missing one drawer, a bed which customarily sleeps two gentlemen, an unsteady deal table upon which to write, a ladderback chair carved with the initials of former guests of the establishment, peeling, dirty blue wallpaper emblazoned with silver fleur-de-lys.

But now, after four glasses of port, I feel triumphant that I occupy such a snug berth. All because Addington envies it and presses his claim, arguing that as leader of our expedition he requires more commodious quarters to plan operations, to spread his maps. A small victory won, not to yield place to him. Addington remains ensconced down the hall in a wretched room no bigger than a cupboard. That will teach him to dally.

Finally, the great man has arrived, assumes command, after keeping me waiting interminably. His domineering presence only softened by five cases of port which he shepherded over the deeps of the Atlantic, across the fruited plains of America, up the Missouri from St. Louis to Fort Benton. It's very good port, the flies like it. I have to place a sheet of notepaper over the mouth of the glass after every sip, otherwise they swarm for the privilege of drowning themselves in it.

Addington, come in high style with stores and equipage unimaginable. His only explanation as to why he is more than a month late, "the difficulties in procuring necessary items in London." Blithely sauntering down the gangplank of the steamer *Resolution* in the early June sun, offering me the coolest of handshakes and introducing his new boon companion, Mr. Caleb Ayto, a horrible, vulgar American stepped right from the pages of Mr. Dickens or Mrs. Trollope. Mr. Ayto playing spaniel, straining to establish his doubtful bona fides to me. "A mere ink-stained wretch is what I am, Mr. Gaunt. An 'articleer' in the Republic of Letters. In short – a newspaperman. But a newspaperman who knows a thing or two about this part of the world. Hard-won knowledge of the useful, practical variety."

Addington is given to taking up with unsavoury characters, but in Ayto he has outdone himself. His motive in collecting this buffoon resplendent in a garish waistcoat a Piccadilly pickpocket would covet is no mystery. Before leaving England, I procured a stack of books written by gentlemen adventurers in order to familiarize myself with conditions in North America. Addington dipped into them as well, a page here, a page there – read just enough to decide his forthcoming escapades will need recording too. I suspect he harbours a notion that this greasy journalist can "work something up" about his forthcoming rambles on the frontier, scribble a flattering portrayal of Captain Addington Gaunt, intrepid British explorer and sportsman, for the delight of the public back home. The man's vanity is incredible, infinite.

So far he evinces not the slightest urgency in getting us under way. Pays no attention when I tell him I have learned nothing of any use after weeks spent interviewing whomever might have a clue to Simon's possible whereabouts. Nothing learned, so how do we proceed? He only shrugs and says, "All in good time. I have things to see to."

The problem is that for the moment, Addington finds Fort Benton too congenial a place to immediately remove himself. There is game to be had a short ride out of the town, and he and Ayto make frequent visits to the pestilential brothels. He immensely enjoys cutting a figure in the bar downstairs, buying rounds of drinks for men who

30

are only too happy to hear him bray and brag as long as he keeps the whisky flowing.

I try to force home to him our position, but he blithely waves me off. Last night, when I caught his ear for a moment and pointed out to him that more than a month has already been lost due to his dilatoriness, he suddenly said, "All work and no play makes Jack a dull boy, Charles. You're being a very dull boy. There's a magic show on the steamer tonight. It'll brighten you."

It did not brighten me, sitting through that endless, preposterous farce. But let Addington have his fun, I thought, and perhaps that will entice him to be more tractable. Allow me to seize an opportunity to talk to him seriously after the performance. But no, that was not to be. It was so in keeping with Addington's character to find the spectacle of yokels galloping that female magician up and down Front Street too amusing to leave. In the end, I walked away and left him there. He was very late getting back to the hotel. I fell asleep waiting to snare him for a conversation when he returned.

All these tedious weeks in Fort Benton I have harboured one delusion. That when Addington arrived, and heard my anxieties and fears, he would dispel them with some bluff, practical soldier's talk. Assure me that Simon is being held captive by tribesmen and can be ransomed. Tell me that he is holed up in the solitary cabin of some prospector or trapper, waiting to be found. No matter how implausible the scenario, Addington could give me faith and courage if he would only act.

My reunion with him has served to forcibly remind me that we never shared one jot of fellow-feeling. My brother does not seem to experience the slightest anxiety for Simon, or be prepared to acknowledge that our reason for being in this godforsaken place is not to entertain him, but to learn what has happened to our brother. Yesterday, at the levee when I attempted to engage him on the topic of Simon, Addington abruptly announced, "I believe the Governor is losing his mind."

I could scarcely credit my ears. "Father losing his mind? What sort of nonsense are you speaking?"

Addington seemed to have already half-forgotten what he had just said, his attention compromised by a likely-looking horse being led along the riverbank. But when I repeated myself, he vaguely answered, "Father's got it in his head there's a conspiracy directed at him." So like Addington to burden me with more uneasiness when what I need is reassurance. To give a twist to my mind as he used to twist my ear when he was fourteen and I was six. "The butler found him on the carpet, beneath the library windows. He assumed the old boy had tripped and taken a tumble, tried to help him to his feet, but Father refused to get off the floor. Said he wasn't about to show himself to anyone lurking about outside. Next day, he ordered the draperies drawn, day and night."

"But who can he suspect of plotting against him?"

Addington simply shrugged. "Yes, that is the question, isn't it."

Thinking of Sythe Grange denied sunlight, that hideous interior, the sitting rooms cluttered with burly mahogany tables, Wanstead sofas, voluminous, dusty curtains of dark-red rep and bottle-green velvet, everything draped in claustral gloom, all I could say is, "The loss of Simon has temporarily driven him to distraction."

"I'm not so sure," Addington replied. After that, I could get no more out of him. He had to meet Ayto for a libation.

Of course, it is Simon. Father cannot really be going mad. Not that sturdy old warhorse. It is for affection that he hungers, the filial love which Simon always openly showed him and which I was chary to display, fearing rebuff. Neither Addington nor I can supply that for him. Yet, strange to say, I did hear Father claim that Addington, too, had once been capable of loving, unbelievable as that seemed to me as a boy of six or seven.

The sound of Father ranting had beckoned me to the door of his study that day. I remember earlier noting the arrival of the family solicitor, Mr. Fry, and catching a few words exchanged among the servants about Master Addington being in trouble at school again. Ear pressed to the door, I kept a lookout for Simon, who disapproved of my taste for eavesdropping. Even at that tender age, what a stickler he was for proper conduct. But not self-righteous, no, never that.

Not once did he reprove my curiosity, but if I attempted to pass on any of the intelligence I gathered, he would stuff his fingers in his ears and run away. I could not stop myself spying, but I did my best to keep it from Simon. His good opinion meant the world to me. We two were still one in everything, undivided souls, and I felt him to be my better half. He had not yet become an embarrassment to me; our adult paths had yet to diverge.

Father was in a rage. "I want you to find a school that will take my son Addington, Mr. Fry! Let 'em beat him, starve him, whatever it takes! I want him well and truly corrected!"

Mr. Fry's quiet reply was unintelligible, but the tone of it was temporizing and placating. Whatever the solicitor said prompted Father to lower his voice. Nonetheless, he could still be heard through the heavy oak door. Father can always be heard; not to share his verdicts with the household is beyond him. "Ah, perhaps you are correct, Mr. Fry," he said. "Perhaps his mother's death did work a change in the boy. Addington worshipped and adored her. When my Eunice died giving birth to the twins, it must have put the worm in the apple."

For the first time, I understood the reason for Addington's hatred of us. Because Simon and I were twins, inseparable, connected by a bond he recognized but could not share. More important, because, with the unswervable conviction of a child, Addington could never forgive us the death of his mother. For years, I turned this over in my mind. Addington hated us, but could he not see how we, too, longed for a mother to warm that cold house? And if Simon and I were equally guilty of murder, why was it only me that Addington relentlessly persecuted? That he mercilessly cuffed, pinched, frog-marched headlong into walls?

Simon he never dared touch, not from fear of Father, but because of something in my twin that stayed Addington's hand. What's more, if Addington happened on us, the "cursed twins" together, he never harmed me, simply stalked off muttering threats of future assaults. If Simon was near me, I was safe. In some way I could not fathom, Simon, weak as he was, was my protector. His spirit affected all of us in a mysterious fashion: in Father, awakening a passionate love; in me, a conscience, however sporadically. In Addington, a check for his savagery. To put a word to Simon's power, to define it, is impossible. But I think Simon *saw* more in us than we realized. We all felt it.

How laughable that Addington should be curbed by the angel of the house, the pet of all the servants, the friend of all. How strange that Simon should be the darling of Father, a man for whom nothing exists if it cannot be measured, while Simon has no interest in calculation, was seven before he could count, ten before he could tell time. A boy content to let his nerves and heart chart the world for him.

Never the least drop of hurry in Simon's soul, his slow way of speaking, a faint, lingering smile on his lips as he wandered about the house. A child who would wind his arms around the leg of a servant, stand rapt, rubbing his face against a skirt. Even indomitable Miss Dowell, the governess, allowed him this intimacy. Often we would find him sound asleep in the hallway with the mastiffs, William the Conqueror and Alfred the Great, his white-blond head pillowed on the gently heaving flank of a dozing dog, lamb lying down with the lions.

And there was his button collection. Father did not approve, not when he spent good money providing suitable toys for the amusement of his boys – a jolly Noah's Ark, tops, hoops and sticks, lead soldiers, a train. Father afraid an eight-year-old's preference for buttons would leave the impression he was a simpleton. Henry Gaunt could not have an idiot son. He confiscated them.

Simon raised no hue and cry, simply started another collection abetted by Mrs. Bullfinch, the housekeeper, who doted on him so much she was willing to run the risk of Father's ire. Soon, Simon had another set of buttons rattling in his pockets. If it were me, I would have hid this from Father, but not Simon. He spread them on the carpet in Father's sight like a jeweller displaying precious gems. And it worked. Father overlooked the flouting of his authority, retreated before Simon's fascination with bits of glass, ivory, jet, bone, mother-of-pearl, wood. Buttons, buttons, ordinary buttons. He spent hours tracing their shapes with his fingers, staring at them, sometimes even popping them into his mouth and sucking them as avidly as he would lemon drops.

One afternoon in the library, he lifted a button of blue glass to the summer light cascading through the tall windows. I heard him murmur two words, "How bright!" and, as he did, a spot of unutterable brilliance, a tiny patch of shimmering, blue, celestial fire winked on his face as he waggled his button in the sunshine.

I edged closer. Simon exchanged a bone button for the glass one. Squeezing it tightly, he exclaimed ecstatically, "How warm it is!" and passed it to me. I felt an animal heat burn in my palm, felt that old, dry piece of bone pulse with living blood and marrow. I hurled the button to the carpet, frightened by Simon's powers of suggestion.

I was not the only one susceptible. Without Simon, Mr. Balducci would never have come to Sythe Grange as drawing master. All my pleas for lessons in art Father rebuffed, scornfully dismissed. He scoffed at the notion that one of his sons could possibly be interested in "daubing paint." Seeing me so crestfallen, Simon intervened on my behalf. Every morning at breakfast he importuned Father. "Please, sir, Charles and I wish to learn to draw."

Father said nothing, dove behind his paper, but in a few weeks, to my astonishment, fat Mr. Balducci came bouncing up the drive on an estate cart stacked with his luggage. When his presence was explained, when I realized the miracle Simon had wrought, I burst into tears. After all, he had no interest in drawing, a boy so awkward his printing could scarcely be read, a boy who covered his shirts in inky blots whenever he touched a pen. And yet he had done this for me. For my sake done the unthinkable. Told a lie.

During Mr. Balducci's tenure at Sythe Grange, Simon always haunted the "studio," encouraging my first crude efforts, declaring them wonderful. And Simon's enthusiasm ignited Mr. Balducci's. The Italian would rub his hands gleefully together and parrot my brother's judgment. "Yes, excellent! Most excellent!" It was not excellent, but it was the first approval I had received from anyone other than Simon for what Father described as "Charles's doodles." My wilted heart drank it in thirstily.

Father attempted to raise all his sons to fully appreciate the advantages which accrue to men with a respect for numbers, for bald information, for hard facts. But facts did not take with Simon. I cannot imagine he would ever be capable of recording the nonsense I see before me, something Father has such a taste for, and which I have only recently begun to post to him daily, yielding to his orders. An account, in his words, "Of weather, temperature, geography, business conducted, occurrences ordinary or unusual pertaining to the enterprise."

Today's letter, on the table, reads, *"Temperature as of seven a.m., sixty-two degrees Fahrenheit. Sky clear, cloudless."* It is as far as I have got. What else to say? Business conducted. What business conducted? And then I dredge up the one decision Addington has taken and cavalierly turned over to me to implement. I begin to write.

"Brief confab with Addington after breakfast yesterday. He wishes to engage scout familiar with topography and tribes of Upper Missouri and North-West Territory. Old frontier hands met by Addington on journey upriver recommend Mr. Jerry Potts, a Scottish half-breed and highly regarded guide, as the man to hire.

"It has fallen to me to locate Mr. Potts, and strike terms with him. Mr. Ayto, a fellow whom Addington met on the steamer to Fort Benton, has volunteered to help us in the search for Simon. Addington has accepted his offer, and agreed to pay Mr. Ayto's expenses. It is Mr. Ayto's advice that on no account should remuneration in excess of fifty dollars a month be offered to a half-breed. They may be had cheap. I shall take Mr. Ayto at his word."

What more can be said?

"Temperature as of midday, eighty-four degrees Fahrenheit. Strong wind all afternoon, dying away shortly before six o'clock. Sixteenth consecutive day with no precipitation. Drouth threatening Fort Benton. No news pertaining to Simon. I press Addington to leave Fort Benton and journey north with all dispatch. If he agrees, this may be the last letter you shall receive in some time. No regular post will be available after we depart. Yours sincerely, Charles Gaunt"

Simon Father loves. Addington he respects because he admires ruthlessness. At his warmest, Father ignores me. So I was surprised when he asked me to paint him a room. Filled with momentary elation, I believed it an opportunity to win a tiny bit of his esteem.

Perhaps he has already examined my effort, opened the room which I locked, carrying the key away with me in my pocket. Despite his solemn oath not to inspect the murals until I was finished, Father would not hesitate to have the servants force the door if curiosity got the better of him.

Father denied me nothing to accomplish my commission. Immense trestle tables, quantities of paint, brushes, dozens of lamps equipped with reflectors, hundreds of beeswax candles to make night bright as day. At first, I worked like a demon. All those exact geometrical calculations, the ruling off of grids on the plaster for my cartoons, grids drawn to scale from those superimposed on preliminary sketches. And yet, the whole project was compromised from the beginning. In my heart, I knew he would never be satisfied, could hear him comparing my work unfavourably to those wall paintings that he saw in that restaurant twenty years ago and that he believes the height of artistic expression. "Well, my boy, it may be 'interesting,' but it is no Polar Latitudes. There was a fellow who could paint!"

No sooner did I begin than I sensed defeat. I would fail Father. From Mr. Balducci's tuition I knew that a mural must be done *buon fresco* to last, painted on a wet, freshly prepared lime-plaster wall. Nevertheless, I applied my oils to a dry wall, not even bothering to size the surface with casein or glue.

From the beginning, I condemned Father's mural to fade, flake, eventually disappear. The certainty of my pictures undergoing such a fate pleases me. Emperor Addington, who refused to sit for me and whom I had to draw from a photograph, the servants who were the models for slaves, praetorian guards, degenerate Roman senators, posterity shall never gaze upon them.

I could not bring myself to paint Father what he wanted, a Soyer's Symposium, a mere entertainment, an amusement. Since I could not hope to please him, I pleased myself. I placed Father on the ceiling as Jove, with fluffy, white side-whiskers, clutching his thunderbolts, sentenced to watch Rome corrode, turn to motes of dusty paint under his very eyes.

I sweep the port from the table for the pleasure of hearing it shatter on the floor. A horde of disturbed flies buzzes angrily on the window-pane, dances ferociously there. This room smells of dust and an unemptied chamber pot. Because Addington wanted it does not mean it is not a horrid place, a cell filled with heat, flies, dust, stinks.

I go to the window. No relief there, just a view of a sun-stunned, deserted road. Like all roads in this Ultima Thule, it runs straight as a die, no cozy twists or eccentric turns which acknowledge human history. A direct route to nowhere. I want Simon.

Down below, a drunken Indian reels out of an alley, holding a barrel stave like a sceptre. I have yet to see the "noble savage" of literature, only what the locals call "post Indians," wretches who hang about the fort begging, slatterns and their debauched consorts in the castoff rags of the white man: frock coats with a single sleeve, rotting hats, tattered trousers. They plead for pennies, or offer their wives to passersby for the price of a glass of whisky.

Though inebriated, this man is better dressed, a primitive Beau Brummel in fringed buckskin trousers and a beaded jacket which flashes in the sunlight like a peacock's tail. European haberdashery, stridently checked shirt, and shiny, high-crowned hat.

Unsteadily, he deposits his buttocks upon the ground, crosses his bandy legs, lifts the barrel stave high above his head. It hangs there suspended, then the Indian slams it down on the roadway, begins to sing. To howl. Yip like a dog run over by a wagon in a London street. In time to his unearthly ululations, he drums the hard, packed earth. A performance of despair, of animal agony – all these things at once. His head rolls slackly back and forth as his raw mouth beseeches the sky, face horribly swollen from drink or a beating, the features so puffy, so bloated he appears to have been born without eyes.

At the sight of the flashing stick a memory rises in me. Shooting season at Sythe Grange. Birds flushed from their coverts by the beaters, the whirl of them in the sky, the bark of guns. All those pheasant chicks Father's gamekeeper hand-raised, coddled with hard-boiled egg and mash only to be driven from the bushes, made to pay the price of their careful nurturing.

That barrel stave slashing the earth and the beater's shrill cry seem meant to drive me into the open. I must take immediate steps to find Potts. I must urge, wheedle, Addington into action. If I do not place our feet upon the road, it will not be done.

Palms flat to the windowpane, I stare down at the Indian eyeless in Gaza, the Indian who sports a bedraggled, wispy moustache above a siren mouth summoning me to be my brother's keeper.

6

CUSTIS STRAW Here I am, caught watering the haystack out back of the livery stable, a pistol at my ear. The cold touch of gunmetal kicks my trickle into a roaring freshet. Fear does wonders for a man's pisser.

"Steady now, Mr. Straw. Finish your business and then tuck it away."

I'd know that bullfrog voice anywhere. "Why, Sheriff Hinckey, I never knew you to be so enterprising. Road agent is a step up from your usual – picking the pockets of drunks you find in the street."

"Hold your sauce, Straw."

"I'll hold my sauce when you take that revolver off me. I don't exercise my right to bear arms. I might piss on your boots, but I'm not equipped to shoot you."

"Come along."

"Where?"

"Justice of the Peace Daniels is waiting on you in the jail."

"I'm arrested?"

No answer, he just waits for me to stow my peter, gives me a bunt with the gun barrel, and commences marching me right down the main pike, Front Street, busiest thoroughfare in Fort Benton. Hinckey's got a goodly audience this morning to troop me by, what with a mule-train forming up outside T. C. Powers's establishment, all the skinners propped against their wagons, gulping a breakfast of cornbread.

"Here!" one of them hollers. "What's Straw done? You catch him pinching Bibles, Sheriff?"

I holler back, "I'm being hauled in for voting Republican, boys!" That old conniver, Justice Daniels, would certain like to see that made a capital crime. Whole damn town's full of Southerners, all of them swearing he was a colonel in the war, proprietor of a plantation with five, six, seven hundred happy Negroes. Nothing but cracker liars who counted themselves lucky to own a mule before the war. Pitiful stories way too big for their sorry selves.

The old adobe jail's directly ahead, run down and crumbly from rain and neglect. Sheriff Hinckey and Justice Daniels stint on the repairs because they don't believe the county ought to be burdened with neither its upkeep nor the expense of feeding prisoners. Anybody commits a felony that isn't a hanging offence, they just run them over the Choteau County line. Good riddance to bad rubbish. They hold on to murderers when they can, which isn't often. A hanging draws a big crowd and is good for business.

"Get in there!" Hinckey barks, ramming me through the door.

Willard Daniels, spiffy in an old claw-hammer coat, is sitting behind a battered rolltop desk, peeling an apple. He doesn't look up, just watches the skin peel off the pippin like a red scarf unwinding.

"Here he is. I brung him," Hinckey announces grandly, looking to get his head patted.

Mr. Justice lifts his yellow eyes to me.

"That's right," I say. "Rover fetched me, but being a dog he can't say why."

Old Daniels likes to play gentleman, Southern-variety. He's wearing a white shirt with ratty ruffles like weeviled-out cotton bolls all down its front, a shirt so threadbare you can see his nipples right through the cloth, brown as pennies. He sets the apple down on a sheet of paper, snaps shut the penknife, wipes his fingers on the sleeve of his coat, and says, "Show him, Hinckey. Show Mr. Straw why he's been brought."

Hinckey starts for a dark corner, tiptoeing in his boots. I follow the high-stepping, chicken-gaited fool with my eyes. Then I spot it, a small body lying covered by a blanket. I make out one pale foot peeking out from underneath, the other wearing a man's brogan. I glance at Daniels. The old man licks his thin lips, nods to Hinckey, and the Sheriff sweeps the blanket off the corpse.

Jesus Christ Almighty. Poor little Marjorie Dray in a homespun dress, sorrel hair fanned out, bits of dried grass and twigs tangled in her curls, a belt pulled tight around her throat. She's bitten her bottom lip clean through.

I have to steady myself against the sight, lean on Daniels's desk, breathing like I aim to suck up all the air in the room. Daniels touches my hand with a cold palm. "That ain't all," he says. "Let Mr. Straw see the rest."

Hinckey lifts the hem of Madge's dress over jutting hip bones. There's streaks of rusty blood, blisters of dried spunk on her thin thighs, a skimpy patch of russet hair. I have to shut my eyes. Daniels's voice presses on me out of the darkness. "She been trifled with, Mr. Straw."

"Goddamn it, cover her up!"

"Do as Mr. Straw says, Sheriff."

Dizziness forces me to open my eyes before I topple over. Daniels grins nastily. "Who do you figure for such a terrible deed, Mr. Straw?" he asks.

"How the hell do I know?"

"You was seen with her last night."

It's an accusation, but I can't find the words to answer it, not with little Madge lying so. Hinckey's only pulled the blanket up to her shoulders. The sight of those teeth clamped cruelly through her lip, the belt that choked the life out of Madge Dray – I can't bear to look upon it. "Take that belt off her."

"No, sir. I ain't going to meddle with evidence."

I move fast, drop to my knees, tear at the belt, rock up on my feet to see the old man with a hand held up to warn Sheriff Hinckey off from interfering with me. The belt is cold in my hand, clammy as the dead flesh I just touched.

Daniels props a boot up on his desk, resumes in an easy, cheerful voice. "Word is you escorted her to that show last night on the riverboat. Had her on your arm. Little wash girl who laundered your stockings and shirts, handkerchiefs and dirty underdrawers, you took her out for a night on the town. Seeing her brother-in-law's away doing business, maybe you thought – cat's away, the mice will play."

"Yessir," agrees Hinckey. "Mr. Abner Stoveall goes off to sell whisky to British Indians, nigger crawls out the woodpile."

"Crawls out," Daniels adds, with a nasty curl of the lip, "to have some fresh, sweet cherry pie."

"Keep that talk to yourself, you filthy old hog." My words sound righteous, stiff, maybe like a man playing innocent. Somebody with something to hide.

Daniels's voice grows stronger, buttery confident. "Man your age puts his eye on a young gal like that – thirteen, fourteen year old – most times he don't sashay about with her. Don't want to look unseemly." Daniels pauses. "Besotted is a danger, Mr. Straw. It's maggots in the brain. You ought to have asked for her hand. Better to do the decent thing." Daniels starts quartering the apple, precise as a watchmaker. "Maybe you and Miz Stoveall had an understanding about her baby sister. Was that how it was, Mr. Straw? Miz Stoveall forced to take up pimping after her husband left her high and dry?" He spears a section of apple with the penknife, pops it in his mouth, chews wetly, noisily.

"You don't know Lucy Stoveall if you think that. She's an upright woman."

"Well, I'm puzzled because this morning when the body was found in that alley between the Four Aces and the livery – just off Front Street where you and Madge was seen watching the boys haul Madame Magique around in that wagon . . ." Cagy old bastard waits to see if I have anything to say about what he's suggesting. I don't. Won't give him the satisfaction. "Well, Hinckey here went to fetch Lucy Stoveall out of her wagon, but Miz Stoveall wouldn't come. She let it drop she had business out at your ranch. Now why is it you're the first person she wants to see after terrible news like she received this morning?" He tilts his head to one side, cocks a curious magpie eye at me.

"I don't know why she would head for my ranch. I keep a room at the Stubhorn."

"Maybe she thought you to be doing an honest day's work for once," Daniels says. "Don't you think it strange you don't know what she wants with you, Straw?"

"I'm no judge of strange."

"Hell, you ask me, you set the standard for it. Everybody knows you're peculiar. You fuck her dead or alive, Straw?" For a moment, I think to hit him, but I hold myself steady, stare back.

Daniels is eyeing me like a cat ready to pounce. "I see you ain't wearing a belt, Mr. Straw."

"I'm a suspenders man." I draw my coat back to show him my red galluses.

"Put the belt on, Mr. Straw," Daniels orders me.

There it is, forgotten in my hand. I slip it around my waist. The tongue of the buckle has to notch in the last punch hole, the one nearest the tip of the tongue, three down from the one showing the wear of use. "If the shoe fits wear it," I say to him. "The shoe doesn't fit, Daniels. Look for yourself."

"Maybe there was two of you. Maybe you had a accomplice. Maybe that piece of leather belongs to him."

This is so stupid that he's got to believe what he's saying, which means he didn't haul me in here just to humiliate or harass me.

"If that's all you've got, I'll be gone."

"I got more. Sheriff Hinckey told me that when that Stoveall woman headed off to your property she went with a big old horse pistol. Maybe she's got a reason to shoot you."

"You best ask her." I turn to leave.

"I will. And until I get an answer I'm putting you under protective custody. Lock you up until we get to the bottom of this."

I swing back on him. "In a pig's eye you're putting me in custody!"

"No? What's going to stop me?"

"Writ of habeas corpus."

Daniels scrapes the sole of his boot off the edge of the desk, hoists himself out of the chair. There's banked fire flickering behind the scum of cataract on his eyes. "Don't you trot no dog Latin at me. I read law for a year with a lawyer in Kentucky. How you think I got this job?"

"You got the job because the great Party of the Democracy doesn't count many hereabouts that know how to read and write."

"If I was a considerate man I'd scrub my arse before you kiss it," says Daniels. "But I ain't." He yanks a stubby parlour gun from his back pocket, holds it up in my face to admire its nickel-plate finish and gutta-percha grip, then slashes me across the mouth with the butt. His blow's an old man's, abrupt and jerky, not much pop to it, it's mostly the surprise of it that staggers me. I wipe blood from my lips. "You son of a bitch."

Daniels strokes the ruffles on his shirt front, gestures with the pistol. "Let me enlighten you, Mr. Straw. Habeas corpus. It is the Latin for 'you must have the body,' if I remember my Blackstone. And you have the body, Straw," he says, poking the pistol barrel at little Marjorie Dray. "I have produced it." He levels the tiny pistol in my face. "That is my reading of the Latin in this case. Do you dispute it?"

I spit blood on the packed-dirt floor.

"If you press me again, Mr. Straw, I shall have *you* for a habeas corpus. Do you understand *my* Latinity, sir?"

"I do. If nothing else, we're clear on that."

LUCY STOVEALL You come awake and it's all a blur. Then the buggy wheel in your mind takes a turn, stops dead on that same spot it's been coming to rest on since the bad news, and everything clicks sharp. You see little yellow and pink flowers on low-growth cactus, crumbs of sand under your nose scurrying with red ants.

My baby sister is dead. Madge is dead.

I laid down on this knoll to spy out the lie of the land, but my mind flew off into blackness. No sleep last night after I found Madge's bed empty. Wondering where she had gone, I walked the streets, then sat waiting for her to come back, kept the lantern burning for the traveller lost in the blizzard. Sweet Madge wasn't a girl to run off. Still wide-eyed awake when Sheriff Hinckey rode up to our wagon. The look on his face, I knew deep down in my heart he only had dreadfulness to announce.

The Sheriff couldn't stop me from lighting out. My mind was set on this. Rightfully it's man's business, but I want the Kelso brothers for myself. After I'm done with them, the law can do with me what they please. That's all I had in my mind, covering three mile this morning from town, running and walking, gunny sack banging against my leg like the devil's fist. Nothing but the Kelsos. Wailed the whole way, wailed like a Virginia nigger sold to Alabama, never stopped until I came up here on Straw's ranch, spotted that soddie where his kin, that scum he hired to ride herd on his horses, squat. Then I had to stick my hand in my mouth so's to break off my lamenting, so's not to give warning.

It's quiet now but for the hum of bugs, the dry scratch of wind in the bunchgrass. Sun laying on my shoulders hot as a stove lid. Nothing shows below, no smoke rising from the tin chimney of the soddie, no Joel and Titus Kelso to be seen about, just Straw's remuda drifting about the brown plain. Mustangs in the corral half-asleep, heads hanging in the heat, lazy tails switching flies.

My poke bonnet's gone, don't know where, but I still got my sack, clutched it so tight while I slept my fingers went stiff. All I got to do now is stand and that buggy wheel in my mind will turn, roll me down the hill past the corral, roll me right to the door of that soddie with the weeds growing out the roof, roll me right up to those slumpy walls, that window winking in the sun like a crazy man's eye.

Go down, Lucy Stoveall.

The horses come crowding to the corral rails, nicker friendly as I pass. I stop dead, wondering if the sound will raise the Kelsos. Then I remember the big Navy Colt is still in the gunny sack. I drag it out. Long as my forearm, the heavy barrel takes a dive for the ground like a dowsing wand. A scorcher breeze peels a mist of dust off the yard, throws it in my teeth. Rusty hammer won't cock, both thumbs pressing hard and it won't set. Then it grinds, clicks into place.

I blink, the wheel commences to roll again, I roll with it over ground soapy with tossed wash water, ashes, old bones and hides, empty Van Camp's bean cans, a rack of charred elk antlers. Shiftless mudsills so lazy they pitch trash on their doorstep.

The soddie door is ajar, listing on leather hinges. I put my eye to the gap, but it's too dark inside to make out anything. I listen, catch whispery snores. I yank the door, plunge in with a sluice of light, and the wind bangs the door shut behind me. I'm blind in a room thick with a terrible stench.

"Where are you!" I shout.

A bit of sunshine leaks through the dusty window on to pink flesh and I throw up the Colt and fire. My nose fills with smoke, my ears clang. The door flaps open and sunlight blasts back in, shows me what I've fired on.

Not one of the Kelsos, but a dead pig. The dirt floor is a jelly of blood and pig shit. The sow's got a rope hitched to a trotter, and a bib of flies tied to the slash across her throat. Bluebottles swirl up, shimmer and buzz, make the snoring noise I heard at the door. Strange. There's a piece of paper on the pig's flank.

Bunks stripped of blankets, shelves bare. A leaky flour sack laying a trail to the doorway. The Kelsos are gone.

I stoop down and see that PITCHER OF DIRTY OLD HOGG BY NAME OF STRAW is scrawled on the paper. When I pick it up, printing on the other side shows through the thin paper. It's one of the handbills the Englishman's been covering Fort Benton with. I flip it and read.

REWARD OF A THOUSAND DOLLARS OFFERED

TO ANY PERSON OR PERSONS HAVING KNOWLEDGE OF THE WHEREABOUTS OR THE FATE OF SIMON GAUNT ESQ., LAST SEEN IN THE COMPANY OF THE REVEREND OBADIAH WITHERSPOON IN FORT BENTON ON OR ABOUT THE 19TH OF OCTOBER LAST.

MR. SIMON GAUNT IS 27 YEARS OF AGE, STANDS FIVE-FOOT-NINE, IS A GENTLEMAN OF SLENDER BUILD. HIS

SPEECH AND DEPORTMENT ARE THOSE OF AN ENGLISH GEN-
TLEMAN, HIS FEATURES REGULAR, EYES PALE BLUE, HAIR
BLOND.

ANYONE WITH INFORMATION PERTAINING TO THIS
MATTER SHOULD MAKE HIMSELF KNOWN TO MR. CHARLES
GAUNT AT THE OVERLAND HOTEL, FORT BENTON. HE IS
MOST ANXIOUS TO LEARN ANYTHING TOUCHING UPON
HIS BROTHER AND ALL THOSE RENDERING INFORMATION
AND ASSISTANCE SHALL FIND THEMSELVES GRATEFULLY AND
AMPLY REWARDED FOR THEIR TROUBLE.

I crumple the paper in my hand, step back through the doorway.
Outside, the wind is groaning and clawing at the grass. Remembering
Madge, I want to groan and claw too. After a bit, I look up and see
Sheriff Hinckey bouncing a rig towards me across the prairie.

❖ ❖ ❖

CUSTIS Justice Daniels has gone to his dinner, Hinckey has gone to
collect Mrs. Stoveall, and I'm left to kick my heels in a cell. Daniels
wouldn't pass on word to Aloysius to fetch me my Bible from the
Stubhorn saloon. He said, "That don't fool nobody, Straw. The devil
can quote Scripture to his own purpose."

He banged the door mighty hard going out when I told him I didn't
want to read Scripture, just wipe my ass with the Book of Judges.

Aloysius Donald Dooley will scold me for not being mindful of
my situation. Say I'm only digging myself into a deeper hole. But I
don't intend to plead and make myself small for that son-of-a-bitch
Daniels. I don't bend for the likes of him.

Aloysius claims I'm contrary, but that's because he's a publican,
and it's a saloon-keeper's job to be pleasant even if he doesn't want
to. Not that he is all that cheerful. To think of it, I've never seen a
bar-keep dole out spirits with such an air of chastening gloom.
Aloysius said he arrived in America from Ireland just a babe in arms,

but once he got off the potato diet, he grew like a weed. He is a prodigious height, six-foot-four in his stockings, and he likes to say he reached that elevation by the time he was fifteen, which made him a foot taller than his Da. He said his old man beat him frequently for the presumption of it. So maybe every drink he pours, he's thinking that he's just gained a dollar on the man who spent it, and fears a thumping for advancing his position in the world.

Aloysius is a fine individual, but he'd be a finer one if he'd leave off trying to reform me and instruct me. The man's a mystery. Five years renting a room from him in the Stubhorn and all I've ever got out of him is that when he turned sixteen he was so tired of the Dooley family fleeing property seizures from landlords and bailiffs that he lit out West to make his fortune. He admits to rattling around various places – Kansas, Nebraska, Missouri – doing exactly what he'll never say. At the end of it, he rolled into Fort Benton with enough cash in his pockets to buy the Stubhorn.

Aloysius and Dr. Andrew Bengough count as my only friends in this town, and they never stop airing their opinions of me. Dr. Bengough said to me once, "Your character, sir, is that of a Mussulman. As Allah wills. Hence your phenomenal patience." Bengough thinks I'm long-suffering because I won't answer the lies said about me. Let them all talk. What they hold against me most is I saw the nickel laying right under their noses and I picked it up. Years ago, when every man-jack in these parts headed off to Helena to prospect gold and make himself a pile, I went into Crow country and set up a trading post. What's worse in their eyes is that I refused to trade whisky to the Indians and kept my thumb off the scale. It's an affront to them for a white man to act in that fashion. But next spring I showed up with eighty head of prime Crow horses ready to sell to fortune hunters when the riverboats docked. And because I had earned the Crow's trust, I had a steady supply of horses until my own herd was established. Horse flesh is always a surer bet than scrabbling in cold water and gravel for a fleck of gold. That's what those scapegraces resent. Their pockets stayed empty and mine didn't.

Nobody says a thing to my face, but Aloysius passes on all the rumours he hears in the saloon. He believes that if I know the impression I leave, it might lead me to change my ways. There's nothing I haven't been accused of. That I was a Mormon once, fled Salt Lake City, left five wives behind and enough kids to fill a school. That I was a hot-eyed abolitionist in Bloody Kansas, a friend of madman John Brown, hacking slavery sympathizers to pieces with a broadsword.

They'll have something else to blab about with poor Marjorie Dray laying there on the dirt floor.

Why would such a thing happen to her? Live forty-five years, and you understand that's a hapless question. In a town chock full of drifters, riverboat men, trappers, muleskinners, bull-whackers, old waddies, and sap-green cowboys, all coming to Benton to get drunk, play house with the whores, blow off steam, there's a bushel of culprits. A boom town draws rogues like a jam jar draws wasps.

Nobody will stop to think about that because I'm handy to blame. And Madge Dray has often been seen delivering my laundry, going up those outside stairs to my room above the Stubhorn. The curious noted how long her visits lasted, wagged their smutty tongues. Aloysius warned me of it. I didn't give a damn. I was too interested in finding out what I could about her sister, Mrs. Stoveall. First time I laid eyes on that fiery hair, those big brown eyes, I was done for. Hiring her and Madge to do my laundry was purely an excuse to see her.

But not once has Lucy Stoveall ever delivered my clothes, she made sure that was Madge's chore. Didn't take me long to learn how Madge loved to talk about her big sister. Worshipped her. I made the most of it. Learned Abner Stoveall had run his tenant farm in Tennessee broke. New start, he said, sold up their stock, borrowed some money from a brother, and took them off in a wagon for St. Louis. Spent the winter there, Madge and Lucy working in a rooming house as chambermaids to pay the room and board while old Abner played cards in the parlour. This spring, they caught the first boat to Benton with the intention to push on down the Mullan Road for Walla Walla, Washington. From a fellow heading downriver, Abner Stoveall bought a wagon cheap, but he got skinned. The reach of the wagon was cracked and right on the edge of town a wheel hit a rock and it snapped like a piece of kindling. It hasn't moved since. "Here we were," Madge had said, "stranded in Fort Benton, Abner so deep in the mopes, feeling so hard done by, he couldn't bring himself to lift a finger and start repairs." But then all the talk of good money to be made peddling whisky to the Indians in British territory recovered his spirits, and in the blink of an eye he bought a new wagon and a store of whisky with all their Washington stake money, left those two poor women penniless in a broke-back wagon to fend for themselves. And that's what they've been doing, living hand to mouth for six weeks, tub-scrubbing anyone's clothes who doesn't want to pay the Chinaman's price. And no sign of Abner Stoveall in all that time.

I let Madge use my hairbrushes and sprinkle herself with my bay rum. It seemed to make her forget herself, and say what I reckon she wasn't supposed to. My heart lifted when she told me outright her sister had no use for her husband. Well, why should she? He's old enough to be her father. He's a tyrant and a woman-whipper. She even confided a secret. If Abner Stoveall ever got them to Walla Walla, Madge said she and Lucy were going to skip out on him, do a flit, make for San Francisco, where there was plenty of work. They'd live quiet in the big city, just the two of them, free of old Abner Stoveall and his abominations. Her eyes shone with the thought of it.

It's a sorry story. Two young women chained to that blackguard. Many times, taking my wash to them, I thought to have a private word with Lucy Stoveall about her situation, maybe offer a loan. But she's a proud and wary woman. Always held herself at a distance, so I couldn't bring myself to speak.

When I invited them, as my guests, to the entertainment on the riverboat, Lucy Stoveall wouldn't take my offer. "I've got no use for make-believe trumpery, but you take Madge." I saw it plain in her face, she suspected I had designs of some kind. I was disappointed in her refusal, but it was too late to back away from my invitation to her little sister.

So on Madge Dray's last night on earth there I was, shelling out three dollars to buy her the best view she could have of Madame

Magique predigistating. Only five chairs on deck and we had two of them, right up front where no one could miss seeing us. We were Fort Benton high society that night. The good doctor Bengough beside us and two strangers behind us, one of them the Englishman who had been posting advertisements for a month, and the other, Dr. Bengough whispered, had newly arrived on the very same boat that had brought the exotic Madame Magique to us. Everybody else standing in a multitude behind the chairs, craning their necks to gawk.

It pains me to remember the happiness on Madge's face, how she loved her outing that night. Clapping her hands when Madame Magique made her flash entry in purple tights, a star-spangled corset wrangling those mighty bosoms into a stupendous vision of ivory pulchritude. Twisting around in her seat, gasping when Madame roamed the audience, pulling double-eagles out of dirty ears. Amazed when she made an ordinary walking stick bloom paper flowers and gave us a bang-up finale to the first act – like Jesus, turning a glass of Missouri River water, too thin to plough and too thick to drink, into whisky, handing it to Sweet Oil Bob to sample and pronounce on its quality, and he pleading for another so plaintive and pitiful Madge laughed until her cheeks ran with tears.

When intermission came I bought her a bottled ginger drink from Madame's assistant. It was her first, she whispered to me, she'd never tasted the like of it.

Madame came out for the second act in black tights and a black doublet, hair tucked up and hidden under a turban. Her assistant informed us sombrely that Madame was sometimes the "unwilling earthly tenement of souls gone over," and that the ghost of the long-dead Hamlet, Prince of Denmark, desired to make a statement to the citizens of Fort Benton.

A skull was whipped from behind Madame's back, up it went into the lamp light, and in a voice manly, foreign, and otherworldly, she cried, "'Alas, poor Yorick!'" and launched into a speech about death that nailed us to our seats.

But just as quick as this prince Hamlet took hold of her, he flew the coop, Madame recovered herself, looked about all bewildered, cried out to her assistant, "Prithee, Horatio, tell me! Where am I?"

"Fort Benton, Madame Magique!" he hollered and poor Yorick's skull banged like a rocket, sent up a cloud of blue smoke that scared the wits out of all and sundry. Madge screamed and hung to my arm, but she didn't lose her nerve like those two prospectors who charged the gunwales and flung themselves overboard into Big Muddy. That set everybody stampeding about the deck, one or two pistols were drawn, and riot threatened. But it didn't faze Madame. She just stood with her handsome face lifted to the stars and proclaimed with tender, calming, womanly emotion, " 'Good night, sweet prince; And flights of angels sing thee to thy rest!' "

Dr. Bengough leapt to his feet to start the huzzahing and cheering, a signal the danger from spooks was past. A handful of rowdies planted Madame Magique on a chair, pranced her around the deck on their shoulders, bucked her down the gangplank, slogged her through the mud of the levee up to Front Street. Dr. Bengough laid hands to a wagon tongue, called for a "chariot of triumph." With all the shoving and pushing, boys disputing for the honour of pulling Madame Magique up and down Front Street, I smelled a donnybrook, but Madame graciously suggested she'd make herself available for as long as necessary, see to it that everybody got their chance to haul her in the torchlight parade. I remember the two Englishmen standing clear of the fray, looking on the way boys watch grasshoppers tussle in a jar. The one with the moustache had a contemptuous smile on his face.

My hands shake now when I think that was the last time I saw Madge, so alive and joyful, face shining among the quick. I don't remember much else beyond that, try as I might. Those tiny hot lights started to spark a warning in the corners of my eyeballs. I knew I'd right soon be blind in swimming black, head athrob with a megrim. Madge had to be got home safe out of that mob of wild rascals while I was still fit to do it. So I took her hand and told her it was time for us to go. She didn't want to and begged me to stay just a bit longer, but I dragged her off.

I can recollect nothing after that. The laudanum bottle was dry this morning. But even if I don't remember how, I know I would have seen Madge Dray home safe and sound as is a gentleman escort's bounden duty.

There comes rain whistling down on the roof. My hands shake all the more, can't even force them into my pockets to get them still. I got to climb up on the bed, hold to the window bars, look away from the corpse of little Madge Dray.

Not much to see, the rain's driven most to cover. A mule train's leaving, ten wagons, jennies straining to turn the wheels in the gumbo, ears standing up like bayonets. A street arab, one of the whores' catchcolts, runs along beside a wagon, him all speckled with mud spitting off the rim, trying to jam a stick into the blur of wheel spokes. Some mongrel dog, patched with hairless skin, keeps darting at the pasterns of the swing mule, making it kick and bray like a cracked trumpet as the teamster tries to whip the dog off.

The kid, the dog, the mule train pass, leave the street empty except for the rain and the younger of the two Englishmen splashing through the mud. I've heard someone speak his name. Gant? Gantry? Whatever the name, he's been the talk of the town for weeks, the lodestone for a tribe of fortune hunters pouring into the Overland Hotel, in the hopes of selling lies about the fate and whereabouts of his brother.

I wished I had my Bible to occupy me. Laying down on my plank bed, closing my eyes, I try to blank my mind. But it won't do as I wish. Death lying near keeps crowding in. The jail starts to feel like that army hospital in Washington D.C., where they carted me off to after my last engagement in the war, the Battle of the Wilderness. Plenty of dead youngsters there. Every morning the beds were full of another night's harvest of them. It came to me there in that hospital that thirty-eight was too old for foot-soldiering. And if I was too damn old, every boy on those rows of straw ticks was too damn young.

Living with a pillow wrapped around my head to shut out the whimpering, the pounding of mattresses, the begging to be given back the arms and legs that were carried away in buckets. I heard these sounds through those long, suffocatingly hot summer days and nights. I heard the soul-savers trooping up and down the aisles, mumbling prayers over dying boys, reading them their letters, leading the hymn singing, holding hands and preaching resignation to the blind, the shattered.

One of these handed me a Bible. Strange to think I'd never dipped into the Good Book before then. Two years of schooling and I could read well enough, even as a boy I chewed every word in any newspaper came my way, even studied Mr. Daniel Webster's Dictionary, had a taste for politicians' stump oratory, loved large words, high-flown phrases. You'd have thought the Bible would have been right up my alley, but I had no interest in it.

Now, lying in this army hospital, miles from home in a swelter of gall and despair I pored over that book, every passage speaking to me of the war and nothing but the war. "And he said unto him, My lord knoweth that the children *are* tender, and the flocks and herds with young *are* with me: and if men should overdrive them one day, all the flock will die." It ran around in my head for days, a prophecy of all those suffering boys around me. I'd study on the Bible continual, think strange thoughts that seemed true to me then. *If man is created in the image of God, then all these men are a picture of the wounded, crucified Jesus. God laid on cots, line after line, each holding up to God a picture of His suffering Self. God staring up at God, and God staring down at God.*

I recall lying in my bed one day, holding the Good Book pressed to my chest. The sun had flinched below the windowsill, the shadows of the trees outside were swaying crazily on the plaster wall when the parson arrived.

I reckon it was a heartening Christian sight for him to see a man with a Bible clasped tight to his breast. Bending down over me, he murmured, "God bless you, sir. Would you like me to pray with you? Is there anything you want?"

I told him plain what I wanted. I pointed that Bible down the row of pallets and said, "I want all these Jesuses to pick up their beds and walk. Matthew 9, verse 6. Jesus said to a suffering man, 'Arise, take up thine bed, and go unto thine house.' And the man did. Well, Jesus is looking down and telling all these poor boys just the same. He's saying, one Jesus to every Jesus, one God to every God. Go home, He's saying to them."

Pressing his hand to my brow, the parson smiled. "Rest now. Sleep," he said, and went slanting off, boots whispering on the floor, certain I was crazed.

Not a particle of sleep or rest for me that night. Staring up into the darkness looking for the face of God peering down upon Himself. I could not find God up there in the dimness, but I did see the shades of boys quitting their beds, shouldering their stinking pallets, shuffling off homeward. I saw them winding up the blue passes of the Adirondacks, fording the black loam of the ploughed fields of Ohio. I saw them drifting along rich river bottoms, every whit as golden as the turning leaves that showered down upon their heads, or blowing grimy-faced as the dirty smoke that came blustering down the broad avenues of New York and Boston.

They were tramping under the buckshot stars that riddled the deep blue sky over Pennsylvania and Rhode Island. An Atlantic storm slapped them sideways, filled their boot prints with cold rain in Massachusetts. Home, they said to themselves as they scrambled over snake fences in Iowa or waded through the ditches of Illinois, grass trailing along their waists. Home.

I saw them resurrecting.

I knew then I would see these boys for all of my natural born days, would never forget them, and that for the rest of my life I would wish it was my fate to take up my bed and go with them.

Now I wish I could witness Madge Dray do the same. In my mind, get up and go home to her sister, Lucy Stoveall.

7

LUCY The sun was so hot bright that when I came in the jail with Sheriff Hinckey, it nigh blinded me, the murk. I could just make out Justice Daniels setting behind a desk, shirt a patch of white in the dusk, and the silhouette of Mr. Straw, pressed up against the bars of the cell. I said nary a word, just stumbled by them, looking for Madge's body. I found her in a corner. Her face was only part-covered, her two bare legs sticking out from the blanket, white, slender peeled willows. Madge's body so thin, so small. Nobody had the decency to close her eyes.

I tried to cover her but the blanket wouldn't reach head to toe. I caught a whiff of horse. The bastards had covered her with a saddle blanket. That she should be used so, the disrespect of it, put me all atremble, swept me with tears. I stood there, my head hanging, clenching down the shake in my throat until I could get my words out clear and strong. "You fetch my sister to our wagon. You get her off this dirt floor and out of this horse stink and you bring her to my wagon." I turned round. The three of them, the law and Straw, were standing stock-still, looking at me.

I said to Mr. Daniels, loud and sharp, "I suppose you heard me?"

He didn't like being spoken to so. It roused him up. "Miz Stoveall, we'll deliver the body directly once you answer us a few questions. I got no interest in it going high here in my office."

He had no business pushing back at me in that fashion. Putting it that way. But it worked. All I could do was fumble out, "What kind of questions?"

"Did Straw bring your sister back last night?"

"Yes, he did."

"You are certain of that?"

"I heard her in the wagon. Felt her come over to kiss me. She always did so before sleep."

"You did not lay eyes on Straw. But you say you felt your sister kiss you. Could be a dream you had."

A sob rose up in me, I tried to choke it down. "No, no, this was no dream. I know what I felt!" I cried out. "But later I woke up and she wasn't there. It scared me."

"Maybe you supposed she'd snuck off to Straw. Tell the truth now, woman."

"My baby sister, she was a good girl. She didn't sneak off with Mr. Straw."

"So where did she go, if it weren't to Straw, do you reckon?"

Mr. Straw spoke up sudden, gave me a chance to collect myself. "Madame Magique. She went back to see more of Madame Magique, those boys parading her up and down Front Street. She had begged to stay."

Mr. Daniels said, "You watch your p's and q's, Mr. Straw. Don't go interfering with a witness."

Mr. Straw said, "Mrs. Stoveall told you how it was and you got no business holding me."

"We'll see about that. I let you out of that cell, I know what you're going to do. Run yourself across the Choteau County line and out of our jurisdiction. Then you're scot-free. You're laughing at us."

I saw how it stood. Sheriff Hinckey could arrest nobody who was off this little parcel of land. By now the Kelsos were beyond the law's short arm. Safe after a couple of hours of hard riding. But if I raised no hue and cry, laid no suspicion on them, they might believe they were free and clear. They might come back to Fort Benton in time, be delivered into my hands.

Mr. Daniels saw me thinking, stroked his fingers slowly up and down those shirt ruffles. It was like he was touching some spot on my body he oughtn't. "Hinckey tells you your sister's dead, but you don't want to go see the body. You light out for Custis Straw's property. Why's that? Took off with a big old horse pistol. Sheriff Hinckey said you looked like you had a use for it." He waited.

"It's clear the law can't keep a woman safe in this town, and it's no use outside it. A body has to protect herself. That's why I carried the gun."

"You were going to settle with Straw yourself?"

"No," I said, most careful, "my sister and me aren't acquainted with many folks around here. Straw was a friendly customer. Only natural I'd turn his direction in time of trouble."

"You ain't being helpful, Miz Stoveall. Out with it."

"I'm done talking to someone who does not listen. But you will listen to this. You see to it that my sister's body is sent to our wagon. Right smartly." Daniels tapped his desktop, Hinckey slouched against a wall, hands in his pockets. I looked at Custis Straw, who was hanging spread-eagled on the bars. There was sunlight coming through a window high up on the wall behind him, but he was blocking the most of it, the man is that wide. When I started for the door Mr. Straw called out to me. I stopped. "A wagon won't do for preparing a body," he said. "My room in the Stubhorn . . . you can have the use of it."

I was about to say no, but then I saw he was right. That wagon is not a fitting place for a proper laying out. And Madge was always bragging on Mr. Straw's hairbrushes, his bottles of sweet-smelling waters. She admired them so. I knew he would have store-bought soap, a dandified man like him. It wouldn't do to wash her soft body with soap the two of us had boiled up out of fat and ashes. She ought to go to the earth sweet.

"I'm grateful," I told Mr. Straw. Then my throat clutched, the fist of grief squeezing down hard, and I had to rush out of that jail.

I ran all the way back to the wagon, hand shielding my face from the looks of passersby, crawled into my gunny-sack bed like a mouse into its nest. I lie here, studying the daylight seeping through the canvas roof.

All my life I've tried not to imagine what might have been, but I can't stop myself from doing so now. If the typhus hadn't carried off Mother and Father when I was sixteen and Madge only seven – what then? Every nastiness seems to have followed from that. My father might have been nought but a Tennessee sharecropper, but he was a worker. We Drays never went hungry, never went cold. A gentle house, no whippings but ones that were earned. They even sent me for a time to the dame school, although plenty said it was a waste, to teach a girl to read. I didn't know how happy I was until seven years ago; the typhoid took Mother and Father off and happiness with it. Next thing I knew, the landlord was on the doorstep telling us that Madge and me had a month to get off the property, he had found another man to work the place.

What choice had I when Abner Stoveall came courting? All our kin gone West, bound for greener pastures. He promised us both a roof over our heads, swearing to treat Madge like she was his own flesh and blood. Sitting in Mother's kitchen, the betraying bastard bounced Madge on his knee, crawling his fingers all over her, tickling happy shrieks out of her.

Fool. A fool I was to take him at his word, sell myself to a man older than my own dead father for the prospect of eighty acres, a team of mules, two milch cows, a runty, screw-horned bull, a dozen scraggly chickens, five skinny hogs, a dirt-floor cabin with greased parchment windows. First time the candle was blown out and he crawled over on to me, I knew the high price I'd paid.

Then to find out the property really belonged to Abner's younger brother Wisdom, who lived three mile down the road, that we were the tenants of a man who people said could skin a rat and sell it for beaver. It was hard to learn my husband was a liar and, worse, a lazy liar.

My, but didn't Wisdom love to lord it over his older brother, bully him and hand out orders. Still, orders couldn't get a lick of work from Abner. He didn't have any more interest in ploughing or planting, in chopping weeds, in fixing fences, in putting up hay, in shucking corn than a hog who gets his rations fed to him regular would. Abner believed God had a purpose for him, and that purpose was to fool with fice dogs, ride a pacing horse, hunt, and drink whisky. With two healthy gals on the place to toil for him, why strain his delicate constitution? And pull our weight we did, pulled like a pair of mules.

You'd think the soft life we provided him would have eased some gratefulness out of Abner. But no, he's always been a moody man. And Wisdom made him worse, brought his meanness to a boil. I used to dread the sight of Wisdom's green-topped buggy coming down the road to check on his property. Abner knew better than to sass his little brother because Wisdom owned a hotter temper even than his own. Knocked Abner down in the yard with a trace chain once for back-talking him.

And after every one of Wisdom's visits, didn't Madge and me know we were going to catch it, that there'd be the very devil to pay for Abner's treatment at his brother's hands? Abner ranting on, the spit flying. "There's my little brother wearing white moleskin gentry pants, and me as naked as Father Adam under a pair of old overhauls. It ain't right, him so high and me so low. Giving me a scolding like I was a schoolboy." Putting on a mincing voice. "'Them calves got the scours, Abner. They been getting their hot bran mash like I said?'" Abner coming at me then, fist doubled up. "Goddamn it, woman, why ain't you been boiling feed up for the cattle!" And when I told him he had never passed on word to me that Wisdom had ordered hot mash, he'd roar all the louder. "By the flaming Jesus, I ordered one or the other of you to see to it! Where's that sister of yours! You won't own up to shying off what I tell you to do, I'll switch the truth out of her."

And he would, lay into Madge with a willow, cross-hatch her legs with stripes because this was his almighty power to bend me. I'd do whatever he asked to spare Madge hurt and harm.

Every slice of bread that man ate was seasoned with the sweat of our brows. I ploughed; Madge sowed seed. I bucked stove wood; Madge stacked it. I milked; Madge churned. The butter went to town for sale, and the buttermilk down Abner's gullet. Him riding off most days at noon, Lord knows where, coming home late for supper, full of whisky, slopping about from side to side in the saddle.

The farm was sinking beneath our feet while me and Madge bailed to keep it afloat. Weeds creeping into the fields, rats scampering in the corn bins, cows limping with hoof rot. Too much work, and too little money, and what cash did come in went riding out again in Abner's pockets for a spree.

And in the end, Wisdom saw the pleasure of an upper hand wasn't worth the losses. He wanted Abner out of his hair so almighty bad he handed him stake money to journey to Washington by the ocean.

But Washington is still hundreds of miles off and none of my sacrifice did a smidgen of good; I couldn't save my baby sister after Abner dropped us in this Sodom and Gomorrah. He put us down among the wolves and the wolves tore Madge. Now I've got nothing left to do but to bare my angry teeth and bite, and when I sink them, they'll feel the grip of my grieving jaw.

I won't be used again. I know what Custis Straw's playing at. I'm not blind. Nobody could miss those moony looks he sends me. You can see through men like a pane of glass, once you learn the trick. Straw's trying to work on me just like Abner did, use Madge to get in my good graces. But I can play him one better.

Titus and Joel Kelso are more than Straw's hired hands. I heard tell they're some description of shirt-tail relations. They're kin to Straw and kin knows kin, how it thinks, what it's apt to do. I can inch what I need to know out of Straw and him not even cotton on to it. If the Kelsos have scampered for home, Straw'll know where home is. If they took themselves off someplace else, he'll have the best guess where that might be. Young fellows talk their plans.

But now I got to lose my anger until I'm done washing Madge, so that when I put my hands on her for the last time, they'll be gentle.

❖ ❖ ❖

CUSTIS I was about to offer Lucy Stoveall my condolences, but she left so abrupt I didn't have time to finish rallying the words in my mind. They needed to be stately and comforting ones. A man can't spur such words out on short notice. From the look of her, worn down so by sorrow, the wrong words would have ripped her apart like thin cloth.

The door banged shut behind her, Daniels got to his feet, paced the room. "That red-hair bitch is a liar. Maybe Straw's been poking her too. Maybe she's glad to have the sister out of the way," he said to Hinckey.

He had more foul opinions to vent, but there came a click of the door latch, a slab of bright light, and Dr. Bengough stepped into the jail and gave me a quick nod of his head. "Dooley," is all he said, meaning Aloysius had heard talk in the saloon I'd been arrested and rousted Bengough to look into it.

I was surely glad to see that stooped old man come edging over the floor like it was ice he was crossing. He shuffled himself over square in front of Daniels, took two snorts from his snuff box, sneezed, wiped his eyes, and said, "Well, Daniels, this is a damnable mess you got yourself into."

"Straw's in the mess, not me. He's the one diddled a little girl, choked the life out of her."

Bengough kept his voice reasonable, even-tempered. "Nonsense. What evidence do you have to support such a charge?"

"I'm getting my evidence."

"Not good enough, Mr. Daniels. You can't lock a man up on a guess or a whim. You must charge him or release him."

"The law ain't your trade, Doctor," Daniels said.

One of Dr. Bengough's hands came up and smoothed his twitch of white beard with a kid glove. I've seen him do that when he loses at cards and wants to disguise his irritation. "No, sir, it is not my trade. The trade I practise is ruled by one maxim, 'Do no harm.' You might adopt it for your own. Now release that man."

The doctor is a man with a spine. The Democratic Party in Fort Benton might be run by Southerners and Fenian Irish, but despite being neither, he's a power to reckon with. During the war, he fought Lincoln's suspension of habeas corpus like a demon, and that gives him standing with the party faithful. You don't want to get Bengough started on tyrant Lincoln, enemy of the rights and liberties of free men. Bengough didn't keep his opinions to himself during the war and he paid the price for it – muck thrown at him in the streets of Illinois, and one or two spells in jail. Which makes him a hero to the Democrats hereabouts. It's a point of pride for those rascals to number one man of principle amongst their sorry tribe.

It was no mystery what Daniels was thinking faced with the doctor. Willard Daniels had fished his job out of the pork barrel, and it doesn't do to forget that Bengough has influence with the men who lift the lid on that barrel. If Justice Daniels wants to keep earning fifty cents for every paper he signs as notary public, and two dollars for each court session, he best not defy the good doctor.

Still, you could see Daniels struggling with the bitterness of his choice. Which was bigger, his love for his pocketbook or his hate for me? In the end, he motioned to Hinckey and said grudgingly, "Let Mr. Straw go."

There was a rattling of keys, the rusty door screeched open, and I was sprung. "You'll be back, Bible Reader," Daniels said.

I laughed in his face. Bengough gave a yank on my arm, tugged me towards the door. "Behave yourself," he said.

I wasn't finished with Daniels yet. "I'm going to send some men to bring that poor girl to the Stubhorn. Be sure somebody's here when they come."

"Good Lord, don't you beat all. You aim to have the pleasure of washing your little Madge?" Daniels said.

I took a step towards him, but Bengough held me tight. "Leave him be, Custis. Walk away."

There was no profit in it, so I went along with Bengough, docile. The din and glare of the street was a blow to my senses; I leaned up against a hitching post while the wagon traffic grumbled by.

"You think it wise to have her taken to the Stubhorn on your say so? People will talk," Bengough suggested mildly.

I was tired of questions; I'd had my fill of them. And sunshine was thumping my head, causing me to lose my bearings. Bengough put a glove to my shoulder. "You're bound on going to perdition, aren't you, Custis? Why not try to explain yourself?"

"I don't want to be understood. It's no concern of mine to be understood."

"If a man won't be understood, people think the worst of him. The worst is what happened to Madge Dray." I just stood blinking, feeling sick. Bengough shook his head. "A little philosophy might broaden your outlook. As Epictetus says, In walking about, as you take care not to step on a nail or to sprain your foot, so take care not to damage your ruling faculty. The situation calls for you to exercise common sense."

"Maybe," was all I said. Though he's often right, he puts too much store in book education. It's irksome for a grown man to be expected to sit at his feet and polish him an apple, just because forty years ago he could read Latin and Greek. I was in no mood to yield. What I was willing to do was give him my hand. "I'm obliged for your help," I said. "It was timely and welcome."

Bengough gave my fingers a thoughtful squeeze and threw a tag from some scholar at me, all signs that I was forgiven. "'Anyone can stop a man's life, but no one his death; a thousand doors open on to it.'"

"Doctor, that doesn't apply."

"No, Custis, I speak to myself, not you. Seneca corrects the vanity of doctors. I must remind myself there is nothing I can do for Dutchie Hertog, his kidneys are failing, but he insists on a house call. I had better go and leave you to your own devices."

Bengough drew himself up as straight as he is able and departed. Watching him go, I had a sneaking feeling his last words were a chastisement no matter how he denied it.

There was a large serving of disruption in my mind as soon as he left me. All at once, I felt the murderer's belt around my waist, realized I'd never taken it off, had walked out of the jail still wearing it. For a second, it felt as if a girdle of fire circled my belly. I turned to go back, intending to hand it over to Daniels. But then I stopped myself. It was plain if Daniels and Hinckey couldn't pin this on me, they had no interest in pinning it on anybody. Whoever killed little Madge was most likely long gone, and the law was only too happy to wash their hands of it. Some things are easy to overlook. And a poor stranger girl doesn't warrant taking any pains to find her some justice.

I pulled that burning belt off me, rolled it, and shoved it in my pocket. I had a right to it. This wasn't the common sense Bengough urged on me, but I couldn't do otherwise. I wasn't about to forget Madge Dray as soon as Daniels and Hinckey would – in an hour's time, a day at most. If they want the belt back, they'll have to ask for it. I'm its keeper now.

Then I headed off for the Stubhorn. I had my room to get ready. Arrangements to make for a wagon to bring Madge Dray's body from the jail. Lucy Stoveall to summon to lay her sister out. My friend Aloysius to soothe. I knew he would not be happy to learn I was about to turn his establishment into a funeral parlour.

And I was correct. So now I hide in my room from Dooley's ire, wait for Lucy Stoveall, wait for her sister's body.

8

Fort Benton was not a godly town, it had no church, counted no ordained clergy among its citizenry. Due to these circumstances, Custis Straw improvised a burial service for the murdered girl, persuading Aloysius Dooley to volunteer his saloon for the obsequies, and asking the Methodist lay preacher Chauncey Clumb to conduct them. Lucy Stoveall did not approve nor object to these arrangements, and she certainly did not show any gratitude to Straw for making them. She seemed determined to stand remote and distant from the proceedings. Straw took her aloofness in stride, telling himself grief runs hot or cold, and every temperature in between. It wasn't for him to judge.

A sparse congregation gathered in the Stubhorn. Mr. Clumb's wife planted herself down beside Lucy Stoveall with that hopeful look some women wear when they're readying themselves to shine in a crisis. There were no other ladies present; the sporting women from Rotten Row stayed away because they knew their presence was likely to set Mr. Clumb off. He was a great one for preaching against whores on street corners. The rest of the mourners were a few men whose laundry Madge and Lucy had done, and a contingent of the curious who were eager to see how Straw would conduct himself at the girl's funeral. They had heard rumours he had been taken in for her murder.

Straw and Dooley sat side by side, the latter with his chin tucked in his chest and his long legs splayed out in front of him like travois poles. He kept clearing his throat, sniffing the air with his red nose, and casting anxious glances at the mirror over the bar. It had taken him all morning to hunt up a sheet of canvas big enough to drape over the forty feet of tobacco-yellowed glass and Straw knew he was worried that it might come undone and float off. For Aloysius Dooley, to leave a mirror uncovered in the presence of the dead was to court the worst possible luck.

Straw noted that pudgy Mr. Clumb was sending signals that he was ready to begin the service. He was shifting from foot to foot, his fat little hands cuddled up to his waistcoat like hairless kittens. By the look on his face, the Methodist was confident he was about to dazzle the congregation.

And he did, after a fashion. "Someone has gone to Jesus!" Clumb suddenly shouted, causing Dooley's outstretched legs to give an involuntary jerk. Clumb's voice managed to do two surprising things at one and the same time, simper and penetrate. "Let us sing her home," he urged and launched into "Diamonds in the Rough." Clumb was not dismayed by those who didn't know the words and could only softly moan along through their noses. He carried the burden himself, with a will loud enough to drown out a boat whistle. This sacred composition by C. W. Byron, a former carnival man who had made his way to the Glorious Light, struck Clumb as a very apt choice, since the unfortunate girl had spent her last hours at a frolic.

"I used to dance the polka, the schottische and the waltz;
I used to love the theatre, its glitter vain and false;
And Jesus, when he found me, he found me very tough,
But, praise the Lord, he saved me, I'm a diamond in
     the rough."

Clumb paraded back and forth, scooping up bushels of air to toss heavenward, as if lending a boost to Madge Dray's soul, help send it flying upward to Paradise. Straw noticed that Lucy Stoveall had not risen to join in the singing. She stayed put, head bowed under the sludge of words washing over her. The pallor of the woman was enough to break his heart.

> "The day will soon be over, when digging will be done,
> And no more gems be gathered, so let us all press on;
> When Jesus comes to claim us, and says, 'It is enough,'
> The diamonds will be shining, no longer in the rough."

After he waded through the hymn, Clumb began to hop about, nimble as a flea, taking a bite from Holy Scripture wherever he landed. Straw could make no sense of any of it, although one old waddie nodded away as if Clumb was clearing up each and every religious doubt or problem that had ever plagued him. On and on the preacher went in full spate.

Lucy Stoveall was doing her best to shut out the preacher's holy babble. She had sworn to herself not to let any picture of Madge creep into her thoughts that might cause her to collapse and make a spectacle of herself. But this fool was working up a portrait of her sister that was so wrong she could not help but correct it in her mind. Now Clumb was singing "Jesus Loves Me." As if that had anything to do with Madge. Wasn't her big sister the only one who had ever loved Madge after their mother and father had been carried off at one stroke? And as far as Lucy Stoveall could see, the typhoid had to be laid on Jesus' doorstep. Besides, it wasn't Jesus who had raised Madge from her seventh year on, that had fallen to her.

Madge was an angel with a gift for happiness. Just having someone brush her hair could make her grateful, make her sing to the strokes of the brush. Her breath had smelled of milk, like a baby's. The milk of human kindness, the simple scent of goodness.

The sudden scrape of a chair on the puncheon floor arrested Clumb's peroration. Lucy Stoveall, up on her feet, was facing him. "Mrs. Stoveall?" he said, bewildered.

She took three deep breaths to ease the ache in her throat. "Finish with it," she said. "Make an end, Preacher."

Lucy stood amidst a great hush, a shocked and humming stillness. Then, all at once, a tumult broke on the roof like the beating of a multitude of wings. Every face lifted upward, then turned to the windows. Rain was thundering on the glass; a door of beaten silver swung shut on the view of the road.

Lucy was headed for the saloon door. "Bring her," she said. The assembly rippled with indecision. Then Straw and Dooley rose, went to the casket, gripped the rope handles. Several others followed their example. Madge's coffin lifted from the sawhorses on which it rested.

They found Lucy outside, holding the bridle of one of the undertaker's team. The cloudburst suddenly slackened, as if its peremptory signal, being answered, had lost the need to insist. The assembly filed out of the saloon doors into a fine shower, gentle and feathery, cloudy as muslin in the distance. The pallbearers slid the coffin into the wagon and before the driver could climb up on his seat, Lucy gave a tug to the team and started the funeral cortege towards the cemetery. Everyone fell in behind the wagon, slogging along wordlessly through the gumbo. The wagon wheels crusted thickly with mud, and then unwound in long bandages of greasy clay to the accompaniment of the low groans of the wagon box, the soft chatter of a loose tailgate. Pedestrians on the boardwalk came to attention and bared their heads to the rain. A squat man with a hand of cards fanned in his fist came to the door of the Wild Turkey and peered out; a head bobbed above his shoulder. A teamster pulled his mules to the side of Front Street to give the funeral procession free passage. "God walk with you, ma'am," he said, doffing his hat as Lucy Stoveall went by, eyes on her feet.

Numbed by a great tiredness, she did not see or hear him. When she lifted her feet from the mud, she felt hands clutching at her ankles, trying to hold her back. It was as if she was dragging it all along behind her: horses, wagon, casket, mourners. But the weight of this was nothing compared to the burden of sorrow inside her, heavy, ponderous as lead. She glanced up and saw the Missouri to her right, the river current pulling in the opposite direction to the one in which she trudged. It was slate grey under the overcast sky, and it seemed to

Lucy that it was threatening to take hold of her and Madge, sweep them back down-current, deny her sister a resting place.

Custis Straw kept his eyes fixed on Lucy, full of wonder at her determination, the way she plodded on in a haze of rain, earnest as a prayer, head bowed to the mud.

Now they were beyond the outskirts of town, ahead a crop of wooden crosses sprouted above the sage and tumbleweed, the needle-grass and wild rye. The two men Straw had hired as gravediggers were leaning on their shovels by a mound of freshly turned earth, jute sacks thrown over their shoulders to stave off the rain.

The casket was unloaded, lowered into the grave. Silence reigned for a moment before a single bird in a nearby bush began to call the sun back out from behind the clouds. Mr. Clumb led them in the singing of yet another hymn.

Straw saw Lucy stoop to the pile of wet dirt heaped beside the grave. She took up a fistful of mud. He watched her hand tighten, dirty rivulets of water streaming from between her fingers, dripping on to her skirt.

"Whence we came, and whither wending;
Soon we must through darkness go,
To inherit bliss unending,
Or eternity of woe."

She drew back her arm, face working, and hurled the ball of clay down into the pit. It hit the casket lid with dreadful force.

"Mrs. Stoveall," Clumb admonished sternly, "collect yourself."

"Dust to dust, ashes to ashes, mud to mud, Preacher," Lucy scraped out hoarsely. "That's all there is to say. Cover her."

When she swung away, blundering blindly through the tilting crosses and rank wet grass, Straw hurried after her. Gaining the muddy track, Lucy broke into a slithering run, lost her footing, slid to her knees.

"Mrs. Stoveall, Mrs. Stoveall, have a care. You go easy now," Custis murmured as he helped her to her feet. Lucy was sobbing, her face crumpled and red. "Listen," he said, "listen to me, girl. Where are you bound in this fashion?"

The answer was nowhere. She could not form a reply. A sudden gust cast a spatter of cold rain in their faces. Straw put his arm around her shoulders, drew her into the shelter of his chest. "You come along with me, Mrs. Stoveall," he whispered. "Let me take you to the Stubhorn."

The wind and rain returned with a vengeance, driving everyone off Front Street just as Straw and Mrs. Stoveall reached Dooley's saloon. Straw installed Lucy at a table beside the pot-belly stove, got a fire of cottonwood chunks going, set a kettle to boil, rustled up cups, a bottle of Monongahela whisky and rock sugar for hot toddies. Lucy hadn't spoken a word since they had left the grave-yard; she was sitting hunch-shouldered, hands clamped between her knees, gnawing at her lips, shuddering. For Straw, her condition brought to mind scenes he had witnessed during the war, men who had passed through the worst of trials and then broke apart on a safer shore.

When he handed Lucy the toddy, her shaking hand splashed hot whisky on the table. Straw took the mug from her, held it to her lips, let her gulp a bit. "Easy," he cautioned. "Take a breath."

Lucy whispered, "I'm all aquiver. I can't stop." Strands of wet hair hung in her face.

"You're just cold," Straw lied to her.

Lucy pried the cup from him. "I'm steadier now."

The door flew open and Dooley lurched in, shaking the rain from himself, stamping his boots, blowing like a grampus. Straw was happy to see him. It was a chore to hold a conversation with Lucy Stoveall aloft by himself.

"Hasn't let up yet, has it, Aloysius?" he called out.

Dooley didn't answer. At the best of times females tongue-tied him. He needed a plausible reason to avoid chat, so assuming an air of great purpose, he marched across the floor and set to tearing down the canvas tarp cloaking the mirror over the bar.

"Leave that alone, Aloysius," said Straw. "Come and take a drink with us."

The canvas came off the mirror with a ripping sound, bellied out and wafted down to the floor. "Let it be," said Straw sharply. "I'll help you fold it later."

"Hold your horses." Dooley's eyes scurried to the oil painting that he'd taken down and hidden behind the bar to keep it away from the disapproving eyes of the Methodist. Snatching it up, he rushed to the vacant nail and slammed the picture on the wall. Stepping back to judge whether it was hanging straight, he realized what he had gone and done.

The painting was of a naked woman lying on a shocking scarlet divan in a pose of languorous abandonment. There she was, all lust and invitation, flaunting her rose and alabaster flesh, her round belly and pert-nippled bosoms.

Dooley, beginning his mortified excuses, couldn't bring himself to turn and face Lucy. "It come with the saloon when I bought it from old Jew Jake. I don't hold with nudities, but the boys wouldn't hear of me taking her down. The fellow who painted this picture called her Clara, and they said he was from Philadelphia. That's all I know about this picture."

Behind him, Straw cleared his throat.

Dooley thought of another mitigating circumstance. "There was a prospector named Giles offered to buy her off me for a hundred dollars. He wanted to put her up in his cabin. I'd have sold her to him too, but the rest of the fellows drinking here that night took up a subscription and outbid Giles by forty dollars. They wanted Clara left up on the wall. So I'm under obligation. I taken the money."

Lucy said, "Mr. Dooley, I want to thank you for letting me have the use of your saloon for the funeral. You are a good man. Come and join us." Straw heard the whisky in her voice for the first time. Most probably, she was not accustomed to drink. Her words were a tiny bit slurred, a throaty purr.

Dooley's relief at being forgiven was boundless. It made him forget for a moment his wariness of women. He went to the bar, collected a bottle, and bashfully joined them. "I don't want to trouble your conversation," he said, sinking into a chair six feet off. When he realized Lucy was looking at him, he smiled to the ceiling, lifted the bottle to his lips, and took a long drink.

Straw asked him, "Everything settled at the cemetery?"

Dooley nodded. "Clumb was still singing some, but the gravediggers didn't wait on him to finish. They wanted to get out the rain so they started to fill the hole."

"What that Methodist lacked in sense he tried to make up for with singing," Lucy said coldly.

Dooley crouched forward like a cat offering its head to be petted. "I won't have a piano in here," Dooley declared, "for fear it might encourage singing. The worst for singing is them Frenchies off the St. Louis boats. Only thing worst than singing is singing you can't understand because it ain't English." Dooley pelted on. "In my experience, Southerners are near as bad for tunes as the Frenchies. There was a fellow from Louisiana used to come in here, get drunk, and sing darky songs. Generally, darky songs ain't cheerful tunes. I had to put him out. He was bad for business. As a rule, singing is bad for business. It oppresses the spirits. Drinking ought to be a cheerful occupation."

"Madge had a sweet voice," Lucy said, slopping another generous measure of Monongahela into her cup. "She purely loved to sing. If she heard a tune once and it pleased her, she never forgot it." Her eyes filled as she lowered her mouth to the mug. Bad sign, thought Straw, a drunkard's caution, to lower and not lift. "We ought to have sung one of Madge's favourite tunes at the funeral instead of that Jesus malarkey."

Dooley pitched right back in, couldn't stop himself now the dam had broken. "Yes, that would have pleased Madge. I'm sure of it."

Straw was growing annoyed with Dooley's presumption. "What are you sure of? You didn't even know the girl. You never laid eyes on Madge except when she delivered my washing."

"Maybe he didn't know Madge," said Lucy. "But maybe Mr. Dooley knows the human heart. Maybe that's what Mr. Dooley knows."

"That's right," said Dooley. "I was raised up in a family of twelve. There's a lesson in human nature for you."

"The only nature you know is your own, Aloysius, and that ain't deep," Straw remarked.

Lucy Stoveall saw her opportunity. "Human nature is a puzzle. I was right surprised, Mr. Straw, when your kin – those Kelso boys – ran off on you, first sign of your trouble with the law."

Straw was taken by surprise. "What do you mean, run off on me?"

Lucy leaned her face across the table, close enough for him to touch. She peered at him intently before slumping back in her chair, evidently disappointed. "I declare. You really don't know, do you?"

"What is it I don't know?"

"When I went out to your horse ranch, the soddie was cleaned out. All but for a dead hog in the parlour."

"Dead hog?"

"The pig had a note stuck to it. *Old hog by the name of Custis Straw*. That's a hard opinion coming from relations."

"Bastards," said Dooley under his breath.

Straw was shaken. What with the trouble with Justice Daniels and preparations for the funeral, he hadn't been out to check on his wranglers for two days. Worse, the Kelsos abandoning him might suggest to the town he was guilty. "Well, they are hard boys," he said. "They asked me for another advance on wages and I turned them down. I suppose that made them mad enough to quit me." He remembered the hog. "And the pig – they were always crying for fresh meat. So I bought them a butchering hog." He smiled lamely. "Maybe they were trying to tell me they don't like pork."

"I'd have give them pork," Dooley muttered.

Lucy turned to Straw. "Where do you figure they went? Back home?"

"Kansas? I doubt it. Titus got himself in a spot of trouble there. His mother remarried and there were bad feelings between the boys and their stepdaddy. Titus shoved a pitchfork into him, and the fellow damn near died. Both boys did a skedaddle. Their mother's a cousin of mine. I guess they heard talk I was selling horses here. Showed up on my doorstep one day looking for work."

Lucy nodded to herself, lips pressed tight as she thought. "So where do you reckon they went – if they aren't welcome home?"

"Probably north to British territory. Titus was always threatening to make for there and sign on with a whisky post. It's a job would suit his temperament – drink poteen all day, and put his boots to drunk Indians. Don't worry about those two, if they were dropped into hell Titus would claim the window with the cool breeze for the two of them." Straw stopped himself then, realizing he had ventured in to rocky territory. This was a tender subject for her.

"Like Abner," said Lucy, "cut from the same bad cloth." Lucy's eyes wandered aimlessly about the saloon, then came back to rest on him. "Mr. Straw, I have a boon to ask of you."

"Just you ask, Mrs. Stoveall. I'd be pleased to do whatever I can."

She poured herself another dollop of whisky before speaking. "I want you to take me up north and help me find my husband. He ought to know what befell my sister."

Dooley jingled the coins in his pocket, a warning to Straw. He didn't need it. "Mrs. Stoveall, that's not a good idea," Straw said. "The country up there isn't fit for a woman."

"I'll be the judge of that."

Straw was treading carefully. "I traded in that country for a short while. It wasn't easy country then, and it's got a damn sight worse. The Indians are dying in droves up there from smallpox. Whisky has made them beggars. They know who brought both to them. White folks aren't welcome." He paused. "I'll be damned if I take a white woman into that."

Straw's refusal, the whisky in her, caused Lucy to loose the grip on her smouldering anger. Lips twisted, she remarked to Dooley, "He's kindness itself, Mr. Dooley, isn't he? He'll talk good deeds every which way. But he won't deliver." She swung round to Straw. "Don't think I don't know your kind, do-gooder," she said, voice climbing dangerously high. "I see through you."

Dooley broke in, trying to bend her from her course. "Think it might rain again, Miz Stoveall?"

But Lucy Stoveall was not about to be deflected. "I know your kind," she said, keeping her attention fixed on Straw.

"Understand me, Mrs. Stoveall, I'm not taking you to chase after your husband in that country. But if you want, I'll go and look for him myself. That I'll do."

"He wouldn't come back for the likes of you," Lucy said. "You aren't the sort of man to get a point across. You're a creeping Christer, Bible-reader, do-gooder like that Clumb."

It was an unkind comparison, but Straw told himself she was unmoored because of the funeral. "Mrs. Stoveall, you aren't going to get a rise out of me, I can promise you that."

"No, sir, I won't get a rise out of you," she shot back. "Because you're a cheek-turner. You let everybody run over you – old Daniels, even your hired hands."

Dooley was inching his chair towards them, bumping the legs over the floorboards. "Miz Stoveall," he said, proceeding carefully, "Custis only has your interests at heart. And he's right –"

Lucy flared. "I don't give a damn if he's right! You think Custis Straw's being right means anything to me!"

"I want you to listen to me, Mrs. Stoveall," Straw said, ever so softly. "It's true, you want me to be wrong, but wanting doesn't make a thing so. It's best you wait on your husband here. It can't be too long before he turns up. Until he does, you ought to move out of that busted-up wagon and into more comfortable quarters. I want you to have my room here in the Stubhorn."

Just then, Dooley's question to Lucy about the possibility of more rain was answered. Sheet lightning sent a flicker through the room that played a blue-white jig on all their faces. Thunder rolled an empty, groaning barrel over the roof and set the windowpanes to rattling in their frames.

Straw saw that the liquor had finally got the better of Lucy Stoveall. There was no more life in those lovely brown eyes than in a doll's. She was no longer with them. He said to Dooley, "Take Mrs. Stoveall upstairs to my room. She needs to rest. See her settled."

Dooley fingered Lucy's elbow delicately. She rose, took a few faltering steps. There was a sharp crack of thunder, but she didn't register that, nor the sizzle of light that danced through the saloon. Straw took a small bottle from his jacket pocket and pressed it into her hand. "Laudanum. If you wake, Mrs. Stoveall, take a draft. It's a soporific."

Lucy accepted it numbly. Dooley led her upstairs.

Lucy groped her way out of an opiate dream. She could not locate Madge, kept reaching for her. Ever since Abner had left them, they had shared a bed for warmth, for comfort. She could smell the familiar scent of her sister. Her palms ran over the sheets, fumbling for her.

Then Lucy remembered Madge was dead. She sat straight up with the shock of it. It was the lye soap her sister had scrubbed Straw's laundry with that she was smelling; it was there in Straw's sheets, the same harsh, cleanly odour that had worked its way into her sister's hands. A picture rose in Lucy's mind: her little sister's raw red fingers toying with the buttons of her dress as she sang.

Lucy lit a lamp to chase away the picture. The room had no clock, but she could feel the lateness of the hour. She had obliterated the afternoon, the evening, most of the night in dreamless sleep.

She saw herself in the mirror above the bureau, saw how much Madge and she had resembled one another. The white bodies scattered with russet freckles they had tried to fade with buttermilk poultices, laughing at their foolishness. The high, slanted cheekbones. Madge's sorrel hair just a tad darker than her own tousled red mane. Lucy's grief was a mother's grief. The longing to mark changes in her child. My baby, she thought. My baby that I mothered, that I raised up. My baby that they took from me.

A brush lay beside the lamp on the bureau, beckoning. Lucy took it up. It had a silver back, streaked with tarnish. The weight of the silver was the weight of sorrow. Slowly, she flexed her wrist, watching the lamplight slide to and fro from the brightness of the metal to its dark tarnish. She made a pass through the air and felt the abundant heaviness of Madge's hair under the brush. She heard singing, a purely pitched voice. Felt pleasure as she brushed Madge's hair and her sister sang. Lucy's lips began to move.

Straw had waited all afternoon and evening in case Lucy came back downstairs. She didn't. Around ten o'clock, Dooley called it a day and took to his cot in the backroom of the Stubhorn. Straw made a mattress from the folded tarp and lay down to sleep in his clothes. But he could feel every board in the floor. The pain of the old war wounds to his legs stabbed him awake each time he tossed and turned. It rose from his body like revenants from a graveyard.

Straw knew there was no point in coaxing sleep any longer. Stealing through the darkness of the saloon in his stockinged feet, he went out the back door. The storm was over and the sky was clear of clouds. Straw stood in the wet grass under a mass of seething stars, countless sparks in the pitch-black night, drawing the coolness of rain-freshened air deep into his lungs.

Above him, the lamp came on in his room. He shifted to where the light from the window lay spread on the ground, gleaming on the wet grass, and checked his pocket watch. Four o'clock. For several minutes he stood begging the lamp to go out, for Lucy Stoveall to ease back into sleep.

Suddenly there came a faint voice, a tune afloat, drifting all around the light in which he stood. He strained to catch it, the voice slowly strengthening under his attention; the words finally making the darkness ring.

> "Let us pause in life's pleasures
> And count its many tears
> While we all sup sorrow with the poor.
> There's a song that will linger forever in our ears;
> Oh, hard times come again no more . . ."

Lucy Stoveall was singing up there, in his room. The voice was familiar, but it was not hers. A light voice, a young girl's voice.

He was hearing Madge. As Lucy had said, no one had sung for her sister. Now it seemed Madge was singing for herself.

"'Tis the song, the sigh of the weary
Hard times, hard times, come again no more
Many days you have lingered around my cabin door;
Oh hard times come again no more."

The singing stopped. The light went out and they all returned to their respective darkness.

9

CHARLES   Yesterday evening, urged into action by the tattoo of the native drummer, I threw on my hat and coat and rushed off to the I. G. Baker Company, the firm engaged by Father's New York business agent to act as our expedition's treasury, seeking there dependable advice and assistance in the matter of locating Jerry Potts.

In my excitement, I had not stopped to think that given the lateness of the hour – somewhere around nine o'clock – that Mr. Baker would not be at the helm of his establishment. A foreman supervising the unloading of a shipment of goods informed me the proprietor had gone home, but, if I wished, I could speak to a Mr. Jabez Cooke. In the grip of my newly found resolve, I said, "Yes, at once."

Directed to his office in the warehouse, I found Mr. Cooke presiding over a cluttered, filthy room with windrows of dead flies banked on every window sash. Mr. Cooke is typical of the specimens of American frontier manhood I have so far encountered, lanky, gaunt, most likely malarial. After offering him a cheroot, the end of which he bit off and began to chew, setting the remainder aside, I stated that I had come to him, a gentleman representing one of the great mercantile firms of Fort Benton, to make an inquiry about one of its citizens.

"Who might that be?" he asked, making himself comfortable, slinging a sinewy arm over the side of his chair and hoisting a cuspidor into his lap into which he squirted a stream of cheroot juice from between his front teeth.

"Mr. Jerry Potts. Do you know where I can find him?"

Mr. Cooke mumbled that he didn't have time to keep track of half-breeds and their damn peregrinations. Then, rather impudently I thought, he asked what I wanted with Potts. I told him my brother and I wished to engage this Potts as a scout for our forthcoming expedition north. I added that it would prove useful to me if he could provide me with any information about this individual's suitability and character.

Mr. Cooke, as it turned out, was only too willing to oblige. After twenty-five years involved in the trade with the Indians of the Upper Missouri, his and Jerry Potts's paths have crossed often. He embarked unbidden on an interminable tale of Potts's ancestry and upbringing, which, as I listened to it, seemed to rival one of Mr. Charles Dickens's own novels, not only in its length, but as a chronicle of childhood hardship and ill-usage. Jerry Potts, I learned, is the son of a respectable Scot, Mr. Andrew Potts, who some thirty years ago was an employee of the American Fur Company during the time of the great trade in beaver pelts. Andrew Potts took an Indian woman to his bed, a Blood of the Blackfoot Nation, called Crooked Back, who, in due time, delivered him a son christened Jerry Potts. Sadly, while the child was still an infant, Andrew Potts was murdered by a disgruntled Blackfoot who shoved a musket through the trading wicket of Fort Mackenzie and shot him dead.

Crooked Back then formed another liaison with a Scottish trader, Alexander Harvey, who, in Cooke's florid telling, seems to have exceeded the brutality and depravity of Dickens's Bill Sykes. Crooked Back soon fled Harvey to return to the Blood tribe, leaving behind her baby son in Harvey's charge.

When, bewildered, I asked why a woman would do such a thing, Mr. Cooke simply remarked with a nonchalant shrug, "Maybe Harvey wouldn't surrender the boy so's to punish her. Maybe Crooked Back thought it would be best if her son was raised white."

Mr. Cooke spat into the cuspidor on his lap with an air of reflection, leaned towards me across his scarred desk, and with great relish launched into a series of gruesome anecdotes touching upon Harvey's depravity. The heat of the close, stuffy office threatened to overwhelm me as these blood-soaked yarns were related. It was a struggle to curtail my impatience, but being determined to find Potts, I hoped that if I bore with Mr. Cooke, in the end he might impart some useful information that would be of assistance in locating the scout.

Everyone, it seemed, had been terrified of Alexander Harvey, white and Indian alike. When the American Fur Company engages at Fort Mackenzie could no longer bear his presence, they organized a petition to company headquarters in St. Louis, asking that he be removed. Harvey caught wind of it, beat every signer to a pulp, and went so far as to murder one of the petitioners within the very walls of the fort.

Harvey was a law unto himself. When a Blackfoot took a pig which he found wandering outside the walls of the fort, the Scot tracked him down and put a musket ball in his leg. "He sauntered up to the wounded brave, cool as you please," Mr. Cooke continued, "lit a pipe and offered it to the groaning Indian. While the Blackfoot smoked, Harvey commented on the pleasing warmth of the sun, the prettiness of the view. When the Blackfoot had finished the pipe, Harvey said, 'Take one last look at this fine world and think of how you're going to miss it.' Put his musket to the Indian's ear and blew his brains out."

But according to Mr. Cooke, the escapade which brought this madman's career in the fur trade to an end involved a slave owned by one of the managers of the American Fur Company. In the depths of winter, the poor Negro was sent out to cut fuel in the woods near Fort Mackenzie. There he was discovered by Blackfoot who killed and scalped him. For Harvey, the murder of a black man was of no consequence, but the destruction of a piece of valuable company property was. He was determined to teach the Blackfoot a lesson. The next spring when they rode up to the fort ready to trade their skins, Harvey met them with a loaded cannon and, without warning, fired into their party, killing and wounding a score of them. Apparently, these particular Indians were not the perpetrators of the crime in question, but that did not matter to Harvey. However, his action did not instill in the Blackfoot a respect for the white man's property, but only a great hatred for the American Fur Company. The Indians inaugurated a campaign of harassment and murder of such ferocity against the traders that the fort had to be evacuated and abandoned.

Cooke gave me a yellow-toothed grin after relating this incident. "There was mighty hard feelings towards Harvey after that. The one thing you don't want to interfere with is a man's pockets. It was decided the only way to be rid of Harvey was to kill him. For every one of them put a knife into him at the same time. But Harvey was too cute and canny for them bumblers. He got wind of the plot, stole a boat, and headed downstream. The bastard purely disappeared without leaving a trace."

"And Jerry Potts? What of the boy?"

"Well, it's a hard thing, but a man's life is precious to him and I reckon a kid so young would have only slowed him down so Harvey left him behind. There's some who say the only soft spot Harvey had in his black heart was for the little tyke. But for him, Harvey didn't have a friend in the world. I've heard from engages at Fort Mackenzie that when Harvey got drunk he'd keep the boy up all night playing cards with him in his quarters, they could hear him ranting to young Potts how everybody was against Alexander Harvey, how he didn't dare turn his back on a man-jack of them for fear of getting shot or stabbed. Would Jerry stand by him? Could he count on him?"

Delicately, I made the observation that the fashion in which Potts was raised surely must have encouraged criminal tendencies in the boy. The more I heard, the more I wondered how suitable a guide Jerry Potts would be.

"How he was raised did toughen him some," Mr. Cooke remarked matter-of-factly. "I'll grant you that. Rumour has it that after Harvey lit out on him, Potts lived like a stray dog at the company posts, sleeping in any corner, eating whatever table scraps he got thrown. But he survived it, and that recommends him in this part of the world. And then another Scotchman, Andrew Dawson, came along and took him under his wing, put him to work in the trade, tried his best to make a honest, sober Scotchman out of him."

"And the experiment was a success?" I said, growing more hopeful.

"Up to a point," said Mr. Cooke. "Over the years, Potts had occasionally seen his mother when the Bloods came in to trade. Finally, she decided to take him off to live with her and her people for a time. The Bloods watered down the white in him a good deal, I reckon. Taught him to hunt like a Indian, ride like a Indian, read land like a Indian, fight like a Indian. They taught him Blackfoot religion. So he's neither fish nor fowl. No man can tell where the white in him stops and the red starts."

The question needed to be asked of Mr. Cooke. If he were in my position, would he hire Potts?

"Potts carries a map of every river, every butte, every coulee, every pimple on the prairie's ass up there in his head. But, more important, once you set foot into Blackfoot country he's your safe passage. Potts is worth a troop of cavalry. He stands mighty high in their estimation. The Blackfoot call him Bear Child, and that's more than just a name like John or Joe, it's a title of honour. They gave it to him after he led them in a mighty battle with the Crow. If Jerry Potts is with you and your party keeps its nose clean, don't give offence, the Blackfoot won't touch a hair on your heads."

Mr. Cooke lit the remainder of my cheroot. His tiny office had all along been an oven, but now it was becoming a smoky oven. I could tolerate it no longer. "What you must tell me, Mr. Cooke, is how to find Potts. It is a matter of great urgency."

"Well," said Mr. Cooke, "if he's anywheres about town, or near town, I'd recommend a tour of the drinking establishments. Sooner or later Potts will turn up in one of them, or some barfly will have seen him. Jerry Potts is a boy with the taste for the booze."

After thanking Mr. Cooke, I hastened to apply his advice. However, I did not find Jerry Potts last night in any of the saloons and taverns I visited. And none of the patrons were very helpful when I attempted to solicit information. They treated me with thinly veiled contempt, calling me pilgrim, tinhorn, and tenderfoot to my face.

This morning I must resume my quest for the dipsomaniac frontiersman despite my reservations about employing such a man as Mr. Cooke described to me. But a fire must be lit under Addington and so, whatever Potts's deficiencies of character, he must do.

❖ ❖ ❖

ALOYSIUS DOOLEY It's good to have the funeral parlour closed and the Stubhorn back to business. Lucy Stoveall left yesterday, cleared out of Custis's room upstairs. He tried to hold her, but lost that battle. I like her style, she's about the only one I know can knock Custis back on his heels. Right now, he's setting over at his regular table by the window, just short of noon and sucking up whisky, reading his pocket Bible. I don't know what he hopes to find in it.

Custis Straw does his best to hide his bruises. He took it hard that Lucy Stoveall brushed off his charity, and I know the tittle-tattle blowing round town about him and Madge is eating at his guts like lime. That fool business with the belt proved that. Last two days he's scarcely set foot outside the Stubhorn, whisky and that black book his only occupations.

This hour of the day, I got nothing to do but think about doleful Straw, rinse glasses, and hop for Danny Rand, that wet-behind-the-ears young tough, pal to the Kelsos. I got no use for anybody who sticks himself at the far end of a counter just to make a man walk to pour a drink. Though maybe the distance between us is a benefit, seeing how he stinks. Filthy jacket and filthier shirt, trousers stiff with dirt, horsehair, and sweat. Rand's been riding bareback, meaning either he lost his saddle in a poker game, or he's helped himself to somebody's stray horse. Little wonder he's so friendly with those scapegrace Kelso boys. Rand carries himself with the same nasty swagger as Titus Kelso. Walks around with a chip on his shoulder, just asking for somebody to knock it off.

Everybody is entitled to make a mistake, but Custis runs to big ones. Maybe there's some excuse for him hiring Joel Kelso, but how Custis could miss Titus's nature is a mystery. He is a nasty piece of work altogether, one of them little gamecocks set on proving he's got the sharpest spurs in the barnyard, and the biggest crow. Custis might have seen it too, if he weren't so damned lazy, happy to be a rocking-chair horse dealer, whiling away his days with a glass in his hand, instead of minding to his own property and his business concerns. I told him that straight to his face, but he just flashed a toothy grin and said, "You rate money too high, Aloysius. You want to be rich and I only ask to be comfortable. 'Consider the lilies of the field, how they grow; they toil not, neither do they spin: And yet I say unto you, That even Solomon in all his glory was not arrayed like one of these.'" What I ought to say to him now is, "What you're arrayed in, Custis Straw, is shit. Head to toe. And nobody thinks you smell like a lily."

But to make excuses for him, I reckon the Kelsos pulled their horns in whenever Custis took the trouble to hoist his big arse out of a easy chair and sally out to the ranch. But that was infrequent enough. I don't know how the man makes a dollar with his carefree ways.

The day McIntyre came in here looking for Custis to buy a string of pack horses off him, it was me, out of the goodness of my heart, that drove out to Custis's property on the off-chance he might actually be found overseeing his concern and I could bring him back to town so's he wouldn't lose a opportunity to cut a deal with McIntyre.

Rolled up to the breaking corral just as Titus was bucking out a buckskin gelding every bit as cantankerous as himself. Set my buggy brake just in time to receive the joy of seeing that mustang flop himself to the ground with Titus's boot hung in the stirrup and go for a roll, mash Titus between saddle and hardpan like he was a boiled spud. When Titus was ready for a ladle of gravy, up that horse bounced to his feet, cinch broken and saddle half-twisted off his back. Couple of bucks and the surcingle snapped, and there went the saddle, flying high as a mortar round.

Titus was a pitiful, broken sight. He tried to gather his legs under him, but they'd collapse and plunk down he'd drop to his hands and knees. Joel and me went over the rails to help him, but Titus just cursed us, pawing through the horseshit like a crawling baby, nose sprinkling blood in the dust. Joel tiptoeing after him, squeaking, "Tite, how you doing? How you doing, Tite?"

Tite weren't doing too good, but after a bit he got himself upright and said to Joel, "I'm going to burn that whoreson to the ground. Get me that other saddle and a spade bit." Joel hopped to it, he takes orders from Titus like his brother was the resurrected Christ.

Titus edged up on the horse with a lariat. When he dropped a loop on him, the gelding took off like a scalded cat, skidded him around the corral on his boot heels, teeth jolting in his jaws. Titus ploughed a lot of ground before the buckskin quit his fight, planted himself spraddle-legged, and stood watching Titus pull himself hand over hand down the rope towards him. Soon as Titus got to within five feet of the buckskin, that mustang laid his ears back and struck like a snake. Sank them big, ugly teeth in Titus's chest, shook him like a terrier on a rat, Titus screeching and flopping. My, but wasn't that a sweet serenade to Aloysius Donald Dooley's ears.

After the horse had his chew, he let Titus loose. Titus reeled away, ripping at his shirt buttons. The bite mark was big as a soup plate and bloody. Once he seen the damage, Titus hugged his chest, scrunched himself up around the pain of it for a fair while, uttering blasphemies.

Joel was doing his best to persuade Titus to see sense. "Hell, you don't need this, Tite. He ain't about to quit fighting you. Just leave him be."

Well, that was not the approach to take. I reckon Joel was saying the last thing Titus could tolerate, that this was too much horse for him. "Latch on to that rope," Titus snapped at him. "And hold him." Off he stomped in a rage.

Joel obliged, but he kept a respectful distance between himself and those teeth. The horse never stirred a foot awaiting the next eventuality.

Titus come back with a pair of hoof clippers. "All right," he told Joel, "give me that son of a bitch." Joel made tracks out of harm's way and Titus commenced dragging himself back down that lariat. Same as before, the horse went for Titus, but this time Titus was ready, he chopped them clippers smack into the gelding's head, flung all his weight on the rope, and yanked the mustang down hard to the ground. You could hear the breath whistle out of that horse when he hit.

Titus dropped down on the buckskin's neck, and sat there panting for a spell, hefting them clippers in his hand as the horse heaved under him, trying to rise. Then Titus starts to pounding on its neck, smack smack, no more expression on his mean little mug than if he were shingling a roof. Every time them clippers landed they popped a grunt out of that horse that shook him all the way down to his legs.

Joel was giggling beside me. "That old horse run fire ants up Tite's pants. He gone be sorry. When Tite's finished licking on that neck, it's gone be soft as butter. You could rein him with a thread."

I called out, "That horse ain't your property, Titus."

Titus just kept whaling away. About the time I feared he was going to kill that horse, Titus scooted his buttocks off the mustang's neck. It come up like a colt on new legs, dazed, all atremble, coat slippery with sweat.

The Kelsos swarmed him. Joel clamped teeth to a ear; Titus snared a hind leg with a rope, jacked it up, tied it off fast and neat. Left standing on three legs that horse weren't about to fight. They bridled him with the spade bit, threw on the saddle, Titus swung up, settled his seat, gathered the reins. Joel whipped the rope off the hind leg.

The mustang fired straight up, slithery as a eel, slammed down stiff-legged and squealing, timing its kick to pitch Titus over its head. But Titus righted himself, flopped back in the saddle, nailed the rowels of his spurs to the mustang's shoulders, raked it back to the flanks, gouging hard. They whirligigged round that corral, Joel bellowing, "Burr on a blanket! Stick him, Tite! Stick him!"

Titus can ride, dirty little tick. That mustang gave it his all, but when he couldn't buck his torment he tried to outrun it. Dog with a tin can rattling on its tail, it fairly flew, eyes wild and bulging, hooves drumming panic clear to where I hung on the rails.

Titus just let the buckskin gallop, reins slack, yipping, spurring cruel, leaning into the turns as they tore around the corral. Made me think of a crazy man's mind going in circles. All at once, Titus hollered for a way out the asylum. "Open the gate!"

Joel cracked it wide. The mustang cut for the gate directly, legs churning, nostrils flared. Titus Kelso sitting the horse easy, no more expression on his face than a face on a coin.

Almost at the gate, horse going hard for open prairie, Titus jerks the gee rein hard to his hip. Spade bit caught the mustang's mouth like a fish hook, bent that butter-soft neck like a bow. Horse slid to his haunches in a spray of dust and dirt, eyes rolling. Titus braced himself, toes aimed skyward in the stirrups. Rail splintered when they crashed into it, a dry crack flat as a rifle shot. Felt the corral fence jolt even where I stood, jumped like a live thing under my hand. Everything went slow, Titus sliding out of the saddle, horse turning jelly-spined, a piece of broken rail sticking out of its chest, one hoof tapping the corral poles as he slumped like a mudslide.

Joel and me scrambled over the fence; Titus lifted his eyes to us as we run to him. All he had to say for himself was, "Son of a bitch shied straight into the fence."

"You reined him into that fence!" I shouted.

Titus flattened a thumb on the side of his nose, snorted blood from it. "Ain't you going to ask me how I'm faring, Mr. Dooley?" He was cold as a witch's teat.

"I seen how you turned that horse into that fence, you mean little chigger!"

"I turn what I turn for a reason. Man or horse," was all he said.

I considered telling Custis what had happened, but I held my peace. I don't believe I could have persuaded him there was intention to what Titus Kelso did. Custis would have explained it away as mishap. He fancies himself the expert on human nature, but he don't examine himself. Many a time I've heard him say, "A soft answer turneth away wrath." But he's short on soft answers himself. Custis just had to contradict Lucy Stoveall where she was sore, which is dangerous to do with a woman as wrathful as she is at present. He couldn't help but tell her she's crazy to moulder in that busted wagon when she can have his room and feather bed just for the asking. Or that he ain't going to cart her off up north to find her worthless husband.

I ain't no authority on the fair sex, but I know better than to go controverting a angry woman. With her sister so foully murdered, how does Custis expect Lucy Stoveall to see reason, be anything but bitter mad? Her last grip on Madge is the rage she's feeling, and she ain't about to let it go. Custis's talking sense to her isn't about to pour cold water on it, only stoke it stronger.

Unlike Lucy Stoveall, Custis won't let his anger show. It's the war he's mad about, the waste of it. He sits on his hoard of precious fury like a miser sitting on his gold. Neither Lucy Stoveall nor Custis Straw are ready yet to forget the dead. In quiet moments, I've seen all them dead soldiers walk across his face.

It drives him to distraction that he can't hide himself from me like he does everybody else. It's a burr under his foreskin that I know his thoughts so well. He's forever boasting he owns a cross-bench mind, but he don't fool Aloysius Dooley. What Custis calls thinking for himself is just a excuse to poke a stick in somebody's eye, stir up trouble. He jokes about going unarmed, says a empty holster is his guardian angel because the only thing certain to get somebody hanged in lawless parts is to shoot a man who don't carry a weapon. But that ain't the whole truth. He's scared to trust himself with a gun. I reckon the war taught him a man can develop a taste for killing just like he can for whores, cards, or whisky. So Custis won't touch a weapon, for fear it will tempt him.

He's all affection and pity for tail-enders because when he's taking their side or uplifting them, he don't feel his own shortfallings. I told him a sociable, sensible man keeps off certain topics, and don't take the part of unpopular folk.

"Give me an instance," he says, "where I did that."

"Well, like arguing with the Missouri man who said the niggers ought to be shipped back to Africa and you saying that if we paid them passage and back wages owed for a couple hundred years of labour they'd likely jump at the offer."

"What else was I supposed to say? I happen to believe it," he barks at me.

"It's a dangerous opinion to offer to a man of strong convictions primed with three-quarters of a bottle of whisky."

"I got my rights," is all he says.

Well, I got my rights too. He's got no business aggravating my customers, making the whisky go sour in their bellies. And he hogs that table to himself by the window like he homesteaded the spot. What's more, Bible reading is worst than darky music for spreading glumness. I've seen jolly fellows flinch at the sight of his Bible. Makes them think of their mothers praying for them somewheres.

Speaking of customers, there goes that blamed Danny Rand, rapping a coin on the bar-top for service. A man wants a drink, he ought to ask for it pleasant, not crack away with his money, waggle his empty glass at me like a whore's ass. A saloon-keeper's life is a cross.

❖ ❖ ❖

CUSTIS Maybe carrying that belt off with me wasn't such a good idea. I can't stop worrying over it in my mind and worrying over it with my fingers. Aloysius once said to me his old Mam was always clicking her rosary and when she wasn't, she was always thinking she ought to be. He said those beads were the bane of her life. I reckon that the belt that murdered Madge Dray is turning into my dusky rosary. I know every inch of it by heart already, same as Mrs. Dooley knew her prayers. I see it in my sleep, can't escape it waking. A length of wide, thick leather, black, stained, nicked, scarred. Ordinary, clumsy brass buckle. Three brass studs on the tip of it as if they'd been put there to add sting to a whipping. The sight of them stings me, makes me regret I took Madge away from her pleasure that evening. If I hadn't, she might be alive today. A working man's belt, cinch for a roustabout, trapper, muleskinner, saddle tramp. That doesn't narrow things down. You could fit Fort Benton's quality in a canoe; the ordinary folk would fill a couple of steamboats.

I can scarce keep from fingering it in my pocket now, but Aloysius's watching me from behind the bar like an old mother hen. It was a mistake to have shown him the belt as soon as I got back from the jail and to have inquired of him if he had seen anyone wearing it. First thing he asked was what was behind my question. When I told him it had choked the life out of that poor girl, Aloysius shook his head hard and kept repeating, "No, I ain't seen that on none of my customers, and I don't want to see it again. Put that out of sight. My sight and yours, Custis. That ain't a keepsake a sane man clings to."

It's risky to question too many about the belt because I don't want those with an unfavourable opinion of me to be reminded of my association with little Madge. But last night I took it down to Mr. Robert E. Lee's laundry and bathhouse, inquired whether he'd seen this particular item when stowing the clothes of his customers who'd come to him for a soak. The Chinaman smiled at me and shook his head, saying he didn't look too close at any of the duds came into his care for fear of seeing the wildlife in them. After that, we smoked two pipes of opium. When I got back to the Stubhorn, I sat on my bed staring at that belt, trying to summon up some recollection of it on my own.

Two pipes of opium and that belt before bed were a bad combination. No sooner had I dropped off into a light sleep than those torches that had led Madame Magique's parade started to wave in my dreams, blobs of fiery jelly marching up and down Front Street, over and over.

Next and all of a sudden, Madge Dray was on top of me, naked, tiny-breasted, squatting over my hips, lewdly parting her sex, sliding down on me, mewing like a cat. I tried to lift her off me. But then my pleasure rose up in me too fierce and I gave way to it. When I did, she started to shrink smaller and smaller until she was scarcely bigger than my prick, just a silky sleeve stroking my lust, a doll not a girl. And all the time this was happening, I knew how wrong a thing it was.

This morning my drawers were stiff with the stains of a callow boy. I can't stop wondering where that terrible, evil dream arose from. The Bible says, "For as he thinketh in his heart, so is he." A dream isn't a thought, but it surely is a close cousin to one. Last night made me feel almost as ashamed as if I'd really done the thing people accuse me of.

A shadow falls across my table, I feel a gush of warm air, hear the flap of swinging doors. Who's paused on the threshold of the Stubhorn but that English bill poster, looking fresh as a new-picked daisy. A real, genuine English toff, the kind of handsome young man women whisper about behind their fans when he swans into a room. Tall, slim, clean-shaven, pale-blue eyes, one of those Roman beaks that whichever lady it points at, it points at willing prey. Lounge jacket, fawn waistcoat, Shepherd's plaid trousers, low-crowned bowler cocked jauntily to the side of his head. A whiff of lemon verbena. English tailoring and courage in your costume – it makes a man stand out. I've never dared further than black broadcloth.

Aloysius is awestruck by the Englishman's glory, and the dirty gunsel draped over the bar, garments rotting off him, pastes a sneer on his mouth on account of all that finery. The Englishman's polished ankle boots head for the bar. Same as fresh shit gathers flies, he's made to attract trouble.

"If I might impose on you," the Englishman says to Aloysius, "I'm seeking a Mr. Potts. Have you seen the gentleman this morning?"

The saddle tramp wades in before Aloysius can answer. "Hey, darling, be polite and buy a drink from the man before you jump all over him with your goddamn questions."

"Quite so," the Englishman says coolly. "A gin, if you please, landlord."

Aloysius ducks down under the counter; there's a great clinking of glass and he produces a bottle of oily-looking gin that must have been distilled about the time Noah built the ark. It's an apology the way Aloysius pours it.

The Englishman pays and lifts his drink to Aloysius. "Cheers," he says.

The rowdy at the bar passes comment. "Gin's a whore's drink."

I'm not sure the Englishman understands where the hardcase is pushing towards. If he does, I've got to admire him, he's bland as custard to the offence.

"A drink for whores and bugger boys," adds the saddle tramp.

"I daresay," remarks the Englishman, picks his glass up and ambles towards an empty table.

"Don't prance away from me," says the hardcase. "I'm talking to you."

I catch the Englishman's eye. "Care to join me?"

"Honoured and delighted." He takes a chair. "Charles Gaunt."

I give him my hand. "Custis Straw."

I hoist a looksee over Mr. Gaunt's shoulder. The fellow at the bar is muttering something to Aloysius. Aloysius shakes his head in disgust and turns away from him. Mr. Gaunt takes out a snowy hand-kerchief and dabs at the sweat on his upper lip. The day promises to be a scorcher; in a couple of hours the Stubhorn will be hotter than the hubs of hell.

Mr. Gaunt nods to my Bible. "You were at your devotions when I entered, sir. I have interrupted them."

"Well, it's a life's study. I don't reckon I'll ever get to the bottom of it. It can wait."

"My brother is devout." The way he says it, devout on his lips sounds like a disease.

"That the one that went missioning to the Indians?"

Mr. Gaunt nods. "You've seen my circulars?"

"Hard to miss, Mr. Gaunt."

He fidgets with his waistcoat, sips his gin. "As you may have overheard, I am looking for a Mr. Potts. Do you know if he has a res-idence in town?"

"I hear he's camped upriver, about five or six miles from Benton. I can take you there if you like."

A look of surprise and relief flits across Mr. Gaunt's face. He sends me a thankful smile. "That is most welcome news, sir. Very hospitable of you. I am at your disposal whenever it is convenient."

He's all eagerness, but good manners covers it so only the hem shows. I've put down five whiskies in my belly and I don't relish shaking them up in a hot afternoon ride. Mr. Gaunt can wait. "Tomorrow then. Early. Meet me here."

"My brother Addington will certainly wish to accompany us, if you are agreeable to that."

"The more the merrier."

He starts to thank me again when the sound of broken-down boots slapping the puncheon floor makes him turn round in his chair. The barfly is teetering over him.

"You walked away from me. Who the hell you think you are?"

From behind the bar, Aloysius shouts, "Clear off out of there, Rand."

Rand ignores him. "Don't turn your high and mighty nose up at me – not when you keep this sort of company," he says to Mr. Gaunt, pointing at me.

"Go away, son," I say. "You weren't invited to this party."

"And if I don't?" Just like that, Rand's dragged a Smith & Wesson topbreak .38 out of his jacket pocket and has it aimed at me. He's swaying so wildly from the effects of drink that the gun barrel moves like a pendulum in front of my face. "Little girl diddler," he says.

I see Aloysius, five paces to the side of Rand. I don't know how he got to that position so fast and so quiet. Aloysius stands on those long legs of his as still as a blue heron peering into water, beak poised to strike. A twelve-gauge sawed-off rests in the crook of his arm. It's not pointed at Rand, it's just propped there comfortable and ready. The Irishman doesn't say a word.

The young rowdy's eyes flick from Aloysius to me, back to Aloysius. Rand laughs too loudly, pockets the pistol, walks unsteadily to the swing doors. They flap and wheeze on their rusty hinges as he passes through them.

In the sudden quiet when the doors stop swinging, I hear the building creak and breathe, more alive than I will ever be.

10

On the bank of the Missouri, Jerry Potts sits under a moulting cottonwood, surrounded by a blizzard of drifting fluff, clothes speckled white, head hoary. The gnarled tree's cotton lies thick on the ground, eddies and squirms with every breath of breeze, swirls down to settle onto the ash-coloured surface of the river, where plumes of mist lazily rise and disperse. Dawn breaks dove grey, a pearly sun squinting at Potts's herd of horses watering in the shallows. Silence is peppered with soft sounds, the suck of a hoof extricated from mud, the snuffle and gulp of drinking horses, the quiet patter of water dripping from a lifted muzzle, the tentative song of birds hopping about in the brush.

A man notoriously close-mouthed, infamous for one-word answers, he is practising thinking in English. Resting his hand on the grip of the pistol jammed in his belt, he laboriously retrieves all the English names for the weapon. Revolver. Six-shooter. Side arm. Equalizer. Firearm. .45. Short gun. Hog-leg. Roscoe. Peacemaker. Colt. It is a difficult task to recall them all. English is a stubborn, balky tongue. It moves in his mind in fits and starts, often planting its feet and refusing to budge.

He wonders why it does so. His two Almost Fathers, Harvey and Dawson, spoke nothing to him but English. Maybe his head is like the buffalo paunches in which the Blackfoot store water. Maybe his mother, Crooked Back, poured so many Kanai words into his baby-ear that he has room in his head for only a few drops of English. Thinking in English is too hard, too wearisome, and he allows his mind to slip gratefully into the tongue of his mother's people.

Nothing exists for white men unless they give it a name in their own language. His mother's people, the Kanai, they call Bloods. The Nitsi-tapi, they call the Blackfoot. Once they give a name to a thing they think that is enough to understand it.

The Nitsi-tapi accept him as one of their own, despite his Scotchman father. The whites will never do the same. The whites are proud of their blood, always boasting that theirs is stronger than the blood of any other people. So how is it that the strong blood doesn't overcome the weaker? If they believe what they say, why isn't he a Scotchman? But even Dawson, the Almost Father he loved, never believed him a true Scotchman. He thought like all whites. One drop of black blood makes a man a nigger, and one drop of Kanai blood makes Jerry Potts a red nigger.

He lifts his face to the cloud of falling cotton, delighting in its gentle, tickling touch. It feels like baby Mitchell's soft black hair brushing against his throat in the days when he could hold his son close. To give his son an English name had been a mistake. Bad luck for them all. For Mary, for Mitchell, for him.

It has been two long years since he last saw his boy, since Mary took Mitchell south to the basin of the Powder and Bighorn rivers to live in the lodges of the River Crow. By now, Mitchell will have forgotten the face of his father, just as he himself has forgotten the face of Andrew Potts, long dead in the ground. In a little time, Mitchell will be playing the hoop-and-arrow game, herding horses with the other Crow boys. A few more winters will pass and he will be tall and strong enough to go on his first horse-stealing raid, perhaps as servant to the pipeholder. It is a great sorrow to Potts to think his son will grow up to be a Crow-speaker, will never learn more than a few simple words of the beautiful language of the Kanai, just enough to hurl insults at them when they meet in battle. It is even sadder to know that his son is being raised to hate the blood of his own veins, being taught to call the Real People the Treacherous Ones in the fashion of the Crow. His son's spirit will be divided like his own is, never at rest. Mitchell the

Crow-Kanai, Jerry Potts the Scotchman-Kanai.

How foolish desire is, Potts thinks, to have led him to lose all reason, to take a Crow woman to his bed. Mary, eighteen, in a green trader dress that rattled with rows of elk teeth, her glossy hair black as the obsidian points the Nez Perce tribe trade from behind the Backbone of the World. Mary, graceful, quiet, gentle. Mary who once teased him about the skimpy whiskers of his moustache, calling him Mouse.

He had given her father, wily Talker Drum, a present of twenty horses, a Spencer carbine, ten ropes of tobacco, a dozen silk handkerchiefs before he would consent to the marriage. Talker Drum bargained hard, but in the end he was very pleased to have a son-in-law who was the Almost Child of Dawson, a fine connection that ensured Talker Drum would be supplied with much powder and shot, plenty of coffee and sugar. But not long after Potts had taken Mary as his wife, the American Fur Company had fallen on hard times. The white men in England and the States were not pleased to wear beaver hats any more. Dawson, "King of the Missouri," the Almost Father who had been so kind to him, went back downriver, just as Harvey had done years before. What was Jerry Potts to Talker Drum then, with Dawson gone and his trade goods with him?

After Mary left him, he had wanted to believe it was because he had no more gifts for her family, no more silver earrings for her. Bitterly, he had told himself greed had worked in her like a cactus thorn burrowing deep in the flesh, spreading poison.

Now he understands the fault was not all Mary's. When, in the night-darkness, under the buffalo robes, she had taught him to speak the Crow language, she never dreamed how he would use it. Neither did he. It was simply a game, Mary laughing at the strange way Mouse pronounced her mother-words, pulling his whiskers when he made a mistake, both of them laughing, hugging each other tight under the robes. But now Potts knows that to speak English or to speak Crow does not lend you the heart of the stranger. He had used Mary's loving words, the tongue of her own people, to lick the flesh from their bones and make them skeletons.

He does not regret that the Crow words saved his life, but the words Mary taught him also made a sharp knife that sliced her heart in half – one raw piece mourning those he had sent to the Other Side Camp of the Crow to sit in the darkness beside the dead, The Without Fires; the other piece glad that the knowledge she had given him brought her husband safely back to her and their child. Potts knows now that to live divided is dangerous, a confusion that sickens the spirit.

The winter day the gulf opened between Mary and him was one of strong cold, the snowdrifts scabbed with icy skin tough as a warrior's parfleche shield. He had left camp to hunt a little after the midday meal; frost crystals were dancing in the air, a mist of small stars that burned his nose and lungs with every breath. The Big Hairys would be gathered in the coulee bottoms to shelter from the cold, to huddle together in the belly-deep snow. A few shots would reward him with plenty of meat and fleecy head-tail robes in prime condition.

He rode the bank of Shonkin Creek, following every twist of the stream until thick, bristling brush overhanging a bend blocked his way, forcing him to turn his pony down on to the frozen creek. The footing was slippery, chancy, and he let his horse feel its way while he kept his eyes down, looking for muskrat runs where the ice would be thin. His pony skittered round the bend, and when Potts glanced up, there they were, a party of mounted Crow warriors on the bank above him, silhouetted against the steely sky. For an instant, he was about to quirt his pony and run for it, but then he checked his hand, left it resting on his thigh. If he galloped the horse on the ice, it would surely slip and fall, leaving him helpless.

He stared up at his enemies, weighing the danger. Seven of them. Three armed with horn bows, four with breechloader One Shots. He had his Many Shots Henry repeater, but the odds were still not in his favour. He made the sign of peace, twice, waiting tensely for them to reply.

An answer was slow in coming. The Crow had the upper hand and knew it. He could see contempt for him on the red-painted faces and in the cold eyes with their vermilion-tinted lids. The warriors' long hair was fanned out on the rumps of their ponies, their roached forelocks stood up, menacing as porcupine quills. He picked out their leader immediately. A man whose nose had once been badly broken and that had mended crookedly. A man who wore ten scalp locks stitched to the seams of his leggings, dead men's hair ruffling in the wind. Strings of sea shells dangled from his earlobes, turning green then blue in the winter light, twinkling with the slightest movement of Broken Nose's pony. Potts knew it was in this man's hands whether he lived or died. He saw the pipeholder was full of excitement, despite the arrogant stillness in which he held his face. Broken Nose's breath was coming in short, sharp pants, steam jerking from his nostrils.

Once more, Potts signed friendship and finally Broken Nose began to hand talk. Their camp was a short ride off. Would he come with them and pay a visit to the chief? Smoke a pipe, warm himself at their fires, feast on boss ribs? Potts had no choice but to accept the invitation with a nod of agreement. He kept his gaze fixed on Broken's Nose's blazing eyes.

Laughing and motioning, the Crow beckoned him to join them. Potts dug his heels into his pony and scrambled up the bank, skin prickled in fear of the first arrow, bullet, knife thrust, blow. But nothing happened. Smelling its rider's fear, his pony began to mill about and snort, jostling the Crow's horses. This made the warriors encircling him laugh all the harder.

They set off down a narrow game trail wending its way through the thicket, the three bowmen leading, Broken Nose and the riflemen at his back. The poplar and brush were so thick they hemmed him in tight. It was impossible to try to escape.

Behind him, the Crow were talking, unaware he knew their language. Broken Nose said he did not know what to make of Potts. His jacket was decorated with Blackfoot designs, but he had white man's hair on his lip. The others sniggered at this.

Potts slipped the mitten from his right hand, forced it inside his shirt to warm his fingers, to take the stiffness from them. He fondled his cat-skin medicine, begging it to lend him its power. He gave thanks to the cat for sending him the dream. Searching Fort Benton high and low, he had found the black tom atop a fence behind T. C. Powers's warehouse. It had humped its back, bristled, howled, hissed, spat, the bull's-eye lamps of its eyes burning with spirit power.

One clean shot through a glaring eye, and then he had skinned it on the spot, and given Mary the pelt to tan. For years he had worn it close to his chest, drawing the tom cat's hunting stealth, its fierceness into his own heart. As he prayed to it, everything became keen and clear as if the creature was lending him its eyes. Each bobbing ice crystal blazed with a separate fire; the naked limbs of the poplars glistened like white bones. The hair on the nape of his neck lifted.

The trail emerged from the trees; the party turned towards a slough where a stand of bulrushes poked through the snow.

They were heading directly west, into the low-riding winter sun that was stoking the frost particles hanging in the air with a stabbing brightness. He pressed the cat skin hard to him, giving thanks to his medicine for sending the blinding light into the eyes of the men at his back.

The bowmen were leaping their ponies through the high drifts, splashing snow, making trail. Potts tucked at his reins, slowing his horse, forcing the four Crow behind him to check their ponies to stay at his back. The bowmen were gaining ground on them fast, drawing farther and farther ahead.

He and the riflemen rode into the cat-tails; the dry stalks and leaves brushing their leggings made a low, sinister hiss. His ears strained for the sound he expected to come any moment. He took his hand out of his shirt, slid his forefinger into the trigger guard of the Henry carbine. The cold metal burned like fire.

Above the hiss of the rustling stalks he heard the click of a hammer cocking and flung himself from the back of his pony, crashing blindly into the cat-tails just as a rifle cracked and a bullet whined overhead.

He floundered to his knees amid a tumult of Crow war cries, flicking the lever of the Henry and firing up into the bellies of his enemy's horses. A pony reared, hooves tearing sky. The rider fell an arm's-length from him. Still on his knees, he shot the Crow twice, his muzzle so close to the man's chest that the barrel flame made the jacket burn and smoke.

Scrambling to his feet, he plunged through the bulrushes. A gut-shot pony spun in a crazed circle, blood spraying from its wound, sewing red beads on the snow. The whirling horse presented its rider's back and Potts fired a single shot between the warrior's shoulder blades.

He stumbled through the snow, chopping aside the bulrushes with his rifle barrel, chasing his nervous horse, snatching at the trailing reins. His fingers were about to close on them when he heard a bullet whistle over his shoulder. Swinging around he came face to face with a twisted, screaming red mask, with glittering, terrified eyes; a boy fumbling to jam another shell into the breech of his One Shot. Potts speared him in the ribs with the barrel of the Henry; the jolt snapped his finger down hard on the trigger and cast one more Crow into the darkness of The Without Fires.

He flung a glance over his shoulder and saw Broken Nose charging him, his pony trampling down the dry stalks in a storm of fluff, Broken Nose ducked low in the saddle, his breechloader aimed along the pony's neck. Potts shifted his side to him, making a smaller target of himself, and cranked another shell into the chamber of the Henry. The war pony was coming at him hard, heaving through the heavy snow like it was swimming a fast river, the bulrushes tossing madly.

Broken Nose fired. There was a little gasp of fizzling flame in the mouth of the barrel and then it thumped and exploded. Potts stood his ground as the Crow brandished his gun like a club. When Broken Nose was almost on top of him, he snapped three shots off so quickly they ran together as one, lifting the Crow out of the saddle just as if a spirit hand had snatched him up by his long, wild hair.

He stepped aside and let the pony gallop past him. It was bound for the three bowmen who, summoned by the gunshots, had just topped a ridge two hundred yards off.

The power swelled in his chest, knotted in his throat. His cat medicine had caused Broken Nose's carbine to misfire, had kept him safe in the shimmer of a cold, radiant day. Today, no man's hand could harm him. He shouted up the hill to the stupefied Crow, mocking them in their own tongue.

One of the Crow gave a despairing cry and loosed an arrow. It fell far short of him, the range was too great for a horn bow. Potts slowly, deliberately raised his rifle, and the Crow and the riderless horse wheeled, disappeared behind the brow of the hill.

With their going, he felt an insistent urge to make water. His urine rushed out of him, steaming in the frigid air, filling his nostrils with the smell of his own body, the smell of fear departing him in a cloud of steam.

A quick cut, a foot braced to the corpse, a sharp tug, and the hair ripped free. The blood froze dark to the blade of his skinning knife. He fashioned a bundle of bulrushes and draped it with the scalps. The stalks bent with the weight of his trophies.

When he rode into the Blackfoot camp on the Marias chanting his victory song, the people poured out excitedly from their lodges to heap insults on the Crow hair. Everyone but Mary, who turned back into their teepee when she saw what he waved aloft.

Strikes the Enemy at Night had given him a new name that day, Bear Child, because he had fought like a grizzly, clawing to pieces those who were foolish enough to attack him, snapping their bones in his powerful jaws. Around and around the village Potts rode as the warriors angrily shouted that the Crows must be punished for their evil tricks and lying ways.

Potts could feel his spirit sinking. With every round he made of the camp, the anger was passing out of him just as the fear had passed out of his body when he had made his water. All he could think was, Why does Mary shame me? Refuse to sing my bravery? His eye continually drifted to the door flap of his teepee that hung closed, a silent rebuke to him.

Although he wanted to be part of no more killing, he rode off with the rest of the Blackfoot warriors. They caught the Crow camp on the move, a straggling column hurrying to reach the safety of their own land and kind, making a panicked rush through the winter dark, the butts of their travois poles slashing the pale skin of the snow.

It was a great slaughter. The Crow fought a stiff rearguard action, but bit by bit they were forced to give way. By the dozens, their broken bodies lay strewn on the plain. The coyotes and prairie wolves restlessly paced the horizon, howling to taste the freshly killed meat.

Nothing between him and his wife had ever been the same after that night. How could Mary forgive him for riding through the blue dusk, for seeking to turn even more of her people into shadows? How could he forgive her for betraying his honour, for refusing to celebrate his bravery?

For a long time neither spoke of it, the wound slowly turning bad, festering. One night when he was drunk, full of resentment, the bitter taste of buffalo gall sour at the root of his tongue, he had taunted Mary, asking, "If I die, will you keep the custom of your people, chop off a finger joint for me? Is Jerry Potts worth a finger joint to you?"

For a moment, she stirred the ashes of the fire with a smoking stick and then replied, "And what am I to call you now? Jerry Potts or Bear Child? What do you wish to be, White or Kanai?"

She knew his secret. He wanted to be both and could not pardon her for reminding him of the impossibility of it. For another year they floated in a wider, deeper silence. Then Johnny Healy proposed that Potts go to work for him supplying meat for the crew that was to build Healy's big fort at the junction of the St. Mary and Belly rivers, in the very heart of Blackfoot country. Mary said she would not live in the midst of Crow-haters. He must not do this work for the white man Johnny Healy.

"I will," he said.

"Then it is time for me to return to my people," was her answer.

Burying his fury, he only smiled and said, "Do as you wish."

Before Mary left for her father's country, he had presented her with many gifts, bolts of calico, coils of brass wire, tea, sugar, jars of marmalade, a hundred weight of flour. He said to her, "I will not have the Crow say my son and wife came to them because I could not feed them. In a little while, you will think of how good life was in my lodge and bring Mitchell back."

Mary did not bring Mitchell back. The leaves of the poplars yellowed and blew away, every morning a thick pelt of frost lay on the grass. Winter drew down and Potts sulked in his lodge, day after day drinking cheap "Indian whisky." All that winter it seemed to him the sun was reluctant to rise in the morning and hurried out of sight as fast as it could, as if it was ashamed to be seen.

Spring came and still he loitered about Fort Benton, waiting for the Crow to come in to trade. They came, but there was no Mary, no Mitchell. The days were soft and sunny, the new grass light green. It would soon be time for him to leave with Healy and the bull train full of tools and supplies.

Be no more divided, he warned himself, then he saddled his horse and rode off. In a week he returned to Fort Benton with two new wives, Panther Woman and Spotted Killer, daughters of Sitting in the Middle. Blackfoot wives who would remind him with every word they spoke that he, too, was a Blackfoot, a Real Person. Good women who would help him settle the confusion in his blood that Mary had stirred up.

The rasp of someone moving through dry grass shakes him out of his thoughts. Turning, he sees Panther Woman approaching, a strong, squat girl in a man's hat, a battered Trilby.

"Three riders coming," she tells him. "Hairy Faces."

Careful not to frighten her, he only nods. But he wonders why white men ride out to his camp. Two days ago he had gone on a spree in Fort Benton, nothing of it remembered. When the whisky gets hold of him, he often quarrels with the whites because of how they look at him and what they say. They call him Chamber Potts and laugh. They call him Mormon Jerry because he has two wives. He cannot remember, but maybe when he was drunk the other night he gave some white blowhard a lesson. Maybe the white man and his friends are coming to take revenge.

He gets to his feet and follows Panther Woman up the path worn in the river bluff by his horses. When his spacious teepee painted with the red grizzly cub comes into sight, he is filled with pleasure. A man who owns such a lodge, who owns a herd of a hundred horses, who carries the name Bear Child, who has taken a dozen scalp locks, is a man of consequence. Let the white men see him as he really is.

The grey of the morning is almost gone. Spotted Killer is hanging thin strips of venison on the meat rack to dry in the sun.

In the distance, Potts sees three riders making little puffs of dust. Two ride strangely even for whites, bobbing like bull boats attempting to cross a choppy river. Spotted Killer hangs the last of the meat and joins Potts and Panther Woman. Spotted Killer tugs the blue calico dress he bought for her in Fort Benton into place, shapes it with her palms. He knows she is proud to welcome visitors in her fine new dress. Panther Woman straightens her hat.

Potts recognizes one of the horsemen. Custis Straw, on his big chestnut gelding. The others he does not know. But if they come with the horse dealer, they mean him no harm. He returns the pistol he has been holding behind his leg to his belt, and walks out to greet his guests.

11

CHARLES Mr. Potts is hired and I am jubilant. No more excuses for Addington. The prospect of our departure after a few days of preparation invigorates me. It also causes me to reflect upon my missing brother's deficiencies. Simon always had a weakness for madcap, pious schemes but, if it were not for Oxford, he might have restricted them to England and safer ground. It is the university I blame for sowing those romantic seeds in him that sprouted his ridiculous desire to uplift the Indian.

Oxford, "home of lost causes, and forsaken beliefs, and unpopular names, and impossible loyalties!" Matthew Arnold is not my cup of tea, but he certainly proved to be Simon's favourite sugary, tepid beverage. Impossible loyalties, indeed. A very apt description for my brother's willingness to sacrifice himself for primitives who never asked for his help, or could be improved by it.

I often think the university has ripened more mush-headed fruit than the rest of England's orchards put together. Addle-headed dons and tutors jabbering bosh. Simon, a prime candidate for the catatonia induced by that "sweet city with her dreaming spires . . ." Dreaming so deeply as to be incapable of wakening to reality. The most preposterous dreamer of them all, Sir Henry Acland, Regius Professor of Medicine. Simple Sir Henry toddling off with the Prince Consort, uxorious Albert, on his grand tour of North America. And the good doctor insisting that he must visit the Indians to investigate their habits, customs, and condition. Having had his wish granted, it seems Dr. Acland discoursed at length to a conclave of chiefs and supernumeraries upon the history, beauties, wonders, and wisdom of the doctor's great alma mater, and concluded his peroration with a hearty invitation for any of those assembled to call upon him at Oxford the next time they happened to be in the vicinity.

How absurd, if the consequences had not been so disastrous for Simon. Once back home, Dr. Acland inaugurated his famous series of lectures, "The Myth of Hiawatha," talks lavishly illustrated with his sketches and artifacts, and zealously attended by many Oxford boobies. Simon was among those entranced by Dr. Acland. Being of sounder mind, I eschewed this weekly entertainment, despite my brother's entreaties.

A year later, word began to circulate that an individual arrayed in moccasins and deer hide had made his appearance at Dr. Acland's house on Broad Street, announcing himself to the dismayed house-keeper as Dr. Acland's good friend, Oronhyatekha. I could not contain my hilarity on hearing the story of how the doctor, summoned posthaste by the terrified domestic, was informed by Oronhyatekha that the professor's description of Oxford had so filled him with a burning passion for learning that he had prevailed upon his tribesmen in Upper Canada to raise a collection for his journey to the seat of knowledge. Presto, he had arrived with exactly four shillings and a ha'penny in his pocket!

Any sane man would have been aghast, but not Dr. Acland. Oronhyatekha was just the "lost cause" a true Oxford man so dearly loves. The doctor paraded him around the university, had him sign the visitors' book in the reading room of the Bodleian, feted and lionized him. Many were deeply touched by this Indian's arduous pil-grimage to drink from the well of the university's wisdom and wished to make his acquaintance. Without my hearing of it, Simon wangled an invitation to a soiree where Oronhyatekha was the principal attraction. One of the guests provided me with a full report, gleefully relating how Simon and Oronhyatekha passed much of the evening in a corner of the drawing room, engrossed in a heartfelt tête-à-tête.

I was wrong to think this encounter insignificant, of a piece with Simon's penchant for handing out shillings to able-bodied beggars and pence to street-urchin pests. It came as a great shock to me a few weeks later when Simon told me he had contributed twenty pounds to a subscription to enable Oronhyatekha to enter St. Edmund Hall as a student.

Doing my best to check my exasperation, I pointed out to him that this sum was half his quarterly allowance. He told me not to worry, he would economize. Economize how? I demanded. On wine and clothes, he said. I told him his clothes did not do now, he cut a very poor figure. He smiled and remarked I did not know Oronhyatekha, had no inkling of how desperately he wished to pursue an education.

"Fools are very often sincere. I have not seen his signature in the Bodleian, but I can imagine it," I said, laboriously forming letters in the air. "How is he possibly to benefit from an Oxford education?"

"When one feels a lack, one must take steps to remedy it," Simon replied.

"A lack of what? Homer in the Greek?"

"That is unkind, Charles. Who among us does not feel he is wanting something to make himself complete?"

"I am aware of no such deficit."

"Then you are a fortunate fellow. I cannot say the same."

We left it at that. I was finding that as Simon grew older, he also grew more enigmatic and cryptic. How often since that day have I berated myself for not questioning him further.

Was it friendship Simon felt he lacked? At Oxford, he was indeed a solitary figure. But was not I, who had always been his inseparable companion, close at hand? If Simon had turned to me for advice, allowed me to offer suggestions about his dress and manner, he need not have been lonely. I could have made him acceptable.

But no, Simon preferred time spent with his new protégé. They strolled arm in arm through the quadrangles. He gave the Indian private lessons in his rooms, fed him biscuits and tea. He taught Oronhyatekha to ride a velocipede, a comedy fully appreciated by all who witnessed it.

My childhood protector was now the one in need of protection. I was capable of navigating my way through our new life, but Simon remained as innocent as he was at ten, as oblivious to other's opinions as he had been to Father's distaste for his button collection. Where once he had been tolerated as Charles Gaunt's amusingly high-minded brother, his friendship with the red man prompted those who counted in Oxford to ridicule him. My heart bled to know my brother was dismissed as a buffoon. One day, I overheard Dearborne refer to him as "the Mad Gaunt." But in spite of all my attempts to persuade him to cut his ties with the stranger, he stubbornly refused.

One night, entering a local establishment, I spotted Simon and Oronhyatekha occupying a table that put them on full display in the very centre of the public bar. Dreading my brother would insist on introducing me to his new bosom friend, I took a seat behind a pillar from which I could observe them undetected. They were deep in conversation, Simon's face exalted and vivid. Perhaps he was enlightening the Indian on the Athanasian Creed.

Something very peculiar and disturbing ensued. I saw Oronhyatekha reach out and gently touch a lock of Simon's yellow hair. There was a look of inquiry on the Indian's face. Just as a scientist might be swept up in curiosity by an unusual specimen, it seemed he was unable to stop himself from examining the phenomena of Simon's fine, curly blond hair. I could forgive a savage's manners, but Simon's willingness to allow such familiarity with his person, to meet such presumption with a willing smile was another matter. The exchange was so fleeting that no one else appeared to have noted what had occurred. But I had. After that incident, my course was decided.

The end of term was near, so I did nothing until my brother and I returned to Sythe Grange. Upon arriving, I went directly to Father and reported my brother's unfortunate association with Oronhyatekha, as well as the extravagant contribution Simon had made for his support.

Father summoned Simon to the library. I circled back to listen with bated breath at the door. Only father's voice was audible, booming a King Lear–like soliloquy on the ingratitude of children. I could not hear Simon's quiet responses, but with Father growing louder as each minute passed, I knew my brother was not proving amenable to reason. Seconds before the interview finally concluded, Father shouted like a madman, "No, sir, I shall not have it! Make an end of it! That is my final word! Make an end of it!"

I skipped down the corridor to a window. The door of the library swung open and Simon emerged looking very pale but calm. He came up to me where I stood feigning interest in the deer below. Quietly, he said, "I will not be going up to Oxford with you next term, Charles. Father has forbidden it."

He walked on, leaving me rooted to the floor. This was not the outcome I had hoped for. Giving myself a shake, I hurried after Simon and found him in his room, seated on his bed, Bible already opened on his lap. "Why?" I asked him. "Why has Father forbidden it?"

He looked up and subjected me to a searching look. "You know very well, Charles." He waited for me to deny my culpability. I could not. He shook his head sadly. "Because I have not conducted myself as a gentleman should. Because I have become a laughingstock, and in doing so made the Gaunt name a laughingstock. Last of all, because I would not give my word of honour never to see Oronhyatekha again."

Instantly, I regretted what I had done. With the force of a blow, it struck me how insupportable life in Oxford would be without him. How dreadful it would be to be separated for the first time in my life from my twin, the best part of myself. "I shall speak to Father," I said.

"He will not be moved," said Simon. "But please understand, you have no need to feel jealousy. Surely you know how dear you are to me and ever will be."

It was the way Simon spoke to me, so naturally and so kindly, which heaped coals upon my head. The tender, guilty spot that he had touched caused me to wince.

"You accuse me of jealousy? You think that I could be jealous of your savage? How very unchristian of you to make such an accusation."

Simon got to his feet. His rumpled suit suddenly seemed to me to signal the disorder which he had allowed to creep into his life. "I am very far from walking in Christ's footsteps. But I wish to add to the sum of love in the world. Do you not desire to love and be loved, Charles?"

The question was so direct, so genuine, I could not evade it. "I hope to be loved, but if I am not, I shall settle for affection. I cannot be a saint, so I shall endeavour to be a gentleman. I cannot comprehend metaphysics and theology, so I shall place my faith in reason and logic. I do not aim as high as you, but I shall be content."

"I think you will never be a great painter until you surrender to love," was all my brother said, and that was enough.

Nothing more of Oronhyatekha was ever mentioned, but I refused to return to Oxford without Simon. Two years at university was sufficient buffing and polishing for me, and twenty years would never have been long enough to put a shine on Simon.

Today, riding back to Fort Benton with Mr. Straw and Addington from the half-breed's squalid camp, I pondered on a remarkable coincidence. Jerry Potts and the drunken savage that I saw howling and beating the road with a barrel stave are one and the same man. However, I am beyond second thoughts, eagerness to be underway suppresses them.

I said nothing of this to Addington, who was too intent on impressing Mr. Straw with how soundly he had planned our pending operations to look kindly on any interruption from me. My brother was explaining to Mr. Straw how his military experience had taught him that ample stores and suitable transport are of paramount importance. "I set that Potts fellow straight, Mr. Straw, about the necessity of wagons, didn't I? What did the half-breed say? 'I don't like wagons. Wagons are not good when the time comes to run away from enemies.'"

Running away. What my dear twin has done. Run from Father. Fled me.

Forgive me, Simon.

12

Two horsemen lead the line of march. Captain Addington Gaunt, proud as a Cossack, towers on a sorrel blood-horse while Jerry Potts slouches on a piebald, hammer-headed mustang. Two wagons following, each carrying a passenger and hired teamster, Charles Gaunt beside Grunewald, Mr. Ayto next to Barker, spare horses tethered to the tailgates of the Conestogas. The little town of Fort Benton grows smaller below as the procession makes a long, clamorous climb out of the river valley of the Missouri, wagons juddering along the pot-holed freight trail. Axles shrieking, the chirp and squeal of wagon boards sawing against one another, the tintinnabulation of enamel-ware clanking in the back, drivers shouting, "Hyup! Hyup!" slapping reins to teams surging in their collars up the arid, canvas-coloured hill, the blue sky lurching above them, flapping like a matador's cape, teasing them to charge forward.

Finally, they roll over the crest, pause to give the tired horses a blow. Ahead, the plain topples north, breakers of grass pitching in the wind, buffalo wallows filled by last night's rain glinting like new dimes in the sun, little smudges of whorled cloud, fingerprints on a windowpane. Far off, tiny antelope – scurrying ants. Above, hawks sailing the updrafts – flakes of ash.

Addington Gaunt twists around in the saddle to see the last member of the expedition clear the ridge. Lucy Stoveall, trudging with her head down, a gunny sack slung over her shoulder holding all

her gear, two linsey woolsey dresses, a bone comb, her sister's daguer-
rotype, a bar of lye soap, and the Navy Colt.

They move off.

❖ ❖ ❖

ALOYSIUS Just my good fortune: heading down to the levee to make
sure them roustabouts didn't pilfer one of my kegs of beer off the
steamboat, I saw Lucy Stoveall pleading with the English. It falls to
me to break the bad tidings to Straw.

Rode back with my shipment on the freight wagon, unlocked the
saloon so the men could unload, and I discover Straw already in his
spot by the window, a glass in hand. Whisky at eleven in the morning
on a empty stomach, couldn't wait for me to open up, served himself.

I eased into what I had to say. "I seen the English setting out this
morning," I told him.

"They aren't going to find anything," Custis remarked. "I didn't
have the heart to tell Charles Gaunt that. And I didn't bother to waste
an opinion on the Captain. I had two hours of his company visiting
Potts. Addington Gaunt taught me that after a stint in the British
army, a man knows everything there is to know."

"The whole troop of them was gathered in Front Street, extra
horses, wagons bulging with provisions. They looked to go to China
and back."

"Well," said Custis, "the Captain seems to be a man who likes to
do things in a superior style."

"Mrs. Stoveall was there." He didn't catch what I was leading
up to.

"Maybe she likes hoopla as much as you do, Aloysius."

I said, "I seen her asking them to let her work her way, cook and
scrub for them. Said she could make a firebread light as angel food.
Just give her a chance, take her along."

That got his attention. "What?" he snarled.

"Lord, I could scarce believe my eyes, but she dropped down on
her knees in the dust and horseshit and begged them. Held up her

hands like this" – I stretched out my arms and crooked my fingers pitiful so he could see how Lucy Stoveall had acted – "said she'd lost her sister recent, was bereaved without a soul in the world to lean on. Said her husband was up north and she was desperate to find him. Please to lend her a helping hand."

"I don't believe it," Custis said. "Lucy Stoveall isn't a woman to pull that sort of monkey business." That's what he claimed, but he looked doubtful nonetheless.

I went on. "And when she was done beseeching, the Captain swung down off his handsome horse, and he took her by the hand, and he lifted her up from her knees and he says, 'Madame, an officer and a gentleman cannot refuse to comfort a lady in distress. It would give me the greatest pleasure to see you safely into the arms of your husband.' And that's how she got aid and succour from the English." I let Custis take it in for a moment. "They left four hours ago."

He let fly at me. "Goddamn it, Dooley, why didn't you come tell me!"

"Because I had to guard my goods from them light-fingered dock thieves. And why am I obliged to report every little matter to you, lickety-split?"

Custis sat thinking for a time, sliding his glass backwards and forwards on the tabletop. Finally, he said, "When I went out to Jerry Potts's camp with the Englishmen, Potts told them if they didn't find the corpse of their brother at the Whitemud River, they ought to turn for the whisky posts in Whoop-Up country. Maybe they could learn something about him there. Captain Gaunt has likely blabbed their plans in every saloon in town. Mrs. Stoveall must have got wind of it somehow. I reckon she's figuring that if Abner Stoveall has sold his store of whisky, he'll have to rely on one of the posts to replenish it. She must hope to find her husband at one of them."

I didn't say yea or nay to Custis's speculations. He was in no mood for any more words from me. He glanced up and said, "Aloysius, I am disappointed in you. You should have stopped her."

"Well, I didn't because it ain't none of my business what Lucy Stoveall chooses to do, nor yours neither."

Custis got to his feet, scowled at me, took the bottle, and charged off to his room. I could see he was suffering mightily from my bulletin. He is like that, oftentimes afflicted with sudden gloom.

Hard on the heels of his leaving, a swarm of bullwhackers back from a haul to Helena trooped in so I didn't have the time to spare to coax and jolly Custis out of the mopes. Ox drivers and mule men are fine customers; eating dust from dawn till dark is parching work. They was pleasant, tolerably well-behaved fellows except for one knothead who wouldn't trouble himself to go outside and piss, but used a cuspidor to relieve himself. I got to get me a dog for that. A fellow sees some hound ready to be sicked on his peeder, he'll quit sprinkling in the spittoons.

About midnight the bull-train boss came in swinging a ox goad and drove the diehards out. He wanted them sober because they're hauling blast powder tomorrow. A welcome sight he was, as Custis was on my mind. Soon as the boss rousted them, I blew out the lights and barred the door in case any escaped him and doubled back for one last drink.

Then I give Custis's predicament a think. With that Stoveall woman gone he is better off, no matter how dismal it makes him. Entertaining such disorderly, passionate feelings at his time of life is unbecoming in a man. He ought to know better. A middle-aged man with quim, with cunny on the brain, is a pitiful sight to behold.

My old Da said to me once, "Aloysius, God gave you a eejit's face. Put it to your advantage. Hide behind it and ambush people." Well, it rests on Aloysius Dooley's shoulders to point out to Custis Straw Esquire the consequences of pining after another man's wife.

Custis's always more welcoming if you approach with whisky, so I gather a bottle, tuck two shot glasses in my coat pockets, and step outside. Jew Jake weren't fortunate in the carpenter he hired to build the Stubhorn. He told me the fellow didn't leave no room for a indoor staircase so he just run one up the side of the building. I reckon that's how things get done in Fort Benton, and you got to learn to live with what you're handed. That's Straw's problem. He won't learn that simple lesson.

His room still shows a light. Going up the stairs I tramp them hard to give him warning, but when I knock at his door, he don't answer. Could be he's dead drunk, or ploughed under on laudanum or opium. I don't no more approve of dirty, foreign habits like opium smoking than I do chasing a skirt that's spoken for. I rap again, no answer, so I just let myself in.

Custis's sprawled out on the bed, nightshirt rucked up above his knees, sweat on a furrowed face like a woman in the throes of labour. Tragic, Dr. Bengough would say. Custis don't hand me so much as a glance. "Long day – thought we'd close it with a tot," I say, holding up the bottle.

Custis answers back sharp, "I don't want whisky. Nor company neither."

I drag a cane-bottomed chair over to the bed, settle myself, fill our glasses. Custis takes the one I hand him, but he don't taste it, just holds it propped on his chest. I see the bottle he carried to the room lying on the floor empty, but I suspect that went down his throat hours ago, so he's had space to sober up.

"Lucy Stoveall took a vow," I say. "The moment she promised 'I do,' that's all she wrote. You're too late on the scene, Custis. Forget this nonsense. And if you ain't noticed, she's wilful besides."

"I like a wilful woman."

"Wilful women need leeway. She ain't going to get it with you. You're wilful yourself."

"Furthest thing from it."

"I admit Lucy Stoveall's got her points of interest. She's a looker." I'm hoping to mollify him by complimenting her.

Straw takes his first drink. "I noticed you noticing, Aloysius. After the funeral you buzzed around her like a fly around the sugar bowl."

"Maybe, but I know better than to settle in it and try to help myself to that sweetness. You got to forget certain things. Soon as you do, you'll brighten some."

"How am I supposed to forget this?" And he reaches under the bed covers and pulls out that dirty black belt, dangles it before my eyes.

"Custis Straw, you get more peculiar every day. Whyever are you cuddling up to that loathsome thing?"

His eyes narrow. "Tell the truth. You sure you never saw anybody wearing this in the Stubhorn?"

"Goddamn it, Custis, I told you no. I don't let my eyes go that low on customers. I don't want them wondering if I'm staring at what I oughtn't to be."

Custis lets the belt drop to the floor. "Lucy Stoveall and I have this in common," he says, "neither of us can put her sister's death out of mind. I understand her. Not knowing who murdered her sister is oppressing her spirits. She might rest easier if she knew who the culprit was."

I leave that alone.

"I've tried almighty hard to change myself," Custis says. "I tinker with the particulars of my life, but I don't seem to make much headway. You think that's a thing a man can do, Aloysius – change himself?"

Custis is veering about tonight. As far as I can see, one thing don't follow another. "I got no opinion on that. I never attempted it."

"It's why I enlisted during the war. A man needs to serve something bigger than himself. It enlarges him." Custis ponders for a moment. "It's my nature to keep my distance. But when I favour someone, I don't change my mind."

"No, I did change once, I remember now," I offer. "I used to gamble, but I give it up."

"That isn't a change of nature. You love money, Aloysius. You figured gambling was a way of getting your hands on more of it. But it was a losing proposition – that's why you swore off it."

"Well, when I was a little babby I hated peas. I can eat them now."

"A dog can learn to eat peas. The question is bigger than peas. I thought on it all day. Keeping my distance is the sensible thing to do, but I'm going after Lucy Stoveall. I intend to persuade her to come back to Fort Benton with me."

"And what if she don't persuade?"

"It's a dangerous business for a woman out there, shepherded by English bumblers. I'll make her come. For her own good." Saying this, Custis's face changes in a way I never seen before. I'm glad Justice Daniels never saw him staring so fearsome. A jury might convict a man on the evidence of that look alone.

"I'd think twice about it if I was you. All you done since you quit the Indian trade is sit on your arse and eat fat pork. Could be you've gone too soft for rescuing women."

"We'll see."

My temper rises. "Everybody chasing after everybody else. Those Englishmen chasing their brother. Lucy Stoveall chasing her husband. You after Lucy Stoveall. A game of fox and hounds."

"It isn't a game," says Straw. "Not to me."

I can see he ain't about to be talked out of his nonsense. I set the whisky on the floor in easy reach of his bed. "I think you ought to suckle down this bottle. Maybe then when you wake up, you'll have forgot this damn lunatic notion." It's late and I've had enough of Custis Straw. I'm a working man, not a freebooting horse trader. I need my rest. I got glasses to wash and floors to sweep come morning. I make for the door.

"I won't forget," says Custis.

That halts me, hand on the doorknob. "Those times you tried to change, Custis. What were you aiming to be?"

"I wanted to be better," he says. "That's all. Just a better man who aimed himself a little higher."

I leave him with the last word, which is how things generally fall out between us, but I slam the door hard so he knows I ain't happy about it.

❖ ❖ ❖

CUSTIS   After Aloysius's meddling visit I didn't touch the gift of whisky nor did I sleep either. I thought about Lucy Stoveall's grief and the cause of it, the belt laying on the floor beside my bed. I watched the dawn creep into my window and let it light my mind. The Gaunts will have a two-day start before I've cleared my affairs here, but wagons travel slow. Besides, I know their first destination is the

Whitemud River, where the bones of the English preacher were found. No trouble overtaking them.

Daniel Thibault will keep an eye on my horses until I get back. All the fifty-cent pieces I've handed that old bum, he owes me a favour. Aloysius won't approve. I can hear him now, "It's just like you, Straw, hiring the first one-eye, seventy-year-old Frenchie half-breed you can find. All his relatives are known horse thieves. I hope you took that into account."

Coming to a firm decision is a heartening thing. Roll the dice, take the consequences. I wash and shave, brush my best broadcloth suit, take my St. Louis hat out of its box. A new hat fit for a new outlook. Something special shipped from the finest haberdashery emporium they got down there. A black silk bowler. After a few attempts, I discover the right angle for it in the mirror and head off to the livery.

I need a mount to bring Mrs. Stoveall back to Benton, and all the horses out at my place are rough stock, not fit for ladies. It tickles me to see D. C. Harding, proprietor, mucking out stalls. He's been short on help ever since that enterprising blackamoor, Pompey, stole off with Abner Stoveall to make a fortune in the Queen's country. Harding's a cautious, haggling soul, but I don't have the patience for it this morning. I know what I want and I'll have it – a quiet Morgan mare that I've seen one of Mule Jenny's whores ride when she takes the air. It costs me five hundred dollars, but I get D. C. to throw in a bridle and a second-hand saddle to boot. He frowns, but that's for appearance's sake. D. C. knows well enough my impatience has skinned me.

A little after eight, I see Danny Howard unlocking his General Merchandise, and I cross the street. I'm the first customer of the day. By the time I'm done shopping, I've bought a hunting knife, a hatchet, hardtack, jerked beef, one cured buffalo ham, salt, sugar, coffee, matches, blankets, a duster, a ground sheet, wool stockings, four flannel shirts, and a pea jacket. The cash I've dropped in his establishment, he makes no fuss when I tell him I want my supplies delivered to the Stubhorn.

Last call is the gunsmith's. Karl Hofstedder doesn't look up when the cowbell hung above the door clangs. He's working on a Remington percussion revolver, converting it for cartridge loads, busy fitting a recoil plate into the pistol frame. I appreciate a man who does a tidy job, and the German is tidy to an extreme. He doesn't favour me with his attention until he's finished the chore at hand, lays his tools aside, pushes his glasses up on his forehead, and says, "Ja?"

"That's a nice job," I say. "Who's the pistol for?"

"Nobodies. I fix him to sell."

"I'll take it off your hands if you can finish it today."

"Sure," says Hofstedder. "Nothing to do but fit him the cylinder."

I pick out a flapped holster for the revolver and a Henry repeater. But I give most care to choosing a buffalo gun. Last night Aloysius suggested I'd gone soft riding a chair, and that's got the ring of truth to it because I sure as hell don't intend to run buffalo to put meat in my larder. Plunging into a badger hole at a gallop is too risky for a man of my age. I'll do my hunting afoot, thank you, and for that I'll need a weapon with more range and wallop than a Henry.

Hofstedder and I consult on my requirements. I finally settle on a Sharps. Thirty-two-inch octagonal barrel, a .45-calibre bullet weighing 550 grains, and a black powder charge of 120. That ought to do me proud. I order two hundred cartridges, hand-loaded with the best English powder money can buy.

"I finish the revolver quick for you," clucks Hofstedder. "My son, Otto, comes soon. Otto makes the beautiful cartridge. Not one grain too much, not one grain too little. Just so," Hofstedder says, pinching his thumb and forefinger together, grinning with the beauty of Otto's workmanship. "This afternoon he delivers for you."

Back in my room, armaments stowed, I try to nap, but I'm too stirred up. Every time I close my eyes, I see myself approaching the Gaunts' camp, and Lucy standing by a wagon, hand shading her eyes to see who's come calling. She's likely to be curious about the saddled Morgan I'll be leading. Mr. Straw, did some mishap befall your fellow traveller? No? Then why are you leading a horse?

It's for you, Mrs. Stoveall. A lunatic is asking you to ride off with him.

A man gets to my age, there isn't much he has to offer a younger woman but property and the promise of good treatment. If Lucy gave me the chance, I'd stick to her, loyal as a dog, see her safe. I hear myself promising it to the ceiling. "Custis Straw'll hold to you, girl."

Charm and dash I never could learn. You are born with those, the same as blue eyes or sound teeth. Not that some didn't try to instruct me in them. Such as Mother's friend, Mrs. Conkin, the two of us sitting together on a settee at a parlour dance back home in civilized Indiana, and she asks me why I'm not waltzing when there's so fine a supply of pretty girls on hand. Nineteen and bashful, all I could do was shrug. "Custis," she advised me, "a woman is attracted to a man who directs his heart to her. Genuine interest is all that is required."

"I like women fine," I remember saying to her, "but I get no return of it."

She shed a motherly smile on me. "You like women, Custis. But you behave towards them just as you do towards the men you like. You must recognize the distinctions that separate the sexes. To do so is pleasing to a lady."

I suppose what she meant was I oughtn't talk to women as I did to men. Bluntly. I should bow, hand out compliments about their eyes, their hands, their hair. Dance attendance instead of trying to plumb their real and lasting qualities.

About four o'clock, Hofstedder's son, Otto, delivers the Sharps. He's a surprise. The boy's cross-eyed. I don't know about his future, a cross-eyed gunsmith isn't likely to inspire confidence. One look at him and I decide to make a dry run with the cartridges he loaded. I collect my horse, Dan, at the livery and ride out of town to the big old boulder that sits like a cue ball on a billiard-table-level plain.

The rock's the height of a man and round, a buffalo stone polished smooth as glass by thousands of cows and bulls who've been coming here to rub winter wool from their coats for hundreds of years. There's a deep trench circling it made by the herds milling about to have their scratch. The bottom of it's carpeted deep with hair, dust, and old, powdery dung.

I pace off three hundred yards from the stone and drive the iron shooting rest for the Sharps into the ground. I chamber a round, settle on my haunches, lay the heavy barrel in the V of the rest, and set the sight on the tang strap to three hundred yards. I'm all ready to fire when I realize I've forgot to bring something for a target.

I sit here, looking down the sights with the buttplate snug in my shoulder, smooth walnut stock cool on my cheek, sights resting on a boulder big as a barn door. This is no test. Even Aloysius could hit it. With the sun hot on my shoulders, the gun pressed into me, a memory springs into my mind, another afternoon years ago, our company on a knoll tangled up in a lackadaisical skirmish with Rebels below. They couldn't shake us from the height, our position was too strong for them to risk an uphill charge, and we had no reason to go down, not with the Confederates secure behind a snake fence and a stone wall.

The only fly in the ointment was the federal mortar the Rebels had captured and turned against us. The injury the shells they lobbed at us was slight, we'd done our spade work, dug in, and all that was necessary was to keep our heads down. But we had a smooth-cheeked boy for a captain, some green slip who'd won a commission through political pull. Full of himself, he considered it cowardly to sit and wait things out. I could see him and the lieutenant with their heads together, a bad sign because the lieutenant would sooner kiss arse than eat breakfast. Then they called for me.

The captain didn't know my name, and didn't ask for it, just called me "Uncle," the handle the young fellows had fastened on me because to them I was as old as Methusaleh. "Uncle," he said, "Lieutenant Deschere tells me you're a fine shot. I want you to make your way down that hill and pester their battery with sniper fire. They are making far too free with us."

He was a stiff little prick, with a jut to his jaw and a court-martialling eye, so I did as I was ordered without argument. Got on my belly and wriggled down the slope, Spencer carbine strapped to my back. I snaked through whatever would give me cover, slithered through briars, cane, nettles, thinking that scrapes and scratches were better than the bite of Confederate bullets.

It took me half an hour to reach a brake close enough to the mortar. My tunic was torn to rags and so was I. Laying in the welcome shade, soaked in sweat and blood, gulping air like a wind-broken horse, I watched the men's heads bobbing up and down behind the stone wall as they worked the mortar. Better still, my position showed me an officer in plain view, pacing back and forth behind that captured gun.

I took the field glass that the captain had given me and trained it on the Confederate. He looked even younger than the boy who had sent me down the hill. A child of the quality, his uniform bought by Father, no butternut grey for him but the finest tailoring, a yellow sash cinched about his waist, a planter's hat with one side of the brim turned up and pinned, and with a pheasant cock feather waving like a banner. He had locks down to his shoulders, every bit as bright and yellow as his sash.

I counted the boy's clockwork paces. He would stride five steps, do an about-face, stride five more, about-face again. Back and forth he went like a wolf in a cage. The jitters wouldn't let him keep still. He was trying to burn it off marching.

I steadied my carbine on a tree branch, laid the sights to the spot where the boy halted his parade to spin around and tramp back. I sat there for a long time, the grey breast of his tunic swinging into my sights and disappearing, arriving and departing over and over. I heard the mortar pounding on, and knew my captain was up there on the hill, cursing me for a tardy coward, but I couldn't bring myself to pull the trigger on that boy. Not when he was frozen in my sights like a duck on a pond. At the least, he deserved the same chance as a game bird, to be shot on the wing.

I dealt him sporting odds, a shot to the temple while he was on the move. Down the line he came, taking long limber strides. I waited, counted his steps, the Spencer aimed to where his bouncing, jaunty hat would soon arrive. Leading a pheasant in flight; leading that brave, twitching cock feather on his hat. I counted to four, eased down on the trigger. It blew his hat off with the breath of Almighty God Himself.

I might as easy have missed, but I didn't.

That planter's hat's been tumbling in my mind for ages now. It sails up at the oddest times, turning slow and heavy in the air. I've been waiting years for it to fall. It never does.

I put the Sharps by, jerk the rest out of the ground, walk it to the rock, thrust it in the sod. I leave my silk bowler hanging on it.

I pace off a hundred yards and I set my front sight to that black speck. I own a pair of old man's eyes now, reading Scripture print is a trial, but at longer distances I see things clear as ever. I haven't discharged a weapon in three years, but I hear the words my old musketry instructor whispered in my ear. "Mister, squeeze that trigger like your lady's nipple. Just hard enough to get results, but not hard enough to make her jump."

One deep breath, ease half of it from the lungs, coax the trigger. My St. Louis hat jolts and twitches. Cross-eyed Otto packs a true load. I slip another cartridge into the breech, cock the Sharps, draw a bead, fire, and the hat bucks again. Then I start to miss, the Sharps is too heavy a gun to hold steady without a rest. But I keep firing and reloading, determined to make that hat take flight. The barrel grows hot in my hand, too hot to load. Just like the rifles of the 6th Wisconsin did at South Mountain, the day McClellan, watching the men of the West hold back the Confederates, dubbed us the Iron Brigade.

I drop the Sharps. I'm light-headed, haven't had a bite of grub today. The Remington revolver has come out of its holster and into my hand, and I'm advancing on the bowler. I hear myself counting steps just like I did that Confederate boy's. I snap a shot off. I'm shaking, the pistol waving up and down on the end of my arm like a trainman's flag. I break into a trot, a slow clumsy charge through all those years of battle, firing fast and wild. I'm back in the woods of the Wilderness with that other pistol in my hand. One bullet left in the cylinder when I stumble up to the bowler, shove the barrel of the revolver up under the riddled crown, and blow it to kingdom come.

I see it land.

13

Jerry Potts is the sensitive antennae of the caravan. He feels their way for them, heavily laden wagons creeping behind him, the slow, fumbling body of a cumbersome insect. From dawn to dusk they crawl past ravines and low prominences, inch over muddy river fords. After two days they gain British territory, steal past the southern flanks of the Cypress Hills, squirm round Old Man On His Back Hills, nosing their way towards the Whitemud River. There, last November, an itinerant prospector had found the body of the Reverend Obadiah Witherspoon. The only thing that identified the preacher was an engraved communion cup beside his corpse. "Presented to Reverend Witherspoon by a grateful congregation. Godspeed you in your work." When the prospector had brought his news and the silver cup back to Fort Benton, word of it reached I. G. Baker. A sum of money had been forwarded to Baker two months before from a Mr. Henry Gaunt with instructions that he was to offer it to Mr. Simon Gaunt when he and the preacher arrived in Fort Benton. The money was to be surrendered on one condition. That Henry Gaunt's son promise to buy passage back to England with it. The boy refused outright.

Following the discovery of Witherspoon's corpse, Baker had felt obliged to apprise Henry Gaunt of the turn of events, to inform him that there had been some disaster in the wilds and that although the body of his son had not been found, everything pointed to his death. The message took three months to reach Sythe Grange.

Baker's letter had set all this in motion: the delirious monotony of travel, the passage through heat and dust, swarms of flies and mosquitoes, the spine-jolting bumps of wagons crossing an ochre prairie under the indifferent regard of a vast sky.

By afternoon, sun-scalded eyes drop to the rumps of the teams, seeking relief from limitless distances. The weary horses plod on, hauling their strange cargo: cases of Madeira, claret, port, brandy, half-bottles of champagne wine; delicacies of the well-stocked English pantry: pickled walnuts, marmalade, fish pâté, dried figs, blocks of dark chocolate, potted meats; the gear of the sportsman: a collapsible bath, shooting sticks, Belgian shotguns, rifles of every calibre, boxing gloves, an English longbow, clothyard arrows. Wagon boxes wail under the burden, and their drivers, Grunewald and Barker, uneasily contemplate the crash if they should tip.

Covered in fine sallow dust, Madge Stoveall's grieving sister, Lucy, follows the caravan, a wan, sickly ghost who refuses to ride.

❖ ❖ ❖

LUCY   Three days trailing these tailgates and I've about walked out of Abner's castoff boots. Big toe's so blistered it looks like a chunk of boiled okra. Mr. Charles asks me nicely to take a seat in his wagon, but I just smile and shake my head no, which makes him peer back at me from under his straw hat, all befuddled. Howsoever kind he is, I need to punish and wear down my body so I can sleep dreamless when night falls.

The hidden hand is at work in me. The very night of little Madge's funeral, singing that song for her, Sister's voice rose up in my throat. Then old Granny Timmin's blood started to rustle in my veins, day by day growing stronger, speaking from the marrow of my bones.

Granny Timmin, who dowsed lost things. All of the neighbours coming to her from miles around, asking her to help recover their valuables, rings, cufflinks, pocket watches, brooches, earrings, cash money – any variety of metal truck gone missing. That old woman in her best black dress and a white hanky on her head, walking through front parlours, through barns, through ploughed fields with the wish-bone stick in her hands until it went on point like a hunting dog, the sap in the green limb all aquiver with the tug of lost silver, lost gold.

Mother's gift was of a different kind. Precious metal did not answer to her, but water did. All about the county she witched wells and springs, water bending her bough.

I know Abner hoped to profit by me. He was sure witching was in our family, and he aimed to turn me loose to find lost trinkets, or water for a fee. But I never turned up so much as a penny coin or a cupful of brackish water. It mightily displeased him.

But, laying there mournful and sad in that wagon three nights after Madge's funeral, tossing and turning in a muddle of blankets, the notion took hold of me that if water and metal could be witched, why couldn't flesh?

I pitched out of my bed, took up a knife, and ran for that clump of bush growing hard by my wagon, hacked off a pincherry wish-bone. A big old swollen moon was spreading a chilly, quicksilver light so bright I could see my bare feet brushing through the dew-soaked grass. A cur howled some complaint to the town, a tinny piano knocked out music, drunks were raising a ruckus in the street. It felt like a swoony spell.

Did it just as I'd seen Granny and Mother do. Slow, I turned to the east, elbows set on my hips, tip of the pincherry sniffing for scent of my sister's murderers. Nothing answered. Straw had said the Kelsos had come from Kansas, so southward I shifted. The wand stood firm. I shuffled to face west, and the green stick stayed just the same in my hands.

I swung my shoulders north, threw my eyes up to the pole star, and a tiny trembling ran through the pincherry, came stronger and ever stronger, the wishbone leaping, jumping, wrestling about in my hands so's I could hardly hold to it. It frightened me to see the tip of the wand twitching with a horrible palsy in the cold, blue moonlight. And the palsy ran up my arms, tremors spreading, my whole body quaking like it was beset with St. Vitus's dance, my skin all gooseflesh. And then my mouth snapping open so wide I feared the joints of my jaws would crack, and my tongue tapping the roof of my mouth, stuttering fast as a telegraph key. And a strange voice groaned far back in my throat, a deep voice, a man's voice foully cursing Titus and Joel Kelso. I fainted dead away then, but I woke up fresh and filled with purpose, near bursting with it. The stick had pointed north. I had the promise I would find my sister's murderers there.

CHARLES   Tonight I wrote, not for Father's sake, but for myself. I recorded the splendid endurance and tenacity of the remarkable Mrs. Stoveall. For days she has obdurately insisted on hiking behind the wagons from dawn until dusk, no reasons for her stubbornness supplied, never yielding when I importuned her to ride. Now at the end of a taxing, arduous day, she has gathered dried buffalo dung for a cooking fire, dressed the antelope Addington killed, and prepared a delicious repast of steaks and "corn dodgers" smothered in molasses. My brother could not get enough of this American sweet. She may be cooking them for an eternity.

Our evenings have assumed an unvarying pattern. Mrs. Stoveall drudges like a slavey, cooks, serves, washes up. Mr. Ayto and Addington guzzle wine. This open-air life has invigorated Addington, he is completely in his element. Six months ago he was liverish and out of sorts, complexion poor, teeth strangely discoloured; he constantly sponged saliva from his lips with a handkerchief. But now he appears to be in the pink of health, the only one of us whose energy is a match for the indefatigable Mrs. Stoveall.

Even now, despite the lateness of the hour, my brother's high spirits blow gale force. Like a pampered child, he desires to be the centre of attention, is voluble and demanding, greedy for admiration and esteem, particularly that of our guide, Jerry Potts. But the taciturn native refuses to tip his hat to my brother's antics. Last night, when Addington played gymnast, stripping to the waist and walking a circle around the fire on his hands, sparks raining down on his bare back, a truly embarrassing display, Mr. Potts sat with a blanket drawn around his shoulders, impassive as an owl. Not so much as a hoot of approbation from him. His failure to applaud Addington's athletic prowess put a painful thorn in my brother's paw which even fawning Mr. Ayto could not draw, no matter how lavishly he praised him. If Mr. Potts is not careful to mend his ways, he shall find he has made an enemy of Addington.

Having failed once to impress our scout, tonight Addington broke out his beloved longbow, and regaled his captive audience with tales of the brave English archers at Crecy and Agincourt whose strong arms drove shafts through the plate armour of French knights, sent arrows whistling clean through the bellies of their destriers. I suppose we were to infer that Addington is their equal. He stood by the fire, flexing the bow to its utmost, bending it to the breaking point, and boasting he would soon bag a grizzly bear with it. When he invited Mr. Potts to see if he was strong enough to draw the string to his ear as Addington had, the half-breed walked off into the night without a word. My brother and Mr. Ayto found this extremely amusing, but I saw Grunewald and Barker exchange anxious glances. Certainly Addington would argue that the opinions of hirelings matter not a whit, but we are all dependent on one another in the wilds, and it does not do to sow dissension in the ranks. Grunewald and Barker owe allegiance to my brother, but there is no doubt that our scout is the man the teamsters truly fear and respect.

Mr. Potts has assured us that one day more of travel shall bring us to the Whitemud River.

Tomorrow, I will walk the banks of the river, wander the copses, comb the prairie grass for my brother's body. How can I measure which part of me is filled with hope of discovery, to put to rest the matter, against the fervent prayer that our search will yield nothing at all.

This fourth day of travel began in darkness at Mr. Potts's insistence, stars simmering in the sky, land humped dark and foreboding under the paler firmament. I had been awake for hours, lying in my blankets, impatient for his summons. My mood lightened as our scout led the way, swinging a lantern, a beacon to guide the drivers. After an hour's journey, a spectacular mulberry dawn dyed the billowy cloud which lay about the sky in fluffy mounds like wool at an English sheep shearing. If only I could have gathered it up in sacks to paint later. Such clouds that perhaps only Turner could have done justice to their livid majesty. Nevertheless, my fingers itched for a brush.

We rumbled on, Grunewald breaking wind expressively, spitting, and hugging his thoughts to himself.

Now it is noon, and after eight hours of journeying, Addington has decreed a halt. He and our guide are in dispute. The half-breed keeps pointing off to the northeast and repeating emphatically, "Couple more hours, Whitemud. Water and wood. We rest then."

Addington adopts a firm hand. "My good man, the decision is not yours to make. I am in command and I say we do not take another step until we have eaten and rested. Is that clear?"

"Addington," I say, "reconsider."

"And you be quiet, Charles. I shall not brook insubordination from whatever quarter it comes."

The inscrutable Mr. Potts shrugs. "You stop here. I go on," he blithely announces and trots off, setting a spark to my brother's fuse. "Potts! Come back, damn you! D'you hear!"

Our guide's abrupt departure produces a ripple of consternation. Grunewald's hands twitch on the reins. "It ain't much farther, Cap'n. We better follow him."

Barker simply cries, "Step up!" and his team rattles after the rapidly dwindling figure of our guide. Alarm infects Grunewald, who lashes his horses, jostling aside Addington. I throw a questioning glance back to my brother, who holds himself stiffly erect in the saddle, like a witness to a shameful battlefield rout.

But then he collects himself, decisively spurs his horse and over-takes us. "Press on, men!" he shouts above the din made by the careering wagons. "Show the half-breed your mettle! Press on!" If panic cannot be suppressed, it must be bent to Addington's will, made to seem something other than what it is.

All at once, I recall Mrs. Stoveall, and twist round on the wagon seat. There she stands, staring after us, camp follower abandoned by the fleeing troops. I shout at Grunewald to stop, but he doesn't heed me. Scrambling into the back, I frantically wave and cry out, "Mrs. Stoveall! Mrs. Stoveall! Hurry!" There is an instant of hesitation on her part, then she kicks off her preposterous boots, snatches them up, and flies after us, skirt fluttering, white feet flashing as she leaps sage brush, bounding like a deer. I drop the tailgate, stretch out a hand, give her arm a tug, pull her on, and we fall in a heap on the floorboards of the wagon.

My hand inadvertently grazes a plump breast as we struggle to our knees, swaying wildly from side to side. She catches hold of my shoulders to prevent herself from toppling over. Locked face to face, I confront the most marvellous eyes, a deep brown, the irises flecked with tiny grains of gold. Her face is flushed, hair in fiery disarray. "How swift you are! A veritable Amazon!" I shout, dreadfully excited by my part in her rescue. "A very near thing!"

Lucy Stoveall laughs with an unladylike, animal exuberance. But then I wonder if she isn't laughing at asinine me, hat ludicrously askew, stirred up by the most piddling of adventures and shouting like an inmate of Bedlam.

❖ ❖ ❖

LUCY   All sheepish he says, "Excuse my outburst, Mrs. Stoveall. All the Gaunts are mad. Although I daresay Addington is the maddest of us all, madder than Caligula."

How like a boy Mr. Charles looks. Nose burned red as a cherry, eyes blue as a cornflower. I take my hands from his shoulders, lean back against the wagon box. Pulling off his straw Panama, he fans himself, showing his fine brown hair, all damp, plastered tight to his skull.

"You all can't be crazier than this. A galloping pantry beats all for craziness." I point to the provisions threatening to crash down on our heads, cases of corned beef, Borden's condensed milk, Van Camp's beans, never mind the toothsome English dainties. I didn't believe my eyes the first time I poked my head into the glory of this supply wagon.

"Ah, yes," says Mr. Charles, helping himself to a jar of orange marmalade rolling loose about the floor. He waves it under my nose. "Addington, like Napoleon, believes his army marches on its stomach. But he gives so little credit to you, who keeps us content with your kitchen."

It's the first word of thanks or praise I've heard from the lot of them. I reckoned Mr. Addington, an expansive man in every way, would be the one to pass out compliments, not Mr. Charles, who's mostly still as a mill pond. "Well, the makings are fine. It's hard to put your foot wrong when you start with quality scratch," I tell him.

Mr. Charles unscrews the marmalade jar, dips his fingers in it, and sucks a dollop into his mouth. "My brother's personal store. He's addicted to his marmalade. I commit noblesse oblige. Is my secret safe with you?"

He offers the jar, but I'm shy to sample. Mr. Charles's brother strikes me as a fellow who might not want strange fingers mucking about in his jam. But Mr. Charles keeps tempting me. "Just a taste, Mrs. Stoveall. Share my guilt. Otherwise, I fear you will report my crime."

I don't want to spoil his lark, so I take a scoop. It tastes wonderful strong of orange, sweet and bitter both. "I ate an orange last Christmas," I blurt. "Took a quarter from my husband's pocket, and bought me and my sister two. Never had an orange before. That was St. Louis. Seems a long time ago."

"I am no corrupter of innocence then. It appears, Mrs. Stoveall, that you are already a hardened felon."

I'm not sure of his description of me, not sure whether he means to chastise me for pilfering Abner's pockets. "If you're calling me a thief, you're wrong. Every nickel that old rake jingled in his pockets came from me and my sister's sweat. He owed us our treat."

"A jest on my part, but an indelicate one. No criticism implied. Accept my apologies, Mrs. Stoveall." He bows his head to me. His crown looks tender as a baby's topknot, hair all swirled and soft. I'm sorry I mistook his meaning.

"I'm a touchy woman, Mr. Charles. So I ask pardon from you."

He nods and smiles, falls back against a bag of flour, getting himself comfortable. We're friends again. "I have been observing you closely, Mrs. Stoveall," he remarks, "and I like what I see. You are an admirable addition to our company."

I feel a blush spread on my face. "Well, that's handsome of you to think so."

Mr. Charles smiles. "Shall I confess something to you?"

"If you got the need."

"Do not think ill of me, Mrs. Stoveall, but when you made your proposal to join us – I did not think it wise of my brother to accede."

"Yes, and why was that?"

"I was concerned for the reputation of a woman travelling with men who were unknown to her." He reaches up and taps a skillet hanging from the wagon hoops with his fingertips, as if it helps him find his words. "But I was very wrong. You have been a great boon to our morale and well-being. I am most genuinely grateful for your presence."

"I do my best to make you gentlemen comfortable." He's got more to say, it's writ large on his face.

"Yes." He ponders a moment, fingertips still tapping the skillet. "Permit me to say a few words about my brother – in strictest confidence. In Fort Benton, his offer of protection may have appeared the height of chivalry. But keep in mind, my brother is a very impulsive man. He likes to cut a grand figure before an audience." Mr. Charles leaves it there for a bit. "His character is erratic . . . not entirely dependable. If I were you, I should keep my distance from Addington. And if you should ever require assistance – for any reason whatsoever – it would be better if you came to me."

I study on this, study on the look he wears. Mr. Charles can't bring himself to put it straight to a woman, even a married one. "All right," I say, "I've been warned."

❖ ❖ ❖

CHARLES   For most of a blazing hot afternoon Mr. Potts led us a merry, foxy chase. Dawdling until our wagons drew into sight, and then showing us his brush, galloping off just beyond our grasp. Several times Addington attempted to overtake him, but his thoroughbred was no match for our scout's knock-kneed, tireless pony.

Now, in late afternoon, we have finally reached our destination, a river valley collapsed like a toothless mouth in the face of the plain. As our wagons zigzag down the slope, I spy our guide, his horse unsaddled, a fire lit beside the Whitemud River, a disconsolate trickle of brown water dotted with muddy bars covered in brush. On the tops of the willow thickets which thrive on these tiny islands, red-winged and yellow-headed blackbirds flick about in the wind like diminutive pennants. The white clay cutbanks are riddled with the nest-holes of some species of swallow, thousands of which skim the surface of the water, curvet, cut elaborate arabesques of flight. An explosion of ducks erupts from the river at our noisy approach.

Addington immediately beards Mr. Potts. "You did not give us the slip, sir. I persevered. The deserter is overtaken."

"Now we rest," says our guide.

Mr. Potts's imperturbable demeanour has the most maddening effect on Addington. "No," he growls, "we do not rest. We search for Reverend Witherspoon's grave. We make use of the remaining hours of light."

"Maybe we eat first."

The exhausted horses droop in a lather of soapy sweat. The rest of us are equally exhausted. Everyone is of the same opinion as our guide, that we rest, that we sup. Only Mr. Ayto gleams a look of encouragement to my brother.

Mrs. Stoveall says, "I can whip something up quick – with the tinned goods."

Addington turns on her. "Our course of action is settled, Mrs. Stoveall. You may, for the present, occupy yourself watering the horses. The rest of us shall conduct a search of the vicinity."

"Addington, that is no way to speak to a lady."

My brother rounds on me, face brick-red, an ominous bulge to his eyes which I remember so well from childhood. "You, sir, are a milksop."

Mr. Ayto makes an untimely intervention. "Yes, it is not wise to undermine the Captain's authority –"

Mr. Potts suddenly says, "Over there." He points to a ravine several hundred yards off.

Addington, voice shrill with exasperation, demands, "Over there! Over there! What are you talking about, man!"

"The English preacher man is over there."

"What do you mean, 'Over there'?"

"I reckon over there you find him."

"Oh, I see," says Addington disdainfully. "A case of mental telepathy. Native clairvoyance."

"Just so," chimes Ayto.

Mr. Potts simply follows his own undivulged logic and heads for the coulee. After a moment of indecision, we follow, Addington furious, the rest of us puzzled and inquisitive.

It seems impossible that our guide should be so certain, even though he was present when Addington and I interviewed the prospector who had stumbled upon Reverend Witherspoon's body, a meeting arranged by Mr. Baker two days before we set out. The prospector had offered very vague information. He could not pinpoint for us where he had found the body, beyond saying he had come across it on the Whitemud River, perhaps a half-day's ride from the Cypress Hills. A hard spell of cold had settled in, the prospector told us, and he had seen tracks of Indian ponies about, and that decided him not to linger in the locality. He hadn't buried the clergyman, just hastily erected a cairn of logs over him as a protection from scavengers, and lit out as fast as he could for Fort Benton. "That fool was dead, and I wasn't about to join him. I smelled Sioux, so I rode out of there fast."

The coulee into which Mr. Potts leads us is choked with brush and spindly poplar, impeding everybody's progress except for our narrow-shouldered, bandy-legged guide, who seems to pass through it without disturbing so much as a twig. In moments, he disappears from sight, and leaves us to claw our way through crackling undergrowth. Then a reprieve, a small clearing presents itself, and in it stands our scout, nonchalantly posed beside an impressive jumble of logs.

Addington seems nonplussed, falls into a brown study. No doubt he meditates on the diminishment of his self-importance occasioned by our guide's miraculous success in locating what appears to be Witherspoon's resting place. I ask, "Mr. Potts, tell me how you knew to come here – exactly here?"

He circles the logs, thoughtfully poking them with a moccasined foot. "Not much timber round here," is his obscure explanation.

I press him further. "I don't understand. But how did you *know*?"

"Don't let him pull the wool over your eyes," Addington snaps. "This is no great mystery. Potts was here an hour before we arrived, and he had the good fortune to stumble across the cairn. Now he's trying to amaze us by playing the shaman." Addington shoots Mr. Potts a dark look. "Am I right, Potts?"

Mr. Potts grins broadly. "You cracking smart, Cap'n."

For the first time today, Addington overlooks the scout's insolence. "Pull those logs apart," he says to the teamsters. "Let us see if what we find is indeed Witherspoon."

It is Witherspoon, although I would not have recognized the blackened, half-rotten, leering corpse Grunewald and Barker uncover as the man who had once sat in the sitting room of Simon's and my house in Grosvenor Square, expounding the bizarre dogmas of his church.

His cadaver excites horrible images in my mind – Simon in a similar state, his gentle face blistered by corruption, his teeth bared in a grinning rictus, his skull a mess of haphazard tufts of hair. But I try to keep at bay a horror that seems more real – that this vast and empty land will remain mute, will never yield an answer to Simon's fate.

My stomach turns and sends me blundering back to the wagons.

Addington found inexcusable my refusal to take part in the burial service for Obadiah Witherspoon. But I wanted to hear no words said over his corpse. I will not feign sympathy or respect for the man who deluded my brother with fanatical doctrines and led him to renounce his family in favour of this accursed place.

In any case, Addington was only observing the formalities. No sooner had Witherspoon been interred than my brother announced he was off to hunt, and made some reference to Mr. Ayto about "baked funeral meats" for our supper.

Mr. Potts remarked to him, "Maybe you get lost. Maybe we starve before we get our supper."

Addington patted his coat pocket. "Never fear me getting lost, my good fellow. I navigate with a compass. A compass doesn't lie." Well-satisfied with having had the best of the exchange, my brother departed grandly, leaving us to our various amusements, Grunewald and Barker to gamble with the money my brother paid them to play sexton, Mr. Ayto to trim his toenails with a clasp knife, Mrs. Stoveall to see to domestic arrangements, and Mr. Potts, seemingly impervious to my brother's insult, to doze beneath a wagon.

A little while ago, when Grunewald and Barker were conducting their own crude inquest into Witherspoon's death, I overheard them say that they believe Witherspoon was not dispatched by savages, but met his death by misadventure. If Simon had been present at the time of Witherspoon's mishap, he certainly would have seen that the man was decently buried. Somehow, they must have become separated. But how and why? And what chance would my delicate and unworldly brother have of surviving on his own? I will not allow myself to lose hope.

Sitting here, on the bank of the Whitemud, I have decided to take refuge in my watercolours.

The half-sheet of Imperial, best linen ragcloth paper, spots with bits of debris. The water from the river is slop, straining it through cheesecloth has not removed all particulate.

The methods which Mr. Balducci drummed into me are not of much use in depicting western skies. Lay down a yellowish or reddish wash first to mute the brilliance of the succeeding blue, to lend it a pleasing softness, he always said. Very correct for rendering a hazy, moist English sky. But here, the heavens are of a crystalline brilliance and daunting depth.

So I lay down a wash of blue followed by a second coat of azure, hoping to thrum the optic nerve of the viewer. As my second application dries, I pick away at the filth speckling the surface of the paper. As my concentration takes a recess, I find myself visited by eerie thoughts. That Simon may have set his feet on the very spot where I sit. That he may be watching me this moment, hidden in the stand of trees confronting me from the opposite bank of the Whitemud, waiting for me to cry out to him.

I catch a rustling of grass, the snap of a breaking twig, and look up, half-expecting to see Simon smiling fondly down upon me. But it is Lucy Stoveall who greets me.

"Do you mind?"

"Please do." I shift to make room for her on my patch of grass, and she settles down, hugs her knees, peering with undisguised interest at the paper pinned to my board. I was rather pleased by my efforts, but with Mrs. Stoveall staring at the painting, my sky suddenly seems bland and insipid.

"Well," she says, "aren't you the clever fellow."

"No, not clever. But I had a good many lessons."

"It's a pretty picture."

"A picture certainly. But pretty was not really my goal. You see, I'm rather at a loss as to how to render the scene. It's the sky that confounds me. These skies are not what I'm used to in England." I point and her gaze follows my finger. "Now how do you paint that?" We both squint into a cloudless heaven that seems to spill a fierce, pale blue light on our upturned faces. "When your training no longer answers – why then you must experiment. And it is not the skies alone, the quality of light here changes everything, even the shadows." I trace our silhouettes, crisply etched on the ground. "I was taught to bleed the edges of shadows. But here, on this land, a shadow is a cameo, cut from black tin, sharply defined, stark." I rummage for a more expressive word. "Heavy."

Lucy examines our figures, dark on the ground. "You're right," she says. "Black as stovepipe tin. I never thought it before."

I realize how much I've said and with what urgency I've said it. My first heartfelt words in a month. "You must forgive me, Mrs. Stoveall. Art has always been my chief concern – until these last difficult months," I say.

"Your brother. I saw your face. I wondered if it was right to interrupt."

I cast my eyes about me. "I had the most uncanny feeling that somehow Simon was present. I was almost tempted to call out to him."

Suddenly her eyes brim with tears; she shakes her head. "Madge hovers near me too."

"Your sister," I say, "I'm sorry." Awkwardly, I place my hand on her shoulder. Through the thin cloth I can feel the heat of her sorrow.

Lucy asks quietly, "If you could talk to your brother, what would you say?"

"Ah. I would beg forgiveness for how we parted. I was very angry with Simon at the time. I berated him for his damnable idealism. My brother was very sweet-natured."

"My sister was a right good girl too. The best I could imagine."

I hazard a smile. "A point of similarity, Mrs. Stoveall. We were both encumbered by virtuous siblings."

"Madge was no encumbrance. Not to me. They could have stopped my own breath and I'd have missed it less."

We sit in silence, each thinking our own thoughts, as the sluggard river creeps by us. A great noise intrudes. Back in camp the men are shouting, "Buff! Buff!" Huzzahs for Addington. Apparently, our mighty Nimrod has slain his first bison.

Success in the field has helped Addington to recover his sang-froid. Over buffalo steaks and claret, he recounts the exploit for us. "There were ten or twelve grazing. I charged at them, loosed my horse pell. The beasts broke headlong with me hot on their tails. I picked out the biggest of the brutes, hump like a boulder, head like a bank safe, pulled abreast, leaned down, put one shot behind his shoulder, and turned him head over heels!" he exults, snapping his fingers in summation.

Mr. Ayto, my brother, and I, after disposing of three bottles of the ruby, are well into the port. No celebratory wine was offered to the others which, from their faces, looks to have been a mistake. But Addington's stance is that the cellar is restricted to the gentlemen, so let him bear the brunt of their displeasure.

Mr. Ayto, complacently tipsy, holds the floor. He and Addington have been flattering each other for the past half-hour. The question now under discussion is who exerts the greatest influence on the affairs of the world, the thinker or the man of action.

"I disagree most strenuously, Captain," declares insufferable Ayto. "The pen is *not* mightier than the sword. The pen *relies* on the sword. Look at Rome, sir. When the legions failed, civilization failed. No more scribblers then, sir. No more poems and plays then. No, indeed. And it is for this reason, Captain, that I have always admired, cele-brated – in my humble fashion *sung* – the praises of men of action such as yourself." Mr. Ayto strikes his hightop boots with the flat of his hand for emphasis. "I am a man, sir. And I admire men. A good many of these romancers and poets are women in trousers. On the other hand, a journalist – why he's a practical fellow – he has a knowl-edge of the world. He bends his elbow with men of business, profes-sional men, soldiers like yourself. Active fellows. He gets his hands dirty with the work of the world, throws himself into the broil, the questions of the day." Mr. Ayto leans forward to share a confidence. "Some years ago I wrote a small but influential pamphlet. The title was 'A Wolf in Sheep's Clothing.'" He allows us a moment to express our awe, as if he had said, "I once wrote a small poem, the title of which was *Paradise Lost*."

"The allusion is lost on me, Mr. Ayto. Please do elucidate," I say, wishing to prick the gasbag.

"Well," Mr. Ayto hooks thumbs in his garish waistcoat, "my script was a call to resist President Grant's Indian policy. You see, Charles, the president appointed an Indian, an Iroquois no less, as commissioner of Indian Affairs, a fellow just one remove from barbarism by name of Ely Parker, formerly known as Donehogawa. We Westerners wouldn't have it, sir. An Indian Bureau filled with pacifist Quakers and directed by a redman. We raised a proper hue and cry. Wolf in sheep's clothing? You catch the meaning of my title?"

Addington confesses comprehension. "Most certainly."

"We drove old Donehogawa out. Sent him packing. Gone like that," Mr. Ayto declares, waving goodbye. "I maintained then, have done so until this very day, that the army must deal with the Indians, not civilians. No nonsense from our red friends then. Let the logic of lead persuade them to mend their ways." Mr. Ayto lifts his glass high above his head where it flashes in the firelight. "Here's to the sword! Charles, here's to men such as your brother! The cream of Anglo-Saxon civilization!"

"Come now," Addington murmurs modestly, flushed with pleasure.

I raise my glass, propose my own toast. "To the power of the press. To influence bought for a penny a line. To the milk of Anglo-Saxon civilization which floats the cream."

For a moment, Mr. Ayto and Addington are left drunkenly blinking. Then Addington recovers and, like a good elder brother, steps in to correct me. "You are inebriated, sir. Mind your manners."

He is correct, but my intoxication does not invalidate my point. "Let me remind you, Addington, that your good self and Mr. Ayto have matched me glass for glass."

"Some can hold their wine."

"Ah, well," I grin foolishly at them. "Put my bad behaviour down to envy. A painter feels his superfluousness when confronted with two monumental pillars of civilization such as yourselves."

Both the milk and cream have turned very sour. "I thought my story might instruct you upon the necessity of using a firm hand with the redman," Mr. Ayto says. "We had an example of their failings today. Potts's disregard for duty. The phrenology of his skull displays a very limited capacity for responsibility. The cranium is tiny."

"Hold your tongue, he can hear you," I say sharply.

Both Addington and Mr. Ayto turn to Jerry Potts, who is sitting at the edge of the illumination cast by the fire.

"I daresay he can hear. But can he understand?" To prove his point, Mr. Ayto blares at him, "Potts, do you know what the word 'phrenology' means?"

Mr. Potts shrugs noncommittally.

"The Latin *cranium*, from the Greek *kranion*?"

"For God's sake," I say to Mr. Ayto. "Leave him in peace. He's done nothing to you."

Mr. Potts gets to his feet. "I take a piss," he proclaims.

"Yes, Jerry," says Mr. Ayto. "Do urinate."

Mr. Potts slinks off into the shadows.

Potts halts on the edge of the plateau overlooking the Whitemud, peers down into the valley where the campfire is a small orange flower, a prairie lily blowing in the night. A coyote yaps feverishly. Potts hunkers, pulls a bottle out from under his jacket, works away at the cork. Four days and not once have the English offered him a drink. Tonight, he has helped himself to a bottle from the supply wagon.

The cork releases with a surprising pop, liquor foams and he clamps his lips to the neck to capture it. The drink froths up his nose, making him gulp, sneeze. It tastes like yeasty bread, or maybe the stomach salts old Dr. Bengough gave him once for the bellyache.

Finally the bottle is quiet. No more fizz. The Captain and Ayto are like this bubbly liquor. It gives a man a heavy feeling to have to listen to the chatter of silly children all day long. One day, maybe he will have to push a cork into Ayto, stuff it right down his neck to stop his blather.

The Captain froths over also, but he is a different bottle. A cork would not go down his neck so easy. Potts has been watching him. The man can ride and he can shoot. He is strong, quick, nimble.

The Captain's weak spot is that he has no eye for the lie of the land. He trusts his compass too much. But it is not wise to put such stake in whatever can be lost or broken.

It made the Captain very angry that he had found the grave of the English preacher so easily. What the Captain does not know is that two years ago, he and his Kanai cousin Red Horse had hunted here on the Whitemud, killed themselves a big elk on the turtle-shaped bar across from where the wagons sit now. The elk was fat; all afternoon they had grilled steaks and roasted the bull's rack in a slow fire, feasting until dusk on its rich marrow.

When night fell they had slipped into that ravine to hide themselves from the eyes of enemies. There they found an old war lodge built years ago by a party of raiders. Deadfall and river driftwood crossed like teepee poles, stacked tight, timber to timber, and covered with cottonwood bark so no glint of fire from within could shine through a chink.

The prospector in Benton said he had piled timber on the preacher's grave to protect the body. Potts had guessed where he had got it. Logs from the war lodge.

Keeping these fools safe weighs on him heavily. They would never find their way home unless he took their hands and led them. Except maybe the woman. He has been watching that one. For three days she has walked behind the wagons without complaint like a Kanai woman behind the travois. When the day's work is done, she sits quietly by herself. She sleeps little, rises early in darkness to boil their coffee, to fry their meat, to bake bread. When it comes time to move on, she is always ready to start, waiting with her gunny sack hung over her shoulder.

There is something else he has seen. The woman is stealing food, storing it in that bag. Food that will not spoil. Biscuits, dried meat. He does not know what she is up to.

He takes another drink. This liquor is not as cheering as whisky; it does not wipe away Ayto's insult. He may not understand the meaning of Ayto's words, but there was no mistaking the ridicule in his voice.

Tomorrow the sun will come up, but the land will still be dark to the English, a mystery, even in the light of day. Just as their words are dark, a mystery to him.

❖ ❖ ❖

LUCY After two days scouring for sign of Simon Gaunt, the men have given up the search. They tramped the banks of the river for miles, rifled through the thickets, rode the prairie up top every which way. They did all that could be done, Mr. Charles in particular. He was in a passion. Somebody had to drag him back to camp every night, else he would have kept roaming about in the dark. I kept his supper warm for him as best I could.

Despite Mr. Addington's almighty airs, Mr. Charles is the true Nature's gentleman. He's the only one of them who shaves every day – even Mr. Addington has slackened off there – and he is a stickler for neatness and cleanliness, the way he brushes his coat every morning, wipes his boots clean. Everything from him is please and thank you, Mrs. Stoveall. Grunewald and Barker call me woman, like I didn't have a name. One of these days I might have an accident, spill a little hot grease on them. Ayto thinks I'm at his beck and call. Mr. Addington mostly ignores me.

Mr. Charles is a scholar. By the fire, he scribbles away in a book on a writing desk you can hold in your lap. While he does that, his brother and Mr. Ayto get drunk. Mr. Addington is full of scampish tricks, turning his somersaults, doing cartwheels, walking about on his hands. I can see Mr. Charles doesn't approve of his brother cutting up such capers like a dog in a medicine show.

When Mr. Charles saw the state of Abner's boots, split and gaping, he pressed on me a pair of his own shoes and two pair of soft, thick stockings to wear to help make them fit. Tomorrow, when we strike out again, I'll step a good deal lighter for his gift.

14

CUSTIS Splashing across the Milk River last night I was mighty puffed up with myself for crossing into British territory after one day's long, tough ride. Not that the Medicine Line means anything. No difference to remark between here and there, dirt isn't patriotic, doesn't wave the flag. The war taught me that much.

But this morning when I crawled out of my kit I soon learned the penalty for pushing beyond my limits. I'm so damned chafed and stiff I can scarcely walk. Worse, the Morgan's come up lame. So here I am, gulping a pot of hot coffee, legs held to the fire, roasting the cramp out of them, the sun peeping at me with a drunkard's bloodshot eye. Prospects aren't near so cheerful as yesterday's when Lucy Stoveall beckoned on a fine day. Bright and breezy, grass mottled with cloud shadows, sun and shade snapping on and off as I went along.

I knew a man who once said bad luck the first day of a journey was nothing, but misfortune on the second sticks like a cocklebur, it's not to be shook. If that's true, things are shaping up bad for me. Right off, I noticed the Morgan favouring her right back leg as she grazed, but when I inspected it, I found nothing, not so much as a hoof crack or stone bruise.

What can't be diagnosed, can't be cured. So I drink my coffee and fashion a lunge line from my lariat, then set the mare to circling me so I can study her gait. She's hesitant to take the lead and that's what makes her look awkward on the follow. The trouble has to be in the front legs, not the back. A little scraping with my pocketknife and I find it quick enough, a damp spot near the V of the frog on the left front hoof. A pocket of ripe infection.

This needs to be thought through. The mare's too lame to travel today. If I cut her loose and press on, I'm short a mount to bring Lucy Stoveall back to Fort Benton. The best bet is to ease the pressure on the mare's hoof, and to see if she might be able to travel at an easy pace tomorrow.

I've got an awl in my saddlebags for making simple repairs to my saddle and harness. Once I've sharpened it to a needle-point, I have a lancet. I prick carefully all around the rim of the corruption, press down on it with my thumb, drain a teacup's worth of pus and pinkish blood. Next step is to douse the sole with whisky, and bind it up in my handkerchief to keep it clean. Now there's nothing to do but wait and hope she recuperates by tomorrow.

Problem is I'm so warm to catch up to Lucy Stoveall, to wait is vexing hard. My thoughts keep darting off to her in the wilderness, and the whisky in the bottle in my hand keeps inching down.

When I find her, what I'll say is this: "Lucy Stoveall, I've got ten thousand dollars in a bank in St. Louis and another two thousand stashed in I. G. Baker's safe. I own two hundred head of horses; even sold cheap they'll bring fifty dollars a head. I know you had a notion once to escape your husband. So fly with me. I'll take you to San Francisco in style. We'll look on the Pacific Ocean. I've seen it from the Oregon view, and it's as fine a thing as there is in creation. But if you don't care for the Pacific Ocean, I'll take you wherever you want to go – just you point me. I'm not much, but I reckon I'm a good deal better than Abner Stoveall. Run with me and I'll get you clear of his clutches. I don't ask but to help you. I know your fineness and I know I'm not worthy of it. But I'll treat you right. I swear it."

I tell myself I've got to hold my fire as I was taught in the 19th Indiana. The youngsters there took me for the steadiest of soldiers because of how I did everything with the utmost care and deliberation before going into battle – fixing a bayonet, checking my loads, rolling a cigarette. They called me Uncle Ice, thinking I felt no fear, but my guts were seething and I was reckless for action. I played a part like an actor because if I didn't, the real Custis Straw would have snapped from impatience.

I had to save myself from my own nature then, and I have to do it now. So I hold myself quiet as quiet can be, lift the bottle slowly to my lips, just as slowly settle it back down betwixt my feet. I stare at the horizon line like a man lashed to a mast.

Morning passes to the swish of a horse's tail, the sound of Dan and the mare cropping grass, the buzzing of a fly. Now the sun squats directly over my head. It's unusual hot, sweltering, sticky for these parts, drops of sweat plop off the end of my nose, trickle down my ribs.

Miles south of the Milk, bloated purple thunderheads are rearing up, sheet lightning commencing to flash, followed by a growl like a far-off artillery barrage. The whisky's finished. I heave the bottle into the river, watch it popple and sink, take out my pocket watch. Every move slow, calculated, measured. It's one o'clock. I've been keeping guard on my nerves for close on five hours.

The storm rolls towards me, bringing darkness with it like a baggage train raises dust. Less than a mile off, it will soon be on top of me. There's no place to seek shelter, so I just wait for whatever it brings. I feel the temperature suddenly drop, see the grass start to thrash. There's more lightning running yellow, forked cracks in the sky. The clouds are on the boil. A water spout whirls up on the Milk River, spins like a shiny tin siphon, and suddenly is stamped flat.

I pull off my hat, shove it under my haunches, sit firm on it. The wind shrieks, fills my jacket like it was a sail, drives a tumbleweed on to my chest, wrestles it off. Rain and wind and flying dust tear at me all at once, claw my face, shake me. I duck down, clutch the grass, rock back and forth as the storm roars and batters me. A terrible crash claps in my ears, a hot, blue-green light spurts in my eyes, cuts out, pulling down a blind. Leaning into the charging wind, grape-shot rain peppering my face, I hold on, howling like a child. Thunder covers my screams, but I feel them scraping up my windpipe.

And then, as quickly as it came, the thunder passes, muttering, grousing off to the north and there's only a heavy rain tramping down my back. I hear what's left of my bellowing, a sickly lament, a low, monotonous drone.

The downpour keeps up, but I sit patient under it. I keep telling myself fear made no other part of me break and run, only my voice did that. Hold ground, Custis.

Bit by bit, the rain eases off, whimpering in the mud. I lift my face to the long prospect south. The sky is rinsed clean, a weak sun breaks on miles of wet plain patched with apple green, new penny copper, glints of silver. On that plain, a tiny black horse and its rider are making towards me as if the Apocalypse had shaken one of the Four Horsemen out of the clouds and down to earth.

I drag my mashed hat out from under my buttocks, punch the crown into some sort of shape, set it on my head, straighten my back and shoulders, and wait for the horseman to deliver his face to me.

The rider who fords the waters of the Milk and draws rein in front of me is none other than a sopping-wet Aloysius Dooley.

❖ ❖ ❖

CHARLES It is now two days since we abandoned our fruitless search of the Whitemud and began to trek westward, headed for the many lawless whisky posts that Potts says have recently sprung up in British territory north of the Sweetgrass Hills. He claims that the ruffians who infest this region have constant intercourse with the Blackfoot, and so I cling to the slender possibility that the whisky traders may have learned something of Simon's fate from the natives. Hope based on such a weak foundation may be delusion, but I have recourse to nothing else. We must pursue every avenue until winter threatens and turns us back to England.

My only reprieve from doubt and despondency is furnished by Lucy Stoveall. I find her a cheering companion. Her talk is unrestrained and genial, her manner forthright and sensible, tempered by an undercurrent of melancholy which we both share. She is unlike any woman I have ever met. It is very pleasant to stretch my legs with Mrs. Stoveall and pass an hour or two in conversation that is agreeable, but not frivolous. As all Americans are, she is a natural democrat, but a refreshing and charming one. Several times she has brought me up short with astute remarks upon the character of our companions, a reminder that one may be ignorant but not necessarily unintelligent.

Yesterday, as we rambled in the wake of the wagon, I was moved to reflect upon how difficult it is to set the boundaries with Mrs. Stoveall, to decide exactly what position she occupies, that of our servant or damsel in distress.

Today, the weather was glorious, not too warm for an extended stroll, and I took full advantage of it to spend several pleasant hours in Lucy Stoveall's society. With so many more hard miles yet to cover, Mr. Potts advised relaxing the pace of our caravan so as to husband the strength of the horses for the rough terrain that lies ahead. Grunewald and Barker took him at his word, let the horses amble as the drivers dozed on their seats. Addington for once did not contradict Mr. Potts but, full of restless energy, seized the opportunity to ride off with Mr. Ayto to hunt.

Mrs. Stoveall and I were left free to meander and botanize. Lucy, as she has now enjoined me to call her, walked along eyes fastened to the ground, her red hair streaming in the breeze, pointing out to me and naming many small, delicately coloured flowers hidden in the prairie grasses: scarlet mallow, broomweed, sunflower, blue beardtongue. In the sheltered coulees we explored, there were the ominously named yellow death camas and the pinkish-white bearberry. Once, I caught her deep in contemplation at the bottom of a gully, a small nosegay of native flowers clasped in her hand. A figure of sombre beauty amid the shadows, a subject for a Pre-Raphaelite. I slipped away so as not to interrupt her rumination, and waited on the prairie for her to emerge. She strode out of the declivity very purposefully, announcing she feared I had got myself lost.

A little later, my attention was directed by her to a colony of burrowing owls, tiny feathered troglodytes who make their home in abandoned gopher holes. I was astounded and intrigued that creatures of the air would choose to make their home deep in the earth. The birds were as curious of me as I was of them. From the mouths of their lairs they stared back at me with a comical intensity. I enjoyed a hearty laugh at their expense.

We strolled on and heard a lovely song, the singer of which Lucy identified as a meadowlark. As I stood enjoying the lark's concert, Lucy shyly inquired whether I would care to see a portrait of Madge taken in St. Louis. I said I would be delighted. She took it out of the sack which was slung over her shoulder and placed it reverently in my hands.

The daguerreotype revealed a comely young girl, dressed in a simple white blouse and skirt, her hair coiled on the top of her head in a crown of plaits.

Lucy asked, "Do you note a resemblance to me?"

I did not. Her sister left an impression of fragility very unlike Lucy's robustness, the fragility of a Meissen figurine. The girl's smile was timid, her teeth small, her chin deferentially dipped. Not at all like Lucy except, perhaps, for the hair. Lucy's slightly hooded, slanting eyes, and high, curving cheekbones were certainly not in evidence in the daguerreotype. Madge, unlike her sister, could not be called handsome, a word applied to women of an unconventional beauty and a word so descriptive of the unconventional Lucy.

"Very like you," I said, returning the portrait. "A very striking girl."

She did not seem aware I had handed her a compliment, but she beamed, happy that I had claimed to have seen so much of herself in her sister.

It was then she asked if I had a portrait of Simon she might view. Tonight I showed it to her. Not the one Father judged the best likeness: Simon posed in the library of Sythe Grange, feet planted on a Turkey rug, playing the stiff English gentleman. Just as a wax work might be said to capture the original, to that degree Simon had been captured. But not his true, animating spirit. Not a trace of it.

The photograph I showed to Lucy was the one taken our first year at Oxford. When she saw it, she could not help exclaiming, "Why, your brother looks like a beggar!"

Simon, draped in a worsted cloak fashionable at the turn of the last century, smiling equably out at the world from under a shapeless, felt hat. This costume had been acquired at a second-hand clothes dealer because Simon had fallen under the spell of Matthew Arnold's elegiac poetry. Like so many other Oxford students who rambled the banks of "the stripling Thames," and mooned about the Cumner Hills with copies of "The Scholar Gypsy" and "Thyrsis" stuffed in their pockets, he had caught the disease of romanticism. How like my brother to carry his fantasies even further than they and adopt the dress of Arnold's legendary scholar gypsy, a "hat of antique shape, and cloak of grey." To believe that by wafting about the countryside, Nature would imbue him with a more mysterious and authentic knowledge than the university could offer.

All this flummery was bad enough, but then he proposed that the two of us should make an overnight trek on foot from Oxford to London when the moon was full, in an attempt to recapture the questing soul and open-air life of the gypsy scholar. From this scheme there was no dissuading him. He said if I could not be prevailed upon to join him, he must make his pilgrimage alone. That threw me into a quandary. Left to his own devices, my guileless brother could not escape disaster. If he wasn't mauled by farmers' dogs in the dead of night, he would be mistaken for a poacher, or taken in charge as a vagrant. A threadbare cloak and pulverized, moth-eaten hat would not recommend him to a local magistrate. Despite my exasperation and foreboding, I felt I had no choice but to go.

So one evening in the midst of a bronze dusk we set off from Oxford. Simon in his ridiculous rags, clutching a pilgrim's staff he had cut in Wychwood days before, a satchel slung over his shoulder packed with porter, bread, and cheese. In an attempt to add an aspect of respectability to the outing, I had dressed myself in the garb of a genteel sportsman.

Down the narrow streets Simon blithely advanced while I hugged the walls and slunk along under the gables, trying to make myself as inconspicuous and small as possible. After an eternity, we escaped the bemused eyes of the townspeople. It was a warm evening, very still, cloudless, and as we made our way the moon peeped above the hedges and lit our way like a lantern. Miles outside of Oxford we encountered a farmer's cart on the road. He doffed his cap to me, stared uncomprehendingly at my strange companion, was still peering back at us dumbfounded as his cart rounded a bend.

For two hours we briskly strode along in silence, Simon's pale face aglow with joy and the bright lunar light. At our feet the white lane gleamed like paper cross-hatched with the shadows of beeches and elms. Here and there a window shed its light or a dog barked as we passed a silent cottage, but these were the only signs of life.

Solitude salved my embarrassment, and I began to feel that, just as once we had shared unspoken thoughts and feelings in childhood, I was entering into a wordless communion with my brother. Impulsively, I threw my arm over his shoulder and was rewarded with a smile of sheer delight. He whispered to me, "This is the world. Not that."

Like so much of what Simon said, this was not comprehensible. "Not that" might refer to the university, or perhaps my reluctance to be seen by amused onlookers as we left the town. But the implied criticism caused me to remove my arm from his shoulders and say, "Surely the world is everywhere."

My brother stopped and gazed about him. "Yes, you are right," he conceded. "But it is difficult to feel and know the world in certain places."

"Perhaps I feel the world, hear it, under different conditions than yourself. You must not be dogmatic, Simon." I felt it would be false of me to be anything but perfectly frank.

"I am filled with happiness here. Does your perception of the world promote your happiness?"

I sidestepped the question of happiness. "My perception promotes my comfort. It permits me to make my way in the world." I thought for a moment and attempted to reverse the pressure he was bringing to bear. "If you continue as you seem intent on doing, you will pay a price. Your path –" I hesitated, gesturing to the road, "will not be as easy and plain as this byway. Fairy moonbeams do not provide a steady light." He slowly nodded. It was painful to watch. I feared I had wounded him dreadfully. "I have hurt you," I said.

"You grow more like Father every day."

"Nonsense. How can you possibly say that?"

Without answering my question, Simon resumed walking. "You were made to marry, I think," he said, another impenetrable remark.

I retorted, "I mean to be a painter. Don't you know? Painters keep mistresses."

"We are a family of dissemblers," he said. My brother gravely pursed his lips, a judge momentously weighing a sentence. "And I am the greatest dissembler of us all," he said at last.

I could not help but laugh at this self-accusation. Nothing could be more patently ludicrous than his claim of dissembling. From childhood on, Simon had never been capable of concealing any of this thoughts or motives. But my dismissal of his claims to dishonesty had upset him. Once more he halted, tapping his staff on the ground. His voice rose. "You are more obvious than I, and always have been. You have always yearned for love, Charles. Father's love. But you were ashamed to ask it of anyone but me. You felt your need a weakness, a weakness that could only be revealed to someone weaker than yourself. You took me for that person. But now my peculiarities, as you would describe them, have made our attachment a burden to you. So you must seek love, affection elsewhere. Do not follow your present course. It is a dead end. The dead end of the perfect English gentleman. Go away. Go to Italy, or to France," he said forcefully. "You are not strong enough to resist Father, to find love and freedom here. You care too much for the approbation of others."

I shot back, "So your vast experience with the fair sex recommends to me a foreign wife. Which is your preference? The Italian or the French?"

"Both of us," he said, "frozen in a pose." Simon touched his hat, his cloak significantly. "I edge towards honesty. But this is only a first step. I must learn courage by degrees."

"Riddles."

My brother reached out, clasped his hand to the back of my neck, and drew me close, so near I could feel his warm breath on my face. "I would not have you think ill of me. Do not think ill of me, whatever happens," he said. At that moment, he looked so beseechingly into my eyes that I can recall his expression even now, years later, the swollen moon and tiny stars riding above his shoulder. With vehement emphasis he recited to me, " 'To the just-pausing Genius we remit / Our worn-out life, and are – what we have been.' "

"Arnold," I said.

"Arnold."

"And what does it signify?"

"We are not alone, Charles. Given time, the spirit of the universe will accept us. For the present, it asks us simply to be. To be ourselves and not someone else's dream of us."

"Is this the speech of a Christian?"

He avoided justifying himself. "Why are we on this road? To arrive at London. We think London exists because we have seen it with our own eyes; we believe it still stands on the strength of daily reports – articles in the newspaper, your friend Tom Budge's stories about his visit to Kew Gardens a fortnight ago. But we cannot know for sure it still stands until we reach it ourselves. There may be no city awaiting us at the end of the road."

"That is preposterous," I said.

"And the universal spirit, Genius, God, where is It, He?" Simon said. "He, It, is to be found in the reports that we poor human beings have been filing for centuries, reports of encounters, reports of intimations, reports written and spoken in every language known to man. None of them the same, but all sincere. To pursue the 'just-pausing Genius' is the only proper aim of life." Concluding his homily, Simon was immediately lightened. He released his hold on me and was himself – old, happy Simon. "Remember Mr. Jacks?" he said. I nodded. Jacks, the head gardener at Sythe Grange, dead for years.

"Remember when we were ten or eleven, and he gave us porter to drink?"

"Yes. I remember."

"It made me drunk, Charles. I have never been drunk since. But I have never forgotten the feeling. Lying in the grass with the sun on my face. I tell you, I felt equal to anything." He patted the satchel that hung at his side. "I have bread and cheese and porter. Let us break our journey."

And we did. I in my kerseyside trousers, soaking my buttocks on wet grass under a hawthorn bush. We ate contentedly and then walked on contentedly, walked on through the hind end of night, through the false dawn, and through the morning sunshine until, bone-weary, we glimpsed the smoke rising from the chimneys of London, and at last entered the city, saw the men and women bustling about the streets, bent on their own purposes. That sight of London at the end of the road was the closest I have ever come to belief.

And I must confess to myself, if no one else, that despite my best efforts to keep hope alive, and my determination to pursue the search for him, with every day that passes the conviction grows that I shall never see Simon alive again. Perhaps I am already what the old country people call the left twin. The survivor of the cruellest separation: those who shared a womb torn from one another in the world.

Jacks once told Simon and me a story about a young woman who suffered from the dark thrush, whose mouth was filled with ulcers and infection. And a small boy, whose twin had died only a year before, was brought to her, and when he had blown his breath in her mouth three times, she was cured. The left twin, it is said, has the power to heal. But not himself.

15

It being Sunday, and over his brother's strenuous objections that they keep to the task, press on, Addington has magnanimously granted the men a day of rest. He has decided to mark the Sabbath with a rousing good gallop. After a two-mile run, the sorrel straining under him, the chuff of lungs, the chuck of legs, he savagely reins him up. The gelding sidles, dances, switches his hindquarters while Addington clucks his tongue soothingly. Finally, the animal settles, drops his head to graze, and Addington surveys his surroundings with approval. Mile upon unimpeded mile of firm turf over which to race. All it lacks is a few hedges and gates to sail over and it would be the peak of perfection.

Addington is in high spirits, certain that in a short time he will be in the pink of condition, fit as Nero's fiddle. The rash that mottled his thighs all last year is gone and with it the ache in his joints. So much for Dr. Andrews and his simpered warnings. *Captain Addington, a venereal complaint is a most indolent disease. It will sleep, sir, it will lull you, but when it awakes . . . I have made a most thorough study of its character. And what I recommend to my patients is a strict regime of regularly administered medicaments – mercury, antimony, and iodide of potassium. A most efficacious and salutary prophylactic against the advance of the ailment, don't you know.* Emphatically, *We must be vigilant, Captain.* So the vigilant dosing began, went on month after month, without any improvement in his symptoms or his well-being. Injections of mercury and applications of it to the skin.

Going out to dine, his body smeared with mercury, gleaming like a sardine under evening dress.

It is a mistake to surrender oneself into another's hands. Day by day, he had felt himself grow more feeble, more lethargic, more *womanish*. But that is finished. No more poisoning himself. No more mercury, no more iodide of potassium, no more antimony. Nothing but a touch of Fowler's Solution, three drops in a glass of port before sleep, the lightest of medicines. Placing himself in the hands of the sovereign physician, healing Nature, that is the ticket. Strenuous exercise, sunshine, invigorating air, game freshly killed and freshly prepared, there's the true remedy.

All those doses of quicksilver can destroy a man. Heavy droplets of mercury circulating through the body, infesting the brain, weighing down every thought, here was surely the root of his dark imaginings, the explanation for the bony-ribbed, scabby, grey horse upon which he had sat so many nights at Sythe Grange.

Who was that chap at school, the one with the ampoule of mercury? Edson. Its properties fascinated the little beggar. He would slide it out of the vial in a single, shivering globule and, with a mad look in his eye, mash down hard on it with his thumb, sending myriad drops scurrying all about the tabletop like tiny silver mice. Then, playing cat, Edson would carefully bat them back together into a gleaming orb, shatter them all over again, giggling to himself.

But now the grey horse fades night by night, becoming at worst a fitful phantom compounded out of the dregs of quicksilver still circulating in his system, a small, treacherous whirlpool spinning round memories of Dunvargan: a twisted face here, a hand clenching him there, hollow whispers.

But he is confident this too will pass like the sores, the discolouration of his teeth. Ghosts are banished by daylight corporeality, by clamping his legs to the barrel of a horse, by basking in hot sun, by inhaling fresh air.

This is what he was born to do. Live like a Mongol khan. Eight hours in the saddle, a return to camp with quarry slung across the saddle-bow, a crackling fire, meat, wine, laughter, stories. The business at Sythe Grange, stealing into the night with a longbow, dodging the gamekeeper and his minions, risking mantraps and spring guns, all that had simply been an invalid's attempt to combat torpor, to stir sluggish blood with a dose of artificial danger. The red deer a sacrifice to propitiate the savage gods of his malady.

How else was an active man to keep on his mettle? The old men had taken his career from him. Colonel Oates berating him after the Irish rioted. After Oates had dressed him down like that, treated him like a schoolboy, thoroughly humiliated him, what choice had he but to resign? Elderly officers pushing down the strong for fear of losing their places and, if you dared to stand up for yourself, they cast you down even further. Reminded you of your place.

So be it. He has found his place, his element. No longer suffocated by the stale breath of old duffers, finally at liberty to fill his lungs freely. At last, in command. See how he'd brought that half-breed neatly to heel.

Of course, Charles is an annoyance. He, too, needs to be taught it is not his place to carp at every decision made, nag him to rush about looking for Simon. Only fools like Charles and Father cling to the ridiculous hope he is alive. There is nothing to be found but a corpse, and small chance of that. Charles ought to enjoy this jaunt, like he is doing.

The hunting is wonderful. Three antelope, a dozen prairie chicken, a mule deer bagged yesterday. A sportsman's paradise under his very nose and Charles chooses to pick flowers with that woman.

No sign yet of any grizzlies, *Ursus arctos horribilis*. Let the county toxophilites call Horace Alfred Ford the greatest English archer after they learn the Captain has brought down one of the great bears armed with nothing but a longbow. Face it, overcome it, that's what defines a man.

Mr. Ayto will write that exploit up very thrillingly and he is certain Charles can be prevailed upon to do him a capital illustration for the book. There it is in his mind's eye, ravening bear erect on its hind legs, pawing the shaft buried in its throat, and there he is, a mere arm's-length away from those terrible teeth and claws, cool and collected.

He often mulls over titles for his book in moments such as this. *A Gentleman Nomad in the Great American Desert. The Rambles and Adventures of Captain Gaunt.* Perhaps Mr. Ayto can do those one better; he is, after all, the man of letters.

With the exception of the impudent guide, Addington is well pleased with the band he has assembled. Grunewald and Barker are steady, plodding oxen. The woman a diligent dogsbody. It is irksome to see her so much in the company of Charles, who tags after her like a fawning spaniel. But no fear of Charles being first into port. His milksop brother would sooner request a wench to sit for a portrait than fall on her back for him.

He sees the bitch, her legs in the air. But he must be careful. A moment of impulse, of unexpected pressure, and the mercury in his brain might squirt into a thousand pieces as it had in Fort Benton. He knows this is the only possible explanation for what had occurred there. He is, after all, a very disciplined fellow, whatever Colonel Oates might have said about his conduct in Ireland. Castigating old bugger.

Certain thoughts are unmanageable, too distressing. Suddenly he feels the need of company. Mr. Ayto is a congenial chap; the two of them shall open a bottle. Addington jerks up the horse's head, gouges with his spurs, pounds off back to camp.

❖ ❖ ❖

ALOYSIUS A man might have expected some thanks from Custis, but no, it weren't forthcoming. I find him half-drunk, squatting in a puddle, and he don't even have the good manners to say, "Hello, Aloysius, glad to see you." All he wants from me is my horse, demands I trade it for the Morgan.

I told him straight. "Not in a month of Sundays."

He ripped and snorted, threatened and begged, but I didn't budge. Straw needs a cool head around to try to put a check on him, even if he don't know it. His state of mind is unpredictable of late. He seems set on making a nuisance of himself, courting trouble. When I finally got through to him I weren't about to yield the horse, and I weren't about to turn around and go home, he turned nasty.

"I don't know what you think you're up to," Straw said. "Imposing yourself on a body who doesn't want you. I advise you to go home and look after your precious business. I suspect the riff-raff are breaking into the Stubhorn this very minute. Helping themselves to your store of spirits. Glug glug. Aloysius Dooley comes home and finds himself bankrupt. 'Woe is me!' he cries."

Sometimes being a friend to Custis Straw is like hammering spikes into your forehead. You don't do it because it feels good. "Nobody ain't going to break into my place."

"Oh, I see. Every layabout, ruffian, and rascal in Fort Benton has such a high regard for the great Aloysius Dooley they wouldn't think of despoiling his property. Whatever was I thinking?"

"It's taken care of. I rented me a fighting dog," I told him. "Alphonse Miller's fighting dog. That big black one that's all nuts and teeth. We locked him in the Stubhorn. Any burglar pokes himself into my saloon'll get a piece chewed off. Miller promised he'd only feed him every second day. Just to keep his mood dark."

"You're disgusting," said Straw. "Starving a dumb animal. Think of him locked up. The loneliness of it."

"He's bred to fight. They don't like company. Loneliness is cheerful to them."

After that, Straw wouldn't talk no more, just sat and brooded. It was getting dark, so I made a fire. Custis sat reading his Bible while I fried us a pan of bacon. I served him his share. "I want you to hear this, Aloysius," he says. " 'Greater love has no man than this, that a man lay down his life for his friends.' " He claps the book shut. "And all I'm asking from you is a horse."

Well, I shut down my business for him. I wouldn't do that for any other man. I can't say how Custis worked himself under my skin like he done, except there's never a dull day in his company. It keeps you on the jump just trying to figure out how his mind works and where it's going to veer off to next. And most times he's good-hearted. The truest thing I ever heard anybody say about Custis Straw came from Dr. Bengough, who remarked, "Straw is the only man I know who does his best to harm no one but himself." I aim to see, he don't do too much damage to his contrary person.

The morning after I caught up with him, Custis's mood improved immediately once he judged the Morgan fit to travel. Going in easy stages, we reached the Whitemud River in two days, rode the bank until we struck where the Gaunts camped. They'd left, nothing there but cold ashes and wagon tracks leading west. Custis kicked the charred sticks and fire ring to pieces, muttering and cursing to himself.

For two days we trailed after them, Custis as impatient as a bride-groom on his wedding night. Even heavy-laden wagons ain't easy to track on the prairie. Soon as they pass over the wiry grass it springs up, and we had to do a good deal of casting about to pick up the smallest trace of their passage.

Now this morning, Custis's sure we're closing on them. We find horseshit with rind on it, but the turds are green and moist inside. After he's done pinching and smelling the road apples, Custis scrambles back up on Dan, full of determination to overtake them.

Just before noon, we come over a hog's back and, five hundred yards off, there they are. Custis halts us atop the ridge with a thoughtful look on his face. I suspicion he's running through his mind how he's going to get his way with Lucy Stoveall.

The Gaunts' horses are grazing peaceful in their hobbles. The wagons are parked tongue overlapping tongue in what I take to be the English Captain's idea of defence against marauding Indians. In the open ground between the Conestogas I spot three men, little in the distance. Two are watching the third, who's going round and round in a tight circle, waving his arms above his head, legs jerking like he's dancing a hornpipe.

Custis and me start down the slope. Our approach ain't noticed. Everybody's too busy gawking at the dance. It ain't until we're almost on them that Grunewald and Barker hear our hoof beats and swing about to face us. The other one keeps hopping.

I see what the jigging's about. Jerry Potts's buckskins make him hard to spot laying in the tan grass. He's sprawled face to the ground and some bastard is putting the boots to his ribs. Suddenly the fellow realizes company has come to call, and he looks up shocked, appears ready to take flight, probably thinking we're road agents bearing down with pillage on our minds. But Grunewald hails us by name and that's reassurance enough to stop Jerry Potts's attacker from scampering.

Custis rides us right up to where Potts is laying. The man standing over him says, "Gentlemen, welcome. The leader of our party is absent at the moment, but I am, as it were, *in loco parentis*. Caleb Ayto is the name." He sticks up his hand for Custis to shake, but Custis gives it a flick with the rein. Ayto jumps back, startled, rubbing his wrist as if he'd been touched by a hot poker.

"Don't you offer your hand to me. I don't want it. Why are you abusing Jerry Potts so?"

Caleb Ayto's face goes white and pasty, but he summons up enough yeast to give the dough a rise. "The man's a thief! Pinched two bottles of the Captain's port and drank himself insensible! He needed to be taught a lesson!"

Custis dismounts. "This lesson is over," he says. "Next time, if you've got the courage, you can try and give him a lesson when he's sober."

Caleb Ayto ain't about to be lectured. He pivots on his heel and fires the toe of his boot into Potts's flank so hard he shifts him along the ground.

One quick step and Custis's laid into Ayto's face with a back-hander that staggers him. Ayto trips over a wagon tongue, and lands on his arse, dazed, blood creeping down his upper lip. Tight-lipped with fury, Custis rounds on Grunewald and Barker. "You get Potts out of the sun! Put him under yonder wagon! Now!" The teamsters gather up the half-breed with a guilty air and start stowing him away careful like he was a case of china, fussing, tucking, and patting at him to show Custis how interested they are in Jerry Potts's welfare. Custis has other concerns though. "Where's Mrs. Stoveall?" he demands.

Meek and mild, Grunewald answers, "Off picking flowers with Charles Gaunt, I reckon."

You can see this ain't pleasing news to Custis, but before he can follow up his question, the Captain gallops into camp. Reinforcements encourage Caleb Ayto to get himself back up on his hind legs. He starts to bawl, "This man assaulted me, sir! Attacked me without provocation! Hit me before I could get my guard up!"

The Captain trots his horse right up to Custis; the gelding near butts him with his head. "Mr. Straw, I never expected our paths to cross so soon. And in such circumstances. Tell me, did you strike this gentleman?" says Gaunt, very severe.

"I struck somebody – but I did not strike a gentleman."

At that, the Captain comes down off the horse. He ripples like a cat. "Won't do," he says. "Apologize to Mr. Ayto immediately."

Custis has spotted Charles Gaunt and Lucy Stoveall headed our way. She's carrying a harvest of flowers in the lap of her skirt, and her calves is showing. Gaunt and Mrs. Stoveall together, laughing and happy, has pinned all of Custis's attention.

"Do you hear me?" says the Captain and prods Custis with his forefinger. Custis slaps his hand aside.

Things are running away like a overloaded wagon down a steep hill. Somebody needs to hang on the brake. "Goddamn it," I say to Custis, "give him his apology."

Charles Gaunt finally spots Custis and calls out, "Mr. Straw, what a pleasant surprise!" Lucy is startled to see us and bobs her head in greeting.

The Captain is peeling off his jacket and shirt, readying to do battle. Amazed by this, Charles Gaunt asks, "Addington, whatever are you doing?" In a flash, the Captain is stripped, all lean and bumpy with muscle. But Custis don't give him a glance, he's staring directly at Lucy Stoveall with a fixed, weird, off-kilter shine to his eyes, a look that makes Mrs. Stoveall sidle up closer to Charles Gaunt, as if to shield herself from the steady glare Custis has turned on her.

"Put your clothes back on," I tell the Captain. "Nobody's about to fight you."

"Not if they know what's good for them!" cries Caleb Ayto. "Captain Gaunt is a master of the pugilistic arts!"

Charles Gaunt has noticed Jerry Potts stretched out under the wagon. Baffled, he asks his brother, "What is the matter with our guide? Has he fallen ill?"

"Yes – ill on stolen wine."

"That's a filthy lie," says Custis. He ain't got no justification for saying it, but his temper's run riot on him. The words are sneering and hot and seem directed as much at Charles Gaunt as the Captain. They are scarcely out of his mouth when the Captain hands Custis a cuff to the ear for the insult. It knocks him a step to the side. Charles throws his arms around the Captain, and I latch on to Custis, but the Captain flings off his brother like a dog shakes water from his coat. I hang to Custis's arm, but he ain't struggling to get at the Captain. He's just waiting on what happens next.

The Captain taunts him. "Let us see what you're made of, Mr. Straw."

"Walk away," I whisper to Custis. I give a tug to his arm, but he don't move a step. Custis has settled down on his foundation, and he's purely stubborn at bedrock. "Here now, let's shake hands, boys, and forget this foolishness. Captain, your friend Ayto took a smack and now Straw's had one too. Ain't you all even?"

Everybody's crowding in close, waiting on a soft word from either of them. Excepting Ayto, who has a bloodthirsty look to him. "In a matter of honour," Mr. High and Mighty Englishman announces, "I cannot be satisfied until Mr. Straw begs my pardon for calling me a liar."

Custis bows low. It's a mockery.

The Captain strikes a pose, arms crooked, one fist under the chin, the other ready to fence and parry. "Then you intend to fight," he says. Custis don't move a muscle, don't lift his arms. Grunewald, Barker, and Ayto draw back, clear a space. Lucy Stoveall and Charles stay rooted to the spot. "Stand aside," the Captain says to them.

Lucy Stoveall don't move. "Mr. Straw's no match for you, Captain. Let him be."

"We are in this man's debt, Addington," says Charles. "Don't forget that."

"I intend to fight," Custis says. He don't wish to be in Charles Gaunt's debt, don't want sheltering from him. Seeing Lucy leaning into him was more than he could swallow.

For the Captain, hearing that Custis is ready to fight is the best of news. "Grunewald," he cries, "get my boxing gloves from the wagon!"

One look at Custis and I see he ain't going to be turned from this. I got to take charge as best I can and give him a chance. "No mufflers," I say. "If Straw fights, he fights London Prize Rules. Any man knocked down or thrown – end of round. Thirty seconds breather. Eight more seconds to come to scratch."

The Captain grins. "Old rules. I see you are a student of the Noble Art."

"My old Da, Ignatius Dooley, was a pug. A miller of the old school, a bareknuckler, a claret spiller."

"Ah," says the Captain, "you are a son of the Wild Goose Nation. I know the Irish well." It's a jeer. I let it pass. The Captain goes up and down on his toes, bouncing on the spot. "A warning to Mr. Straw and you. I was trained by an old pugilist who once sat at the feet of the great Daniel Mendoza."

I don't let him have the satisfaction of seeing me surprised. All I say is, "I know the Jousting Jew's reputation."

"You will act as Mr. Straw's corner?"

I nod.

"Mr. Ayto will second me. I propose my brother Charles as time-keeper. Are you agreeable?"

"No objections."

Charles says, "I want no part of this ridiculous farce."

Custis looks him straight in the eye. "Keep the time, Mr. Gaunt." Charles hesitates, then nods, giving way to Custis's forceful stare.

"Strip your man." The Captain turns on his heel and walks to his place with Ayto.

I grab Custis by the arm and lead him out of their earshot, talking fast. "The Captain's been schooled in the game. It's why I asked for London Prize Rules. Next thing to a barroom brawl. Everything allowed but kicking, biting, and head-butting. He looks to be fast on his feet, so catch hold of him anywheres you can, clamp to him, pick him up and throw him to the ground. Make sure you land on top of him. Land heavy. You might stove in a couple of ribs." I start unbuttoning Custis's shirt, jerk it off him. He peers down at himself and folds his arms over his chest, covering up. He don't want Lucy Stoveall to see him naked, paunch and baby titties, white and wobbly. Old. I smack his arms to bring him back to business, to make him listen. "Hit with the back of your hand so as not to break a knuckle. Don't chase him, not with them gimpy legs of yours. If you're catching it bad, drop to your knee. Man goes down, round is over, and you got thirty seconds to recover." Custis gives me a look that says he won't take a knee. I grab the hairs on the nape of his neck and pull hard so he remembers. "Not a one of the best of the old pugs didn't go to his knee to save himself. No shame, Custis. Remember. Go down."

"You figure him to whip me, don't you, Aloysius?" he asks. Custis has read my face. If the Captain were trained by a disciple of Daniel Mendoza, Custis's prospects ain't good. But I hold my peace. You don't tell a man he's going to take a beating just before he sets foot in the ring, it disheartens him. "You'll do fine – if you catch hold of him," I say.

"Well, I been whipped before," Custis sighs gloomily.

The Captain's eager to start, flinging his arms impatient back and forth across his chest. "Is your man ready, Mr. Dooley? Or does he care to reconsider and make an apology?"

"Well?" I ask Custis. "I'd think about saying I were sorry. No harm in it."

Custis clenches his teeth, that's his answer. I throw my jacket to the ground. "Scratch," I say, pointing to it. "Gentlemen, one foot to the coat and bear up." Charles holds a pocket watch open, Lucy Stoveall huddles beside him. Grunewald and Barker lean forward and peer. Ayto shouts, "Slash him, Captain!"

I signal to Charles. "First round!" he cries, and I hurry to Custis's corner.

It's bad. Gaunt is quick and light on his feet as a waterwalker bug. He raps Custis's face like a door, short, sharp jabs, and retreats. He been taught well, lets Custis come to him and catches him coming, then dances aside, and smacks him on the kidneys when he blunders by.

"Stand ground!" I shout to Custis. "Don't let him draw you!" Custis takes heed, plants himself. The Captain circles him, cocking his eye at the red splotches he's painted on Custis's face. Custis snatches for a handful of hair, but comes up empty.

Ayto hoots and laughs. Grunewald and Barker join in. Gaunt bores away, the smack of his fists on Custis's face is like a butcher slapping steaks on a counter. He drops Custis straight to the dirt and stands astride him.

"Give him room, Gaunt! Back to your damn corner! End of round!" I shout.

Custis's sitting dazed on the ground, a bad cut over his right eye streaming blood. The Captain points. "First claret," he says with a laugh, and saunters back to his corner. Ayto claps his back and congratulates him. I heave Custis to his feet. He's groggy, pouring blood. I pinch the cut as tight as I can. "Listen to me, the next time he shoots a facer at you, hit him with your wrist bone on the inside of his arm, just above the elbow. Like this." I show him how to chop Gaunt. "You might be able to break his arm and end this thing."

Custis ain't paying me no mind. He's staring at Lucy Stoveall and she's staring back. The flowers she picked lie in a bright heap at her feet. Custis's right eye's juicy and puffy, already squeezing shut, but I reckon he owns a even more tender spot. Straw don't like to be shamed, lose his dignity, and anybody can read Lucy Stoveall's thoughts from the look on her face. She's thinking, Why, you poor old stubborn fool.

"Next time the Captain pastes you, go down and stay down. Don't come to scratch."

"No," he says, so quiet I can scarce hear him.

Charles Gaunt calls out, "Second round!" He don't look happy saying it.

"Go down and stay down," I remind Custis.

This time, the Captain toys with Custis a good five minutes, playing all the tricks, drumming Custis's ribs to make him tuck his arms, then up to his face, twisting punches so as to split Custis's skin on the eye sockets. He slashes him like he would with a razor, mashes his viz to a swimming, bloody bog. Then the Englishman steps back, his work pure pleasure to him, measuring Custis for the next shot. When it comes, a rattling blow to the head with his hip behind it, Custis's legs fold. Down he sinks, slow and dreamy to his knees, arms sagged at his sides. I got to lead him, half-blind, off the field. "We're throwing in the towel," I say. "Enough's enough."

Custis sucks wind like a rotten-lunged consumptive, can't catch his breath. Lucy calls out to me, waving her arm. "Stop him! Don't let him go on!" Custis's head snaps up at the sound of her voice. He wipes his bloody eye with his forearm and lurches up. The Captain's waiting with his foot on scratch. Charles calls a new round in a faint voice. "We ain't answering!" I shout, holding Custis by the belt, but he tears himself loose and sways towards the Captain.

They're face to face, fists milling when Custis rushes the Captain surprising sudden, snatches hold of the Englishman's windpipe. With the Captain caught fast in his fist, Custis's legs churn, he leans all his weight behind his stiff arm and ploughs him backwards. Hurly-burly he drives the Captain, faster and faster, until the Captain smacks into one of the Conestogas so punishing hard crates crash and the wagon rocks on its wheels.

The charge has near done Custis in. He's just laying there against the Captain, gulping air, dead weight pressing the Englishman to the wagon box, fingers still knotted on his throat. The Captain's face is one big mulberry birthmark, stringy veins popping out on his forehead. He plucks at Custis's fingers, trying to pry his hand off.

Custis raises his head from the Englishman's breastbone and clubs him on the temple with his fist. Once, twice, three, four times.

Someone hollers, "Foul! Foul!" and out the corner of my eye, I see Ayto rushing up behind Custis, a stick of firewood in his hand. He lays into the back of Custis's legs with it like he was chopping a tree. Down Custis goes.

I run for Ayto, but Grunewald and Barker come between us. They're slung all over me, dragging me back. Ayto's still bellowing, "A foul! He fouled the Captain! Everybody saw!"

"Hold and hit is fair! London Rules! You cowardly, backstabbing son of a bitch!" I holler.

The Captain is doubled up hacking, hand to his windpipe. I look about for Custis and spot him on his hands and knees, crawling towards my jacket on the ground.

Custis Straw heading for scratch.

Maybe because I've gone so still, eyes following him, they all turn and look. Custis is raising himself upright, bit by bit, gingerly. He wobbles, but he stands.

"Scratch," he says.

Nobody stirs. Not Ayto, not Grunewald, not Charles, not Lucy. Barker's still got his arms wrapped about me. The Captain lifts his head slowly, hand pressed to his throat.

"Scratch!" Custis repeats. Good and loud.

But Lucy Stoveall's louder. "Give it up, Mr. Straw!"

Barker looses his grip on me. The Captain takes his hand from his throat and starts to walk forward, cold and deliberate. Perfidious Albion, my Da used to call England.

I shout a warning. "Custis!" But the Captain is already on him swift and savage, crumples him with a hail of blows.

Then Lucy Stoveall is there between them, shrieking at the Englishman, "Are you blind! Step back! He's had enough!" Custis fumbles up against her skirts and buries his face in them like he's a child hiding from some terrible sight. Custis clings to her legs because there's nothing else to cling to. "This is done! This is finished!" she screams.

"No," Custis mumbles. "Scratch."

"Mr. Straw, you're finished."

He lifts his bloody face up to her. "I'm not finished."

I sail my hat into the ring. It lands with a crow hop. "The towel!" I shout. "We throw in the towel!"

Custis jerks away from Lucy, walks to my hat on his knees, flings it back at me. "Scratch," he says.

He puts one hand on the ground to steady himself, tries to lift himself. He can't. I run to him. "Aloysius?" he asks.

I bend down to him. "Yes, Custis, it's Aloysius."

He paws at my shoulder. "I can't see you too well."

I lift him to his feet, sling his arm over my shoulder. He's walking peculiar, stepping high, like he fears a stalk of grass could trip him. "That was good of Lucy Stoveall. What she done. Taking my part," he says, and faints dead away.

16

Jerry Potts forges into the night with fierce, hot determination. Ayto has shamed him, kicked him like a pot-licking dog. He must get far away from the sight of Ayto's fat face so it doesn't badger him into sending the man to smile up at a coffin lid.

Killing an American would bring him before a white judge and he wants no part of that. A year ago, two Blackfoot were murdered in Fort Benton and the law looked the other way. But when the Blackfoot took their revenge on Malcolm Clarke in the valley of the Prickly Pear, the army was called out, and Major Baker's troop of cavalry fell on the village of Heavy Runner on the Marias. A hundred and seventy Blackfoot, most of them women and children, were put to sleep that January morning, smothered in burning teepees, shot and hacked to pieces. It did not matter that Heavy Runner was a friendly, had never harmed a white man. A price must be paid and the price was a hundred and seventy Blackfoot for one white man. Buckets of blood for a cupful.

It is a bad memory, but the worst part of it is Joe Kipps. Kipps, a Blackfoot half-breed like himself, scouting for the whites, leading Major Baker down on his mother's people, sitting on his horse and never lifting a hand to stop the soldiers while they dyed the snow red with blood.

Is this what a half-breed must do now? Turn his back on one portion of himself? Sell himself to the strongest side? Take white money and sniff a trail for them like a dog? He is finished with that.

What finally made up his mind to leave the English was the Captain's sudden decision to abandon the route to the whisky posts and make for the Sand Hills. Barker had dropped an innocent remark about the country of the big dunes and the Captain had become all ears, full of questions, on fire to see the Sand Hills. The Captain and his brother had argued over this a long time, but in the end Addington Gaunt had got the last word as he always does. A short excursion of several days. What does it matter? he had said.

So let him find the dwelling place of the dead, the country of skeletons for himself. All the Captain thinks about is the book that Ayto is to write that will make the Englishman famous. Famous for what? Traipsing over a small piece of ground, his wagons stuffed with goods like a sutler's store. What is the Captain's journey compared to the one Bull's Forehead made? Nothing.

Sixty years ago, the Blackfoot, hungry for horses, had gone on a raid far to the south, past the big Salt Lake, deep into unknown lands. They had no one to guide them, nothing to rely on but their wits and courage. Potts can see them travelling by night, crossing the territory of many Indian nations; fighting some, singing and feasting with others. For a year they had suffered much hardship and danger until they reached the place where the Spai'yu, the Dark White Men lived, and where it was rumoured there were many ponies. There in Spai'yu ksah'ku, they hit the Dark White Men hard, ran off many fat horses and mules. They had crossed a thousand miles for Spai'yu horses, and they had travelled back a thousand miles to bring them home. No one would ever write this story in a book, but that did not make it any less true. He and Dawson had seen with their own eyes weapons taken from the bodies of the dead Spai'yu, weapons that the Americans and English had never traded in the north, steel lance heads, a thin-bladed sword that bent in your hands, sprang back with a twang, that had beautiful flowers of gold decorating the blade. Dawson called this long knife a rapier, said it was made from the best steel the white men could forge, a steel called Toledo. He said it proved Bull's Forehead had reached Mexico.

Bull's Forehead was an old blind man when he told them this story, but the many strange things he had encountered on his trip were still bright in his mind. The bitter Salt Lake, the Indians who lived like white men in houses made of clay, had impressed him deeply. What amazed Bull's Forehead most were the caves he had seen high up on cliff faces where, long-ago, Indians lived the life of bank-swallows. Bull's Forehead had said he did not know if those Indians could fly like birds, but he supposed they must have been able to.

Captain Gaunt could never match the exploits of Bull's Forehead and the Blackfoot raiders. He is brave, but a fool. He tries to rule everyone with a word. Discipline. But he has no discipline himself. He rides off to hunt whenever it pleases him, even when there is more meat in camp than they can eat. Potts thinks of the Captain's harsh words to him. How he had said it was proper for Ayto to kick him because he had stolen liquor and got drunk. Yet Ayto himself scarcely draws a sober breath, and he often sneaks the Captain's bottles from the wagon.

How can the Captain expect to command men when he shows so little dignity, walks on his hands by the fire, boasts of how he will kill a grizzly with his tall English bow? The Englishman does not understand it is only correct to speak this way after the thing is accomplished, when the right to do so has been earned.

The Captain wants to go to the Sand Hills where the ghosts of the Blackfoot live. He has been told that in the Sand Hills he may bump up against a furious, broken people, and find his own death. He laughed at the warning. He is too stupid to understand that when warriors sell their buffalo runners for red eye, when children cry because of empty bellies, when their mothers lie down with traders for a pint of whisky, their shame quickly turns to rage.

And the white scabs disease is back. The young men murmur that the traders spread it by selling infected blankets, some claim an evil old white man covered with sores spits his sickness into every bottle of whisky before it is sold to Indians. Everywhere the young men talk of how the Hairy Faces must be made to pay for the despair, the hunger, the illness they bring to the lodges of the Real People. This is what the Captain is ready to lead his wagons into.

Potts draws his pony to a halt. The port is sour, curdled in his gut; he empties his belly from the saddle, wipes his mouth and lifts his face to the stars. The Milky Way is spread like the white fleece of a mountain goat across the black sky.

Climbing down from his pony, he knows he has not convinced himself to abandon them. He only needs to think of Custis Straw stretched out in that wagon, half-crippled, half-blind, and he knows it is wrong to leave behind the man who did his best to help him, to protect him from Ayto. In all Straw's years trading with the Indians, no one ever accused him of dishonesty, or false speaking.

To save white men from themselves is the burden Andrew Potts's blood places on his son. At Sun River, he rescued two prospectors when the Sioux attacked them. Holed up in a ramshackle cabin, the prospectors loading for him because he was the better shot, he had been able to hold the Sioux warriors at bay until night came. Then it fell to him to walk through the Sioux camp wrapped in a blanket to hide himself from the eyes of the enemy, risking his life to steal horses so he and the two white men could escape.

Potts lies down on the ground to rest, reins looped around his wrist. The pony pokes its nose into his sore ribs and gives a snuffle.

He will sleep until A-pi-su'-ahts, the Early Riser, the Morning Star, greets him. When Early Riser looks down, he will ask the Child of Sun to lend him the necessary strength to continue on with the Englishmen.

❖ ❖ ❖

CHARLES   Addington's rashness and arrogance has brought our enterprise to the brink of disaster. Our guide's absconding in the dead of night badly rattled Grunewald and Barker. Only his unexpected return late this morning squelched their uneasiness. I am sure if Potts had not reappeared, the teamsters would have insisted on our immediate return to Fort Benton. True to form, Addington seemed completely unaware of their demoralized and anxious state.

When I tried to talk sense to my brother, make him see that to allow Ayto to persecute our scout was, at best, impolitic, he would not grasp my point, would not acknowledge that Potts is essential to our expedition.

"There's no harm in Mr. Ayto," was Addington's response. "I find him amusing."

"He does not amuse Mr. Potts. Have you not remarked how his face darkens when Ayto refers to him as Mr. Moses and you cackle?"

"I do not cackle and no, I did not remark it. It would be like noting boot polish darken."

At least Addington accepted my suggestion that Straw recuperate in one of the goods wagons until he is fit to travel to Fort Benton on horseback. Generous in victory the way he never would be in defeat, Addington even instructed Lucy to prepare Straw some beef tea, and contributed a bottle of his own barley water for the recuperation of the invalid. But admit the foolishness of his actions, promise to mend his ways? Most certainly not.

Since the debacle yesterday, Straw has kept to his wagon like Achilles to his tent, the saloon-keeper Dooley playing nursemaid. A while ago, Potts clambered into Straw's wagon on the heels of my brother's reprimands for the trouble he'd caused, and has yet to emerge.

So here we sit like the ship becalmed in *The Rime of the Ancient Mariner*. Addington has gone to give Mr. Ayto an archery lesson, the teams are not yet hitched, it is almost noon. The day will be frittered away, wasted for naught. Our trip to the Sand Hills, so much an object of controversy between Addington and me yesterday, is no longer a matter of urgency to him. He was deaf to my argument that the barren waste described by Barker could neither harbour Simon nor anyone with news of him. I see now that the issue is not necessarily our destination, but my brother's need to assert himself, and assert himself he will. We go to the Sand Hills – today, tomorrow, the next day. Who can predict? The only thing that is certain is that we shall depart at his pleasure.

Meanwhile, I stew in this heat, figuratively and literally. At eleven o'clock, when I took the daily reading of temperature for Father's records, the thermometer already showed eighty-eight degrees. We will loiter about here and at the end of the day have nothing to show for it but sunstroke and bad temper.

If nothing else, I might seize this opportunity to repair the damage Addington has so recklessly wreaked. Now, while all the disaffected are gathered in conclave in Straw's wagon.

I hear an earnest murmuring from inside the wagon as I prepare to announce myself. "Mr. Straw, it is Charles Gaunt. May I speak with you?"

A silence ensues, followed by an ejaculation difficult to construe as either a yea or a nay. Peering into the dim interior, it is just possible to make them out; Straw propped against a sack, his friend Dooley towering on a keg, Jerry Potts seated cross-legged on the floorboards. They radiate wariness, hostility.

"May I?" I repeat.

"Hell, why not," Straw finally answers.

I climb up. The heat inside the wagon is terrific, singes my nostrils with the odour of scorched canvas and unwashed men. In an instant, I find my shirt soaked in perspiration.

"I have come to tender an apology for what transpired yesterday." They wait alertly, but show no eagerness to accept the olive branch. "Mr. Ayto's behaviour was inexcusable, as was my brother's. I ask you to pardon them."

Straw gingerly shifts his bulk. His battered, swollen features are the face of a monster. His eyes peer inscrutably at me through livid fissures; his lips resemble sausages. "Well, maybe that ought to come from your brother and his friend Ayto," is his blunt, just comment.

"I have my own apologies to make. I should have prevented it."

"No stopping it," Straw says simply. "It had a mind of its own."

"Are you comfortable, Mr. Straw? Is there anything I can do for you?"

Straw's face does not change; perhaps his visage is incapable of alteration in its present state. "You can ask Mrs. Stoveall to pay me a visit."

A ticklish topic in light of the fact Lucy refused to bring Straw his beef tea yesterday. She confessed to me that she suspects Straw pursued our entourage with the aim of persuading her to return to Fort Benton. There was a suggestion that he has amorous designs she does not wish to encourage. "I shall pass on your request," is all I can say.

"Something in your voice tells me you reckon she won't."

"I cannot speak for Mrs. Stoveall."

"Are you sure? From what I saw yesterday it looked to me like you two have become mighty good friends."

I do not care for his insinuating tone. "Perhaps Mrs. Stoveall finds your attentions unwelcome."

"What about your attentions, Mr. Gaunt? Is she welcoming them?"

"We was just saying that maybe you ought to take another crack at persuading your brother not to go to the Sand Hills," Dooley says loudly and dramatically, trying to steer Straw off this indelicate course.

Straw refuses to yield the floor. "Tell me, Mr. Gaunt, has Mrs. Stoveall gone sweet on you?"

"Oh, for Christ's sake, Custis," Dooley remonstrates him.

"I do not think my brother can be dissuaded from going to the Sand Hills. Barker's description of them has excited his interest." I pause. "More to the point, I think it unwise to press him on the matter."

"Bad place," Potts suddenly says. This is the first time I have heard the taciturn half-breed ever condescend to volunteer information. His gaze wanders about the wagon. "Sta-au'. Plenty of Sta-au' there," he mutters.

"I do not understand what you are saying, Mr. Potts. What does this word mean?"

"Blackfoot for ghosts or skeletons," Straw says. "The Sand Hills is the land of the dead. The home of ghosts."

I noted immediately Potts's reluctance to speak of the Sand Hills. This naturally excited my interest and, with much coaxing, I cajoled him into divulging something more about it. Despite the heat and stifling atmosphere, listening to him recount his weird tale in awkward English, I was brought suddenly back to my childhood, to those dreary, winter nights when Simon and I would gather in the kitchen to listen to the servants, simple country girls, talk of spirits. They told of a strange man who had once come to the door of a poor cottage to beg bread, and was sent away with imprecations. And of how when the bread box was opened the next morning, a huge rat leapt upon the hand of the householder and bit him to the bone, leading him into a slow and painful decline, capped with an excruciating death. Or Mrs. Bullfinch's report of the corpse of a suicide seen wandering about the countryside seeking holy ground in which it could lay itself down. Or the strange knocking in the headboard of Meredith Wilson's bed which had announced the impending death of her betrothed.

While Simon took these accounts as gospel, I tried to debunk them. Yet my childish attempts to dismiss them only succeeded in inducing in me a profound terror. It was as if by trying to reason them away, I lent them greater life, while Simon, by accepting the existence of unseen presences, made them his friends. Night after night, I trembled and shivered under the counterpane, stubbornly refusing to confess that I was troubled by thoughts of ghosts. And Simon would cross the floor of our room, curl up in my bed to thaw my icy fear with the warmth of his body.

Now, hours after Potts concluded his story, it still weighs upon me. I felt compelled to record it in my journal, as a way perhaps of beckoning Simon's spirit. Hopeful that by dwelling on a ghost story I would reawaken my brother's comforting presence. What I wrote was Potts's story, but in my own words, so as to draw Simon nearer to me.

Long ago, there was a man and a wife. In time she bore him a son. The husband loved his mate very much but she grew ill of a wasting sickness and died. Grief-stricken, the husband would put his little boy on his back, wander the lonely hills, both of them wailing aloud, day after day. Finally, the man could bear his loneliness no more so he left his son with the boy's grandmother, and set off to the Sand Hills to bring his wife back from the dead.

He walked and walked until he met an old crone living in a tiny lodge scarcely bigger than an ant hill, and heart-sick and weary he told her of his troubles. The old woman pitied his plight and made him the present of a magic bundle to help him in his struggle to recover his wife. That night when the man went to sleep he dreamed the old hag had gone to the Sand Hills and returned with one of his dead relatives to guide him to the Camp of the Dead.

When he awoke the man learned his dream was true and that a long-dead uncle had come to take him where he wished to go. But the old woman would not let him look on his uncle, she told him that on this trip he must keep his eyes tightly shut, and let the ghost lead him. The man did as he was told and walked for days until the ghost told him he could at last open his eyes. When he did, he shivered in terror because all about him was a great crowd of ghosts, moaning and gibbering, a gruesome sight which turned his blood cold. They rattled their bones and plucked their ribs to make frightening, eerie music, but no matter what they did, they could not make him run away.

At last the ghosts despaired of driving him off and began to question him, asking why a Person, a living being, would willingly make a journey to the Sand Hills, a place from which no one ever escaped. The man said he had come for his wife and was determined to return her to the land of the living and the son who so dearly loved her.

Hearing this, one of the skeletons strode through the Camp of the Dead, calling to all the man's dead relatives to come to his lodge for a feast to welcome one of their descendants to his new shadowy home. This tricked the man's relatives, but when they came near the lodge they could smell the odour of a living being, and were afraid to go in. They sniffed the lodge skins and cried out, "There is a Person here! I smell a Person!" and were much alarmed. But the owner of the lodge burned sweet pine to cover the smell of life, and at last the skeletons reluctantly entered, one by one.

When they were all finally gathered, their host told them that the man's great daring must be rewarded. The ghosts were sorry for the man's broken heart and promised to do what they could. They brought his wife to him, but she was not as she had been, she was a skeleton, and horrible to look at with her empty eye sockets and protruding ribs. His father-in-law offered to lead them back to the living, but he said the man must do as he had done before, walk four days with his eyes closed. If he lost his nerve and opened his eyes, he would die, and become a skeleton like the rest of them.

For four days the man walked like a blind man, and listened to the voice of his father-in-law instructing him. He was taught that before he and his wife could return to the world of Persons, it was necessary to wash themselves thoroughly. There was something about the Sand Hills that was very difficult to remove, he said, and the smallest spot of dust must be washed off, or they would die. Last of all, his father-in-law told him he must never strike his wife. If he did, she would instantly turn into a skeleton and go to the Sand Hills, lost for ever and ever.

Shortly after this, the father-in-law left his daughter and son-in-law. The wife told her husband it was time to open his eyes. When he did, he recognized his wife had once again become a Person, but he still could not embrace her. This was because he had lost some part of himself in the Sand Hills and was not a complete living being.

In his upset, he looked around and spied the tiny lodge of the old hag who had given him his sacred bundle. Suddenly she was there, demanding her powerful magic bundle back. Gratefully, he returned it to her, and when he did, he became fully a Person again, able to touch and hold his wife.

After the two embraced long and lovingly, they took the last necessary step before returning to the Land of the Living. They made a sweat lodge and scrubbed the ghost stink off them. Together they entered their village to the amazement and happiness of all, and their little son ran to them, laughing with boundless joy.

❖ ❖ ❖

Potts sits, head covered in a blanket, listening to the mosquitoes whine, wheedle for a taste of his blood. His spirits are very low. He should not have given in to Charles Gaunt. Nothing of the Sand Hills can be explained in the English tongue. How do you speak of skeletons whose feet do not touch the ground when they walk? Skeletons who make war on the skeletons of old enemies, who hunt the skeletons of buffalo, gnaw their dry, meatless bones? The sad, empty life of the Sand Hills, he thinks. Ghosts longing to join the living. Whistling down lodge smoke holes in the night, tapping on teepees, begging to be let in.

He could not tell of it in a way the Englishman could understand, so he told him a story, one he had heard many times in the lodges of the Peigans. It was the tale of how the sacred bundle of the Worm People was brought to them by the man who had gone to seek his wife in the Camp of the Dead. But he had decided not to speak of the bundle or the sacred things that an unbeliever, an Englishman, could never accept.

But when he began the story, at the first mention of the dearly loved wife, his skin prickled, for he realized he was speaking to himself and not to the Englishman. He felt the weight of Mitchell on his back, could hear himself and his son crying as they wandered the barren hills. A cold dread filled him that in saying these words, they would come true, and Mary would die in the country of the Crow. Maybe she was already dead, and her ghost was speaking to him out of his own mouth.

But still he could not stop himself from talking. He hurried on, wanting to end the story as quickly as possible. He trimmed it here and there, but as he did, it became more and more his own story. Then suddenly he could not go on, could not unstick his tongue to tell the last terrible part.

In the story, shortly after the couple returns to the Land of the Living, the husband asks his wife to perform a task. When she does not rush to do it, he loses his temper, picks a stick from the fire, threatens to strike her with it. As he waves the flaming torch in her face, his wife vanishes before his very eyes, flung by his own hand back to the Sand Hills.

It fills Potts with sadness to understand how one instant of anger, one moment of unkindness, is enough to drive what you love far beyond your reach.

17

Seven days pass and the Conestogas begin to cross a blasted landscape, dreary knolls, hollows bristling with stubborn brush, dun
bunchgrass, and low-lying sage and juniper that yield a pungent
incense when crushed under the wheels of the wagons. Powdery clay
steams into the air, cloaks men and beasts in a choking, sallow cloud.
Everyone is too dry-mouthed to speak, the only sounds accompanying the advance are the faint music of jangling trace chains, the plan-
gent protest of axles, the dull plod of hooves. They creep along
drowsily until the terrain begins to undergo subtle alteration, to
demand notice. Fingers of sand appear. The fingers become ridges,
the ridges become drifts. Vehicles slew about, horses paw and strain,
Grunewald and Barker rouse themselves, croak encouragement to
their teams. The heat doubles, the sun presses heavily down on their
heads, reflects from the sand into their faces. A broiling march through
a vast, gritty oven.

A little before seven o'clock, the peremptory smack of gunshots is
heard from where the Captain has dropped from view. Jerry Potts
yanks his rifle from its scabbard, alarm spreads, the rest of the company
retrieve weapons and hasten forward. Rattling round the flank of a
baldy-topped, wind-scoured hill, they encounter a huge dune, an
immense steep ramp that bunts a fierce sun with its shimmering brow.
The dune is pocked with the Captain's footprints. Halfway up the slope

he waves gleefully down at them, sweeps the scene with his pistol barrel, and shouts, "Arabia Deserta! Magnificent!"

To a chorus of mutters and curses, Captain Gaunt begins a leisurely stroll back to them, a man descending his very own stairway of gold.

❖ ❖ ❖

CUSTIS Aloysius and I clamber out of the wagon to the sight of the Captain sashaying down a dune, so proud and swollen with what he's found his buttons are popping. The fool thinks he's the hub everything turns round. Even imagines the black face I wore the past few days was because I took a licking from him in our boxing match, went so far as to say to me, "Mr. Straw, no disgrace in being defeated by me. I am recognized as an expert." I never minded taking a whipping from any man. What I do mind is Lucy Stoveall dodging me at every turn in favour of Charles Gaunt. Last night I caught her for a word or two about returning to Fort Benton, but she was too stubborn to move. No remedy for that but time. I reckon to play cripple so as to keep an eye on her for as long as I can. The Captain can't order me off in good conscience if I'm lame. Ayto bust my legs up pretty good, but they're in better shape than I let on. I just lean on a stick, totter about, twist my mouth, fake godawful agony whenever I'm afoot. Aloysius's fretting for home, and if he was to know I could manage to sit a horse he'd make an almighty fuss to be gone.

Seeing Addington Gaunt prink and preen is a most grievous pain in the fundament. Here comes the famous explorer himself, down from his dune. "Mr. Straw, testing your legs again, I see. You should scale my discovery," he says. "The vista is splendid. Waves of sand for miles."

"I don't believe I'm up to the climb," I tell him.

"Ah well, your loss."

I hear Aloysius's breath whistle in his nose as he watches the Captain float off. "I'm glad the Englishman enjoys the scenery. But you can't drink it. There's no water hereabouts," Aloysius grunts.

"The shine'll soon wear off Captain Gaunt's toy, and he'll be looking for another," I say, settling myself on the foot of the dune, rolling up my trouser legs, and packing hot sand on my aching limbs. Dooley's staring at the musket ball scar on my calf. The worst of my wounds are covered, the bayonet thrusts to the thigh the greyback gave me in the Wilderness before he left me to burn.

Jerry Potts is making to join us. When Ayto and the Captain catch sight of him, Ayto brays, "You are to be congratulated, Captain, on introducing Mr. Moses to his native element! Sinai!" Poor Potts just scurries on by them, ducking his head under their laughter.

Potts hunkers, angrily spits. He doesn't like the Captain, likes Ayto less, and the Sand Hills even less than Ayto.

The hot sand sucks the throb from my legs. "Damn, this is just what the doctor ordered. You ought to try it, Aloysius."

"No thank you," he says. "I ain't sitting in no sand. Sand up the crack of your ass makes a man itch."

"What makes you itch, Aloysius, is any happy suggestion. It rubs you the wrong way to think of enjoying a simple pleasure that can't be bought."

Potts is biting at the ends of his moustache. "Too many people joke," he says. "They think I don't know about Moses. I heard of Moses. He killed the man called Far Away."

I follow his eyes. Potts is looking up the big sand dune. The Captain has pranced back to the top and struck a pose – wide-legged stance, arms akimbo, fists planted on his hips. Charles Gaunt's with him, sketching away like a demon.

The baleful gaze Potts is turning on the Captain makes me a tad uneasy. Rumours are that in his day the half-breed's only killed one white man, a French engagé at one of the American Fur Company posts who made life miserable for him when Potts was just a youngster of fifteen or sixteen. Maybe Jerry Potts is thinking it's time he sent another white man to join the majority. Addington Gaunt conducts himself like a high and mighty pharaoh and I wouldn't want the resemblance to lodge itself in Potts's mind.

"Moses never killed Pharaoh," I tell Potts. "The Bible doesn't even say Pharaoh died. What Moses did was drown Pharaoh's soldiers." I best correct that. "Well, really, it was God drowned them. The hand of God."

"Leave it alone," mutters Aloysius, "don't Sunday-school him. He don't have a clue what you're talking about."

"Dawson told me the story," Potts says. "Moses killed Far Away. Far Away treated Moses' people bad. Moses drowned him in a river of blood."

"Jesus, Joseph, and Mary," Aloysius mutters. He doesn't approve of churching Indians.

The evening sun is bouncing off the sand, turning Potts to hot bronze, even his hat glows. "You got it wrong, Jerry. Moses didn't lay a hand on anybody. All he did –" I lift up my walking stick to give him an illustration of it, "was he held a stick to command the waters to keep off his own people, and then he brought it down, and the waters closed over Pharaoh's soldiers chasing the Hebrews. The Egyptians all drowned. There was no river of blood. It's only the name that threw you – the waters Moses brought down on the soldiers was called the Red Sea. And Gaunt is no Pharaoh. He's nothing but a niggling pissant of an Englishman. Moses wouldn't pay him the least mind. You follow me, Jerry?"

"I remember a river of blood," says Potts.

❖ ❖ ❖

LUCY The moon is bright tonight, so I have to sneak out of camp behind the wagons, keep them betwixt me and the men gathered round the fire, hug the coal-black shadows hanging off the big dune.

I need to tramp the fuss and fret out of me, lose my bother.

I keep to the dark side of the dune until even Ayto speechifying like a circuit rider is lost to my ears, step out into the brightness, let that wall-eye moon goggle me. It's grim as winter all about. Cold blue light, sand banked like snow, litter of dead leaves, scrub and grass dying, the life choked out of it. Makes me shiver.

It was such a night that Madge's and my trouble started. The night they came, there was a big bald-faced moon riding high too. Madge and me woke from our slumbers by the sound of horses moving outside, sniggers, whispers.

Madge sitting up on her pallet, asking, "What's that, Lucy? Who's out there!"

"Don't you mind. Just some drunks lost their way home. I'm here beside you."

Singing commences when they hear us. Nasty singing, like drops of dirty water running down the back of your neck. "'Buffalo Gals, won't you come out tonight, Come out tonight, come out tonight. Buffalo Gals, won't you come out tonight, and dance by the light of the moon!'"

Madge clinging so tight to me I can feel her heart pounding, me roaring loud as I could, "Clear off! Begone! Hear me?"

A teetery whisky-soaked voice calling out, "Don't be like that, girls. Why's old Custis got to hog all his candy to himself? Why can't he let his kin have a taste!"

I knew it was the Kelsos outside. Madge had told me Titus Kelso had been hanging round her. Cantering by the wagon, mean and rat-faced, handing out winks and smirks, doffing his hat. It made her mighty uneasy, she said.

"Titus Kelso, scat! Clear off my property!" I shout.

And his slippery voice answers, "Hear that? Miz Stoveall gone and laid claim to the mud flat she's setting on. She's a prope'ty holder, Joel, *and* a woman of business."

His brother's laugh. No merriment to it. Weak and forced out of him for fear of Titus, so's to please a bully boy. But it was enough to egg Titus on, because on he came. "Now tell me, Miz Stoveall, why do you and your sister got such a taste for them no-class old fellers? That dusty old husband of yours and then salted-down, over-cured Straw who gets sweet young Madge. Why does your little sister have to settle for dried-up jerked meat when she can have it fresh, with a powerful lot of juice in it?"

It started Madge to sobbing. I can bear a lot, but never could I bear her anguish.

The Kelsos crowding their horses up against the wagon, bumping it, making things shake inside: everything going shifty, unsteady. All at once somebody slapped the canvas top hard, and the loud pop made Madge jump and shriek.

She tried to hold to me, but I plucked away her hands, untangled myself, went digging through our gear, determined on Abner's pistol. But the dark hid it, and when a glint of moonlight pointed me to something else I snatched it up.

"Stay put," I said to Madge. "Just you see if I don't run those scoundrels off in short order." Madge shook her head no, I mustn't, but my mind was set.

I shouted, "Leave off rocking this wagon! We're coming out!" Madge took me at my word, started to push aside her blankets, but I held her down, put my finger to her lips.

They quit their thumping when I said we were going to show ourselves. I unhooked the tailgate, let it drop down on its chains. Once I was clear of the canvas I could stand tall on it, look down at them. I held dead still, one arm behind my back, didn't allow myself to shiver in that thin nightdress as they stared up at me.

That big shiny moon behind them. Funny to think, but I found it beautiful. It won't ever be so again. Like food you have sickened on, the moon's eye doesn't sit right with me no more. But that night it drew my gaze, tipped up there in the sky like one of those beaten brass plates on a mantel, hammer dents plain on its sheeny face. A breeze flapping my nightdress and wrinkling the river, scattering silver on the water like thousands of half-dimes spilled from the storeman's till. For two breaths I almost forgot why I had come out.

But Titus Kelso brought me back to it. "Miz Stoveall, let me compliment you on your nightdress. I admire how it sets off your titties."

Cool as you please, he was sitting slouched in the saddle, his brother Joel hanging a little to the rear off his flank.

I sprang down; the startlement of it sent their horses jittery, to throwing their heads, to champing their bits. "Easy there, Missus," Titus said, tucking his reins. "This stud horse of mine been sniffing mare on the air all night. It makes him feisty."

"I won't say it again. Pull foot."

"Folks says you and your sister does washing for gentlemen. What's it cost?"

"Make yourself scarce, you dirty little field tackie."

"Me and my brother need washing awful bad. What say we pay fifty cents above what you charge old Straw? I'm willing to go that high." He flashed a grin. "Just so long as the young one soaps my sock. Joel will have to make do with a rough scrub from you. But I'm fine, delicate material. Nothing but gentle hand-washing for me."

Madge sent up a pitiful cry, calling me back to her in the wagon.

"There," said Titus, "I believe she thinks you're getting the pick of the litter." He called over my head to Madge. "Just hold on, darling. Titus will be there to comfort you in a wink."

Joel was looking uncomfortable. I spoke direct to him, hoping to sway him to do good. "Listen, son, why do you boys want to scare her? She never did you any harm. Why do you want to upset a young thing like her?"

"Oh, she ain't too young," said Titus. "If they're old enough to bleed, they're old enough to butcher."

Maybe I ought not to have done it. Taken that one step forward, swung the reaping hook I'd pressed to my back. But it was a fine, relieving sight, that sickle blade streaking in the pale light, slashing through his off rein, the stud horse rearing. Titus yanking back on the lines and the cut rein unfurling like a girl's hair ribbon in the wind. Down he thumped, hard to his back in the dirt, the stud galloping off. And me over Titus, reaping hook raised.

He got a fright put into him then, same as he'd put into Madge. He stuck up his hand to fend off the next blow and cried out, "Mercy, woman! No need for this!"

"You scamper," I said, stepping away to let him up. He scuffled to his feet, backed away. Joel was just sitting his horse, all agog. Titus swung on him. "Goddamn, catch my horse!" and Joel went pelting after the runaway.

There was only the two of us then, him still retreating slow through the buckbrush. When he reckoned he was out of reach of my blade, he stopped to have the last word and put a judgment on me. "I'll be back. Don't think I won't. A woman don't run Titus Kelso off from what he's set his mind on."

Then he hitched his shoulders, trotted off into the night, shouting after his brother.

A big dune blocking my way starts me out of my thoughts. How I came to be here I can't fathom. I go at the steep pitch of it, digging with the toes of Mr. Charles's shoes, scrabbling with my hands as I climb until I'm atop it. Looking down, I see a deep crater in the sand cupping a few scrawny bushes, scraps of grass, jimson weed, tumbleweed. The moon paints them with white hoarfrost.

Something is tugging panic in my guts. I fight the tightness in my chest; take quick breaths that don't fill my lungs as I slide myself down into the hollow.

I should have chopped that weed Titus Kelso. I should have made his days grass. But I didn't. That was my mistake and Madge paid for it. Now I have to hold to my purpose, keep Madge and what they did to her shoving me on until the day comes I can put the muzzle of Abner's pistol on the two of them.

Last night I dreamed Madge was alive, but there was no comfort in it. I'm walking by a house, one that's tiny small, like it was built for children. Oh, it's lovely and perfect. I stand in the street admiring it, windows of crystal glass, neat green shutters standing open to let the sun in. Slowly it dawns on me this is where Madge and Mr. Charles live as husband and wife.

I have to stoop to get through the door. I hallo the place but nobody answers. In the parlour, there's a window open, curtains stirring in a breeze. I smell peonies. I smell salt, which makes me think the house stands near the sea, that maybe this is San Francisco.

I start up the staircase, bent over so's not to knock my head on the low ceiling. The banister's polished with beeswax, smooth to my hand. I go down the upstairs hallway and see a door standing ajar on a tidy bedroom. I recognize Madge's old nightdress folded across the foot of the bed. I finger the cloth, soft from so many washings.

Then I catch footsteps hurrying down the stairs. I know it's Madge. I turn and run after her, quick down the hallway to the stairs. I hear her steps patter faster and faster, like a shower of rain, and happy laughter. It's a game to her, she's playing hide and seek on me.

I put my foot to the staircase and suddenly it turns like the threads of a screw, spins my body round so fast my hand jerks off the railing, I'm swirling in a tornado, heels flying behind me, kicking like I'm swimming the wind.

And then I am swimming, but in water, my clothes gone, purely naked. The water's peaceful and warm, it's stroking my breasts and belly, nuzzling between my legs. My thighs drift apart to its touch.

I don't hear anything more of Madge. She's gone and there's just my body. I open my eyes. I'm floating over Mr. Charles. His face is looking up at my nakedness and his hands are touching me, hands light on my breasts and my belly, fingers teasing me. And I feel the wrongness of it because Madge is his wife, but I've gone too far to ask him to stop.

Now, even awake, it starts up all over again. The hunger of the body. My sister scarcely cold in the ground, and me in such a shameful state. Feeling choked and burning, a pulse tapping a vein in my neck. Wanting to lift my dress above my hips, fall back on the sand, open my thighs, just like I did in the dream.

But my body gives a jolt, like a body does when it snatches you from the brink of sleep. A wild rose bush at my feet, branches furred with tiny spikes, sharp, cruel thorns, has brought me back to what I ought to be about. I grab it, squeeze it hard, tear at it, twist it, break it free of the ground. Strip the branches until I have a dowsing wand. My hand's bleeding, speckling my dress with blood.

A long shadow nailed to my toes ripples over the washboard sand, walks me to the middle of the crater. I start to turn, waiting for the twitch, the bending bough to point my way, bring me back to my senses, lead me to the Kelsos and to what I'm meant to do.

❖ ❖ ❖

CHARLES Addington informs me Lucy is missing from camp. Alarm rises. "When?"

"She slipped off an hour ago. Perhaps she has an assignation with her erstwhile beau, Mr. Straw."

He knows this is preposterous. Straw and Dooley returned to the wagon after supper, have remained there ever since.

"You must help me find her."

Having incited my anxiety, it gives him great pleasure to blithely dismiss it. "Likely she has gone off to pine. For whom I cannot say. Straw? Grunewald? Barker? Perhaps the inestimable Mr. Moses."

He is ragging me as he did when I was a child. I long to slap the smirk from his face.

"You are an ass, Addington." I set off immediately.

Beneath the towering ramparts of the dune, the sand is crisp and firm under my feet, but Lucy's footprints are not easy to discern until they break out into the sapphire light shed by the moon. Waves of sand calved from the giant mother dune roll away, patchy grass and stunted brush rasps in the evening breeze. Above, an overwrought, pregnant moon presides over all. When one forsakes the magic circle of the fire, these empty expanses deflate confidence. Instinctively, my shoulders hunch. The coyotes sing an eerie, mocking song. Or perhaps it is the skeletons. A howl from an empty rib cage.

Moving as quickly as I can, I still do not lose the sensation of someone following me. I throw a glance over my shoulder. Feeling exposed and vulnerable, suddenly I am covered in sweat, can scarcely breathe. I halt, unbutton my shirt to cool myself, compulsively look behind me. Nothing but two sets of footprints. Lucy's and my own. I take heart, convince myself it is a premonition of our return to camp, the two of us walking side by side, her teasing, indulgent laughter chaffing me because I was so needlessly worried.

I start off again. It is all I can do to restrain myself from bolting after her in a headlong rush. Her name bursts on my lips. "Mrs. Stoveall! Mrs. Stoveall!" I freeze, waiting for some answer, however faint. Nothing. Even the madrigal of the coyotes ceases, quelled by the sound of a human voice.

There comes a flap of angry air, scant feet above my head. I duck, eyes falling to a swoop of shadow. Shadow and flesh spring together in a violent convulsion, a puff of sand, a fanfare of beating wings that subsides into stillness.

Two gold discs, the yellow eyes of an owl, stare back at me as some small thing writhes at its feet.

A broken human wail quavers beyond the waves of sand, sending the owl into flight, the tail of a mouse wriggling in its talons. I sprint towards the cry, encounter an enormous dune, fly at it, slip and fall, stagger to the summit. Below me is Lucy Stoveall, a stick thrust out from her waist as if she holds at bay an invisible adversary. Her body shudders and the stick partners her in a spasmodic dance.

I shout to her, but she seems locked in a catalepsy beyond my reach. I plunge down the drift, feet churning in the loose sand, plunge through the tearing brush. I snatch her shoulder, shake her, shouting her name. Her mouth opens to protest, then slowly closes as recognition stirs.

I pull her close, clasp her to me. Her hands reach up, fumbling for my face, and I taste the surprise of salty blood as her fingers touch my lips. Her hands slip inside my shirt, the soft undersides of her wrists glide along my ribs, her fingers fondle my spine.

"I want to swim on you. Let me swim on you," she pleads.

We stagger, clutching one another. I fumble her bodice open, she shrugs her arms from its sleeves, and begins to strip me of my trousers. Falling to her knees she hugs my thighs, the bounty of her red hair teasing my prick.

"Come down. Come down to me," she whispers. There is a small gasp as I enter her and then I am left whimpering in the grip of desire.

The cold eye of the moon at my back. The sensation of being exposed – no walls, no curtains – the immodesty of an animal, naked of everything but instinct and need, there is only this. She smiles at me, turns her head away as I lose myself completely in the throb of release.

The Captain has never dreamed his curiosity would be so well paid, so well satisfied. His brother, an actor in a thrilling pose plastique, a stimulating tableau vivant. He lowers his head below the dune and buttons up his fly.

18

CHARLES With every day that passes, it is brought home to me ever more clearly and discouragingly that my brother regards the search for his own brother as nothing more than an opportunity to exercise his taste for outdoor life and adventure. He is a character in a boy's book. The several days he spent playing intrepid explorer in the Sand Hills has necessitated we make a detour. The dunes have proven to be impassable by wagon and Potts informs us that we must skirt them to reach Fort Whoop-Up and the other whisky posts that lie to the west, beyond the Saskatchewan River. This dictates turning either north or south to avoid the thirty miles of sand that block our way. Addington has chosen the northern route, most likely because he wishes a glimpse of the great Saskatchewan River. Yet Addington's wilful opposition, his willingness to sidetrack from Simon's possible trail, makes me hold ever more tenaciously, beyond all reason, to some shred of hope.

A little experience of this vast land should bring me closer to the unthinkable, closer to admitting that any hope of finding Simon alive may be nothing more than that. It grows ever more likely that Addington and I shall return to England empty-handed. We shall return to face Father, who is sure to accept no excuses for failure since he cannot conceive of the impossibility of the task he set his sons to perform.

This is all I contemplate. Or, rather, this and Lucy Stoveall. What uncharted waters I find myself in with her, far different from my previous situations, where things were always clear. Though there was always a price to pay, in some fashion, I always understood the terms. But matters are on a different footing with Lucy. There is nothing about it that is defined. But linked by our respective losses, so often discussed in the past weeks, she has supported me with a quiet, unflagging sympathy that I have done my best to return. Like Simon's in earlier days, her simple presence, even her silence, has been consolation in my times of trouble. But when a helpmeet becomes a lover, what then? Can the word "mistress" be spoken to a woman like her. I think not.

We must be discreet. If Addington detects our feelings, our erotic indulgence, there will be the very devil to pay. I can hear him now, reporting to Father. "Sir, I consider it my duty to relate to you that Charles pays his attentions to a woman who wears his boots."

Could I expect Father to understand what I cannot fully understand myself? Father, who would have had his sons fear the very act of love itself? How tactful of him to present Simon and me with Dr. J. L. Milton's masterwork, *On the Pathology and Treatment of Gonorrhoea and Spermatorrhoea*, for our fourteenth birthday. A chastening medical volume outlining the dire consequences of a lavish expenditure of seminal fluid and what it results in, inevitable imbecility and early death.

But young men are not necessarily dogs. After a suitable lapse of time to allow Father to cool after my refusal to return to Oxford without Simon, my brother somehow worked his way with him, managed to prevail upon Father to let us take up bachelor quarters in Grosvenor Square. And we certainly did not sink into depravity when freed from his strict supervision. No, instead we studied assiduously. For two years forswearing the pleasures of youth, refusing to entertain or to be entertained, living the pact we had made, to prove to Father his sons were not wastrels or dilettantes but fellows of serious purpose. We strove and we laboured, Simon to find God, I to make myself a painter.

So like the idyll of our early childhood those days now seem, the two of us supporting one another's pursuits and hopes. Shut up in that house, happy monks. Simon leaving it only to buy more books, or to occupy a back pew in some dank church. And at tea time, the two of us sharing the day's successes and failures. I, displaying my sketches for Simon and he briefing me on his reading, theology, Fourier, Thomas Carlyle, William Blake.

How he loved Blake. I had my reservations about where Simon's tastes were leading him, but his enthusiasms so delighted him I did not have it in me to contradict them. After all, he gave so much more than he received. It was Simon who insisted I take the large room with the French windows for a studio and helped me set it up. Simon who sacrificed time from his own pursuits to model for me. Simon who, despite his natural modesty, stripped to shiver uncomplaining in the winter damp.

But surely I was wrong not to attempt to inoculate him against the mysticism of Blake, so dangerous for one of Simon's temperament. Or against those clanking volumes of sermons by rural vicars and those pious effusions of old maids printed up in pamphlets at their own expense. It seems so now. Let him have the bombast of Carlyle, but not the piffle of those second-rate mystics who cultivated the ground for my brother's susceptible mind to be poisoned by the charlatan Witherspoon. And all the time, without my realizing it, the small crack between us which first appeared at Oxford was slowly, imperceptibly widening into a gulf wide as the Bosporus.

Certainly I had a hand in the breach. The little white lies concerning my immoralities, they may have prompted Simon to feel he, too, deserved his own secret life. Telling him I would spend the day at the British Museum or Gambart's gallery, deflecting him when he wanted to accompany me. The flimsy excuses. "You do not enjoy Gambart's, because you do not approve of gossip, and that is why I go, for that as much as the pictures." The subterfuges. A quick visit to the viewing rooms in case he later asked questions about the exhibitions. Then off to other viewing rooms with a more infamous reputation: the Alhambra, the Argyll in Great Windmill Street, the Holborn Assembly

Hall. Or a leisurely coast up and down Regent Street enjoying the sights, the luxurious shops, the choice restaurants, the concert halls, the dusk slashed with golden light streaming from their windows. The most expensive courtesans in London on display, resplendent in silk and satin, strolling about arm in arm. Or summer excursions to Cremorne Gardens, a place I had never heard tell of until I saw the print, *Derby Night at the Cremorne*, hung in Tom Budge's room at Oxford, his souvenir of jolly evenings spent with jolly girls.

To make excuses for oneself is petty, but I was not debauched. Intervals of many months sometimes passed between my escapades. And it was the strain of work as much as carnal desire which sent me into the streets, the need to forget the drawings which always left me disappointed. The endless drudgery which I now understand is the price of ambition married to a small talent.

I spent most of my time with dollymops rather than hardened whores. Dollymops had more life to them. Girls for whom entertaining men was a sideline, not their life work. Always adamant they were not "gay," not on the game, charming milliners, maids, seamstresses, shop assistants willing to share a gentleman's pleasures on their day off. A good dinner and a bottle of wine, a handsome present, two pounds here and there, where was the harm?

My favourite among them, Iris, I never bedded. It would have put us on too blatantly mercenary terms. I liked to think she went about with me simply for my company. The first time we met, she stoutly declared, "I decide whose arm I take, sir. I don't go about with ruby-nosed gentlemen for the sake of a bit extra. I'm after a spot of fun, I am."

And fun we had, although I suppose I did not learn all I might have from those poor girls who had the courage to seize the moment with reckless good humour and thumb their nose at tomorrow. Their independence, their frankness, their lack of airs struck me as healthy and vital. Perhaps I see the same qualities in Lucy.

It delighted me the way Iris mocked my "nobbish airs" and dragged me off to her favourite haunts, penny gaffs where bibulous patrons pilloried men of my sort in ribald ballads. I shall never forget the shock of hearing the Royal Family itself sent up in the song about the coster-monger and his donkey. Iris, her arm hooked in mine, swaying to the melody, the comic on stage winking and leering as he bellowed,

"I'm quite a sporting character
I wisits flashy places,
Last year, my old woman washed my ass,
An' I vent to Ascot races,
I got jist by the royal booth,
And there – it is no farce, sirs,
The king, he often bowed at me,
While the queen looked at my ass, sirs."

This undercurrent of turbulent, tongue-in-cheek anarchy rife among the lower orders was something I had never suspected. All about me, I felt the audience slyly gauging my reaction to the scandalous tune, endeavouring to provoke me by tugging their forelocks, by winking at the toff in the silk top hat. One fellow had the impudence to stagger up and pant stale beer into my face. "Does a coster-monger's opera tickle the gentleman's fancy?"

As a matter of fact, it did. Enormously.

My overweening affection for these girls was not *nostalgie de la boue* but a recognition they were cleaner clay than myself. Charles Gaunt was truly the kept creature, incapable of asserting himself, incapable of bending the golden bars of his father's cage and making his escape.

Iris sometimes seemed offended that I made no advances, asked nothing in return for the little treats I gave her, scent, flowers, champagne dinners. But her good humour always returned once we embarked on an outing. She would mockingly refer to me as "Champagne Charlie" and tickle me in public. Sexual intercourse with Iris would never be a chilly transaction. It was the reason I was saving her for another.

As does Lucy Stoveall, Iris had passion, passion coupled with an attractive strength and self-reliance entirely foreign to respectable drawing rooms where ladies engineer marital prospects like Metternich balancing the power of great states at the Congress of Vienna.

So how to account for the circumstances I found Lucy in the other night? The perplexing scene she enacted with the stick, her behaviour verging on hysterical frenzy. Even when she recognized who I was, the fashion in which she gave herself to me created disquiet in my mind, as excessive emotion always has.

When I questioned her later, tried to draw her out about what had led to the inner storm which shattered her strong exterior, I recognized the look which stole over her face. There was something in it of Simon's expression the night I came upon him and the Reverend Witherspoon in the drawing room. Something guarded and hostile, as if I were being refused admission to a reality I had not earned.

Of course, in Simon's case I deserved his distrust after the unfortunate incident with Iris. I had truly thought I was doing him a favour when I gave the servants a half-day off, slipped Iris into his room to await his arrival, and took myself off. An antidote to Dr. Milton, one might say.

But when I returned later that afternoon, Iris was gone and Simon in a terrible state, white with fury, unwilling to accept any excuse or apology from me.

"I have sat here waiting for you to return, Charles," he said, "thinking how I can impress on you the heartless, dreadful thing you did to that girl."

"I'll thank you to use my friend's name," I shot back. "It is Iris. She is a kind, affectionate girl with a warm heart and she would have done you a lot of good if you had let her. I only hope you were not so rude as to pray over her."

Simon crossed the room to a table from which he retrieved a book. He marched back to me rigid with anger. "I have marked a relevant passage. Perhaps it will show you the error of your ways," he said.

Naturally, I expected it would be some high-minded bosh, but when I turned it over I saw it was Jean-Jacques Rousseau's *Confessions*. My surprise could not have been greater if he had handed me a copy of *The New Lady's Tickler*.

"What are you doing with this?"

"Read, please!" he said vehemently.

Skimming those few pages, I found nothing which touched upon my particular transgression. What Simon had marked was a description of an attempt by a sodomite to seduce the young Rousseau. I closed the book. With some asperity I said, "I fail to understand the point you wish to make."

"Rousseau observes that the man's advances upon him allowed him to see men as women must. The brutality of their lust. Put yourself in that girl's place. Think of what you subjected her to."

"Apparently neither of us subjected her to anything. You saw to that. You make too much of this," I said. "And I am very much surprised by your taste in immoral French literature. I offer you a jolly, healthy girl and you prefer this."

"At least Rousseau's honesty saves him from true immorality."

"So I am dishonest?"

Simon hesitated.

"Say it. Be what you advocate. Play Rousseau, Simon."

"You are dishonest to yourself when you scratch no deeper than the surface of things."

It was a piercing betrayal. In that instant I noticed his hand was resting on one of the sketches I had left lying on the desk. As soon as the words were out of his mouth, I saw he regretted them, but that only drove home even more forcibly that his opinion was genuine.

"Thank you," I said.

He flushed to the roots of his hair. "I beg your forgiveness, Charles."

"And I yours," I returned. But this was a falsehood. I hid my anger because to reveal it would have exposed the depth of my humiliation. If Simon, the naif, said such things, what was being said behind my back by the gossips of the art world? The little confidence I had stored up crumbled with the lightest of touches, my brother's white hand laid on a drawing. Suddenly, what I had taken such pride in – that in all of England there might not be more that two or three draftsmen better than I – became a paltry achievement. I saw that the true artist required more than an exquisite touch.

"Let us go to bed," Simon coaxed. "Hard words forgotten and forgiven."

I offered a conterfeit smile. "In a bit," I told him. "I am not sleepy yet."

Simon left. It was past midnight. I turned off the gas lamps and stared into the unsteady blue flames of the fire. A story Gambart, the picture dealer and infamous rumour monger, had related about Charles Collins burned as hotly in my mind as the coals on the grate. Like me, Collins was an artist of care and patience. A great future was predicted for him. For weeks, he worked out of doors in all weathers to capture a quaint, tumble-down shed, holes gaping in its roof, planks missing from its walls, light streaming through the tottering wreck. But when Collins finally finished rendering the shed after much painstaking labour, he was at a loss as how to proceed. The shed was always intended to be a background, but for what, he could not say. For the rest of his short life, he debated what he might place in the foreground and dismissed all ideas. An old shed was all he had, ever would have. "Poor fellow never painted again," Gambart confided to me. "And here's a romantic touch. Collins died with the unfinished canvas lying on his bed."

The fire went cold and still I sat, smarting. Why had my brother encouraged and applauded me if this was his true opinion of me? Was Collins's story mine? Was I all background, an empty foreground? Industrious as an ant, and just as artful? At five in the morning I got up and went to my studio, lit the gas lamps. There was my answer. Piles of sketches, studies, and not one painting finished. Like Collins. Heaps of paper and canvas through which I feverishly sifted. Here a hand, here a torso, here a leg, here a head. The offal of a crude autopsy.

At dawn I carried the body parts into the garden. It began to rain as I set fire to them. I stood there hat in hand, watching the flames fizzle in the downpour. No more successful in destroying the wretched things than I had been in making them.

I walked into the streets of London, into the fitful coming and going of rain. If the downpour became intolerable I crept into a public house or a shop and waited for it to decrease. The rest of the time I tramped without direction or purpose, adrift in crowds hurrying to escape the wet and the cold, hastening to win the warmth of their own cozy parlours. London in February, winter darkness, my feet counting greasy flagstones as I stumbled down a very English Via Dolorosa, thoughts as cluttered and grey as the dismal streets.

A little after eight o'clock, having taken not so much as a morsel of food all day, I found myself faint and weary outside the British Museum, drops of rain pattering lightly on my hat like a madman's babble, feet soaked. The museum shut and locked as if its custodians had known of my coming, had expressly barred the doors to me and me alone.

I recalled more of Gambart's gossip. Behind those locked doors the doting mother of the young painter John Everett Millais had done the research for his historical paintings. Had pressed his copies of Hogarth on President Shee of the Royal Academy, launching his career. At ten, the prodigy was accepted into the Royal Academy; a few years later, he was presented the Gold Medal in the Antique School, such a small boy that the members had passed him hand over hand and plunked him down on the dais to roars of approbation. The hope of English art they had called him then, and what had become of him? The painter of "Sermons." Not fit to wipe Turner's and Constable's brushes, but rich. Because he could draw, do an admirable likeness.

I knew by heart the envious tittle-tattle circulating about Millais, the man who made twenty-five-thousand pounds a year, rode to hounds, fished salmon, hunted deer on a grand estate in Scotland. Every inch a gentleman. If I could not whole-heartedly admire his paintings, his personal style appealed to me. I have always loathed Bohemianism, the buffoonery, the insufferable pretence, blouses besmirched with paint, grown men in silly hats.

I made a decision that night, hands gripping the cold bars of the museum gates. If I was already a sham, better to be a sham like Millais and have the world at my feet. I was a prodigious drawer. At ten, I could reproduce Durer almost as well as Millais did Hogarth. Henceforth likenesses for the wealthy and eminent would be my trade. There is always a demand for portraits. I might not be a graduate of the academy, but I possessed other qualities. I was presentable, the son of a man with a fortune and a country house; if I chose to be, I was adept at agreeable conversation. I must go about, make myself known in the right circles.

And this I did. To the men I had known at Oxford I announced that the hermit had renounced the hermitage. I joined a club, accepted invitations to dine. If the overly polite inquired after my twin, I explained he was of an evangelical temper, did not drink wine or dance. Hostesses were apt to declare this admirable but privately judge him unsuitable for the sort of parties they gave. One William Wilberforce in society had been enough.

So I withdrew myself from Simon. Our conspiracy against the larger world was finished, no more colloquies over tea and buns. I was always out, cultivating patrons and artists of whom society approved. Of course, Millais and Leighton, the gods of English painting's Olympus, were not to be approached by the likes of me, but there were other lesser beings whom I might gather to my cause. I frequented the home of a shrill bluestocking who drew sullen poets and fashionable painters around her commodious skirts. At one of her afternoons I made the acquaintance of Pemberton Stall, portraitist of choice for the Men of the North, cotton manufacturers, iron mongers, ship builders with plenty of loose coin and a willingness to expend it to have their faces preserved for posterity.

How often I had heard Gambart say no one could polish an apple like Pemberton Stall, an artist who could erase the squint of a rich man's wife, add cream and damask rose to the bad complexion of a much beloved daughter. That day, I polished Pemberton Stall's apple, showed myself well acquainted with his work. In a short conversation I learned his favourite adjective, "charming," and applied it to a portrait of his I had recently seen hanging in a gallery. My reward was an invitation to visit the studio he kept in his home in St. John's Wood and, "Peruse some rather nice little pictures I have recently done."

Two days later, I was ushered into Pemberton Stall's sanctum sanctorum by his wife, Elizabeth, a woman possessing an imperious carriage, a thrilling, husky voice, and round white arms. We spent the afternoon drinking tea while the painter skipped about his studio, feverishly putting up canvases and taking them down, basking in our unstinting applause. I envied the magic Mr. Stall worked on people of every sort, attracting both the attention of this majestic woman as well as the favour of the blunt manufacturers of the north, men who made a fetish of plainspokenness, practicality, and bluff heartiness. His conversation was whimsical, fey, poetical. Tiny and smelling of French scent, he was amusingly erratic. The very antithesis of his patrons and even of his wife, who was statuesque, cool, contained.

After Elizabeth and I became lovers, she never revealed how Pemberton had won her, but she did explain how he enchanted the dour industrialists. "You see," she said to me one afternoon as we lolled about in her bed, "these men like to think they have hired an artist. Not too much of an artist, of course, but someone just a trifle out of the ordinary and beyond their humdrum experience. Someone who will provide them with anecdotes to entertain their friends, but won't take artistic temperament to an excess. A chap a bit exotic, but not so exotic he does not know his place." Cocking her head and smiling roguishly, she said, "Pemby fits the bill very nicely, don't you think?"

I did, and in time came to see how he fit Elizabeth's bill so nicely too. Despite her cool demeanour, Elizabeth was a driving woman who would have inevitably come into conflict with a more conventional husband determined to play paterfamilias. She relished her position as the dragon who guarded the precious treasure, Pemberton Stall. Theirs was a partnership of equals, he plying the brush and seducing clients, Elizabeth negotiating commissions, bringing pressure to bear when payment lagged, arranging and overseeing the dinners and parties which were Pemby's forum, glittering occasions when he sprinkled the company with his witticisms and whimsical lectures on Art. This was a select group. No one of whom Elizabeth Stall disapproved gained admittance to the house in St. John's Wood, even if Pemby protested. She approved highly of me.

Our affair lasted two years, and during the course of it she advanced my career tremendously. No disloyalty to her husband was involved in this, adultery was a minor thing compared to failing to forward his position in the world of art. But work which Pemby disdained, or was too busy to execute, was carefully steered my way. What a surprise to realize that by the second year of our liaison, I was earning two hundred and fifty pounds per annum by my brush. Not a mint certainly, but a noble supplement to my allowance from Father. Of course, it was in Elizabeth's interest to do all she could for me since so much of what I earned was spent on her. Both of us knew how we stood with one another, that ours was a contract based on mutual satisfaction.

How Elizabeth adored the opera, the ballet. Pemby adored them too, but he never seemed available on the evenings she wished to go. She loved good wine, good dinners, and fashionable restaurants. So did Pemby, but he preferred some sycophant to pay for them. Little gifts, flowers, perfume, chocolates, amused her, but on special occasions, she expected jewellery. Pemby, apparently, was forgetful of special occasions. It was my lot to remember them.

Elizabeth found time spent alone unendurable. I must squire her about, or dance attendance at her home in St. John's Wood, play cards with her, read to her. All her friends paid lip service to the fiction that I was a talented young man whom she was assisting to make his way in the world. When surrounded by ladies, Elizabeth talked a good deal about the beauties of platonic friendship.

From the beginning, jaunty Pemberton Stall never once gave the slightest hint that he suspected matters were other than they should be between me and his wife. It took months to realize that in fact he was aiding and abetting his wife's infidelity. One Sunday afternoon, I laid aside the novel which I had been reading aloud to Elizabeth and asked how it was her husband could overlook our affair. Laughing, she kissed me and exclaimed, "Charles, you silly goose! You have not plumbed the reason for Pemby's tact!" Feeling foolish that I had been so blind, I left it at that.

Occupied as I was, Simon hardly entered my thoughts. I had abandoned the make-shift studio in the house, renting premises in artistic

Chelsea, the environs of Carlyle and Rossetti. My clients appreciated the tone of the district. I seldom spent evenings at home. I was off to my club, or gadding about with friends, or escorting Elizabeth to concerts and soirees. My brother and I crossed paths less and less frequently. Once or twice a week we chewed cold toast together at breakfast, or had a brief chat before bed if I stayed in.

Then one morning when Simon was out, Mrs. Murchison came to me in a dreadful dither. Housekeeping money was missing from the locked box she kept in the pantry. She expected me to get to the bottom of it, discover the criminal in our midst. My first thought was that one of the maids had fallen under the sway of some cracksman or burglar, and had been seduced into supplying information and access to the house. But if that were true, much more would have gone missing than the insignificant sum of a pound and a few odd shillings. What's more, Mrs. Murchison swore the box was locked, she had had to use her key to open it. I could not imagine Mary or Sarah, or even Jack, possessing a lockpick's betty, let alone the skill to employ it.

Nevertheless, I called all the servants into the study and interrogated them sternly. There was a flood of tears from the maids, and manly, flustered indignation from Jack, leaving me in no doubt as to their innocence. Briefly, I entertained the idea Mrs. Murchison had been prey to a fit of absent-mindedness, paid some butcher's boy when he delivered the cuts, and forgotten to record the expenditure in the accounts. But on second thought it seemed more probable the Sphinx should bark than Mrs. Murchison be negligent in her bookkeeping.

Although I had an appointment with Elizabeth that morning, I delayed leaving the house until Simon returned from his errand, intending to pass the matter off on him. The servants trusted and loved Simon. I believed him more capable of easing the distress caused by my accusations than I. When I began to explain the situation, he interrupted to say he had opened the locked box with his own key, taken the money because he had been cut short by a financial emergency.

"In that case," I said, "replace it now. You know how Mrs. Murchison fusses over the accounts."

My demand forced an embarrassing disclosure. "I am stony broke, Charles. If you could loan me ten pound until the end of the month when Father remits our quarterly allowance, I would be eternally grateful."

"Broke? You spend nothing on entertainment, you have no club dues, never take a hansom. How can you be penniless?"

With this challenge, his eyes began to shift about the room. "Lend me ten pound, and let the matter drop, Charles," he implored me.

I was glad to make him a loan. I would have parted with fifty guineas for the pleasure of learning my brother, too, had feet of clay, that we were not so very unlike, after all.

Simon's profligacy slid out of my mind only to be resurrected a few days later. I had sent Jack to hail me a cab and was keeping watch for it when I saw Simon descending our front steps. Two figures crossed the street and accosted him. I saw Simon hand money over to them. Then all three walked away together. When they waded through a bright pool of light cast by a street lamp, I saw one of the men casually place his arm over Simon's shoulders. Furthermore, I noted both of Simon's companions were shabbily dressed, marking them as workmen, possibly vagrants.

Was this one of Simon's impulsive acts of charity? Unlikely, the men appeared to be on familiar terms with him. Something about the scene I had witnessed struck me as sinister.

When I confided my tale to Elizabeth, she suggested I consult a Mr. Isidore Sash, who had been so helpful in sorting out a "sticky matter" for Pemby. She offered no details as to what had been Pemby's problem, but by now I could hazard a guess. When I asked if Mr. Sash were a private detective, Elizabeth evaded the question by answering, "No, just an efficient, respectable man. All the best people turn to Mr. Sash when awkward questions arise. For advice as much as anything else, don't you know?" She offered to communicate my problem to Sash and request his assistance.

"Yes," I said to her, "that would be most helpful."

"Very good," she said, adopting a look of resolution which I had come to know so well, "I shall write Mr. Sash this afternoon."

Mr. Sash found my case and my wallet sufficiently interesting to accept me as a client. His address was in Soho, favourite haunt of foreigners, but Mr. Sash was decidedly English. His quarters were threadbare and clean, very much like their occupant, a tall, lean rack of bones upon which a worn, much-brushed black suit hung like coal dust. As we conferred, he downed glass after glass of water poured from a carafe resting on his desk and made gentle, encouraging, commiserating noises as I related my problem to him. When I finished, I felt rather foolish, it all sounded so bland and unremarkable.

Mr. Sash did not treat it as such. He lifted an eyebrow and murmured, "You and your brother are close?"

The inquiry startled me. I hardly knew how to answer. Things had undergone such a change between us. "No," I said at last. "Not close."

"You entertain no supposition as to who the men were who approached him in the street?"

"No, not in the least."

He gulped some more water; it seemed painful for him to proceed. "And you and your brother have been acquainted with Mr. Stall for long?"

"My brother is not acquainted with Mr. Stall. They have never met. It is I who am a friend to Mr. and Mrs. Stall."

Mr. Sash looked disappointed. "I see," he said, reflecting. "You are certain Mr. Stall and your brother are not acquainted?"

I found this line of questioning most irksome. "I would stake my life on it that they are not acquainted," I said.

"Very well then. I shall make inquiries. Under the circumstances, it would not be wise for me to come to your home. If you would be so good to come to me here, at the same hour, in two week's time – unless you hear from me earlier."

At our next appointment I received Mr. Sash's report, which he delivered with great thoroughness, frequently consulting shorthand notes as he soothed himself with water.

"I have followed your brother for a fortnight," he began. "He keeps to the house by day but each night attends a meeting in rooms over a draper's shop in Holborn. Two men frequently accompany him there." Mr. Sash referred to his notes. "Thomas Beckton, a carter, and William Tailor, a costermonger. They customarily meet your brother outside your house before proceeding to the meeting. In all likelihood, they are the same men you saw him with several weeks past."

"My brother has said nothing of any meetings."

"They are of a religious nature. Your brother attends a Non-conformist chapel called the Church of Christian Israel."

"Church of Christian Israel. I've never heard of it."

"Ah, sir," Mr. Sash said, "the body of Christ is most lamentably fractured in the present age. Christian Science, Mormons, Primitive Methodists . . ." He left the long list of heresies hanging uncompleted, as if to enumerate them all would take him an eternity. "The Church of Christian Israel holds nightly services Mondays, Wednesdays, Fridays, and Saturdays. These are open to the public and all are welcomed. The size of the congregation fluctuated," he glanced at his notes. "Between as little as thirty-five to as many as sixty. The church's adherents are drawn largely from the labouring classes. They appear sober and respectable. The women sit apart from the men as the Welsh do in their chapels and the Jews in their synagogues."

I had a hunger for more meat and fewer details. "Go on, man," I urged. "And what of my brother? Anything amiss there?"

"Undoubtedly your brother's attendance at these meetings explains his financial embarrassment. I regret to inform you that the Christian Israelites are communards." He amended his statement with a qualification. "Let us say they practise socialism tempered with Christianity. A collection or love offering is made without fail every evening. Each member of the congregation is expected to contribute what ready money they have. A double tithe is taken from the collection to support missionary activity. What remains is distributed in equal portions to all the Christian Israelites. Since your brother is by far the most prosperous congregant, this system means he gives a great deal and receives back very little. Simple mathematics, sir. He will never gain, only lose."

"If there is such a distribution, and Beckton and Tailor are members of the church, why would he be handing out money to them before service?"

"To fail to make a contribution is a matter of great shame to the Christian Israelites," explained Mr. Sash. "One woman who had nothing for the collection plate was greeted with derisory cries of, 'The Widow's Mite! The Widow's Mite!' I may only speculate, but I assume your brother was shielding his friends from a similar humiliation."

"I see," I said. "Well, keep your own contributions to an acceptable minimum, Mr. Sash. I would not be pleased to find I was supporting these poor, deluded souls too generously when I review your expenses."

Mr. Sash proved himself not only the soul of discretion but also of honesty. Very primly he said, "Visitors are expressly forbidden from participating in the love offering. Only those who have been baptized in the Water of the New World are permitted to take part."

"Water of the New World. What do you mean?"

"Water transported from North America is required for the baptism of adherents. The doctrine of the Church of Christian Israel holds that the Red Indians are descended from the Lost Tribes of Israel. They consider North America a Hidden Holy Land and its waters sacred. It is also their belief that the conversion of the Indian Jews will bring about Christ's return. It is why they double tithe, to fund missionary work in America and hasten that day."

"Astounding," I said. "Very peculiar. But if it amuses Simon, I suppose there is really no harm in it. I don't approve, but he can spend his allowance as he chooses."

"There is more," said Mr. Sash, tapping his fingers on the table.

"Go on."

"The clergyman who leads this flock – Reverend Obadiah Witherspoon is how he styles himself – is a very dodgy character." Mr. Sash's eyebrows went up. "I have friends on the Metropolitan Police force for whom I sometimes perform small favours, and they, in return, afford me timely kindnesses. Someone whom I cannot name, but who occupies a position of great responsibility in the constabulary, informs me that the Reverend Obadiah Witherspoon served a sentence in Coldbath House of Correction for fraud. He was a prater, sir. A bogus clergyman stumping the streets, preaching extempore, fleecing the gullible with claims he was a missionary in the wilds of America. His chief confederate was a dusky-hued Jew raised in the stalls of Houndsditch Exchange. Witherspoon dressed him in feathers and paint and exhibited him as a Red Indian convert to Christianity. When Witherspoon gathered a substantial crowd by his preaching, the Jew would then be introduced, kiss the Bible, and fervently bawl, 'Jesus good! Jesus good!' Sometimes as much as ten or twelve pounds was collected from the unsuspecting. I do not doubt it, having heard Witherspoon speak. His sermons are most rousing." Mr. Sash cleared his throat. "I suspect Witherspoon is preparing to shear your brother's fleece, and it will cost a good deal more than ten or twelve pounds, Mr. Gaunt."

That gave me pause. "You have done very good work, Mr. Sash, and have earned my heartfelt gratitude and respect." He was very gratified by the compliment and we shook hands. Then Mr. Sash presented his fee with many little groans of solicitude and tiny bobs of the head which verged on genuflection. I paid him and immediately repaired to my studio in Chelsea, where I sat thinking of how to announce to Simon that he was the victim of a confidence man.

I debated at length how I would handle this matter, knowing how reluctant Simon was to believe anything bad of anyone. Then one night, when I returned to Grosvenor Square, I found Simon seated in the drawing room with a stranger. One glimpse of his guest and somehow I knew who he was. How fortuitous, I thought, that the scoundrel should be so conveniently delivered into my hands to be exposed before my brother's very eyes.

Seated there in my favourite chair, sipping my port, the Reverend Witherspoon cut an imposing figure. Powerfully built, he had the chest of a coal-heaver. His abundant mane of salt-and-pepper hair was swept back from his forehead, and this, along with a broad, flat nose and piercing eyes, lent him a distinctly leonine appearance. I asked my twin to introduce his guest. Resistance formed in Simon's face as he did the honours, and he announced by his expression that if I had any sense I would not impose myself upon them for long.

I went to the sideboard, poured myself a glass of port, and inquired whether the good Reverend had a London parish or a country living. I was playing the innocent, enjoying the fact that unknown to him, my knowledge gave me the upper hand. Witherspoon answered that he was not a clergyman of the Church of England, that Erastian sore in the sight of God, but a minister of the Church of Christian Israel. I remarked I had not heard of his creed. What were its principal tenets? He gave me a cunning grin; he had an inkling of what was afoot.

"If you are so interested in our faith, Mr. Gaunt, why not attend services with Simon?"

"But I have you here, Reverend Witherspoon, in my drawing room, drinking my port. I thought you would not wish to miss this opportunity to enlighten me."

"The chief work of our church is the conversion of the Red Indians," was all he offered as explanation.

"I have heard you are an old hand at that. It earned you a good dunking in Coldbath prison."

"Charles!" cried Simon furiously. The Reverend Witherspoon turned his penetrating gaze to my twin and settled him. He smiled at me, toyed with his cuffs. They were none too clean. "My unfortunate past is known to Simon and every member of my congregation," he stated. "I have confessed my failings to them many times. Suffering was my due. I earned it with my sins. But from suffering comes wisdom. When you have walked Coldbath's apparatus of penitence, the treadmill, hour after hour – then, sir, you have had a taste of the torments of hell. In the darkness of Coldbath the light broke upon me, and there God's purpose was revealed to me."

"To save the American Jews."

The Reverend Witherspoon emptied his glass. "If you would be so good, dear boy," he said to Simon. "Just another drop of that excellent port." Simon served him, very much the eager disciple. Returning to his seat, my brother mouthed something to me. I could not read his lips.

Witherspoon lifted the glass to the light, tasted, smacked his appreciation. "You think the existence of American Jews is a fancy. Even though you have not investigated the question." And with that Obadiah Witherspoon launched into what I can only describe as a speech, words so often repeated that they rolled out of him by rote. His shield against doubters. A chant of defiance in a harsh, stentorian voice. Once he was truly under way, he could not contain his energy, rose to his feet and began to pace. He said it was a scientific fact the Indians were Jews. In 1587, the Jesuit Nicholas Delttsu discovered a tribe in Argentina who bore Hebrew names, Abraham, David, Moshe. They were circumcised. The trader Isaac Nasic, a Jew, encountered tribes in Surinam whose language was clearly derived from Hebrew and who employed the Hebrew name for God. In 1642, a Jewish convert to Christianity, Antonio de Montezinos, reported to the learned scholar and holy Amsterdam rabbi, Manasseh Ben Israel, that when exploring the mountains of Ecuador, he had met with Indians who greeted him with the Jewish declaration of faith, the Shema Israel, and who claimed descent from the Lost Tribes of Israel.

Several times I tried to interject some reason into this hectoring oration, but each time he flung another "fact" at me. The Mohawks were the lawgivers of the Iroquois just as the tribe of Levi was for the Hebrews. Mohawk was the corruption of the Hebrew word, *Meichokek*. The physiognomy of the Indians testified to their Semitic ancestry. Many had remarked it. It so startled William Penn that he wrote to a friend that the natives bore so lively a resemblance to Jews that Penn could have believed himself in Duke's Place or Berry Street in London.

It was an extraordinary performance. I was not sure whether I was witnessing the well-honed deceptions of Witherspoon's "prating" days or the earnest sincerity of a madman.

I looked over at Simon. He shook his head, as if to warn me not to interrupt the preacher.

"Scripture," Witherspoon said abruptly, shifting the field of battle. "'Go not into the way of the Gentiles, and into any city of the Samaritans enter ye not. But go rather to the lost sheep of the house of Israel.' Christ's specific charge to His church. Forsake the conversion of the European Jews who derive their name from the House of Judah. Go instead to the Ten Lost Tribes who inherited the name Israel. 'And the backsliding Israel hath justified herself more than treacherous Judah.' The Israelites who lost their faith in exile are not tainted with the blood guilt of the House of Judah, those who renounced, reviled, and slew Christ. The House of Israel is acceptable in the eyes of the Lord. And when Israel is gathered into the fold, then and only then shall we see the Second Coming of Christ, the establishment of his Seat of Mercy in the New Jerusalem across the waters."

Perhaps Witherspoon was a little drunk on my port. Suddenly, he had to stop and steady himself on the fireplace mantel. I said, "And what makes you think you will succeed in converting the Indians where so many have failed?"

He looked at me intently for a moment. "I wish to learn before I teach. I shall fall and kiss the feet of the Elder Brothers of Christ because in their salvation is ours. Among the Indian shamans, knowledge of the powers of the Ark of the Covenant and other mysteries of the ancient Hebrew priesthood may exist." He paused momentously. "But above all, what I wish to learn from them is why they share both want and plenty, keep goods in common, live like the early Christians while we cannot."

"Ah yes," I observed, "you are a great proponent of goods held in common. Particularly my brother's."

"That is enough, Charles! What I do with my money is no concern of yours!" Simon shouted at me.

"It is of concern to me when you disrupt the household by pilfering Mrs. Murchison's housekeeping money. It concerns me when the money I lend you goes to line the pockets of the likes of him."

The Reverend Witherspoon sprang to his own defence. "My portion of the love offering is no greater than any other member of the church."

I parried. "Except for the double tithe for mission work. By now that must be a tidy sum."

"I know the suspicions my past excites. It is Simon who collects, counts, and deposits the double tithe. Only he has the right to make withdrawals. It awaits the day when your brother and I set off to begin the long-delayed work. Happily, that day draws very near."

I cried out in disbelief. "Simon, tell me this is not true!"

"It is true, Charles."

"The both of you – why, you are mad as hatters!"

At this, Witherspoon bowed deeply to me, almost to his knees. Then he went to Simon, kissed him on both cheeks. "Thank you for the wine," he said before departing with a monumental gravity, leaving Simon and me to continue the dispute. It was heated and very bitter. I attacked Witherspoon's honesty; I attacked his sanity. Simon would hear nothing of it. I put it to him bluntly, Did he really, for an instant, believe that the Red Indians were the Lost Tribes of Israel. He said he did not. Then why, I wanted to know, was he willing to put himself in Witherspoon's hands?

"Because the Reverend Witherspoon, believing the Indians are the Elder Brothers of Christ, will take the message of Jesus to them with the utmost respect. That is all I ask."

I remembered Simon's Red Indian, how my brother had treated him, as if he were an equal. I believed I knew why. "You pine for more Oronhyatekhas," I said, "because they cannot see you for what you are – preposterous."

The next day Simon moved out of our house in Grosvenor Square and into the Reverend's quarters. It was my cruel words which drove him there and sealed his fate.

19

CUSTIS We finally worked ourselves clear of the Sand Hills a couple of hours back. Travel is more comfortable, the land rolls easy. Low benches dropping away in comfortable dips, slowly climbing to a new view. But now we face a nasty, hot wind whistling down from the north.

All of a sudden, Barker stiffens on the wagon seat beside me, jerks the reins, hollers, "Whoa!" Aloysius's in back, hiding from the scorching wind. The wagon braking so sudden, he sings out, "What is it, Custis?"

Neither Barker nor I answer, we're too busy squinting, facing the blast, eyes smarting and teary-eyed. It's dead quiet except for the wagon canvas, popping in the wind like one of the Captain's champagne corks.

A half-mile off, in the lee of a ridge, stands an Indian camp. I feel Aloysius's shoulders pressing up against my back, wriggling to catch sight of what's stayed us here.

"Indian village directly ahead," I tell Aloysius. He blinks into the wind.

"We oughter turn back," Barker says. "Maybe they ain't seen us yet."

The Captain bustles up on horseback. "Why have you men halted! Move on!"

Barker points. "Indians."

This braces the Captain. He turns ramrod straight in the saddle. "Potts!" he shouts. "I want you!"

Jerry Potts answers the summons, trots up to the Englishman's side, followed by Grunewald's wagon and the rest of the party. One glimpse of the village and Grunewald, Lucy, Charles, and Ayto all fasten their eyes on the Captain and Potts.

"Can you identify those natives for me, Potts?"

Potts sits slumped on his pony, fingers twisting and twining the mane. He wears a godawful unhappy look. "Blackfoot," he answers softly. "Ghost camp. Everybody dead."

It hadn't struck me right off, but nothing is moving down there. No dogs raising Cain. No sign of horses. No fires. No women cooking meat or chipping robes. No children playing. I feel the hairs on the back of my neck stand up.

"Ridiculous," says the Captain. "How can they possibly be all dead?"

Then, as if to support the Captain's assertion, a man stumbles into the middle of the ring of teepees, madly hailing us. The wind blots out most of what he shouts, but one or two words reach us, faint and forlorn. One of them I catch is an English word. Help.

The scene below screws the Captain's mouth tight as a boy winds his first pocket watch. "I smell a trick. Perhaps those Indians intend to draw us down and spring an ambuscade."

"No," says Potts. "Everybody dead."

"That one isn't dead," the Captain says sharply.

"That's a white man. All the Blackfoot are dead. Maybe he brought it to them, the white scabs."

At the mention of white scabs, the Captain gives Potts a blank stare.

"What the Indians call smallpox," I explain.

The Captain pulls a glass out of his saddlebags and aims it at the fellow calling to us. The man's growing more desperate with every second we delay heeding his appeal. Now he's flapping his arms, hopping up and down like a crow tethered to a string.

Gaunt lowers the telescope. "That fellow indeed appears to be a white man. A white man in a most dreadful state. What can it mean?"

I say the obvious. "We aren't going to know unless we go and see."

Barker is having none of it. "Count me out. I don't like the looks of it. I'm hired to drive. Not poke my nose into no Indian business."

The Captain puts the glass back to his eye. Like the generals say, he's studying the ground.

"Well, get yourself off this wagon and I'll take her down," I say to Barker.

Barker gladly resigns the reins. I turn to Aloysius. "You coming, or are you bailing out too?"

Aloysius hoists himself out of the back and on to the wagon seat. "Good man," I say.

Gaunt, the pompous ass, hands out orders. "Potts, stay with the others to protect Mrs. Stoveall. My brother and I shall escort Mr. Straw in case of a ruse. Charles, arm yourself with a weapon from Barker's wagon." His brother hustles over to us and begins ransacking the armoury. He's making a lot of dangerous-sounding noise behind me. I glance back and see him holding an English fowling piece out in front of him like a pikestaff, muzzle directed at my and Aloysius's backs. "Maybe you better point that bird gun over the tailgate," I suggest.

Away we go, Charles riding shotgun in our wagon, the Captain providing cavalry support. The woebegone castaway goes silent and still at the sight of succour approaching, doesn't make so much as a step towards us as we pull up to the outskirts of the village. I notice three lodges blown over by the wind. From under one of them a pair of legs is sticking out. Dogs or coyotes have chewed the meat off them down to the bone. The half-roasted corpse of a warrior is laying in the ashes of a long dead fire. The top of his skull is gone, blown to kingdom come. A musket lies slanted across his chest. No doubt he sat down beside the fire and ended his misery by applying a gun barrel to his mouth. I've heard tell that even Indians who survive the smallpox sometimes turn to suicide when they see their disfigurement.

I don't spot another of the bodies until it's too late to steer clear of it. The wheels clunk over it with a stomach-turning bump, the horses shy at the rankness squashed out of it. It's all I can to do to get the team stopped before they bolt right over the miserable figure patiently waiting on us, so far gone he doesn't have the presence of mind to avoid getting trampled.

He starts to blubber, arms wrapped tight around his chest. "Lord," he croaks, trying to trap his sobs from escaping, "ain't I glad to see you, pards! Have pity on Matt Chisholm, carry him out of this place! Old Matt's run out of rope." Chisholm's a bearded old-timer with a sun-burned bald pate and a fringe of lank, stringy grey hair that straggles down to his shoulders. A hide hunter, or wolfer from the look of him, buckskins stiff with old blood, rancid and shiny with grease. He's bootless, feet cut to pieces, swollen and black. It makes you wonder how he'd been able to spring about so spry signalling us, but the prospect of rescue must have danced the pain right out of his feet.

The Captain fires a question at him. "What has occurred here, sir?"

The old man seems to be collecting himself some, but he's still babbling. "I ran from them, mister. Washed up here when I couldn't go one step further. Mister, don't you let them lay hands on me again."

"Whom do you refer to, Mr. Chisholm? Do you mean Indians? Were you the captive of these Indians?"

Chisholm shakes his head so hard his circlet of filthy hair whips from side to side. "Never was. No sir. Not held by Indians, no. I'd of had a deal kinder treatment from Indians. White devils was the ones that took me captive. Yes, sir, white fiends was what they was."

There comes a lull in the wind, and the stench from the tents suddenly breaks full force in the noonday heat. Rotting flesh, juices stewing in the human gut. I hear Charles Gaunt retch in the back of the wagon and see the Captain go greenish, stop his nostrils with a handkerchief. It turns me just as queasy and makes Aloysius's throat give a jump. The only one the reek doesn't affect is Matt Chisholm, who's been smelling it so long it must have cauterized his nose.

"Perhaps we ought to discuss this in more salubrious surroundings," the Captain proposes, nose buried in his hanky, the only sensible suggestion I've ever heard the Englishman make. I beckon Chisholm up to the wagon. As he slowly winces his way up the spokes of the wheel, Aloysius shifts over to make a place for him and asks, "How you doing, old-timer?" Chisholm looks down despondently at his bloated feet. "I believe my dogs is poisoned," he says. "Do you reckon they'll have to come off? I'd hate to lose them."

"You aren't going to lose them," I say, trying to sound as if I know what I'm talking about. All I know is those feet of his smell as high as anything mouldering in those lodges.

As soon as we get Matt Chisholm back to the wagons, the Captain starts to pepper him with questions, but Lucy steps in and says, "Look at the state of him, Mr. Addington. Leave him be until I get some food into him."

Even the Captain recognizes the sense to this. So everybody holds their peace and watches Chisholm wolf down a pan of bacon and a mess of corn dodgers. A full belly seems to bring him up to the mark pretty quick. He strikes me as old steel many times tested, not likely to lose his temper and shatter. Once Chisholm's swabbed every speck of grease from his plate with the last crumb of dodger, the Captain breaks with custom and serves all the men some highly rectified from a gallon jug. This gives the occasion an air of ceremony. We hunker down in an arc around Chisholm, Ayto with a notebook propped on his knee ready to record one more interesting anecdote of Captain Gaunt's life on the plains. Lucy stands to one side, hands calmly folded under her bosom.

Chisholm, no doubt feeling the weight of our attention, and seeing Ayto with his pencil poised, starts his story with grave dignity. He tells us how he'd spent the winter up on the Isipitsi, the High River, baiting wolves with strychnine, good money to be had with the strong market in the East for wolf pelts. Two weeks ago he'd bailed his furs and cached them. He couldn't freight them out because in March two of his wagon horses had gone through the ice on the river and drowned. So he struck off south to buy himself another team to haul his winter takings back to Fort Benton.

The second day on the trail he met with two fellows who'd been to Fort Whoop-Up, a hundred and fifty miles to the west, trying to get work with Johnny Healy, but it turned out the boss man wasn't hiring. Now they were just drifting, keeping an eye out for an opportunity. Hoped to meet with some other paying proposition. They weren't fussy what they did, so long as it put cash in their pockets. The two asked if it was all right if they rode with Chisholm for a spell, just in case they encountered unfriendly Indians.

"I was agreeable," says Chisholm. "I'd spent four months talking to myself and covered just about every topic under the sun. I was ready for chat. But it turned out only one of them talked, and all his talk was brag. Two brothers, but the younger one might have been deaf and dumb for all he said."

"Brothers?" Lucy interrupts. "What's their names?" She's blanched white; her freckles are rust spots.

"Why, ma'am, they was called Kelso. Titus and Joel Kelso."

Here's a surprise, but then again Titus always professed an interest in the liquor trade.

"Your kin," Lucy spits at me. I don't know what blame I bear for being related to the Kelsos, but her accusation gives a fright to Chisholm; he clamps shut his mouth and eyes me as if Lucy just announced that the dog lying on the rug happens to be rabid.

"They aren't anything to me, those boys," I reassure him. "They shot my pig."

Chisholm looks grateful to hear it. But he tests the ice a little further to make sure it'll hold. "Don't get me wrong," he says. "I don't mean to step on any toes."

"You step where you want. No love lost between me and the Kelsos."

The old man edges back into his tale of woe and misfortune. But he likes to hear himself tell a story, and soon he's deep into it once again. "The three of us journeyed for a day, had no trouble, nor hard words amongst us except that the older one kept pestering me where exactly I'd laid my hoard of pelts up. Offered himself and Joel to help me take them back to Benton once I bought horses. But I kept my mouth closed remembering his gab about opportunity and easy money. Next day we come on a free-trader with a wagonload of whisky. The Kelsos seemed to know him and I could tell Titus had no love for the man. Bold as brass, he asked a drink from the fellow. The trader told him a drink went for a dollar. Titus said he was out of ready money, but what skin was it off that old monkey's ass to be hospitable to white men thirsty in the wilderness and far from the comforts of home? The trader told him to go home and see if they were handing out free drinks there. He didn't risk his neck in dangerous parts just to dole out charity to every beggar came along. We could push off.

"Kelso was spoiling for a dust-up. He started cursing the trader, splashing him with dirty names – no account son of a bitch, dollar-biter, blood-sucking leech. The trader went into the fray too, calling Titus a fort Indian, arse-out-of-the-pants saddle tramp, trash. They was both on the boil, bandying fighting words. Kelso rode his horse into the trader's path, and blocked his team.

"Then just like that, the other Kelso screams, 'Look out, Tite! There's somebody laying for us in the back!' And before I can blink, shit, or go blind, Titus jerks out his pistol and shoots the trader clean off the wagon seat. All Hades broke loose, a nigger comes spilling out the back of the wagon –"

"Negro?" I say, throwing Lucy a glance. Her face is set like stone.

Chisholm nods his head. "Yessir. A nigger black as the ace of spades. He lights out across the prairie, running like the hounds of hell is after him – which you might say they was because Titus Kelso was galloping hard on his heels. The nigger was squirting left and right, cutting back and forth like a jack hare, Kelso blazing away at him with his pistol. The nigger was nimble, he covered a couple hundred yards before Titus brought him down and finished him off – two shots to the back of the neck."

"Abominable curs!" roars the Captain.

Lucy's chewing her lips, brown eyes cold as pennies on ice. She knows, Aloysius knows, and I know who Titus Kelso laid low. Abner Stoveall and Black Pompey. But Lucy Stoveall doesn't say a word, and it's not my place to volunteer information if she's reluctant. Aloysius's gathering himself to blab, but I warn him off it with a toss of my head.

Chisholm takes a mighty swallow of whisky, sloshes it about in his mouth as if he has a bad taste there that needs rinsing, then gulps it down. "The Kelsos had lost their heads and two men was dead because of it. Oh Titus made a great song and dance justifying himself, kept claiming the nigger was about to ambush us, but both me and his brother knew that was a bold-faced lie, even though we was agreeing with him, chirping away, 'Yes, that darky was laying for you. That's for certain,' and so on. I'd just had proof of the quality of the company I'd fallen in with and I weren't about to dispute just cause. No, sir."

The Captain's expression proclaims he thinks he would have conducted himself very differently in the same circumstances, that he would not have stood for the Kelsos committing such an outrage. The rest of us sit quiet and let Chisholm's conscience settle. He takes another mouthful of whisky and sits thinking for a bit. "You can appreciate my predicament, boys," he finally says. "But when that little rat said, 'I declare, opportunity has knocked and we have opened the door. I believe we've fallen into the whisky trade,' I wasn't having no part of it. I told Titus Kelso, thanks but no thanks. The time has come for us to part ways.

"'If that's your stand,' he said, 'you ain't going nowhere. We ain't about to let you spread word of this. Drop your weapons.' Two against one – I didn't have a Chinaman's chance. So I shucked my pistol and my Henry. 'Now make yourself useful,' he ordered me. 'Go scalp that old man and the nigger.' Already he had a plan. Lay the bloody deed on the doorstep of Indians, dissatisfied customers.

"I did as I was told, otherwise I'd have been cold on the ground with them two dead men. I peeled their scalps, and pricked my ears while Titus laid out his plan to his brother. He said the Indian ford they'd passed on the east bank of the Saskatchewan River would prove a profitable spot for a whisky post. Catch the customers coming and going.

"Then we set out for it, me piloting the dead man's wagon. I made myself useful because I reckoned if I didn't, Titus Kelso wouldn't have no compunction about sending me to glory. We made tracks all that day and most of the night. Titus wanted to put distance between ourselves and the scene of the crime. Next morning when we got to where he aimed us, he set his brother and me to work unloading the whisky, provisions, and tools the trader had for building a post. Packed it all up the slope of the riverbank on our backs until midnight. Next morning bright and early he made Joel and me drag the wagon into the river until the current carried it off. The little bastard never lifted a finger himself, just sat on the bank, pulling on a bottle, watching the Conestoga sail off, take on water until it sank.

"After that, it was nothing but days of hard labour, digging a cave into the bluff above the river. I mined for a week; Joel Kelso cut timber and shored the diggings with it while Titus drank whisky and ordered us about like he was a state governor. We had to step lively about it, he was determined to fort the place up good and solid before any Indians showed. He drove us so hard, one day I decided I had had enough, threw my spade down, and told him I wasn't about to lift another spoonful of dirt. Go ahead and shoot me. It'd be a relief. 'All right then,' he said, went and got a can of coal oil, splashed me down with it. 'I ain't going to shoot you,' he said. 'But I give you a choice. Dig or burn.' I dug.

"That was the writing on the wall. I lost any hope then that when I was done the dugout, he'd cut me loose. Sooner or later, I'd be a dead man floating downriver after that wagon. They had my horse and my guns, and every night they took my boots so's I couldn't run off.

"After three weeks of slaving, the whisky post was almost finished and I reckoned so was I. There was no hope of snatching a horse because when night fell they stabled the stock in the dugout. But one night Titus got generous, allowed his brother the treat of some liquor, and they both got piss-eyed drunk. But bad luck for me, they fell asleep across the mouth of the dugout, Titus curled around my boots. And no way could I lead a horse over their bodies without they woke up. Never mind, it was the best chance I'd had yet to scamper, so I tore up my shirt, wrapped my feet in it, and made tracks out of there. I run like I hadn't run since I was a youngster. Kept to the riverbank because there was heavy brush for me to hide in if they discovered me gone and come after me directly.

"When the sun come up, I crawled into a patch of buffalo berry brush, put my head down and slept. Early afternoon, the Kelsos waked me, casting about for some sign of me, but they rode on by. I determined to keep to my hidey hole until dark come down. Dusk was just settling in when I heard them heading back to the dugout, crashing through the willows. Titus was in a bloody mood, upbraiding Joel for not keeping close watch on the prisoner, Joel was making his mealy-mouthed excuses. If Titus hadn't been so occupied in laying blame, they might've seen me. They passed so close I could have counted the stitches on Titus Kelso's riding boots.

"Come full dark, I hightailed it out of that river bottom. I had maybe seven hours to cover ground before the sun raised up. Lord Jesus, I ran, ran the cloths right off my feet, didn't tarry long trying to find them in the pitch-dark. My feet got tore up terrible bad in the cactus. The pricklies was thick everywhere, you couldn't make a step without you landed in a nest of them. But I did a skedaddle as hard as ever I could. I weren't about to let them villains overtake me.

"First light I was fair crippled and winded, about ready to give up the ghost when I spied that Blackfoot camp yonder. I says to myself, best you throw yourself on red mercy, can't be worse than what's following you. So I limped for it, so blamed bust-up and done in, it didn't sink into me there was no cook fires burning, nor nobody astir. I was well into the camp before I seen every blessed soul was dead. Women in teepees laying cold with dead babies in their arms, children and old folks ripe with the corruption, young bucks who'd shot themselves. Faces bubbled and spotted with scabs, clouds of flies buzzing, corpses beset with every variety of creeping, noisome maggoty thing.

"It was a mighty bad place to land, but a man has to find the silver lining in the black cloud. I figured if the Kelsos was still searching for me they'd steer clear of a Blackfoot camp, wouldn't want to court no trouble of that variety. And I hadn't put a scrap of food in my belly for a day and a half. There was feed on hand aplenty, sacks of pemmican and jerked meat, I was faint with hunger, so I sat myself down and supped with the dead.

"I'd had a dose of the smallpox in St. Joe in '46 and survived it, so I wasn't afeared of the contagion. I told myself, 'Sit tight for a spell, let your feet heal, then maybe you can hoof it down to Benton.' But my feet poisoned up on me. I tried to doctor myself, pick out all the thorns I could catch hold of, but some was buried too deep, and my feet just kept blowing up bigger and bigger. Four days ago, you'd have thought I was wearing two loaves of black bread for shoes.

"I had enough meat, but I suffered for want of water. I got so parched I could hardly choke down my victuals. Mornings, I licked dew off the grass. Lucky for me, it rained a few nights ago and I caught some run-off from the teepee skins in a couple old kettles. That kept me going until you folks delivered me. Misters, that's it, that's all she wrote."

"Where is the Kelsos' whisky post?" the Captain demands, blood in his eye.

"I didn't cover too much ground, halt like I was. Maybe about twenty mile northwest, up on high ground overlooking the river ford so they can signal the Indians in and peddle their wares."

"I think we should pay them a visit," declares the Captain, squaring his shoulders, "and bring them to brook for their infamies."

I turn my eyes on Lucy Stoveall. Maybe she's going to speak now, let the cat out of the bag, and if she does the Captain will surely attempt to visit vengeance and fire on the Kelsos. But she sits quiet and still, not a word falls from her lips.

"Mister," says Chisholm, "as much as I'd like to see them boys punished for how they used me, I wouldn't advise folks who'd befriended me to do nothing rash. The Kelsos are situated in a mighty strong bunker. I know, I built it. Titus Kelso made sure any Indians who tried to storm it would pay a heavy price, and you would too."

"What if we invest them?" the Captain suggests, unwilling to abandon his notion. "We have plenty of supplies. We could starve them into surrender."

"Come, come, Addington, let us be sensible," says Charles Gaunt. "Do you think Grunewald, Barker, and Ayto are willing to risk themselves in such an enterprise? I daresay not. The rest – Mr. Straw, Mr. Dooley – are not yours to command. The injured party, Mr. Chisholm, is against it. More telling, we have a woman in our midst whom we cannot put in the way of danger. Let this matter drop. We would face a long delay in reaching the whisky posts, lose precious weeks in a siege."

It isn't like the Captain to back down, but even that trumped-up little martinet can see there's not a trace of enthusiasm showing in any of our faces for venturing life and limb in an assault on the Kelsos.

"Yes, yes, Captain," Ayto murmurs. "Your brother is right. Let us avoid ill-considered adventures."

With that, Chisholm's audience disperses. Ayto and the Captain go off, Ayto leaning into the Captain and chattering away, likely about what a fine light the rescue of Chisholm will throw him in when it is written up in his account of his deeds in America. Grunewald and Barker start up a game of cards, and Aloysius leads off Chisholm to doctor his feet with some of the Captain's store of iodine. Potts is the only one who remains sitting right where he was, all quiet and mournful.

I catch Lucy alone, starting to mix a batch of dough for firebread. I believe my opportunity has finally been handed to me.

"Mrs. Stoveall," I say, "you do know who the Kelsos killed, don't you?"

"I do," she says, giving a wipe to her brow with a floury wrist.

"I give you my condolences. I know from Madge that you and your husband seldom saw eye to eye, but it's still a lamentable thing."

"Abner reaped what he sowed. That's all I got to say."

I summon my courage. "With your husband dead, your business is done here. Come with me back to Fort Benton. Likely Chisholm will want to make for there too. Counting Aloysius, that'll make three men to see you back safe."

She trains those wild brown eyes of hers on mine; the flecks of gold in them burn with a hot glitter. "I'm sticking here."

"Why? Tell me why you insist on staying with the English." It isn't a real question, but I'd like to hear her answer straight off from her own lips.

"None of your concern, Custis Straw." And she goes back to kneading and punching her dough.

It's a strange thing with women, how infrequently they see where their interests lie. She might as well ask for the moon as for Charles Gaunt. Men like him don't hitch themselves to buggies like her except for short trips, a Sunday-afternoon jaunt.

"You think about it," I say. "Tell me what you decide in the morning."

Leaving her, I pass that peacock Charles Gaunt, sketching in one of his books. I say to him, "Tell your brother I'm helping myself to one of his bottles. He'll find the money for it laying on the floorboards of the wagon."

"Very well." He's so lost in his doodling, he didn't hear what I just told him. It's getting to be a habit, people not listening to a word I say.

"All you English can kiss my ass," I tell him. He looks up startled. I go collect the bottle, then I collect Jerry Potts because he needs to dose his misery too. It's his people rotting in the tents. The two of us walk out from the wagons, squat on the ground, share the bottle. We tip back half of it before Potts speaks. "How many dead down there?"

"I didn't count. Could be seventy or eighty."

"I want to burn it all up. Burn away the white scabs. Maybe we get good and drunk and we burn it all up."

"I'm game."

"Cock suck, white scabs," Potts mutters, lips fumbling against the mouth of the bottle. "Dirty bastard, son of a bitch, arse kiss white scabs. White scab English buggers." He goes on like this for a goodly while, stopping and starting. We run out of whisky a long time after he runs out of his stock of English curse words, ways to string them together, arrange and rearrange them.

Then we stagger off, set the lodges alight, torch the whole village to the ground. Aloysius and a few others wander down to investigate the fireworks, but only he and I stay to hear Potts chant some Blackfoot mourning song for the dead. Aloysius keeps his head bowed the whole time, as if he was in church, and when Potts finishes, Aloysius informs me those lodges aflame remind him of the candles his mother used to light to the Virgin Mary.

❖ ❖ ❖

LUCY My chores finished and everything shipshape, as the sun goes down I bundle up a blanket and slip off. When I'm well hid behind a knob of hill, I spread the blanket on the grass, shed every speck of my clothes, lay down on it, let the air play on my skin. I imagine myself white and burning, a lantern in the dark to lead Charles to our meeting in this place. All about, there's a lovely smell, sharp and tangy like that boxwood box I once sniffed in a mercantile when I was a girl.

A pink glow is trembling just above that low ridge to the east. Every once in a while it flicks up in the dusk. The fire the half-breed and Straw started in the Indian camp isn't done burning yet.

Directly above me, the heavens are a black quilt, sewn up tight with more star stitching than a body could ever count. I wonder up at them. A long time stared at, they set to jigging and whirling, cutting capers in my eyes. I recollect when I was still years short of school, one night Mother took her baby girl by the hand, led her outside, pointed to the sky, and said, "Lucy, here's a secret for you. Heaven's lights is the brightness of children's souls gone over. See all them dancing, happy children up there? Not a one of them with a care in the world because they can see everyone they loved below and are waiting for them to rise, join them, fly up from earth to heaven in a streak of light. And God put them there for us to ponder, to help us remember to be good. So we can join them."

Well, not everyone of us is going to shoot to heaven. Abner Stoveall sure as hell didn't. But funny how the dead do change in your heart. Now Abner doesn't seem worth wasting a hard word on. I can't hate him any more. We two struck a bargain, and there's nary a party to a bargain who doesn't suspect they caught the short end of the stick. I know I felt so and I'd be mighty surprised if Abner didn't feel the same.

He had his share of disappointments in life. Wisdom pushing him to the wall, making him feel little and puny. Me no different, I reckon, shoving him off every time he crawled into bed. I used to think Abner couldn't feel a thing, but he must have felt his smallness in the world. Was a time I wanted him harmed, and now I have my wish, it's a thin and sour taste, not a bit of satisfaction to it.

No, Abner wasn't the sort to blaze a path to heaven and neither am I. Me with a sharp tongue to twist his guts, and him with hard hands to raise welts. Madge was the one made to sail up on high, easy as fluff on God's breath. If she's looking down now, what would she make of me, laying stripped and white, waiting for a man? Probably, she'd whisper to me to take my tiny piece of happiness, hold its honey in my mouth till it melts away. Don't risk my short share of it meddling with the Kelsos. I can hear her now. "Leave it to God." Well, I can't leave it to God. I don't see God hereabouts. There's only Lucy Stoveall.

But I'm frightened. Soon as you get hold of a bit of joy, it wants to slip through your fingers. I reckoned me and Madge would be in San Francisco before winter. Charles wants to hold me tight, yet I've got to struggle out of his arms, free myself from them to do my dire work.

So I lay here on my blanket and try to think another matter besides tomorrow. I wonder if maybe to the stars above I might look a star, a little bit of blinking white on this almighty big black plain.

He's here, my Charles. I didn't catch his footsteps with my thoughts drifting in the sky, but now I hear his voice, quiet and tender. "Lucy, darling." He's already busy shucking his clothes in a rush of hurry, and soon he's above me, pale and shimmery in the night, slowly sinking down beside me. Two stars now, I tell myself. Two stars.

His skin is soft as butter to my fingers, his mouth all the sweeter to me for knowing what he doesn't, that it's the last time.

I can count the people I've loved on one hand and he's the only one that's left. Now I've got to turn my thumb down and over. Make a fist.

20

ALOYSIUS I can't plumb it. Lucy Stoveall left a letter for Charles Gaunt saying she's headed back to Fort Benton and does a flit in the middle of the night on Custis's Morgan. Nobody knows why.

Charles Gaunt was terrible wrought up over her departure. He and the rest trooped out after her a while ago, leaving the two invalids and me behind to keep watch over the camp, protect the Captain's precious marmalade from marauders.

In the midst of the hubbub, Custis just sat by the fire, not saying so much as a word, duster draped over his shoulders, poking the embers with a stick, looking like death warmed over. The last couple of days the rims of his eyelids have turned a queer bottle-glass blue; the man's whole colour has gone splotchy and bad. That session of dry heaves he had out behind the wagon this morning, the cause of it weren't all that Scottish whisky he put down his drain last night with Jerry Potts. It's the lack of the laudanum – I believe he's run out.

All of a sudden, Custis gets to his feet, marches quickly to his horse, and tosses a saddle blanket on him. I go to investigate. "What's all this, Custis?"

"I'm going after Lucy Stoveall," he says. "The Gaunts are headed in the wrong direction."

"How do you know?"

"It just came to me."

"I thought you weren't fit to ride."

235

"I am now."

"You reckon to spread your news to the Gaunts?"

"Let the Gaunts go. That hothead Captain would only be a detriment in this situation."

What the situation is he don't say. Custis's tightening his cinch. "I'm in a hurry, Aloysius. I've got no time to answer any more of your questions."

So I get in a hurry too. When Custis sees me collecting my tack, he don't say yea or nay to my going with him. In minutes, we're headed out of camp, and old Chisholm is waving us goodbye, all forlorn and glum at his company abandoning him.

After a bit, I finally get Custis to loosen his tongue. It's his opinion that Lucy Stoveall is making for the Kelso boys' whisky post. That purely flabbergasts me. "Why ever would she do that?"

"Yesterday, she hears they killed her husband and never says a thing. Doesn't that strike you as strange? I offer to take her to Fort Benton and she refuses me. In the middle of the night she steals a horse and takes off."

"Them ain't any kind of convincing reasons."

"Well, I'm not reasoning it, I'm feeling that's the case. That's where she's gone."

He's stumped me with that. You can't argue with a hunch, so I just go quiet and trot along with him, thinking of how unlikely it is that the Kelsos will be glad to see us. At least, Custis's familiar with this country. Five years ago he come up here to try to buy horses from the Blackfoot, which was no success at all because they wouldn't trade for nothing but whisky or guns and he refused to sell them either. So Custis got nothing out of the enterprise excepting a knowledge of the lie of the land, which is handy at the moment. Chisholm said the Kelsos was holed up on the east bank of the Saskatchewan about twenty miles from where we found the old boy in the smallpox camp. What Custis proposes is we strike the juncture of the Red Deer and Saskatchewan, then work our way north until we come upon the dugout.

After a two-hour ride, we reach what Custis calls the Bull's Forehead, a bluff overlooking the spot where the waters of the two rivers mingle. We ease our horses into the shallows so's they can drink. The matted grass on the slope of the Bull's Forehead looks like a tangle of buffalo wool, shines tawny when the sun hits it at the right angle. Custis gives it one quick look, then proceeds to run his eyes over the bare, humped hills on the east riverbank. Once he's satisfied there's no whisky post nigh, he pulls off his hat, wipes his brow, and slumps over the saddle horn, breathing heavy. All the strength just seems to have run clean out of him. "We ought to have brought along a bottle," he remarks.

"No," I says, "we oughtn't to have toted no whisky. Not on this business."

Custis is sick and trembly. Whatever the cause, a shortage of laudanum, or some ailment working in him, some marrow ache or blood souring, only pure stubbornness is keeping him going. I just hope to God it ain't the smallpox.

Straightening up slowly, he settles his hat back to his head. "We best keep down in the brush near the river, Aloysius. It might hide us if the Kelsos are watching above. You take the lead. Dan's a quiet horse, he'll follow yours. I want to keep my eyes trained on the hills, watch to make sure we don't miss that post."

We go on, weaving through the cottonwood and poplar, skirting thickets of willows. Prairie chicken and grouse flush from the grass, whir away. A doe starts from a shady bed under a clump of choke-cherry bush, flashes us her tail, and bounds into a stand of saplings. For such a delicate thing, she rattles a lot of noise out of the brush. There's no lack of game about, and where there's game there's likely to be Indians. God contrived Aloysius Dooley for a trade where his hands stay clean, one conducted under a ceiling for the pleasure and contentment of mankind. That's why he chose me for a publican and not a Indian fighter.

Some rotten windfall blocks our way and we got to shift down to the riverbank to bypass it. I spot hoof prints in the mud. They ain't cracked and dried, they're recent. I call Straw's attention to the tracks and he gives them the once-over. "Indian pony?" I ask.

Wearily, Straw drags himself back into the saddle. "The horse was shod. It's the Morgan." I'm confounded. Straw's guess about Lucy Stoveall was right on the money against all likelihood. "She's no fool," he says. "She was listening careful to what Chisholm had to say. I calculate she had a three- or four-hour headstart on us." He gives me a nod. "Let's shake some hurry out of these horses, Aloysius." He gives Dan a kick and we lope off, the two of us barrelling through the trees, Custis swinging his bulk from side to side in the saddle, hanging his nose to the ground like a bird dog, scanning for the Morgan's marks. After what seems like three or four mile, the valley bottom widens into a stretch of high grass, berry bushes, and big groves of cottonwood growing near the Saskatchewan. The river's gone broader here, the current lazier; the water's low and muddy brown, spotted with sandbars and timber snags. One of the snags looks like a black water beetle ready to scoot off on crazy legs. To our right, there's nothing to see but sky and the dusty river hills piled on one another's shoulders.

Custis reins in, shades his eyes with his hand, inspects the hills. "It smells close," he says, turning to peer at the Saskatchewan where a string of sandbars lays a wobbly line across the river. A man could hop from one to the other, cross and never get his feet wet. Custis points, "That might be the Indian ford. Chisholm did say the Kelsos set up shop near a crossing." Suddenly all his attention fixes on a clump of poplar a couple hundred yards directly ahead of us. "Aloysius," he says quietly, "dismount. But act like you mean to check your cinch. Turn your horse so he's between you and those trees." Already Custis is stepping down from Dan, wheeling him around. I follow suit. Custis draws the big Sharps buffalo gun from its scabbard, eyes the poplars over the saddle seat. I ain't got no weapon but my cutdown shotgun from behind the bar of the Stubhorn. At this range I might just as well chuck rocks.

When I give my lips a lick, my tongue sticks to them. "What's spooked you, Custis?" But before he can answer, I see what it is, sudden, quick flashes of light breaking at the edge of the thicket.

"Could be sunlight shining off rifle barrels," he mutters.

I cast about me, trying to spy some place for us to take cover. There ain't none. Straw carries two rifles on his saddle, the buffalo gun and a Henry repeater. I'm about to ask for the loan of the repeater when he pulls a telescope from his saddlebags. The one I've often seen the English Captain peering through. I know at once that Custis had to have pinched that glass from Addington Gaunt's own saddlebags before they set out this morning. Custis was hatching this plan the very minute he learned Lucy Stoveall was gone. Going after her weren't no sudden notion like he said. He lied to me. It ain't a thing to do to a friend.

Holding the glass on the hot, blinking lights, a smile breaks on his face. "Take a gander, Aloysius." I put my eye to the telescope he hands me. Nothing but empty whisky bottles strung up in trees, dancing in the breeze.

"The Kelsos did some sign-painting Indians could read. Spelled out their wares," Custis says. "Just beyond that grove, up in the hills is where we'll find their dugout." Already he's got his boot in the stirrup. "Let's get into those poplars smartly. With any luck the Kelsos won't spot us."

We gallop to the clump of trees, tether the horses out of sight. All about me bottles are twinkling and tinkling. Custis's turned bone-white, streaming sweat, panting.

"Custis?"

"I've got a touch of stomach complaint," he says. Then he stoops and pukes, mostly air. When he's done, he leans against a sapling for a time, swabbing his face with his sleeve. "I'll be fine," he says. "Let's go." Off he leads me through the bottle-prettied saplings to a spot on the east side of the poplars where we gain a good view of the hills. We crouch there, sunlight spattering our faces while the poplar leaves quake in a breeze so small it don't even dry the sweat on Custis's face.

I can see the Kelso post, the black mouth of the dugout gaping wide in a sugarloaf hill. Three horses picketed near the entrance, one of them the Morgan.

Custis squats on his hams, shoulders hunched, eyes hooded, mouth a slit, staring at the post. Without a word, he rises and starts back to where we tied the horses, slamming his big body through the undergrowth in a desperate rush. I tear after him, brush slapping and clawing me. When I catch him, he's already busy with his pocketknife, stripping twine from bottles he's cut down from the trees, splicing the cords together with reef knots. He holds up about four foot of splicing, snaps it, testing the knots. "Go get your sawed-off," he says.

I go to my horse and collect the twelve gauge, hand it over to him. Custis works neat and quick. Passing the cord through the trigger guard, he ties it off in a sling, shrugs out of his duster, turns the right-hand pocket inside out, slashes the bottom with the clasp knife, slides his hand to and fro through the hole, wriggling his fingers. He slings the sawed-off over his shoulder. The gun hangs straight down flush to his side, the grip of the stock riding level with his hand, the tip of the barrel hanging midway to his calf. He unbuckles his holster, tosses the revolver at my feet. Puts the duster back on. The cut-down shotgun disappears, hid by the length of the coat.

He lifts his eyes to me. "I aim to pay the Kelsos a visit." Flicking a finger to the holster and pistol lying at my feet, he says, "I'm leaving the Remington and the Sharps with you. I've got no idea what Lucy Stoveall's doing up there, but I'm not about to rule out that she's fallen into trouble. Especially if Titus gets it in his head to make some. Give me an hour – if I don't show after that – scoot as fast as ever you can back to the wagons. Get Potts. I reckon by now he'll have figured out Lucy Stoveall's sent them off on a wild goose chase. With any luck, he'll have persuaded that flighty Captain to return to camp. Rely on Potts and only Potts."

I clear my throat. "I ain't about to desert you, Custis."

"If I don't bring Lucy Stoveall out of there, it'll be because I've been stopped. No desertion involved then. If some misfortune has befallen her, and befalls me in turn, you're the only one who'll know it, and know the Kelsos' whereabouts."

There's a long, deadly-feeling moment of silence as he works on me with his eyes, trying to will me to do as he says. Then some woodpecker starts clattering, knocking his brains out for a grub. Custis's doing up his duster careful, patting each button once he gets it into its hole, like it was a baby's head. When we shake hands, I feel how his fingers tremble so. We don't say a word. Custis pulls himself aboard Dan, and turns the gelding for the Kelsos' post. I got nothing to do but watch Custis pick his way up the slope, shoulders sagged, head bobbling loose on his neck.

CUSTIS They must've noticed me by now. Two visitors in the space of half a day – it's got to make them wonder. I only hope Titus doesn't decide to shoot me off this saddle the way he shot Abner Stoveall off his wagon seat before I make it up there.

Dan is intolerant of hurry on hills. He doesn't like climbing them, or going down them. His nature is slow and deliberate and there's a lesson to learn from it. He looks before he places his feet. Yards from their door, I hail the Kelso boys just as any innocent wayfarer might, give honest warning. "Hello there! Titus Kelso! You open for business!" My shout pricks Dan's ears, halts him. We both wait. "Anybody to home!"

"What you want, Straw?" It's Titus, but he doesn't show himself, keeps to the gloom of his cave.

"I see Lucy Stoveall's horse standing by your door. I want a word with her."

Titus steps out of the mouth of the dugout, a carbine levelled at me. "She don't want to be bothered by no visitors. So take yourself off my prope'ty."

"Steady on now, Titus. All I ask is for you to send her out, so I can hear how it stands with her from her own lips."

"I'll send you a bullet through the brain, that's what I'll send you, Straw."

I smile quiet and talk quiet to try to make him easy. "You'd only lose money by acting so hasty, Titus. I have a paying proposition for you. Let's discuss it."

241

The boy has grown himself a beard since he shot my pig and absconded on me. The beard hides his features, but I can read the calculation in his grey eyes. Titus doesn't lower his gun barrel. He is distrustful, but he's also a right greedy bastard, so I keep at him. "Let's go inside and be sociable. Have a drink. Chasing a woman is thirsty work."

He orders me off Dan and wants to see my weapons. I tell him my only firearm is the Henry in the sheath on the saddle. Next, I have to empty my pockets for him. There's nothing in them but my Bible. Last of all, I must open my coat and fan it for him. I move careful as I can, hoping the rig I patched together will work as I hoped. I pinch the twine sling in the cloth of the duster and ease back the coat. The sawed-off shifts with the cloth as I slowly draw it open, settles behind my right leg while I stand there displaying myself so Titus knows I'm not wearing a gun belt.

"All right, come on in," he says grudgingly.

Soon as I step across the threshold, I smell cool, dank earth, a whiff of the grave. I survey the place. Empty whisky boxes for chairs. A wall of crates stacked at the back of the dugout. Directly before the crates, in a pool of light cast by a coal oil lamp, Lucy Stoveall kneels in the dirt, hands tied behind her back, a stick lashed in her mouth. Joel Kelso stands guard beside her, a carbine in his hands. When I take a step towards her, Lucy drops her head to the dirt, as if to hold me off. Joel waves me off with the rifle. His eyes are scared and his mouth is worried. "Hello, Joel," I say. For a moment, he looks about to make reply, but then he tightens his lips and does his best to make his weak mouth and watery eyes look scornful. It doesn't come natural to him as it does his brother. That boy was born to be nothing but a follower.

"There's the parcel you come to pick up," says Titus. "All tied up with sealing wax and string." At the sound of his voice, Lucy lifts her eyes from the dirt floor and glares at him. I've never seen such hate. Two threads of blood run from the corners of her mouth down her chin. There's a lump on her forehead and a bruise on her cheek.

I clench down my anger because I know Titus is goading me, wants to see me flare. "Loose her, Titus," I say, as level as I can.

"No, sir, I won't. That woman has got to learn some manners. Why she just rode up here this morning bold as brass and when I come out to make welcome, she put a big old horse pistol on me and started firing. But thank you, Jesus, the caps was bad and they just popped like an old woman's farts. I dragged the bitch down off her horse, and I handed her a proper good hiding, but she kept on screeching. Nothing for it, but we had to truss her up just to get some quiet. Ever since, Joel and me been turning over in our minds a proper punishment for her. What do you think it ought to be, Straw?"

"Take the stick out of her mouth. She's bleeding."

"You make a dirty accusation against Titus Kelso, that's what you get – a hard bit in the mouth. Why, your blessed parcel said I raped and killed her sister. Hell, I didn't even know the little cunny was dead. It's a shame. I always did want to stick my peeder in her."

Lucy Stoveall starts to cry. I can see her shoulders shaking and the tears spilling down her face, but she doesn't let a sound escape her. My hands won't stop shaking, even the one I've got pushed through the hole in my pocket and latched on to the grip of Aloysius's twelve gauge. I settle down on a box, keep the cutdown tight against my leg. I need medicating bad. "All right then. One thing at a time, Titus. Let us have a drink and be sociable."

"A drink is a dollar, Straw."

Titus learned one lesson from his encounter with Abner Stoveall. No free drinks in the liquor traffic. "All right, set up three. It's on me." I pause. "Just so you don't get the wrong idea – I'm going into my trouser pocket for cash, nothing more." Titus glowers as I pinch a half-eagle out of my pants. "Can you make change?"

"You see a till anywheres about?"

"Well, then we'll drink five dollars' worth the first round. See where it gets us. Take it from there."

Titus gives Joel an abrupt nod and his brother slouches off, brings back three tin mugs of whisky. Looks to me as if he short-poured mine, but Titus probably practised him on light measures. The first swallow braces me, tamps down the tremors a little. Whisky is a mellowing potation and I hope it effects Titus so. He could use it. He's still watching me sharp-eyed, particularly my quivery hands.

"How's business been, boys? Profitable?"

"Fuck you and the horse you rode in on." The angry expression Titus wears tells me that I've touched a tender spot. Apparently, the whisky trade hasn't lived up to Titus Kelso's high expectations. He squints at me. "Keep your questions to yourself so's you can hear mine. Here's the first. How did that woman and you know where we was at?"

I was hoping he might neglect to put that to me. The Bible says the truth shall set you free, so I wager on the truth. "From Matt Chisholm."

"Tite?" squeaks Joel. He's brimful of surprise. Titus shoots him a look.

"Chisholm's alive," I say. "Right now, he's with our party." I pause. "These are lawless parts, gentlemen. I understand you had a falling out with Abner Stoveall and Black Pompey. It's no concern of mine what course it took, or how it was settled. I wouldn't have darkened your door if Mrs. Stoveall hadn't lost all common sense and come here."

"Old Straw had to follow his cunny," Titus sneers.

I aim to keep the talk flowing so anger doesn't find a space to boil over. "However you put it, Titus. Yes, I came after Lucy Stoveall, but with no intention of making trouble. You know my reputation, Titus. I've got no use for guns. I'm a peaceable man. But I want that woman, boys, and I'm willing to pay you to release her. As much as a thousand dollars."

"Time was a man could buy hisself a nigger for a thousand dollars. You don't rate Lucy Stoveall higher'n a nigger, Straw?" sneers Titus.

It's plain how badly Joel wants to get shut of here; it's all over his face. He just needs somebody to frame the reasons for why they ought to pull foot. "Maybe you haven't heard, Titus, but there's smallpox among the Blackfoot. We happened on one of their camps. Everybody in it was dead. My forecast is customers are likely to be scarce. And if they do show, they'll be nettled and take what they want rather than pay for it. This is no place to loiter, boys."

"Take his money, Tite," says Joel.

"Shut your piehole. I'm thinking."

"Just to keep everybody mild and reasonable. I'll season the pot for persuasion. Two thousand."

Joel and I watch him ponder the offer. "All right," Titus says at last. "For cash money, delivered here, you can have the woman."

I've cleared one hurdle, but not the most important one. "No, I won't do that. I have to take Lucy Stoveall with me. I'm sorry to say it, Titus, but you're not a man to leave a woman with."

Titus spits, the gob lands between my feet. "You sit down to sup with the devil, you need a long spoon. You ain't talking to Joel, Straw. How simple you think I am? Once you get her away – what would bring you back with the money?"

"My word."

"Your word ain't worth nothing to me. It's froth on a cup of piss."

"All right then, here is what I'll do. I'll write you a bearer's note to take to I. G. Baker in Fort Benton. He'll cash it, no questions asked. Joel can stay here and keep watch over us until you get back with the money."

"I ain't staying here!" squeals Joel. "Not with smallpox on the rampage through the Blackfoot and them blaming white folks for it!"

"For two thousand dollars you'll sit here until hell freezes over," says Titus. He bobs his head at me, "Write it."

I take the Good Book from my pocket, rip out an endpaper, commence composing the document with a stub of pencil. I doubt either of the Kelsos are handy readers so I print the words, sign, pass it over for approval. Titus lights a tallow candle and stands it on a box, pores over the contents, lips mumbling every word.

A draft in the dugout causes the candle to gutter, bobble its flame. When I look away, tiny coloured dots start to swim in the murk of the cave. There's a familiar tightening at the base of my skull, a dull, dead ache swelling behind my eyeballs.

Then I hear Titus. "You ain't half so smart as you think, Straw."

I look up. Titus is on his feet, the daylight creeping into the mouth of the dugout flaring fuzz above his head and shoulders. The shape of his body is dark, uncertain. He waves the paper, a blurry streak in the air. "I got your note in my hand. I got you in my hand." He moves towards Lucy crouched in the dirt, takes hold of the stick in her mouth, waggles her head back and forth, sends her red hair flying. "I got your woman in my hand."

The megrim is spreading a smudgy haze over my eyes, warping Titus in a carnival mirror. I peer so hard trying to see him that at first it doesn't sink in, what he's said. Then I behold it plain.

"So you mean to kill us, Titus."

I see him through a smeared window, hear a smirking voice. "Custis, what you take me for? I ain't about to kill no woman. You're as bad as her, accusing me of woman-killing. I got to train her out of such evil supposing. Show her what a sweet, considerate rider Titus Kelso is. I got my good reputation with the ladies to consider."

My hand is tight on the twelve gauge. I have to shift him away from Lucy Stovall. "Titus Kelso, the best part of you dripped down your mother's leg."

"What did you say?" Fury is hot and thick in his throat.

"You are a coward, Titus," I say, as even and cool as I am able. "It runs in the Kelsos, cowardice and low behaviour. Your father was the same. But you go him one better, boy. You are a devious, puke-eating dog. You're some desperado, Titus. So far you've murdered a pig, a little girl, an old man, and a Negro you couldn't face up to, but shot in the back."

Slippery, bloated, Titus floats towards me in a pond of wavy light. "We'll see what I can do," he says, and slaps my face so hard he near twists me off my seat. I hear him right over me, panting.

"Why you got your eyes closed, Straw? You praying? Is that it? Asking Jesus to spare you?"

I've shut my eyes against the shifting shapes, the hard pokes of light. I open them and there Titus is, swaying before me. From a far place, I hear my voice. "I thought I was finished with this," it says, taking me by surprise even as I cock the twelve gauge.

"Finished with this? Not by a long shot, Straw. We just got started."

I lift the barrel of the sawed-off under my duster and touch the muzzle to his thigh. Titus jerks with the explosion; fingers rake my neck, tearing at me, trying to break his sudden plunge to the dirt floor. I stagger up, kicking at the arms clutching at my legs, ripping open the duster, directing the barrel to the shadow bobbling in the back of the dugout. "Throw down! Throw down, Joel! Goddamn it, throw down or I'll give you the other barrel!" Something breaks off his silhouette, hits the dirt floor with a thump. He's dropped the carbine. I wave him towards Lucy. "Unbind her! Now! Do it, Joel!"

I feel heat on my leg, glance down to see little flames licking the shredded cloth of my duster that the muzzle flash of my shotgun has set alight. I shrug off the coat, let it drop.

Behind me, Titus starts to shriek. I've heard that sound many times before. The noise a man makes when he clutches bone splinters, mangled flesh. A man doing his best to stem the tide of life running out of him, trying to hold back the loss of two pints of blood a minute, push it back into himself with red, soaked hands. The sight of his wrecked flesh making him scream as much as the pain.

A bleary shape springs at me. "Custis?" Lucy Stoveall says. "Custis, you all right?"

It rises up in me now, rage at her recklessness, and what it brought me to do. Joel is croaking away at his brother from the back of the dugout. "Hold on, Titus. You'll be fine. Just hold on."

Nothing could be further from the truth. I've put Titus beyond earthly help. So I take it out on Joel, holler I don't want to hear another goddamn word from his mouth. He tries to oblige, resorts to little moans and whimpers.

"Collect Joel's gun," I tell Lucy. "Collect the horses. Dooley's waiting down below. Tell him everything's fine. Tell him I'll be out directly."

"I don't take a step until I see Titus Kelso gone from this earth," she says fiercely.

"He's one breath short of dead. Listen."

Lucy Stoveall turns to look at the wounded man, but I refuse to, keep my back to him. Kelso's stopped screaming. A soft muttering crawls over the floor behind me. "This ain't right. This can't be right. What is this? What's all this? How'd this happen? This can't be right."

"It's right," Lucy tells him.

I feel her leave my side, go to collect Joel's carbine. Titus breaks off muttering and there's nothing but the sound of his laboured breathing, short gasps sawing away at the threads of his life. I don't have to look to know that that buckshot blast took the most of his leg away.

Lucy Stoveall's blurred face swings into view, hovers white and wan. "The other one too," she says. "Both of them dead."

I don't respond. My thoughts are scattering on me. I want silence. I want time to remember if I ever saw that belt on Titus Kelso.

"Straw, they killed my sister," she whispers.

Titus Kelso's last breath leaves his lungs, a harsh sigh.

"It's over," I tell her. "Take yourself out of here, woman. You don't need to see what's left to do."

For a moment, Lucy Stoveall hesitates, but then I hear footsteps moving to the entrance of the dugout and the horses nickering a welcome.

I beckon Joel forward. He scrapes his boots across the dirt floor towards me. "Did you have any hand in what happened to Madge Dray?"

He shakes his head violently, it flashes back and forth in my troubled vision.

"Madge Dray was strangled with a belt. Titus ever own a black belt, three brass studs on its tongue?"

"No, sir."

"That came out too quick, Joel. That's how a goddamn liar answers. I'm going to ask you again. Think hard. If you lie, I'll send you after Titus. Did your brother ever own a black belt with brass studs?"

There comes a long pause, then a frightened voice. "Yes," he says.

"All right, son. Get on your belly." He's blubbering now, wheezy, flabby sobs. I realize he must be lying face to face with his brother's corpse on the floor. "Joel? Joel? I'm going to back out of here now. When I get to the door, I'm going to let off a barrel. Lucy Stoveall hears a shot, she'll believe I did what she asked. Killed you. But if you show yourself before we're gone – I can't answer for your life. You understand?" He doesn't reply. "Don't think of returning to Fort Benton. You keep clear of us. Understand?"

I start stepping backward, one heel following another. My boot skids in a puddle of Titus's blood and I almost go down. I keep edging away. The light changes, grows bigger and more hurtful in my head, telling me I'm near the entrance.

All at once, Joel starts to shout. "I lied! I lied! Tite never had no such belt! You wanted me to lie, so I lied, Straw! You murdering bastard!"

I lift the sawed-off, point it into the blackness, pull the trigger, because Lucy Stoveall is waiting for that sound down in the trees, at the bottom of the hill.

21

LUCY Sometimes I feel trouble hangs to my skirts. That I'm a Jonah. By the time we got back to our camp, Straw was all in a sweat, reeling about, hardly able to hold his seat in the saddle. Dooley laid no accusation at my door, but I could see it in his face that somehow he believed what had happened to his friend was my doing. When Dooley and Chisholm took Straw off on that travois, so parlous sick, to get him aid in Fort Benton, it was a sorrow to me to think how I never gave Custis Straw his due, or showed him gratefulness, and now he's broken and laid so low.

Charles said it was outside a woman's character to do as I did. I believe it scared him, thinking I was one thing when I was another. He read me a sermon. I took it without answering back because I saw how afraid for me he had been. I held my tongue when he said, "Even grief has its bounds, Lucy." But my grief delivered the Kelsos into righteous hands. Custis Straw broke them apart like mealy, weeviled biscuits. They're dust and crumbs now. I ought to kiss Straw's hands for it.

That night though, Charles showed me tender forgiveness. Just touched his lips to the bruise Titus Kelso's fist put on my face, said, "Be at peace, dear Lucy. Be at peace." I hid my face in his neck, and shed hot tears for raising disturbance in his mind. I believe he cried then too, glad to have me safe. Charles made me promise that I would never leave again without explaining my reasons, truthfully. I knew his precious regard for me then.

It might be high summer all about but inside me everything is fall. The lonesomeness of a sad, slow closing down, knowing frost is nigh and wind needling through the cabin chinks is just around the bend. That's me, right now. I won't fool myself, no matter how tight he holds to me. What I got for a season is Charles, but I'm not fool enough to think this is going to last. It's but a short walk into winter for me, and I lose him.

For two days we moved north, then cut west to the Saskatchewan River and headed for the old ford I overheard Potts telling the Captain about. The one the Hudson Bay men used to reach Chesterfield House, a post they once had in these parts. According to the guide, the Blackfoot ran them out and burned Chesterfield House to the ground some fifty years ago, but we found the cart tracks plain in the sod, pointing to where it likely stood. Once Mr. Addington saw that, he was hot iron to locate the remains of what he called "Britain's Troy." Said it would be a "momentous discovery." He sent the half-breed gallivanting about the district until Potts spied some low spots, old cellar holes sunk in the ground.

For two days the Captain set Grunewald and Barker to digging, but all they turned up was a few musket balls and lead trade tokens. I don't know what the Captain hoped to find, but he wasn't after musket balls. It was a disappointment to him, and he fast lost his passion for ruins. For the present, however, he's right happy. A big herd of buffalo, the biggest we've seen so far, moved across to this side of the Saskatchewan. The river boiled with them when they came over the ford, you could hardly hear yourself think for the roaring, bellowing din they made. So the Captain has been chasing them over the plains, slaughtering every one he can lay his sights on. Last night, we had nothing but tongues for our supper.

Charles and me took up where the Captain left off digging, relieved Grunewald and Barker of their mattocks and shovels. They were joyful to hand them over. Charles said he wished to show his brother that at least one Gaunt could hold to a purpose and finish a thing, but I figure what he really wanted was to work off his exasperation with yet another delay at his brother's hand. In an hour he blistered his palms, but still he was happy as a lark, the two of us side by side, heaving ground like we were bound for China. But there was no booty found except for a blue bottle stamped *London Town* and a couple of four-foot-long, hand-forged nails for pinning logs.

We shifted to a hummock, attacked that, and uncovered a nest of crumbly buffalo bones stacked three feet high, sign of how those old-time traders once feasted their winters away.

It's peaceful here. It pleasures me to see Charles dig the ground, draw his pictures. When he paints, he talks to me as he goes, explains the why of his lines and colours. He gives me my own paper and I try to do likewise. When I took Madge's portrait and made to draw it, my hand failed me. I thought if I could draw my sister, it would put her in my mind more steady. My hand would help my brain remember her.

Sometimes Charles puts his fingers on mine to help move the pencil, shows me how you're supposed to do, face close to my face. That drawing touch of his is almost as fine to me as his loving touch when we lie together at night, all soft and smooth and hot – until the muscle sob comes that Abner never gave me, the sudden clutch for Charles's seed. After that, the autumn sadness swells up in me. Looking up at the stars, I think about how we sneak about and hide ourselves from the Captain. The secret shame I am.

In the darkness, I borrow Charles's eyes. This is how I am in his sight. His shoes are on my feet. My hands are big-knuckled from pulling cows' teats all my life. Nothing but two dresses to my name. One linsey woolsey, one calico. Neither store-bought. Each one as tatty as the other. I'm freckled all over my body. I never owned a china teapot. I never danced a waltz. I'll do for the wilderness, where nobody who counts can see me. But if Charles Gaunt was to cross my path in some bustly town like St. Louis, he wouldn't notice me for the ladies with parasols and shot-silk dresses capturing his eye. I'd disappear.

Charles is eager to get on Simon's trail, but I've got nothing left to chase. It's over for me. Hot revenge was what used to heat my heart, but now there's nothing to warm me but Charles Gaunt. I'm cold ashes and cinders but for him.

❖ ❖ ❖

Dr. Bengough rises at four a.m., performs his ablutions at the wash basin cursorily, the rest of his toilet fastidiously, combing his goatee, brushing his white hair and black frock coat with the same brush, wiping his silk top hat with the bedsheet. After a bracing draft of snuff, he smooths kid gloves on his hands, takes up his medical bag, closes the door on the rented rooms that serve him both as surgery and living quarters. More than one patient has undergone the extraction of a molar in Dr. Bengough's easy chair. There are blood stains there testifying to countless dental agonies.

Dr. Bengough is about to make a call on Custis Straw in his room above the Stubhorn. Ten days ago, Aloysius Dooley and a man called Chisholm trundled a recumbent Straw into Fort Benton on a jerry-built travois hauled by Straw's horse. Dooley, fearing his friend had been stricken by smallpox, brought him posthaste to medical attention. Chisholm, too, fell into Dr. Bengough's care because of a case of badly infected feet, but despite a good deal of probing for embedded cactus thorns, and dousing with alcohol, the hardy old fellow was soon up and about, a fixture at every saloon in town.

Straw is a different kettle of fish, a most perplexing case. The one thing Dr. Bengough is certain of is that Straw's affliction is not smallpox. There has been no eruption of pustules. What there has been is a plethora of contradictory symptoms. At first, the appearance of premonitory diarrhoea suggested cholera, and Dr. Bengough immediately prescribed twenty-five drops of laudanum mixed with acetate of lead and bismuth to be administered following every movement of the bowels. The only effect of the medicine was to sink Straw into deep insensibility for fourteen hours. The incontinence continued unabated, copious amounts of blood present in the stool.

Deciding a complete, recent medical history was necessary, Dr. Bengough subjected Dooley to a thorough quizzing. The Irishman reported that Straw had been "poorly" immediately before his violent encounter with the Kelsos, but in its aftermath he had gone into a precipitous decline, the fever attacking with full force. Dooley's opinion was that whatever had occurred between the Kelsos and Straw had "unhinged" him. "I know it was justice," Dooley said to Dr. Bengough. "But there was a good deal of time between the first and second shot. Killing Titus was in the region of self-defence, but it troubles me to think Custis executed Joel cold-blooded. We ought to have brought the scoundrel back to Benton and turned him over to the law."

Dr. Bengough dismissed Dooley's conjecture about the genesis of Straw's malady because, for a layman, the hallucinations produced by the fever could easily be mistaken for lunacy. For the first few days, Straw's physical and mental agitation had proved so violent it was necessary to tie him to the bed to prevent him doing injury to himself or anyone attending him.

In forty-five years practising medicine, Dr. Bengough has learned that a physician is more a tactician than a strategist, that illness, like battle, is unpredictable, and that it is best to respond to every advance of a disease with an equally vigorous counter-thrust. He knows that one malady can mask a more dangerous underlying one, present confusing symptoms that lay a false trail for even the most skilful medical practitioner. After a week, he had concluded that Straw's mental and bodily paroxysms suggested the real danger was brain fever.

The barber was summoned, and Dr. Bengough and Dooley held down Straw, kept him as still as possible while his head was shorn. Dr. Bengough had ordered a cooling bath of rubbing alcohol to be applied hourly to the denuded scalp, but after several days this course of treatment did not ameliorate the fever. Straw still continues to thrash about, bellowing, his mind seemingly enmeshed in the bloody snares of former battlefields.

Walking up the still street towards the Stubhorn, Dr. Bengough is at his wit's end as to how to prevail against this mysterious, implacable illness. A professional aloofness in Straw's case is impossible.

There is too great an affection between them. Of all the men in Fort Benton, Straw, despite his lack of formal education, is the most congenial and stimulating. True, he has no Latin, no Greek, and knows little of Shakespeare or Milton. Yet his intelligence is formidable. One day, halfway into a bottle of Monongahela, Straw made a telling remark during one of their philosophical debates. "I may be ignorant, Dr. Bengough, but I'm not stupid. The difference between ignorant and stupid is that ignorance can be corrected and stupidity can't."

Dr. Bengough had saluted Straw by raising his glass and grandly declaiming, " 'The rest to some slight meaning make pretence, / But Shadwell never deviates into sense.' "

"I don't know Shadwell," Straw replied. "But I'll take your word on it." Then he shot his friend one of his wry, knowing smiles and said, "I don't have anything against poetry, so long as you don't use it to put a man in his place."

At present, Dr. Bengough wonders what he himself is about to deviate into – sense or nonsense. His medical training, commenced nearly a half-century ago, and which had immersed him in the principles of Dr. Benjamin Rush, illustrious Professor of the Institutes of Medicine at the University of Pennsylvania, a man regarded reverently by his disciples as the "Hippocrates of American Medicine," has returned to him. Younger physicians now have nothing but contempt for Dr. Rush's theories of "puking and purging." Dr. Bengough has, over the years, departed from Dr. Rush's teaching, so as to be considered a man of science and not a contemptible old fossil.

Now he confronts a crisis. He compares his position to that of the father who has sworn never to resort to the child-rearing practices of his parents. But when driven to the brink, how do such parents behave? They reach for the belt, or buy peace with a stick of candy just as their fathers did. They resort to what they have been taught. Dr. Bengough finds himself returning to where he began, coming full circle to sit at the feet of Dr. Rush. The diagnosis of brain fever does not appear to have been correct. But he has run out of diagnoses. So last night he honed his lancets. They are in his bag. His final, desperate recourse is to open a vein.

Dr. Bengough pauses behind the Stubhorn. Dooley has not opened for business since he returned to Fort Benton, resolutely insisting on keeping vigil by his friend's bedside. A lamp still burns in the sickroom. Dr. Bengough starts to laboriously climb the stairs, stooped, gasping stertorously. The early-morning sunlight bathes the wall in gold, and he is able to watch himself ascend, an old man's shadow steadily creeping up to do its duty.

Dooley, asleep on the floor, immediately springs awake at the sound of the door opening. "How is he?" Dr. Bengough calmly inquires.

"Around three o'clock he stopped bellering," Dooley responds, rising stiffly from the floor. "I think he wore himself down till he didn't have the strength for it no more."

Dr. Bengough quietly approaches the sickbed. Straw is asleep, head resembling a hardboiled egg sprinkled thickly with pepper, now that his hair is coming back. His respiration is subdued, the weak pulse a threnody.

"Bring me the wash basin, Aloysius," Dr. Bengough says.

"I sponged him down after he went quiet," reports Dooley, as if Bengough's command is a reproof, a criticism of his nursing.

"Not for washing," explains the physician. "To catch his blood. I must bleed him."

Dooley hesitates.

"In my judgment, our friend passed the climacteric several hours ago. He is now embarked on the decline. 'Kill or cure,' Aloysius. I shall take a pint, and then we shall wait. This old dog has no more tricks."

As Dooley holds the basin to receive the issue, Dr. Bengough cuts the vein in Straw's arm. He notes that the blood is blackish, costive, the flow miserly. The two men stand and watch Straw's life trickle sluggishly into the receptacle.

❖ ❖ ❖

CHARLES   I believe that Straw's sudden terrible ailment has done much to undermine the morale of Grunewald, Barker, and Ayto. For the past week, I sensed their anxiety that they, too, might be stricken with illness. There was much muttering about smallpox. So when my brother decided, after wasting a week near the former site of Chesterfield House, to alter our plans and set out north for Fort Edmonton rather than the American whisky posts to the west, the men greeted this announcement with approbation. They fear the Blackfoot will have been made restive by the outbreak of smallpox and will wreak summary retribution on any white men they encounter.

When I challenged Addington for reversing a plan we had agreed to, his excuses were so feeble as to be derisory. He said that Edmonton is a likely place of information, a great centre of British commerce, a magnet for all the plains tribes. "Go to the market, if you wish to hear the news," he proclaimed.

I did my best to reason with him. Yes, I said, Fort Edmonton is indeed a British possession, a possession in regular communication with England. Remember, Father wrote to them many months ago, requesting any news they might have of Simon and the reply was that they had none. Would it not be a better use of our time to visit the whisky posts with which Father had not been in communication?

With cold officiousness, he replied, "You are my subordinate, Charles. It was understood by Father that my experience in military matters gives me precedence in the field. It does no good for you to question my every decision. What do you know of conducting and commanding an expedition?"

"Nothing," I said. "But I do recognize this one lacks a brain."

He threatened to strike me. I invited him to. The men crowded round. I saw Ayto grin. Grunewald and Barker were eager for fisticuffs. I walked away.

Addington's moods, his desires, rule the day. He has become obsessed with ticking off the sights other travellers have noted. His motive in going to Fort Edmonton is transparent. All English gentlemen adventurers make a visit there, and just as a Grand Tour of the continent would be incomplete if one missed certain highly celebrated spots, Addington's movements in the North-West must not depart from custom. Hence Fort Edmonton. Palliser, Cheadle, Butler all gazed upon the sublime Rockies. So in good time will Addington. He shall insist upon it.

After Addington's and my angry encounter, Lucy found me standing on the bank of the Saskatchewan, brooding. She slipped a hand inside my shirt, laid it to my chest while I gazed upon the brown and sullen water. It had a direction, and I had none.

22

CUSTIS Dr. Bengough was up to see me again today, sat on a chair beside my bed, back humped and shoulders touching his earlobes like an old vulture with the smell of rotten meat in his nostrils. This morning he said, "I knew from the beginning it wasn't cholera. The cholera movement resembles rice water, clear and copious, whereas yours are sanguinary."

I told him, "Well, I'm plenty copious."

"Pectin and cheese, Custis, you must eat your pectin and cheese. God helps those who help themselves."

That's been my fate for a month now, lie abed and listen to Bengough talk bowels and Aloysius talk blood. "He's taken four pint out of you, Custis, thick and black as blood pudding." Thank God, I prevailed upon Aloysius to open up the Stubhorn again so I wouldn't have to abide him hovering about, clucking and fussing. But he saw to it I wasn't left entirely bereft of tender ministrations. He bought me a whorehouse commode from Catch-all Kate and hired Black Pompey's little son, Garrison, to give me a shoulder to the johnny whenever my guts clutch, which is frequent. Bengough sees to it the boy ties a knot in a string every time I evacuate. He's a thorough man of science, Bengough. Yesterday I did fourteen knots, and today I've already run up six and it hasn't reached noon yet. The boy's got a full-time job knotting string and paring cheddar.

I could use some distraction, but Garrison doesn't talk much. The orphan state is a melancholy one, and tending to a white man and his stinks is bound to lower your spirits even further. I've only got one smile out of him so far. That was when I begged the boy's clay-shooter marble and showed him how it'd fit in that old wound in my leg like a stopper in a bung hole. "Look at that," I said. "If I was my old fat self, I could make it wink like an eye."

Time lies heavy on a man's hands without whisky. Bengough and Aloysius won't bend on that question, so I'm kept dry. A little whisky might help keep me from thinking of Lucy Stoveall and her Englishman. That's a bitterer pill to swallow than Bengough could ever force down my throat. It seems strange to me now that I ever hoped to overcome Charles Gaunt's handsome face with what I got to offer, but I was bound to try. I brought Lucy Stoveall back to him and I shed blood to do it. I suppose that's what Bengough would call irony. I count myself lucky for the megrim, and then the fever that took hold of me on the ride back to the Gaunts' camp because it made everything blur. Just a day or two ago, Aloysius remarked to me Lucy Stoveall looked fierce as a queen coming home from war, the Kelsos vanquished. I have no memory of that, but if I did, I'd be burdened with remembering her face when she and Charles Gaunt saw each other again.

When I'm not squatting on the commode, goose-bumped and shivery, I try to distract myself with the Good Book. Bengough is an unbeliever, which makes him curious about my affection for Scripture and almighty persistent in his questions on the whys and wherefores of my Bible reading.

I have trouble explaining it to myself, but I once tried to answer him. "The first time I read the Bible cover to cover, I was in an army hospital in Washington," I said. "I had a mind to make myself believe every single word was true. The second time I read it to satisfy myself it was all a lie. Now I read it to weigh both sides, and find some truth."

Bengough nodded. "And what in the Good Book have you decided is absolutely and indisputably true?"

I thought for a moment. "That verse that says 'Jesus wept.'"

Bengough sat stroking his nose with his gloved forefinger. "And was it some intimation of mortality in that military hospital – was that what led you to examine spiritual matters?"

"Yes," I said. But that was a lie. It wasn't fear of death. I was empty. As empty as I am now. I'd lost my faith, in the dark, tangly woods of the Wilderness. There I denied Mr. Burns of Gettysburg and everything he stood for, just like Peter did Christ.

I wouldn't have gone to war if Louella hadn't died the year before. She would have seen to it I remained at home milking and ploughing. Louella and me were ill-suited from the start, but a barren womb made our differences worse. A childless man and woman need to be friends, and our natures were opposed. If the quinsy that carried her off hadn't swelled her throat shut, I believe my wife would have died cursing me. I saw it in her eyes when she passed over.

A thirty-five-year-old widower with no prospects. Just as it had Ulysses S. Grant, the coming of war freed me. The general gave up the life of a counterjumper in a leather goods store in Galena, and I walked away from staring up a mule's ass from dawn to dusk. I signed the muster in July of 1861 and walked away from that hateful farm in Indiana and its hateful memories, left it in my brother-in-law's care. Never went back.

That fine, brave summer of bands and parades, General Gibbon set a black Hardee hat on my head, put me in a frock coat, kersey blue trousers, and white gaiters. I figured I wouldn't wear them more than six months. The war would be over by then or so we thought.

Funny to think Gibbon, a North Carolinian, was such a dyed-in-the-wool Union man. Born in the North I fought for the North, that was the long and the short of it for me. Gibbon was a mystery, a man who won the battle in his heart before he ever took it into the field. It takes a brave man to oppose his homeland and his kin for the sake of an idea. Gibbon had principles. I had none, only wanted to escape my dreary situation. But one affray was enough to teach me that a single drop of blood spilled was a sinful outrage unless it could be justified. Soon the blood was raining down thick and fast all about me. Bull Run followed by Second Bull Run. At South Mountain, we

Western Yankees were drenched in it, mired in it, soaked to the tops of our white gaiters in it. South Mountain earned us the nickname the Iron Brigade. Braced by our hard name, braced by that hard Southerner Gibbon, we fought on, wading through the slaughter of Antietam, Fredericksburg, a dozen smaller horrors.

Then came the day Mr. John Burns of Gettysburg came out of the town to join us on McPherson's Ridge. This little old civilian, seventy-five years old if he was a day, stomping up to our lines in an old-fashioned swallowtail coat, brass buttons rubbed bright, a black stovepipe hat on his head, a hunting rifle slanted over his shoulder. I remember how word of his arrival ran up and down the ranks. "Reinforcements!" "Mr. Burns of Gettysburg has come to smash up Lee!" A few of the boys laughed, but the most of us tossed our hats high in the air and hurrahed him, ran to clap him on the back. I was one of those who got close enough to touch him. Felt his bony shoulder blade through the cloth of that down-at-heels swallowtail coat. A veteran of the War of 1812, Mr. Burns had sniffed the peril, knew the fate of the Republic hung in the balance that day, and left his parlour to defend it, to stand with us at Willoughby's Run.

My face ran with tears at the sight of him falling into the ranks of the 7th Wisconsin, struggling to uncrook his bent spine, pull himself as straight as he stood fifty years before when he faced the British. Maybe Mr. Burns was a fire-breathing abolitionist, or maybe he believed the Republic was the light of the world and its holy salvation. I don't know which. But his reason, whatever it was, had to have been deep in the marrow of his bones to risk the shattering of them at Gettysburg.

Mr. Burns heartened me that morning more than flags and bugles. The winter before, I'd been edging my way towards his kind of commitment. In the long doldrums of winter quarters some of the young soldiers with schooling were forming lyceums to discuss politics and the conduct of the war. They arranged debates. I listened close and learned the fancy turns of phrase of high-toned argument – the affirmative, the negative, the "be it resolved." "Be it resolved that the constitutional relations of the Rebel states be fixed by Congress only." "Be it resolved the Rebel states be reduced to territories." I'd always had a taste for oratory and speechifying, and so I never missed a meeting. I'd been sprayed by the spit of word-walloping backwoods politicians and camp preachers, ranters, roarers, suspender-poppers and hat throwers, men who howled to God or the ghost of George Washington to rain brimstone on the Episcopalians or the die-hard Jacksonians. But these men talked quietly, racked their brains to make their meaning clear, often paused before marching into the next sentence. One night I heard two privates argue the case for "The rights of the South" and damn near carry the vote. It made me proud, an army that could consider the hearts of the enemy.

Plenty of muckety-muck officers hated the lyceums, hated ordinary soldiers in time of war wrangling about what the meaning of it all was. But they were wrong. They had no right to ask us to die like dumb cattle led to the butcher's knife by Judas steers. Those days I was reading every newspaper I could lay hands on, mulling over the meaning of our agony. I hadn't turned to the Bible, not yet.

Hell, I even bucked up courage and spoke once. The question was, "Do the signs of the times point to the downfall of our Republic?" I took the affirmative.

A still night, snow sifting down on the assembly. Standing near a torch you could hear the sizzle of the big flakes melting, the sound of white moths frying in the flame. Men hooded in blankets to keep the snow off, pine knots blooming fiery flowers in the dark, everybody silently turning over what was said. Men pondering.

I was the last to speak. Signs of the fall of the Republic were plain in the army like damp on a plaster wall, I said. Too many officers got commissions by pulling political strings, and if it wasn't stopped, the sheep would soon be in charge of the lions. Another thing. It was wrong for provost marshals to drive the broken back into battle with jabs of the bayonet, screaming they must "Show blood!" before they could retreat. We were free men and should not be treated in such a way. Provost marshals were no better than slave drivers flogging Negroes to pick cotton. It was an insult to citizen soldiers.

I could sense the men harkening, still not sure whether their silence was for me or against me. I took a breath and went on. I said rich men buying other men to serve for them was the worst of disgraces. If the rich, who had gained so much from the Republic, wouldn't fight for it, that was proof enough it was rotten. I told them I didn't want to stand beside a bounty man who'd sold his body for three hundred dollars because when danger came he'd sell mine out for even less. Some said this was a rich man's war but a poor man's fight. It was the duty of every soldier to give the lie to this, lay claim to this war as rightfully his own.

I was finished. Nobody moved nor spoke. Then someone shouted, "Traitor!" Three more times I heard the word called out, but each time it was a little fainter than the last, until it was nothing but a bird chirp.

A soldier commenced to march up and down on the spot, stamping his boots. His neighbour followed suit. Then another and another. Down below me, hundreds of men fell into step, into cadence, beating a long, muffled drum roll in the night. A vote for what I'd said by show of feet, not hands. Shoulders heaving and rolling in time to the boots thudding against the frozen earth; gaunt, bearded faces drinking in the light of the torches, adding to it their own inward fire until their countenances blazed.

It was months after that wintry night, on a July day hot as a furnace, that I laid a hand on Mr. Burns's shoulder in the same fashion that those men had laid a hand on mine when I climbed down off that ammunition box pulpit.

Bengough says when I was in the grip of the fever, I raved day and night about the war. I pretend not to remember, but I do. My mind was full of the Wilderness. I reckon what awoke it was the barber who came to shave my head, stropping his razor. Snick, snick, snick. The sound of men sharpening bayonets, an uneasy whisper, the click of stone on steel the night of our last bivouac before crossing the Rapidan River into Virginia.

We had reason to worry going into the godforsaken Wilderness, Satan's roost. Woods and scrub, brambles and briars, heartbreak farms long-abandoned, reclaimed by second growth. Grant ought to have known it was an army's graveyard. Hooker marched his men into it in 1863, and the unburied corpses he left behind when he retreated were waiting for us in the woods, vines twisted around their bones, insects nesting in their skulls. Nothing but a couple of plank roads to move thousands of troops down, one step off them everything became confusion, a meddlesome cat's cradle, no passage for baggage wagons, artillery.

The generals did as generals will. They found themselves a spot for a battle. Saunders Field, four hundred yards wide and eight hundred yards long, a space hemmed tight by forest, a gully slashed across the middle. We Iron Brigaders formed on the left under Cutler.

Sharp at one o'clock came the brisk tattoo of drummer boys calling us to advance. The hottest part of a hot day, everybody awash in sweat, everybody peeling off knapsacks and coats, letting them drop where they may. The field quivering with splinters of silver, the bayonets we had sharpened for this day. The boys on our right catching it bad, Johnny Rebs pouring flanking fire into them from the cover of the thickets, muskets rattling volleys like an idiot boy running a stick back and forth on a picketfence. Tat, tat, tat, tat. Gunsmoke rolling out of the trees, billowing, flooding Saunders Field. The lucky ones of us wading on in the swirling grey sea while the rest sank. Beside me, Hoagy Pinson singing a psalm in his scared tenor voice.

The New Yorkers wheeled to charge the woods on the right and met a fusillade that cut them down like a scythe cuts grass, down they fell, swathes of bodies. Our cannon booming, playing bloody murder with us as much as the Secession men. My foot landed on a pulpy blue chest and I almost slipped and dropped. Where the rest of him was – legs, arms, head – only the good Lord knew. Maybe the angels were carrying that Billy Yank up to Heaven, piece by piece.

We struck Jones's Brigade of Confederates, slugged it out at close range, volley after volley tearing holes in both our ranks. Those of us who didn't taste lead got splashed with the blood of our brothers. We were less than forty yards from Jones's Brigade when the Confederate ranks shivered in a moment of indecision. Then one Butternut turned tail and ran and the rest followed, humping it for the safety of the timber. We whooped a cheer. Officers waved us forward with their swords, licks of glitter beckoning us to pelt into the thickets after Johnny Reb.

Sudden twilight dropping on us under the shady trees, fallen logs, heavy brush blocking our way. The gloom filling with the sound of snapping twigs, crackling undergrowth, men tripping, falling, cursing. At every step snagged and clutched; muskets snared in branches, thorns catching sleeves and trousers. The leaves so thick it was impossible to see farther than two or three yards ahead. Our lines beginning to fray, soldiers losing touch with their platoons, wandering in jungly undergrowth. I yelled to Hoagy Pinson. There was a sabre laying at my feet discarded by some fleeing Confederate officer. I picked it up and started to hack us a path.

We went on for two or three hundred yards before the racket I was raising marked us for enemy fire. A sudden blast, a fringe of flame spurting between the trunks, balls whistling, chipping splinters, snipping buds. Twigs, leaves, a shower of green pattering down on my back as I dropped to my face. Hollering to Hoagy, Was he all right? He whispering back, Yes, but keep my blamed voice down. I lifted my head and saw Greyback spooks slipping between the pines, dissolving in the murk.

Hoagy and I creeping on. Another five hundred yards covered and another salvo sent us diving, more grey spectres dodging among the trees, a mockery to the eyes and nerves, Johnny Reb here, there, gone. A sprinkle of sniper fire kept us flinching as we slunk along, small as we could make ourselves. Every twenty yards a deadfall blocked you, turned you to seek another passage. The smallest sound startling us, playing spoons on our hearts. Hoagy and I floundering forward, slithering on our bellies through the green dusk, murmuring directions to one another. Our dead lying thick on the ground, the wounded mumbling and groaning and begging for water as we crawled by them.

There was no sign of the rest of the Brigade, we had lost them. Up ahead, we could hear a fight building, furious yells, the sporadic pop of muskets growing to a steady thump. Where the pines thinned atop a ridge, we saw a carpet of blue coats pushing up a slope. We scrambled after them, came panting up the rise just as the trees shook with musket fire, spun our boys round, spilled them down on us, a foam of white faces, wild eyes, gaping mouths. They tore past, flinging away cartridge cases, canteens, muskets, anything they could to lighten flight, bounding over fallen logs and fallen comrades.

The sudden rout froze me and Hoagy. I couldn't believe my eyes, the Iron Brigade pulling a cowardly skedaddle. Then I heard the Confederates coming, yodelling like fiends, spotted them streaming down the hill, whirling through the pines. Before I knew it I had caught the terror too, and turned down the hill, chasing the rest of the boys like the fleetest bounty man, legs threatening to run away on me, springy branches lashing my face, thorns ripping my skin. I tossed my rifle aside, jostled and shouldered the slew-foots and the wounded aside, ran for my life in a lily-livered panic.

I busted out of the woods and out on the edge of Saunders Field. More and more soldiers came stumbling out of the woods. By the score they thrust by me, while I stood bent over, hands on my knees, sucking wind.

A terrible stink rose in my nostrils as I panted.

I looked up. Saunders Field was ablaze, parched grass and tinder-dry brush roaring. Black smoke coiling, heavy and greasy, the sickening smell of burned pork.

The dead and wounded roasting, silly firecracker sounds of ammunition exploding in the heat. Someone bellowing the name of Jesus. Hump-backed Johnny Rebs and Billy Yanks desperately pulling themselves along on their bellies, turtles trying to outcrawl the fire. A man, his coat fluttering flame, taking a few steps before falling back down to burn to death.

The sight of it started me for the rear. Plenty were doing the same. Some limped, some hugged shattered arms to their chests, some numbly walked, blood coursing into their eyes.

We came on the Unionist Marylanders of Denison's Brigade readying to go into action. A murmur went up from them when they identified our brigade. "The Black Hats, the Black Hats are retreating."

Consternation spread among the reserves, it made them sore afraid to see the iron of the Army of the Potomac shattered. Officers imploring us to face the enemy, coaxing us, finally threatening, but it did no good. We were finished.

I hadn't seen hide nor hair of Hoagy Pinson since I peeled out of the thicket; I buttonholed anyone who knew him about his possible whereabouts. They all shook their heads until I ran into Jimmy Johnson. "Pinson? Pinson?" Jimmy said. "He took a wound in the woods."

"Did he make it out?" I yelled.

"Not likely," he said, "not likely at all."

I stood in the road like a rock jutting up in a current, reinforcements, artillery, supply wagons swerving around me, swiftly flowing by as I peered up the road I'd come down, praying to catch a glimpse of Hoagy Pinson hobbling towards me.

I made my return to Saunders Field. Everything was confusion and turmoil. Reserve units milled about, trying to assemble for the last assault before nightfall. Sergeants screeched orders, shoved men into formation, officers beat the unwilling into line with the flats of their swords. The fighting on the right of Saunders Field was still under way. Flags tossed, drums rolled, cannons thundered, riderless horses circled the field in a mad gallop.

Saunders Field was black emptiness, the grass scorched away, nothing but smoking earth, the charred remains of corpses.

The thicket I'd scampered out of seemed to be pretty quiet now. But a haze simmered above the treetops. Sparks blown from Saunders Field had ignited a wildfire in the woods. I thought of Hoagy lying wounded in that grim, dim place, burning to a crisp.

I made for the timber. A few yards into the trees I found the body of a young lieutenant with a pistol clamped in his hand. I pried it out of his fingers and continued on. The wood was deathly still, close as a closet. The smoke a light mist stinging my eyes, and putting the bite of burning resin in the back of my throat. I eased along, boots stealthy in the leaves. No sound but the commotion of birds complaining about the fire. Excited trilling, nervous swoops, and sudden drops back into the treetops, wild hopping from bough to bough.

Here and there cadavers lay about, none of them Hoagy. The corpses grew more numerous and the smoke thicker the farther I went. The fire was a shushing noise now, a greedy smacking of lips every time a bush kindled.

My eyes ran and my throat was raw. I tore off my shirt-tail and made a mask. I heard voices. A mix of Yankee twang and Southern drawl. I couldn't make out what they were saying, but their talk drew me to the edge of a clearing. Two Union men were sitting on the ground, taking off their boots. One of them was Hoagy, head bandaged in a shirt spotted with blood. He looked glum and defeated, his face spongy-grey as bread dough rolled out on a dirty board.

Two emaciated, barefoot Greybacks guarded them. They grinned and spat, joyful at the prospect of requisitioning Yankee footwear.

I reconnoitred. Saw nor heard any sign of more Confederates. Rage and shame slowly rising in me. How could the likes of these pitiful, half-starved scarecrows, their bones poking out of rags, put the run on the Iron Brigade? The lightest breeze would blow over these corn-pone-fed wrecks.

I yanked off my mask and sopped up blood from a dead body, daubed my face with it, slipped the pistol inside my tunic and kept my hand to it, so it would look like I was clutching some hurt to my side.

Groaning, I lurched into the clearing. Hoagy's face shot up, fingers knotted in his bootlaces. The other prisoner's jaw dropped. Muskets swung up at me. "Paws in the air!" one of the Confederates hollered. I ignored him, stumbled on, weaving from side to side.

"Custis!" Hoagy called to me. The Greybacks' heads jerked towards his cry. I pulled my pistol and shot the one nearest. His jawbone scattered and sprayed. A musket went off, my leg kicked out from under me, sent me face first into a windrow of dry leaves. Snuffling dust, mould in my mouth. My right leg broken, flopping like a fish when I tried to stand. Hoagy was yelling, one hand clamped to the musket barrel he had snatched to save my life. The other prisoner was barrelling off, untied boots flopping.

The Confederate wrenched his musket free from Hoagy's grip. I snapped a shot at him but missed. Hoagy Pinson was already spitted on a bayonet, twisting and screaming. I cocked and fired, the hammer playing a flat, dead, desperate tune on empty chambers. The lieutenant had died with two rounds left. I'd used them both.

The Butternut was finished with Hoagy and was coming at me, bayonet greased with my friend's blood.

"Yankee son of a bitch," he said, lips flying spit. "Here's for your dirty trick on Clarence."

He lunged, drove the bayonet into my sound leg. Stabbed two more times, grinding the tip of the blade into my thigh bone as I howled and yelped. For a moment, he stood over me, slack-mouthed, slobbery. He swiped his hand across his mouth and found words. "Enjoy the evening breeze," he said pointing up to the treetops waggling in the wind. A weird light pulsed above them, swarming with sparks. Then he turned, loped away.

I dragged my useless legs over to Hoagy. Purple and yellow guts lay heaped in his lap. He was alive, but couldn't, or wouldn't, speak to me. I sat beside him, touching his face, waiting for it to come, watching it move down the slope, the slow smoulder, the blisters of flame swelling in the brush. Smoky vines twining themselves around tree trunks. A pine on a knoll waving a blazing flag. Fire licking its lips at me through the palings of black trees. The rustling of flame in dead leaves, the scurry of bright-eyed mice. A bush fifty feet off spreading its branches in a candelabra. Hot drafts, a swirl of ash stroking my face. I hid from the heat in the shoulder of my tunic.

Then I heard someone calling out the name Danny and I shouted back.

I saw him, a silhouette shuffling out of a furnace, the lumbering, awkward shadow of a stoker. He stooped over me. A face, big and white as a dinner plate, streaked with soot, eyelashes singed away, crown of his Bummer cap smoking.

"You ain't Danny," he said, disappointed. A boy with puffy, red, godawful, empty eyes. An ember was burning on the epaulette of his jacket. He did not seem to feel it. He looked around him. "Danny," he murmured vaguely, "where you at?" He took one determined, jerky step and I flung my arms tight to his leg to keep him from leaving. But he didn't seem to realize I held him, just swung me along with him, a convict dragging a ball and chain.

"Carry me out," I pleaded. "Carry me out, for the love of God."

Like a man remembering something important, he halted and said, "You know where a feller can get a loan of tobacco?"

And I'm pleading, "Carry me out. Don't let me burn here."

His head turning slowly side to side. "I got a hankering for a pipe," he says.

I'm pointing back to the Rapidan, to the pontoon bridges miles off that we crossed days ago. "Back there! Back there!" I shout.

"Back there? You get me some baccy there?"

"Yes. Oh God, carry me out. Carry me out."

The boy drops to his knees, I wrap my arms around his neck. He hoists himself upright, hand over hand on the boughs of a pine, branches cracking in his powerful hands. There's red light all around us, brands and sudden showers of sparks. I rein him like a horse, jerk him back to the Rapidan by the collar.

I ride my man-horse through the trees, whispering over and over to him to take me out. Ride him to an ambulance, ride the ambulance back to Washington, lay in a hospital bed for three months. Get my discharge, deemed unfit for further service.

As often as I tossed in those infirmary sheets, I tossed and turned it over in my mind, telling myself Hoagy was dead, long dead by the time his body burned. Even if he wasn't dead, even if I had surrendered my place on that boy's back to him, what good would it have done? Hoagy was too far gone to steer the boy, and the boy had lost the wits to save himself. I was the brain that directed his legs. Hoagy and he would have burned for sure. If I had saved myself, I had saved that mad boy too.

No argument convinced me. I didn't believe. In the Wilderness I'd proved what I was.

Even old Wadsworth, our division commander, a rich man from New York, had tried to rally the troops, rode his horse into the face of the rebel lines in the hope they would follow him. Me, I rode a befuddled boy to safety. Wadsworth fell with a bullet lodged in the back of his neck and his men left him to be captured by the Rebs. It took him two days to die of his wound. The Butternuts came to gape at the man who had more money than all the Confederate treasury coffers, the rich man who had forsaken ease and comfort for a cause.

So much for my speech before the winter-barracks lyceum.

Here I lie, a little black boy staring big-eyed at me out of the corner, slave to my misery, waiting for me to beckon him. And I tell myself, Custis Straw, next time you're carried out, let it be feet first. It's what you deserve.

23

CHARLES We set off on the Old North Road connecting Fort Benton with Fort Edmonton, a route which Potts has told us is the one preferred by prospectors who have been lured by rumours of gold to be found in the vicinity of the Hudson Bay post. However, after five days of travel we encounter a hellish landscape. As far as the eye can see to the north, the plain has been blackened by a vast prairie fire, the grass reduced to fine, crumbled ash.

With no pasture for our animals, we must seek a new route, and Addington orders us to march northeast to make intersection with the famous Carlton Trail, the thoroughfare of the Hudson Bay men. My brother's only knowledge of this road derives from what he has garnered by skimming the accounts of those Englishmen who have undertaken excursions in the North-West, but it is enough to decide him on this course.

Slowly, the countryside begins to change, becomes more hospitable, pleasant, somehow more English. Between copses of poplar and pine are broad meadows spotted with flowers: lilac bergamot, goldenrod, bluebells, marigold, aster. Water is more plentiful, we encounter many reedy creeks, small lakes teeming with snipe, ducks, geese, and fish. This is a veritable land of milk and honey compared to the arid, sallow, treeless wastes we have left behind. But the lovely landscape poses its own problems, woods and water hamper travel by wagon, forcing us to make tiresome detours, or spend hours extricating heavily laden vehicles bogged to their hubs in quagmires.

Despite the many impediments to travel, the parkland we traverse induces nostalgia. I find myself longing for the accents of home, and despite my initial opposition to visiting Fort Edmonton, I now look forward to conversation with fellow exiles, a sojourn with my own kind. Fort Edmonton bulks large in my mind, a romantic, lonely British settlement, a fragment of "the right little, tight little Island" which will fold this weary traveller in its arms.

Lucy and I pass pleasant hours strolling behind the wagons. Our attachment is no longer a secret, if it ever were. I need only to announce that the two of us are off to pick wildflowers and a knowing smirk forms on Addington's face. " 'Gather ye rosebuds while ye may,' Charles. 'Gather ye rosebuds,' " is his constant, idiotic refrain.

Words which drop so banally from his lips nonetheless do characterize Lucy's and my private interludes. Walks through the dew-soaked grass to gaze upon another dusky bronze, rose madder sunrise; a smear of leaping fire jigging up and down the spine of the horizon, slowly extinguishing the tiny stars, the aubergine sky flooded with light as the egg of the sun hatches a fierce, crowing blaze. Or sheltered in some leafy glade, falling on one another with hungry mouths, the aspen leaves dappling her with shade and sunshine as she disrobes. Yet every happy moment is undermined by the knowledge that all we share is fleeting, temporary. Sadness rising up even in the thrall of desire and passion. Before winter comes, Addington and I must return to England with or without Simon. Does Lucy understand this? Surely, she must. Still, we never speak of it.

So I flee thoughts of our impending separation by lapsing into fantastic daydreams. Lucy and I occupying a humble cabin set amid these tolerant woods, meadows, and bright flowers. Charles Gaunt a simple husbandman out of Virgil's *Eclogues*, keeper of bees, busy in the garden, paintbrush renounced in favour of rustic bliss. And as I grow more and more impractical, Lucy's innate good sense becomes my anchor. One day when I complained that the men never took my side against Addington, she said it was because I kept too much to myself.

"Ah yes, but so is Addington aloof."

"He's in command. So they don't mind so much. But you ought to sit a hand of cards with Grunewald and Barker now and then. Lose a little money to them."

"How ridiculous."

"They'd like you the better for it."

"What do I care if they like me better?"

"The next time you and Mr. Addington come near to blows you may need friends." She gave me a gentle smile. "They're cut from the same cloth as me, Charles. Here, you're the fish out of water."

I try to do as Lucy suggests and cultivate the men, but I fear I have proven a failure in that regard. I lack the common touch. Nevertheless, I may have had some trifling success with our guide. I suspect he feels the absence of Aloysius Dooley and Custis Straw. Perhaps as I do, Potts wonders what was the outcome of his champion's illness, whether the indomitable Straw has survived it. His presence seemed to have a steadying influence on Grunewald and Barker; there was a reassuring manner about Straw which quieted their uneasiness. His bearing suggested that he might be depended on.

Our guide's despondent air has prompted me more than once to take a seat beside him at meal times. His responses to many of my questions are decidedly unforthcoming. He remains inscrutable. The only topics on which he can be drawn are those dealing with the terrain and the various tribes that inhabit it. As Jabez Cooke described it, his knowledge of these matters is encyclopedic, and seems to be a source of considerable pride for the taciturn fellow. I have come to believe he appreciates the interest I have shown in his savage world.

So we have hiked on, in pursuit of the Carlton Trail. This morning, having risen in darkness to take our breakfast, I hear in the distance a horrific groaning reft with hysterical shrieks, as if the inmates of a madhouse are awakening to consciousness, to the realization of their misery, and raising a complaint against the breaking of the new day.

The ghastly cacophony transfixes me in the ruddy light of the fire.

Barker, noting my bewilderment, says matter-of-factly, "I reckon we're nigh to the Carlton Trail, Mr. Charles. That's Manitoba music you're hearing, the plaint of Red River carts. Métis don't waste no grease on their cart axles; they grind dry. Big train by the sound of it, sixty, maybe seventy, carts I'd say. We've gained the trail."

I decide that the spectacle of this caravan is not to be missed, but none of the others, with the exception of Lucy, declares any interest in rushing to view it. A commonplace affair, small beer to the locals. I am rather surprised that Addington does not insist on accompanying us when I announce we shall go ahead on foot and leave our companions to break camp. But my brother is enjoying one of his moods, scowling morbidly at the fire, impervious to the caterwauling of the Red River carts. Of late, his disposition swings like a weather vane. One day, jolly and hectic, the next, gloomy and peevish, snapping at whoever comes in range.

Lucy and I scamper off like children rushing to the noisy sounds of a fair, race through the dew-soaked grass, take turns dragging one another along by the hand, laughing as we splash heedlessly through morasses in the dark, caring not a whit for mud and wet feet.

A mile or two of this and we strike what is indeed the Carlton Trail, a roadway of ruts worn a foot deep in the sod. We stand hanging upon one another, breathless and happy, as the screeching tumult creeps towards us. Minute by minute the din grows more demonic and piercing. It causes me to shiver, sets my teeth on edge. Then we see the first of the carts cresting a knoll, coming into view against a flaming-red backdrop of cloudy sky, then dipping down into blanketing shadow. It is immediately succeeded by a second rickety silhouette which just as rapidly slides from sight, followed by a third, a fourth, a fifth screaming vehicle.

The lead cart has a lantern hanging above it on a long pole that waggles a beckoning light to the rest of the concourse. I step onto the trail to make our presence known and the driver jerks his scrawny nag to a halt and sends a warning shout to those following, a warning relayed back down the line from one throat to another. The column moans to a stop and sudden silence hums in my eardrums.

The leader of the brigade salutes us in a nasal, brutal *patois*. He gives his name as one Baptiste Laliberté, captain of the brigade. Who am I and who is this woman? What are we doing here alone?

In French I introduce myself and Lucy, explaining that we are members of an English party bound for Fort Edmonton. I say that when I heard the sound of their carts, I could not resist the temptation to make myself acquainted with the Métis, of whom I had heard a little in Fort Benton and much more from our guide. Would they be so good as to show me their ingenious vehicles?

This pleases Laliberté no end. Other drivers dismount and join us, chattering among themselves in unbridled excitement. The curiosity of an Englishman seems very gratifying to them and they press in close as Monsieur Laliberté displays for us his rustic phaeton in the strengthening light of dawn, a conveyance which seems to be a distant cousin to the high-wheeled carts loaded with beets and turnips I once encountered in the lanes of Normandy on a walking tour.

Monsieur Laliberté discourses upon the Red River cart at length. He explains they are very easy to mend; if an axle snaps any of his carters can fashion another from a tree with an axe, and be under way again in a matter of hours. Proudly, he shows me there is not so much as a single piece of ironwork to be found in the entire vehicle. It is lashed together with cords of green buffalo hide which, when they have dried, hold everything in place as tightly as if nailed or bolted. Even the wheels of the carts are encased in buffalo leather, Monsieur Laliberté making the point that if a rim is thrown, a green buffalo hide is more easily obtained in the wilderness than a black-smith's forge.

He tells me that they are carrying a shipment of berry pemmican for the Bay men in Fort Edmonton. The carts are stacked high with skin bags the size of coal sacks which contain dried buffalo meat and grease. Monsieur Laliberté passes me one to heft and its unexpected weight staggers me. Apparently, this spring the Métis hunting brigades killed many buffalo south of the Qu'Appelle Valley and the record of the carnage is to be found in their carts. As he relates all this, Laliberté pantomimes the running of the buffalo, firing and reloading an imaginary musket with a wild, expressive grin.

By now, word that a white female is present has passed down the line and Métis women are making a timid approach, squalling infants strapped to their backs and sturdy toddlers towed along by the hand. They shyly smile at Lucy and shake her hand with grave courtesy. To my mind, the Métis closely resemble a tribe of wandering gypsies. Some are very light-complexioned, while others are as dark as any of the Indians I laid eyes on in Fort Benton. Their costumes are like Potts's own, a motley of native and European dress. I see an assortment of blue coats, jackets of dressed skin, wide-brimmed floppy hats, wool trousers, and beaded buckskin pants. All the men wear long bright sashes cinched to their waists, a dash of Gallic élan to challenge the flamboyance of their Indian beadwork. From the medals hung around their necks, from the rosaries some of the women clutch, I deduce these people are as they have been reported to me, resolutely Catholic. Laliberté is showing signs that he wishes to be under way once more so I refrain from delaying him any longer. We shake hands, express our pleasure at having made each other's acquaintance, and the train readies to resume its journey. Laliberté slaps the rump of his skinny pony with the reins, calls out his farewell, and the music of bedlam resumes again. One by one the vehicles toil by, drivers, wives, children wave farewell and shout at the tops of their lungs to make themselves heard, "Adieu, Monsieur! Adieu, Madame! Adieu! Adieu!" Lucy and I receive the salutes of countless Red River carts and return them all. Finally, the last of them drops over the brow of a hill and all that remains is a dolorous, melancholy dirge which lingers long after they are gone from sight.

Lucy and I sit down beside the trail to await the arrival of the rest of our party. The path now lies plain before us, and all we have to do is set our wagon wheels in the ruts and be guided by them, as a locomotive is by rails, directly to Fort Edmonton.

Stirred by what I have seen, I remark to Lucy, "How fine it would be, my dear, if we could only live as those people do! A Métis man and woman, free of the constraints and prohibitions of civilized behaviour!"

Lucy turns a steady gaze upon me, brown eyes liquid, lustrous in the morning light. She studies me as Mr. Darwin must have studied his specimens, searching for the one clue that would be the key to understanding. I know she has remarked the unfortunate words I have employed – constraints, prohibitions, civilization; now she understands I think precisely in those terms. Leaning over, she brushes the corner of my mouth forgivingly with her lips. Nothing more is said. My essential self has been revealed.

In three days, the Carlton Trail brings us to the gates of Fort Edmonton. The chief factor heartily welcomes us and tenders a prodigal hospitality. Potts, Grunewald, and Barker are quartered in the barracks of the engagés, and Ayto, perhaps on the strength of his florid waistcoat, is assigned a room in the gentlemen's quarters. My brother and I, notables from the "Old Country," are invited to take up residence in the factor's immense log house, universally referred to as Rowand's Folly. Distinctions of rank appear to be as nicely calculated here as they are in the Almanac de Gotha and I detect a certain hesitation on the factor's part about where Lucy should be put. But being a white woman, she, too, is offered a room in Rowand's Folly.

As I earlier assured Addington would be the case, the factor has no news of Simon. He was apologetic about this, and most considerate of my feelings as he performed what he obviously felt to be his duty, which was to make me see that I must not entertain false hopes, must face up to the fact that it is likely Simon's fate shall forever remain a mystery. In truth, the factor told me nothing that I had not turned over in my mind many times. But the man's forthrightness has finally brought me closer to admitting the very real possibility that no trace of Simon shall ever be found.

If I chose to now, I could send Father one succinct letter which would make everything in regard to Simon clear, and also make clear to Father that the mere exercise of his will is powerless to get him what he wants. But I cannot bring myself to take such a step because what Father yearns for, he desires more fervently than anything he has ever desired before. And that is to have Simon back.

No, I will not write to him of Simon yet. I will write instead one of those reports that satisfies Father's thirst for facts. I do this as much for myself as him. I should go mad without some occupation, some distraction. As guests in the factor's house, Lucy and I must observe the proprieties. There are no opportunities for discreet assignations in this teeming fort.

We share a little time each day, taking meals at the factor's table, strolling about or conversing as I sketch. When Lucy chooses not to accompany me in my investigations of Fort Edmonton, she enjoys female company, chatters with the Indian wives of the Bay men who have the rudiments of English, and delights to amuse their children while the mothers perform domestic tasks. As much as I long for our former intimate relations, it is still a great pleasure to me to see her so happily engaged.

Meanwhile I have embarked on the task of learning all I can about the post and sketching the life of its inhabitants. I began by drawing the fort itself, which is imposingly located on a bend of the North Saskatchewan, surrounded on three sides by water, and perched some two-hundred-odd feet above the river. Methodically, I paced the dimensions of the fortifications and found they measure two hundred by three hundred feet. The palisades are strongly constructed of timbers sunk deeply in the earth like bridge pilings; they reach to a height of twenty feet. A gallery runs round all four walls and is patrolled by sentinels. At each corner of the fort, there is a bastion armed with six-pound cannon.

To assist me in my endeavours and answer any of my questions, the chief factor has put at my disposal an Orkneyman named McTavish. McTavish has told me that the Indians suspect double dealing in all matters of trade and if they believe they have been cheated are capable of turning violent. He maintains that the Honourable Company has need of this stronghold to ensure the safety of its employees.

I do not doubt these precautions are justified. One morning from the sentinels' gallery, I viewed a huge gathering of Cree and Assiniboine on the river benches below, vast herds of horses, children splashing in the shallows, hunters continually leaving camp and returning with game slung over their ponies' withers, the smoke of countless cooking fires spreading a blue fog over the hollows. I counted two hundred lodges from my vantage point, but many more were obscured from sight. A constant procession of natives arrive at the fort to barter their goods for European manufactures. Robes and pelts pass in through the blockhouse wicket: cloth, powder, shot, steel traps, knives, axes, and beads pass out. A smithy is devoted to the manufacture and repair of countless metal articles, barrel hoops, nails, chains, locks, bolts, knives, hoes, and forks for the company's garden. Vulcan's forge is fed with coal dug from the banks of the North Saskatchewan.

Trees are felled in nearby woods and turned into planks at the sawpit for boat building. From dawn until last light, the fort resounds with the whine of saws and the ringing of hammers. McTavish says the demand for boats was once insatiable. Freight on the river was carried in York boats, ugly, cumbersome vessels propelled by sweeps and a square sail which can only be set if the wind blows favourably. I'm told that they travel downriver easily enough, but ascending it is such arduous work that they were frequently abandoned to rot on riverbanks once their cargo was off-loaded. Consequently, the shipwrights, mostly men from the Scottish Isles, laboured like Sisyphus. No sooner was a craft completed than another needs be replaced.

At first I took the utmost satisfaction and pride in all this activity, viewed it as sterling testimony to British commerce and industry. But as the weeks here have passed I have come to wonder if this place bears less resemblance to Manchester than it does to some Roman outpost huddled forlornly on the periphery of the Empire, a polyglot and bastard village.

The gentlemen occupying positions of responsibility and authority see themselves as exemplars of everything British and are blissfully unaware that we visitors from the "Old Country" soon conclude the barbarians have had greater influence on the character and habits of their rulers than the rulers on those of their subjects. England may speak smugly of an Empire upon which the sun never sets, but what the sun sets upon here would surely wrinkle noses at home. I cannot hazard a guess what this place will become in a hundred years, but I am certain it will be a disappointment to London. Those in command sense the great company is in decline, but will never admit it. The factor, when he has had a glass or two of rum, will glumly grant that trade has fallen off of late, then rouse himself to lay the blame for it on the doorstep of American traders who indulge in the low, cheating, despicable practice of selling whisky to the Indians.

I've witnessed older employees of the company shake their heads and say that in John Rowand's day matters would have been taken in hand, John Rowand would have put the fear of God into Americans and Indians both. They would have been made to sit up and mind their p's and q's. I think it safe to say that a fondness for all things past is a sure sign of creeping rot.

Yesterday, one of the blacksmiths, Angus McDonald, a hale and hearty septuagenarian, pointed a stubby finger at the Hudson's Bay Company flag flying above Rowand's Folly and inquired whether I knew what the initials on it, HBC, stood for. As I opened my mouth to make the obvious answer, he winked and said, "Here Before Christ, laddie. Here Before Christ."

Old hands such as Angus McDonald seem to look back to the days of the tyrant John Rowand with inexplicable fondness. He has been dead these twenty years, but his name is still spoken with awe and reverence. Father would most certainly approve of John Rowand, a man after his own heart, as ruthless and cunning an entrepreneur as Henry Gaunt. Both were builders, both brooked no opposition.

It was Rowand who constructed the looming, three-storey structure of hand-hewn logs which is the chief factor's residence and in which Lucy, Addington, and I are housed. This primitive palace is known as Rowand's Folly, and is famous throughout the North-West. When John Rowand came to build it, he demanded an unheard of extravagance in these parts: glass windows. So voyageurs endured hundreds of miles of back-breaking labour to ship him, by canoe and York boat, three hundred panes of glass. That alone would have made Rowand's Folly the first wonder of Rupert's Land, but he did not stop there. All around the second floor a gallery was run, an imposing stage from which his personal piper serenaded him with Rowand's favourite Highland airs while the autocrat drank rum, schemed and plotted. The interior of the log house is as barbarically grandiose as the exterior. A huge banquet hall dominates the second floor, ceiling and walls covered in painted board, fantastic curlicues, and ornamental scrolls which, I am told, never fail to impress visiting native dignitaries with their gaudy splendour. What is true of the natives is also true of myself. If the doors of the banquet hall stand open, I cannot pass without first stopping to gape.

The final, crowning touch to Rowand's Folly is an enormous ballroom which, some maintain, the factor used as a shooting gallery to perfect his pistol marksmanship during long winter days.

Stories about him abound. He took for his "country wife" an Indian girl who went looking for him after he failed to return to the fort from a buffalo hunt. Finding him defenceless on the prairie with a broken leg, she carried him to the fort, nursed him back to health. On her he sired four daughters and two sons. Of the sons, Chief Trader Mr. Jack, as he is commonly known, seems to be the apple which fell closest to the tree. He rose to command Fort Carlton, whether on the strength of his abilities or because he was Caesar's son it is impossible to say. Remarkably, the second son, Alexander, attended Edinburgh University, and is now a distinguished surgeon who practises medicine in Quebec City.

Like Captain Bligh, John Rowand was a great flogger of men, but unlike Bligh, he never faced mutiny because his cowed underlings were too afraid to chance it. Old men at the fort speak proudly of having been beaten by Rowand or having witnessed one of his notorious rages. When a violent hailstorm smashed hundreds of his precious windows, he is reported to have shaken his fists at the heavens, cursing, howling, threatening God Himself. One wag remarked to me if God had answered the challenge, he wouldn't have known on whom to bet.

In the end, Rowand's incorrigible temper did him in. One spring he accompanied the boats to Fort Carlton to visit his son, Mr. Jack. There, one of Rowand's men quarrelled with one of his son's engages and a fight broke out. Rowand ordered his man to stop but was ignored in the heat of battle. This insubordination drove the old man berserk, sent him rampaging up and down the wharf until suddenly he was struck down by apoplexy.

The question then arose what was to be done with the great factor's body. The old man had always expressed a desire to be returned to the province of Quebec, the place of his birth, so that he could lie in repose beside his father. This obviously presented problems given the vast distances separating Rowand from his wish. It was decided the corpse must be reduced to a skeleton, and an old Indian was hired to boil Mr. Rowand down to his bones. Remuneration was promised – as much rum as the Indian could drink. Many swear that after the task was completed, Indian women used Rowand's fat to make soap.

Rowand's odyssey grew even stranger. His bones were stowed in a keg of rum to preserve them, shipped by boat to York Factory, and from there to London. The Hudson Bay Company wished to provide a fitting memorial service for the good and faithful servant who had earned them so much profit.

When Rowand was decanted in London, it was discovered the voyageurs had drunk the rum he was pickled in and replaced it with water. Not only had Rowand provided soap for the Indians, but he had given cheer to the French Canadians who transported him.

Once the company paid its respects in London, Rowand was shipped back to Canada for burial. Crossing the Atlantic twice before he was finally interred, surely his was one of the most interminable funeral processions ever recorded.

When we first arrived here, Addington basked in the attention of the chief factor and the gentlemen of the fort, drinking away the nights in their company and losing a good deal of money playing cards. He so revelled in the limelight that all my attempts to press him into action were curtly rebuffed. Addington's chief interest, aside from carousing, was pestering Potts to find a grizzly bear for him to slay with his longbow. But this did not prove possible, since Potts said all bears are shot on sight by the men of the fort to prevent attacks on horses and livestock. The shortage of grizzly bears in the vicinity has clearly contributed to my brother's ill humour.

In the past week, Addington has become increasingly gloomy and withdrawn, sometimes not leaving his bed until midday. Often I saw him lounging up against the log wall of Rowand's Folly, hands stuffed in the pockets of his trousers, sunk in a brown study. When we took supper at the chief factor's table, my brother was bad company, sullen, and frequently rude. He drank too much and ate little, scarcely attended to the factor's conversation.

Yesterday, however, I learned from Ayto that Addington has informed the chief factor that we will, in short order, depart for the whisky posts of the south. This was welcome news. Typically, my brother has made no mention of this to me, but as Lucy once suggested, Addington's inconstancy has returned him to the mark. My anxiety is that if we do not move quickly, the onset of winter shall suspend steamer traffic on the Missouri and make our return to England impossible.

This afternoon, Lucy and I had an hour or two alone. In two days, the chief factor intends to send the Gaunt party off in high style with a grand banquet and ball to be held in Rowand's Folly. Lucy took me utterly by surprise when she told me that Addington has invited her to outfit herself for the ball at his expense. This, he said, was a small token of appreciation for all the pains she has taken to make us comfortable on the trail in the past months. I found Addington's unexpected generosity both perplexing and disturbing but said nothing to Lucy, not wanting to dampen her delight in the purchases she had made at the company store. Her ballgown is to be a surprise for me on the night of the dance, and I was required to solemnly swear not to attempt to spy on her sewing it. Lucy's girlish excitement is a side of her I had not seen before and it is most charming. She is positively flirtatious and brims with innocent, feminine glee.

The much heralded night has arrived and I am bored. I had hoped to have Lucy upon my arm for the banquet, but at the last moment her composure fled and she refused to accompany me. No matter how I entreated her, she was most adamant that she would not attend and be the one woman in the midst of "so many Britishers." The dance, she argued, is a different matter, there will be plenty of Métis and Indian women present. But she will not allow herself to fall under the scrutiny of a hall full of men. "They will all think me Charles Gaunt's scarlet woman and stare and whisper," she said. There was nothing I could do to dismiss her fears.

So here I sit at a groaning board, taking my farewell of valiant trenchermen and bibulous clerks, longing for the refreshment of Lucy's company. Course succeeds course with stomach-numbing regularity, gargantuan servings of meat dishes leavened with boiled potatoes and turnips. Buffalo hump, boss ribs, beaver tails, dried moose nose, whitefish fried in buffalo marrow, and the pièce de résistance, a buffalo calf removed from its dam by Caesarean operation, and preserved in the ice house for just such a momentous feast. Gallons of rum and claret have been downed. Our bread pudding shovelled home, now we have embarked on port and oratory.

The factor toasts our health and reviews the pleasures our society has provided him. No sooner does he take his seat than one of his scruffy, drunken clerks seizes the floor and tearfully recites some Robbie Burns. Nothing is as dreadful as a Scot who sheds his dourness. On and on it goes, compliments extended to the English gentlemen, pointless reminiscences of our month's stay at Fort Edmonton, professions of undying friendship, all of which I submit to with a gratified smile pasted to my lips.

Not so my brother, who has remained red-eyed and choleric throughout the festivities, bending a spoon in his hands. It has not penetrated the dim recesses of his tiny mind that the Hudson Bay men eagerly await some equal return of sentiment from the leader of our expedition. But no, Addington keeps silent and holds to his place while dismay spreads among those trying to prompt him to acknowledge the company's unstinting generosity for so many weeks.

I have stubbornly determined not to launch a lifeboat and come to the rescue when, unsteadily, Ayto, glass in hand, rises to his feet and beams upon the hopeful assembly. "Dear friends," he begins, "many of you know I am the Captain's secretary and in that humble capacity I wish to step into the breach. The Captain is a man of action, not of words, and I know how he trembles to address you. It is my most earnest desire to relieve him of that terror." Laughter linked to the mention of his name jolts Addington out of his trance; under glowering brows he regards Ayto as if he has suddenly become aware there is a madman at table. Already in full flight, the Yankee journalist does not register my brother's baleful glare.

"Caleb Ayto," he says, hooking his thumbs in his waistcoat, "a humble citizen of the great republic which abuts your borders, has been deeply moved by the generosity and courtesy shown to me by my cousins to the north. On behalf of the Gaunt expedition, let me tender a few words of heartfelt thanks, not only for the splendid dinner and the overflowing cup we have all partaken of tonight, but for all you have done in the past weeks to relieve the cares and tribulations of weary travellers. We have faced many dangers, been subject to much hardship, tasted the bitterness of hope disappointed as we searched in vain for the noble Captain's lost brother. But you, gentlemen, have lifted our spirits and eased our despair with the balm of true friendship. With renewed vigour, we sally forth on our sacred quest, confident of your prayers for our success in the coming days . . ."

Overwhelmed by this tide of purple bilgewater, I float off on my own thoughts, anticipating the sight of Lucy arrayed in her new gown until a burst of clapping and the cheers of those assembled mark the termination of Ayto's peroration and rouse me from my stupor.

The factor announces the dance is shortly to begin and we gentlemen, led by a piper, enter the ballroom, promenade round to the skirl of the bagpipe, applauded by company employees, stared at by Indian headmen draped in buffalo robes and Hudson Bay blankets. After enduring one more circuit of the room, the most eminent among us are ushered to a half-dozen pine chairs which have been guarded from trespass by several gnarly-fisted French-Canadian boatmen, one of whom has a kerchief tied around his head, lending him a fierce and piratical aspect.

At the factor's signal, three fiddlers and the piper who escorted us into the hall strike up a tempestuous air. The virtuoso of the orchestra is a Métis Paganini arrayed in gorgeous evening dress, snowy-white buckskin frock coat and waistcoat decorated with silk embroidery and beadwork flowers. As he saws his bow, face running with sweat, long hair whipping, the glass beads scatter candlelight, make him shimmer like a rainbow.

Where is Lucy? I cast an anxious glance to the door of the ballroom, jammed with Indian statesmen shrouded in skin togas, but catch not a glimpse of her.

The ball proceeds. Jigs and reels follow hard upon each other, as if dancing were a competition, or a trial of endurance. Every once in a while some dancer flails his feet on the floor so expertly and exuberantly that he gathers an admiring crowd, which then whoops and urges him on to greater feats of terpsichore.

There are no shy, retiring ladies here fanning themselves coyly in a quiet corner. The women are as active and boisterous as the men; their faces shine with sweaty bliss. The Cree and Assiniboine girls who have clearly participated in a white man's dance before perform the intricate steps with a lively confidence, while the novices simply spring up and down on the spot, joy launching them several feet above the floor, as they leap like the bounding hart.

Addington, who is seated on the factor's right, suddenly rises from his chair and begins to prowl the edges of the dance floor. Back and forth, back and forth he paces, swigging from a pocket flask. There is something odd about his gait, the jolting action of a mechanical toy. He stares down at his feet as if willing them to move, as if he must *think* each step before he makes it, as if he is uncertain his foot can be trusted to make contact with the floor. A young Indian women interrupts his sentry duty, makes signs she wishes him as a partner for the next dance, but he waves her off with a disgusted look on his face.

I turn away from my brother's rudeness just in time to see Lucy make her entrance, weave her way towards me through the throng of onlookers. My heart quickens. How pale and self-conscious she appears. How this adds to her loveliness. Her red hair is drawn into a pretty chignon from which an ebony velvet ribbon trails, over her shoulder down to her breast. The velvety sable of the ribbon heightens, deepens, darkens her brown eyes until they appear almost black. The gown is very simple, a high-bodiced, long-skirted white muslin tied with another black ribbon at the waist. A fashion *à la Grecque*, or perhaps the dress of the heroine of a Jane Austen novel. And the shoes, ladies' booties peeping out from under the hem of her skirt, are of a style so defunct as to have become lost in the mists of time. God knows for whom they were ordered, unless perhaps for Mistress John Rowand, or how long they have sat upon a shelf waiting to be claimed, but here they are, carrying Lucy Stoveall to join me.

I rise and bow. "My dear, you are ravishing."

The compliment colours and flusters her.

She asks, "It's all right then?"

"You are the belle of the ball."

Trying to disguise her pleasure, she seats herself. A moment later, her foot begins to tap in time to the raucous music. Is this a signal to me? Am I to request the pleasure of the next dance?

But a young Frenchman with long curly hair tickling the collar of his blouse saves me from attempting to cut these athletic capers. He stands mute before Lucy and offers his hand.

"Go along, Lucy," I say. "I doubt a dancing master could be found in London to cover this ground. And I assure you, it is beyond my poor powers."

And there she is, jigging with the rest of them, feet spattering on the floor, face rosy with effort, eyes joyous as the music increases tempo, as the chinks in the floorboards puff dust. When the dance ends, the young Frenchman surrenders Lucy to a new partner who draws her back into the hooting crowd of dancers. She is transported by the music and to see her transported delights me. Unmindful of all past and future troubles, Lucy is happy to be nothing but a body lost in reckless grace.

The heat in the ballroom is overpowering, dizzying. I take out a handkerchief and mop my face. As I put it away I catch sight of Addington, finally still. Ayto is with him, leaning into his ear, nattering away. My brother pays him not a speck of attention; there is a disturbingly lost look about Addington's flushed face.

Suddenly a shout goes up among a knot of dancers. "Chasse aux lièvres! Chasse aux lièvres!" The cry is taken up by all until the rafters ring with it. Men and women rush about, seizing spectators, dragging them on to the dance floor. A pretty Indian girl with a coppery moon-shaped face effects my kidnapping despite my protests. She wears a red gingham dress decorated with jangling copper bells which jangle all the harder as she hauls me out of my seat, tugging fiercely on my wrist.

All the dancers join hands and we form a huge ring. A blushing, protesting young man is shoved into the centre of it by his rowdy chums. The orchestra strikes up a tune and we all begin to circle the embarrassed lad. Round and round we go until the music abruptly stops and everyone begins to sing:

> "De ma main droite
> Je tiens Rosalie
> Belle Rosalie!
>
> Qui porte la fleur
> Dans le mois de mai,
> Belle Rosalie!
>
> Embrassez qui vous voudrez
> Car j'aurai la moite."

Much abashed, the chap looks down at his feet, then abruptly moves to a young Métis girl on whose cheek he bestows a decorous peck as the crowd roars its approval, flinging risqué *beaux gestes*. The young lady takes the place of the young man, round and round we go, until the melody once more ceases, and we sing the refrain. The girl selects her gallant, kisses him, and the Chasse aux Lièvres continues.

The music once more breaks off, and a shyly grinning, sandy-haired Scot prepares himself to choose his favoured lady when Addington suddenly bustles forward, breaks through the ring, and stalks to the side of the startled Scot. There is astonishment and shock at this breach of custom and good manners. My brother is oblivious to the dancers' reaction. He takes the boy by the shoulder and murmurs something in his ear, claps a hand to his back. The Scot remains rooted to the spot for a brief moment before shuffling away, looking puzzled and downcast.

A strained hush falls on the crowd as Addington slowly begins to circle the ring of dancers, running his eyes over the women with a peculiar, gloating smile. There is lewd calculation in his gaze, as if each woman is being undressed by his eyes, fondled by the hands clenching and unclenching at his sides.

All the girls and women lower their heads to avoid his appraisal. All at once, Addington comes face to face with Lucy. She is the first to refuse to flinch, returns his stare with one of equal intensity. The two of them stand motionless as seconds pass. Then Addington takes two sudden, lurching strides, seizes Lucy, and brutally kisses her mouth.

It is over in a flash. My brother violently thrusts Lucy away from him, she stumbles backward, collides with one of the dancers, is caught in his arms and saved from falling. Addington, head down, bulls his way through the outraged crowd, blindly knocking people aside with shoulders and forearms, striding with that strange, jerky deliberateness.

Just like that, my brother disappears from the scene. I hurry to Lucy's side, my anger checked by concern, take her hand and lead her through the confusion, the whispers, and astonished murmuring.

"Are you injured?" I say. "Please, you must sit." The factor holds a chair for her.

Lucy presses the heel of her hand to her lips. Her eyes are mournful and sad. "Why would your brother want to spoil my gay time? Why would he treat me so?" she asks.

I have no answer. Behind us, the music resumes.

"Wait here," I order her. "I must speak to him about his abominable behaviour."

Lucy grabs my sleeve. "No, let it pass. I don't want to see him rip you like he did Custis Straw. He's a frightful person, your brother."

"Keep Mrs. Stoveall safe," I say to the factor. "I shall be back directly."

I descend to the first floor of Rowand's Folly calling out, "Addington! Addington, damn you! Where are you! Answer me!"

Getting no reply, I push out into the grounds of the deserted fort. The gallery holds no pacing sentinels tonight; all company employees have been given leave to attend the dance. A cadaverous mongrel heaves up from the dirt, trots to my side with a questioning whine, follows me as I make a tour of the outbuildings, testing the silence with my brother's name. I receive no answer.

There is a chill to the night air; I feel the drops of sweat shrinking on my face. A brisk wind has swept the sky clean of clouds. All that is left are millions of scattered, glassy stars pricking out the beadwork of Heaven, the Big and Little Dipper, Hercules, the Hunting Dogs. I gaze up at them for a long interval until they begin to dash my vision with yellow rails of light. When I drop my eyes, I see it, one window lit on the third floor of Rowand's Folly.

Back in the house, I race up the stairs two at a time, the whirlwind music blowing me upward. I come to a brief halt in the passage, gulp air into my lungs after my rush up the staircase. A splinter of illumination shows under Addington's door. I give no warning, lift the latch, and enter his room.

My brother is sitting on the bed. A small table is drawn to the edge of the straw-tick mattress, and on the table stands a lantern. Addington looks up at me without surprise, as if he has been waiting for me to arrive.

I can scarcely credit my eyes. The flame of the lantern completely burnishes his torso and arms with an armorial, chivalric, silvery brightness. He looks as if he has donned a chain-mail shirt. The sight of him drives whatever admonitions I had prepared straight out of my consciousness. Stunned, I drop down on a chair.

Addington says nothing, simply reaches for a vial on the table, shake a few gleaming drops into his hand, and smears it on his face. Then he grimaces; his countenance streaked with what appears to be melting tin.

"Addington –" I say. My brother shrugs his shoulders impatiently, holds up a hand to stay any conversation. So I simply sit and watch him paint his face with meticulous care. His task completed, he turns on me a blank silver mask out of which gape two dead-blue eyes, a red, leering mouth.

"Addington," I say, "what is this? Explain yourself."

In a voice as empty of emotion as are his eyes, he states, "It creeps up on a fellow when he isn't active. I neglected to remember that. But keep on the move and it can't overtake you. So tomorrow, maybe the day after, I shall be in the saddle again. That's the elixir I require."

"You are talking nonsense. I can't grasp what you are trying to tell me."

My brother follows some line of argument evident only to himself. "In the meantime, a fellow has to rely on stopgaps. A defensive posture, hold the line until counterattack is possible." He lifts the bottle, shakes it at me. "Mercury. I've been slothful, no one to blame but myself. Gave it a chance to bore away in me. Lightning pains in the joints, quite terrific. Sleepless nights, etc. But once I get on the go I'll be able to dispense with the quicksilver. As a remedy it isn't all it's claimed to be. Collects in the brain, settles there, muddles a fellow's thoughts. What's more, it drains down into the legs, turns them heavy as lead." Addington looks down at his limbs, pats them sadly. "It's why I didn't dance tonight. Could hardly lift my legs. Everyone would have enjoyed to see me dance, but what does a chap do when he can hardly stir his legs?" His coat of silver shoots reflected light at me. In the silence that follows I can hear him breathing. "I might have sung them a song – one I wrote – but I didn't think of it at the time. I find my thoughts rather scattered these days. I'll give you a treat though, let you hear my composition, Charles."

And to the tune of the "Roast Beef of Old England," Addington begins to sing in an uninflected, monotonous voice.

"When mighty Roast Buffalo
Was the Englishman's food,
It ennobled our brains
And enriched our blood
Our soldiers were brave
And our courtiers were good
Oh the Roast Buffalo of Old England
And old English Roast Buffalo!"

After one verse, he gives up serenading me. "A song to good health," he comments. "I didn't realize my talent for music. The melody just came into my head and then the words were there too. I'm a man of mysterious parts, even to myself."

He shivers. His head hangs for a few moments, regarding the legs too heavy to dance. He lifts the silver mask to me again and says in a childish, earnest voice, "Now, Charles, you're the scholar in the family. I have a question for you. Is it true that syphilis got its name from a character in a poem, a shepherd boy or some such thing. Is that true?"

I clear my throat and say as evenly as I can, "I do not know."

"Well, if it's true it must be a very bad poem to give its name to this thing." My brother snorts laughter. The effect is repellent, a sudden contortion of the muscles of his face which twists the mask queasily.

I lean forward. "Addington, you are ill."

"Ill for the time being, but I shall recover once I am in the open air again."

"No, Addington, do not think that. You must return to England immediately and seek treatment."

"England is not the place for me. England is an indolent place. There is no room for activity there. It loves indolence, my affliction. One must burn it out, you see. Burn it out of the system with a thrill, a touch of danger. That's the ticket." He looks at me closely, to see if I have understood. "The thing is for a man to find himself a place where he fits, Charles," he continues with assurance. "I never fit in England. Too small a parish, no scope. But here – a different story." His head bobs up and down, confirming his own statement as he wipes his fingers restlessly on the counterpane of the bed. "What we must do is go south. At once."

"No," I say, "we must not. You must return to England. You are unwell."

Addington does not hear me. His brain has made another sudden, erratic dart. "You didn't know the chap – Sergeant Carlyle – but he swore by all the gods that the surest remedy for a blood disease was congress with a virgin. A fresh young girl drew the poison right out of your system. Now what do you think of that? There's a prescription a fellow ought to follow. I tried it once, but several dosings might be necessary."

"That's old soldiers' talk – ignorance and superstition. You must put yourself in the hands of a doctor, a specialist in England. It is your only hope."

All at once, his voice trembles. "You must assist and support me, Charles."

I breathe a little easier. "Naturally, I shall do whatever I can."

But he means something else. "I want Father to build me a fort. Not some piddling place like this," he says with a dismissive wave, "but an immense fortification in the south to control the whisky trade, drive competitors from the field. A great fort with granite towers – you could sketch them for him. But, no," he continues, careering off excitedly, "first you must write and explain the soundness of it as an investment. The return on capital which can be had. Pounds and shillings and pence. You must do so immediately." Addington snatches up a piece of paper from the table and thrusts it into my hand. "Tell Father that we leave tomorrow to scout the lie of the land, to select a dominating location for my fort. Explain to him how important it is to overawe the natives with towers."

I place the paper back on the table. "I go nowhere tomorrow, Addington, unless it is to take you back to England."

He stiffens. "You are obliged to do as I say. Father put me in charge."

In this crisis, the evident must be stated. I struggle to contain my tears, to speak softly to Addington. "We must accept that Simon is dead. We must go back to England."

"If you refuse to follow orders, I shall make a report to Father of your immoral relations with that woman. I have suspected for some time that your behaviour was responsible for undermining the men's respect for me, that it has sowed dissension and insubordination. Your conduct brought dishonour to the family name, and made it impossible for me to lead."

My brother's impenetrable glittering shield has deflected everything I have said. As gently as I can, I make another attempt to reach him. "Please consider your condition. You are presently as unsound in your mind as in your body. If you refuse to heed good advice, I have no alternative but to remove Mrs. Stoveall from your company, take her back to Fort Benton. Your actions this evening have made it clear that no woman is safe with you. I shall request Mr. Potts to accompany us."

"You cannot have Potts! Potts is mine!" he cries petulantly. "I have promised him five hundred dollars if he finds me a grizzly, and he will stick by me until he has it. Besides, Potts and I are on the best of terms. Do you not see how he preens since I adopted Mr. Ayto's sobriquet for him, call him Mr. Moses? Potts is a bit of a spaniel. I shall pet him up and have my way with him."

I get to my feet. "I implore you to clear these phantoms from your mind and accept my offer to see you safely back to England. We shall speak again tomorrow morning when you are rested, and better able to think."

My hand is on the door when Addington querulously cries out to me. "I place a respectable woman under my protection and you ruin her! That is despicable! Your infamy shall not be forgiven, Charles!"

I stand for several moments with my hand resting on the latch. Finally, I turn back. Addington is vigorously running a finger around inside his mouth. He takes it out and wipes it on his trousers. "My mouth is full of sores," he declares, sounding puzzled. "Do you think I got them from kissing Mrs. Stoveall?"

24

Jerry Potts would stay with Captain Gaunt. Charles Gaunt and the woman would be well enough off in Fort Edmonton until they could hitch up with some party heading down from the North Saskatchewan to Montana. The Captain's route was more dangerous, he and his men would have to cross several hundred miles of Blackfoot territory to reach Fort Whoop-Up, but once there, Potts reasoned he could wash his hands of him. Whenever the Captain decided to return to Fort Benton, he could travel in safety with one of the bull trains that hauled trade goods between the Upper Missouri and the junction of the St. Mary and Belly rivers. But above all else, Potts had a hankering to spend time among his mother's people, to feast and smoke in their lodges.

On the long trip south to Fort Whoop-Up, the Captain's behaviour had been unpredictable. When he played cards at night, he confused the men with sudden changes of the rules, abruptly turning a game of poker into a game of rummy every few hands. He sang the same song over and over all day long in a loud, tuneless voice.

Now that they have arrived at Fort Whoop-Up, the Captain has grown even more excitable. He vexes strangers with his nonsense about building a big stone fort to steal the liquor trade from the Americans. When he's not describing his fort, he talks continually of killing a grizzly with his bow. Grunewald and Barker do their best to keep clear of the Englishman. Even Ayto, who has always boasted of his friendship with the Captain, seems to avoid him. But each night the Captain demands Ayto copy down his strange thoughts, thoughts that fly about here and there like birds, and are as difficult to catch. Potts can see in Ayto's eyes how he has become afraid of the Captain.

Potts is weary of loud, swaggering men like Addington Gaunt, but in Fort Whoop-Up they are present everywhere, fifty or more of them within the walls, strutting, making empty threats, boasting of the hard things they have done or will do. This is not a restful place. He spends most of his time in the quarters of the McKay brothers – half-breed hunters Johnny Healy has hired to supply meat for his traders – or in the lodges of the Blackfoot camped just outside the fort.

For the moment, he is giving his eyes and ears respite from braggarts. He sits with his back to the log wall of the fort's stable, basking in the last, soothing rays of the September sun, considering whether to find the grizzly the Captain wheedles for like a small child begging for a bright bauble.

At Fort Edmonton, Potts had seen plenty of grizzly sign. One day he had even spotted a big sow feeding on the carcass of a buffalo calf that had drowned and washed up on the banks of the river. But he had told the Captain nothing of this, and when the Captain had pleaded with him to find him a bear, Potts had said there were no grizzlies about. He lied to the Englishman because he was sure the Captain only wanted to kill a grizzly for the sake of the book Ayto is writing about him.

The Englishman is very sick. When he walks he totters like an old man, and pisses like one too. Potts has seen him standing behind a wagon, pulling and coaxing his pizzle to let him make water. There was more sweat and tears on the Englishman's face than there was piss on the ground.

Potts wonders if Gaunt's desire to kill a grizzly is in truth a desire for something very different. Maybe he is asking Potts to help him find an honourable way to rid himself of his own feeble body. The Captain is not a man to accept death on a sickbed. It may be he wants to enter the World of Skeletons like a man, with courage.

Potts cannot decide what to do about this matter. So he sits in the early-autumn sun and watches all the Fort Whoop-Up men walk about as if they own the place. He was here long before any of them, at the very beginning of the fort, hunting game for the thirty men constructing the post. He had not listened to Mary when she asked him not to work for Johnny Healy; he had taken the job and, because of that, had lost her and Mitchell forever. Potts asks himself why he was so stubborn. The money he earned working for Healy was spent a long time ago, and empty pockets are all he has to show for displeasing his wife.

Potts thinks of the man who had directed the raising of the fort, a carpenter Healy had lured away from the Hudson Bay Company. Having been north to Edmonton, Potts can see the hand of the Bay Man everywhere in Fort Whoop-Up, see it in the solid timber stockade, in the shops and warehouses, in the big oak gates, everything on the pattern of the company forts, right down to the two brass cannon mounted kitty-corner on the palisades. The only thing not the same is the flag flying above the palisades, the striped star flag.

The fort is rock solid, but Potts cannot say the same about the men inside it. They are not so easily ruled as the hirelings of the English company. They remind him of his second father Harvey, the rash, reckless, whisky-drinking father. When the big bosses, D. W. Davis and Johnny Healy, leave Fort Whoop-Up, the men act like children, shoot the cannons off, cheer as the three-pound balls splash geysers in the Belly and St. Mary rivers. Sometimes they amuse themselves up on the walls by taking potshots at Indian dogs, or by jeering at the singing, drunken Blackfoot who stumble about down below them. They brag about the time they put a keg of whisky up on the sod roof of the barracks for "Injun bait," as they called it, and "lit candles" under the thieves' feet, firing rifles up into the ceiling to make them hop.

The old Blackfoot name for the junction of the Belly and the St. Mary is Many Ghosts. Before the Americans came, this was a site of many battles, hundreds fell in fights with the Cree. It is still a place of death, but death without honour. From the whites in Fort Whoop-Up, Potts has heard about the most recent outbreak of the white scabs sickness. Stories of wailing men, women, and children who crowded round the fort, rubbing their weeping sores on the gates, wiping blood and pus on the walls, stacking their dead in a great pile near the palisade, hoping to send the disease back to the white men.

Those of the Blackfoot the white scabs doesn't kill, the whisky does. In winter, many fall down in a stupor, freeze stiff in the snow. Whisky robs them of their good sense so they cannot tell right from wrong. Sons kill fathers, husbands murder wives, brothers slay brothers.

Potts sees all this plain when he is sober, but this is also why he does not care to be sober. He likes how whisky puts sun in his belly and lights his head with happiness. When he drinks, he grows tall, feels his bandy legs straighten and raise him up as high in the world as any white man. Whisky makes him every bit as tall as D. W. Davis, the Whoop-Up boss Potts's people call Spityana, Tall Man. When he is sober, Potts barely reaches Spityana's shoulders, but drunk he can look Davis straight in his cold eyes and show him he does not give a damn for what he thinks.

Word reaches Potts that his mother's uncle, Horse Tail, and the old man's wife, Good Blanket, have set up camp on their own down by the St. Mary so as not to get mixed up in the quarrels and drinking in the big Blackfoot camp. They want to live in the old clean way of the Real People, but Horse Tail is blind and cannot hunt, so it is a hungry time for the couple.

Potts buys a sack of flour, some jerked meat, tea and sugar, a rope of tobacco to tide his relatives over until he can kill them some meat. He slings these goods on to his horse and rides to the spot where Horse Tail has pitched camp near a grove of poplar. The leaves have turned and flutter gold with every puff of wind. Soon the air will be full of snow, not yellow leaves. In his bones, Potts can feel winter coming.

He meets Good Blanket coming out of the bush with an armful of wood. She tells him Horse Tail is in the lodge. She says every morning her husband goes to visit his children on the outskirts of the fort to try to persuade them to give up the whisky, but they do not listen to him. Each day he returns home sadder. These are lonely days for Horse Tail, but maybe a talk with a warrior will lift his spirits. Potts presents her with the food he has brought, smiles and says that a good dinner will make all three of them more cheerful.

He stoops through the entrance of the lodge, calling out a greeting, and finds the old man sitting propped in his red willow back rest, medicine bundle dangling above his grey head. Settling across the fire from him, Potts realizes Horse Tail has only recognized him by the sound of his voice. The old man's eyes are covered with a grey-blue film, are sticky with rheum. He makes slow passes in front of his face with an eagle tail fan to keep the season's last drowsy flies from lighting on them.

Potts gives his uncle the gift of tobacco. Horse Tail sniffs it, exclaims over its quality, and the goodness of his nephew's heart, as he prepares to smoke. From the way the old man handles the pipe, pointing the mouthpiece to the Four Directions, upward to the Sky People, down to the Earth, Potts is aware he intends to speak of serious matters with his nephew. The old man smokes a pinch of tobacco in silence, taps out the ash before he speaks. "Bear Child, it is good to see you again."

"And I am glad to see you, Uncle."

"Every day I go to Hope Up," the old man says, stumbling to pronounce the difficult English name for the fort, "and try to talk sense to my sons, but they do not listen to me."

"Ah," Potts says sympathetically.

"The last time I was there, they could talk of nothing else but you, Bear Child. They say there is an Englishman at Hope Up who has promised five hundred dollars to you when you find a bear for him to kill. They say that when you get the Englishman's money, you will throw a great feast and there will be plenty of whisky for all your relatives." There is a note of accusation in Horse Tail's voice, he waits for Potts to respond to it, but his nephew says nothing. The old man clears his throat. "I do not think you should sell a bear to the Englishman. You were given the grizzly's name, you are its child. It would not be proper to do as the Englishman wants. You must consider this carefully."

"Bear Child is not my only name. I have a white name. Jerry Potts."

The old man notes the defensiveness of the reply, nods his head thoughtfully, eyes shining like glass in the firelight. "That is true," he says. "But you earned the name Bear Child. It is an honour name, and you should not bring disgrace to it."

"I have another honour name. The Englishman who wants the bear gave it to me. He named me Mr. Moses."

The old man refills the calumet, fingers feeling the tobacco into the stone bowl. "I do not understand the honour attached to this name. It means nothing to me."

"There was an Englishman called Moses," explains Potts, "who stole away all the English prisoners from where they were held captive. Moses led them across a great desert with his powerful medicine stick. He defeated the enemies of his people."

Potts holds out a flaming twig from the fire to light the old man's pipe. Horse Tail serenely sucks until it draws smoothly. "I have heard bad things about this Englishman who wants you to sell him a bear," he says at last. "But I do not know the truth about him."

Potts studies the seamed face, darkened from years of sun and wind. "He is an angry, proud man. A man of cruelty," Potts begins. Then he stops, and makes to correct himself. "Uncle," he says, "I did not tell you all there is to tell. He calls me Mr. Moses, but there is no honour in the name."

"Ai!" exclaims Horse Tail.

"But I think even though he has shown me no respect, there is a place deep in his mind that recognizes I might be able to lead him to what he really wants. Perhaps he has known there would come a time when I would be able to free him." Potts pauses.

"How will you save him? Did the butterfly come to you? Have you dreamed it?"

Potts wishes that the butterfly, the messenger of the spirits, had come to him in his sleep and brought an answer on its outstretched wings. But this is not the case.

"No, Uncle. The butterfly did not come. That is why I must rely on your wisdom. The Englishman is very sick. His sickness disgusts him, and troubles his mind. I pity him now." Potts stirs the fire with a stick; flecks of dark-red light rise and hover between him and the old man. "I think he does not want to rot away. I believe he asks for something to overcome the illness of his body and mind."

Horse Tail arranges his long braids in his lap. "Yesterday, the American who is a friend to the Englishman came with three armed men from the fort into the village. They tried to buy a very young girl for the Englishman. Her parents would not take what they offered, and drove them away. But maybe soon, it will happen, and the Englishman will get such a young girl."

"Yes," says Potts, "that is like him. As he spoils, he wishes to spoil others."

"Now that I know your mind on this, and how it is with the Englishman, I believe it is right to speak to you of something Good Blanket told me. She saw a grizzly up the river not far from here. She says he is very strong. The tips of his coat hairs are white. To her, he looks very wise. This may be the bear intended to help you accomplish this thing. I think the Englishman needs to meet his bear quickly."

All afternoon, Potts works up and down the Oldman River, searching for evidence of the grizzly. He finds one set of bear tracks in the mud on the riverbank, but they do not show claw marks and the prints are far too small. They belong to a black bear. A little before dusk, in the shade of a clump of trees overhanging the riverbank, he discovers a spot where a deer had made its bed. Blood lies thick on the ground and a trail of crushed grass shows where the carcass has been dragged off into the heart of the bush.

He cocks his carbine and carefully backs off. At dawn, when the grizzly is hungry, the bear will come to feed here again.

❖ ❖ ❖

Potts has brought Addington glad tidings that rouse in him a heady click of excitement. The Captain feels as he did when his mother sent him off to bed on Christmas Eve to face the long hours before he could tear the wrapping paper from his gifts. But now there is no one to calm him. How he longs for her pale, serene face, her tranquil, gentle voice. For years his memories of his mother have retreated and ebbed until all that remains is a vague sense of her – a meek, round face hovering above his bed, her voice coaxing him to please her, to be Mother's best boy.

Long past midnight, the Captain sits watching the firewood crumble in a crucible of ragged, wind-whipped flame, listening. "Dearest child," the voice whispers, "you know how it annoys Father when you break things. You must learn to handle the world more carefully, my angel."

But it is his father who breaks things, not little Addington. It is he who shatters happiness like a bull breaks dishes in a china shop. At Father's age, to be in rut. Filling a delicate woman with those whelps, Charles and Simon, sentencing her to death with his lust. Who was the great destroyer? Who was careless and selfish? The old prattling hypocrite with his lectures on sexual hygiene, his interminable moralizing. What were whores for, if not to save fine women like his mother from the unspeakable attentions of men such as Father?

In time, he loses the sound of her voice in the crackle of the fire and his excitement swells uncontrollably. He goes off and finds Ayto playing cards, informs him he must be ready to set off with him at the break of dawn. Ayto shall be witness to an exploit hitherto unequalled in the annals of toxophily, shall make a record of it for posterity – a grizzly bear, *Ursus arctos horribilis*, dispatched with the ancient arms of the English yeoman.

Without waiting for Ayto to confirm he will attend this signal event, Addington heads off, propelling himself with his unsteady gait. There is tackle to inspect, arrowheads to sharpen, he must flex the longbow stave, test the bowstring. Once all this is seen to, he builds up the fire, huddles, wraps his arms tightly around his knees. The mute white face of his mother hangs in the black sky, lovely and benign as ever it was in the old days. He spends a sleepless night gazing up at it.

Potts comes to him long before dawn, tells him the hour has arrived. They look for Ayto, but he is not in his bed, is nowhere to be found. Curious. The minutes are ticking by. Potts reminds him they must reach the bear's haunt before the sun is up. It seems they must leave without Ayto, which is a pity, but he has Potts to witness the exploit.

The guide leads the way. The grass is stiffened with a hard frost, the horses' nostrils steam as the miles pass beneath their hooves. They approach a lone teepee. Potts says they must leave their mounts here. If the horses catch the scent of bear, they will go wild with terror, there will be no stopping them from stampeding. At first, Addington argues vehemently against giving up his horse. He keeps the reason to himself. Addington doubts whether his untrustworthy legs can be depended on to carry him very far. But in the end, he has to resign himself to the half-breed's wishes. Potts refuses to take him any farther unless he does as he is told.

For the first time, he catches sight of a broad-shouldered, squat old man who has been standing in the darkness listening to them argue. The old man shuffles forward slowly, stooped, braids dangling to his knees, shoulders draped in a striped Hudson Bay blanket. He speaks to Potts in a guttural language as Addington prepares to strike a lucifer and light a cigarette.

"This is Horse Tail," says Potts. "He asks to shake your hand. He is the one who really gives you the bear."

"All right," says the Captain, who is in an expansive, liberal mood this morning. He strikes the lucifer and as it flares, so do the old man's eyes. They remind Addington of two blobs of mercury reflecting light. Quickly, he extinguishes the match. "Shall we set off? Get down to business?" he abruptly asks Potts.

"He wants to shake your hand," Potts repeats.

The old man gropes for his hand, and Addington must take a few steps forward to clasp it. Horse Tail pumps Addington's arm up and down vigorously, muttering something.

"What is he saying?"

"He says goodbye," Potts tells him.

"Goodbye to you too, old fellow."

Potts and Addington set off, the scout cradling a repeater in the crook of his arm, Addington with a quiver of arrows on his back, an unstrung bow in his hand. Addington struggles along, flinging out legs that do not feel any longer as if they belong to him. After a mile of this, he is covered in sweat, but wills himself to soldier on. There is very little time left before full light breaks. Already the east shows a ruddy and saffron glow, the colour of a well-polished pippin.

"Not much farther now," Potts encourages him.

Ahead, the land slopes down to the Belly. Addington can see the fish-hook gleam of a bend in the river in the brown surround.

A few minutes more and they reach a vantage point that presents an unobstructed view of a wood a hundred yards distant. The effort of covering the last stretch has left Addington exhausted, and when Potts motions him to keep down, not show himself, he gratefully drops to his belly and into the embrace of the soaked, chill grass.

There the two men lie, their gaze fixed on the stand of trees and the river. Addington consults his pocket watch. It is now fifteen minutes past five, shapes and colours are growing distinct. He can make out the poplar crowns, sallow in the burgeoning light, a single blue cloud. The full-faced moon is still up in the sky, courted by a retinue of wan stars.

Time passes, moon and stars fade. Potts touches his arm, points. At first, Addington cannot locate what he is supposed to see, but then his straining eyes find a quaking, a ripple in the tall grass near the river, like the disturbance roused by a loaded barge passing sedately through calm water.

Out of it a grizzly emerges, the high hump of his shoulders rolling in time with his pigeon-toed shuffle. The bear pauses, rises erect on his hind legs, towers with his front paws drooping before his chest, head leisurely swinging as he samples the air, sniffing for danger. Finding nothing to alarm him, he drops back on all fours, shambles into the wood, disappears.

The sight of his magnificent quarry has robbed Addington of his breath, left him choked, strangled. Silence deepens as he fights to govern his breathing, the thump of his heart. He says to Potts, "I shall go into the wood from the landward side. Push him up against the river. Deny him all avenues of escape."

Unsteadily, Addington rises to his feet, and Potts stands too.

"In a half-hour you shall be a rich man, Mr. Moses," Addington remarks. Potts offers his hand to shake. Addington smiles. "To seal our bargain? My word is my bond. You shall get your money."

A shower of black birds falls into the wood where the bear has vanished, then shoots skyward, an explosion of jet fireworks. A meadowlark practises scales. A muskrat writes his signature in the water of the Belly.

"I do not want your money," Potts says suddenly.

Impulsively, Addington grips the scout's hand. The clamminess of the half-breed's palm is unexpected. "Very well then."

And, with that, Addington bends and strings his bow, then quickly moves off in the direction of the wood, heading to the point farthest from the river. There he enters the trees with circumspection, placing his faltering boots down as softly as he can in the leaves that litter the ground. Feeling the wood close round him, thicken behind him, he stops and listens for some sound of the grizzly, nocks an arrow to the bowstring. Everything is perfectly quiet. A morning breeze combs the treetops, and a sweet rustling presages a gentle shower of pale-yellow leaves that flicker down around him. In that sound, he hears his mother's voice, and for the first time in years, sees her clearly.

He is walking with her. She always loved to take his hand when they strolled the grounds of Sythe Grange. They amble through a copse. Little Addington wears knickers and a linen blouse. His mother wears a bonnet fastened with a broad silk ribbon tied in a giant bow. The bonnet frames her countenance. He discerns a shocking pallor in her face, her dark eyebrows are etched starkly above haunted blue eyes. A realization stabs him. Mother was ill even then, long before she was pregnant with Charles and Simon.

Mother is her usual self, utterly composed. She speaks kindly to him of a recent misdemeanour. Last night he cast his lead soldiers into the fire, melted Napoleon, Napoleon's Old Guard, the Duke of Wellington, into slag on the grates. "Some day, Addington, you will be a man of property, and with property comes responsibility. Property is a sacred trust, and is not yours to dispose of as you will. It is a gift of God, just as the lead soldiers were a gift from your father. Property entails a duty to preserve it, to husband it. Surely, you can see that."

Mother does not understand that it is exactly because the toy soldiers were a gift from Father that he consigned them to the fire. Yesterday, he heard Father speak to Mother unkindly, his voice a dull roar behind the door of the study, only interrupted by Mother's sobs. So he had thrown Father's gift into the fire, watched it melt and sizzle there.

He and Mother move along, his hand clasped in hers, his eyes on the ground because he knows she wants her best boy to show contrition. Suddenly, he feels her stiffen beside him, hears her gasp. Alarmed, he glances up and sees Mother's mouth pucker with revulsion, her brows furrow. "Horrible!" she says. "Ghastly!"

A grey, weathered outhouse stands aslant in a clearing amid the beeches. The side of it is covered with the corpses of scavengers and predators, rooks, crows, owls. Caitlin, the gamekeeper, whom Addington admires more than anyone but Mother, shoots offenders and nails them up on the wall, wings fanned as a caution to all their kind to give Sythe Grange a wide berth. A warning not to molest the pheasant chicks carefully raised on a diet of grain and chopped hard-boiled egg. The marauders must understand there is a penalty to be paid for spoiling Father's hunting. Addington had passed Caitlin the spikes the day he had crucified this menagerie.

His mother's distress is unbearable to Addington, and he charges the outhouse on his chubby legs, grabs one of the crows within reach of his short arms, tears the half-rotten body from the boards. It comes apart in his hands, a mess of feathers, maggots, putrefying meat. His mother sweeps him into her arms, presses his face to her breast. She heaves, sobs, repeats over and over, "No one can say my boy hasn't a good heart! No one!"

And he weeps too as his mother wipes the awful carrion stench from his hands with her skirts, telling him he is brave, and kind, and tender-hearted, that no one feels for her as he does, or for the suffering of the birds. "My best boy," she murmurs, "my own sweet boy."

He smells the carrion fetor now, oozing from his own body. He wrestles out of the quiver, tugs at his clothes, rips buttons, unloops his suspenders, shucks his trousers, flings off all his garments in single-minded frenzy. Rolling up his shirt, he sponges the foulness from his chest, his legs, wipes down every inch of his skin.

Gradually he grows calmer under the canopy of bustling leaves. The smell is gone and he is nakedly white. The crisp morning air rinses him spotless. Now that he is wholly cleansed, Addington is ready to accomplish what he has come to do. He gathers up the bow, slings the quiver of arrows on his back.

He glides among the trees, wades through weeds, heedless of the scrape of bark, the sting of thistles. The old excitement of the hunts in the deer park is back, but larger, made grander by a more pressing jeopardy than what he braved facing his father's mantraps, the swan shot of the gamekeeper's gun.

This is real and he is clean. His feet move with assurance; for the first time in weeks he does not have to will them to do his bidding, they carry him without thought. He stalks forward soundlessly, creeping towards the river.

A smothered ripping noise, the snapping and cracking of a bone, brings him up short. He presses himself against a shielding tree until he recovers his breath, then slips off, circling the muffled sounds of the bear's feeding. The river is very close now, he can see it glinting between the trees, a stutter of brightness blinking at him. He marks a heap of brush and fallen poplar, something half-hidden behind it, something massively huge, something earnestly at work. He bounces up and down on his toes, alive with an excitement he cannot keep his body from expressing. He feels the blood running in his veins, light and sweet, all the mercury gone. As he struggles to descry the shape of what awaits him, he wants to call out his joy to it. Tenderly, he strokes the goose vanes of the arrow's fletching, smoothing them for a true flight. He catches a low, dull cough, a sucking, gulping frenzy of feeding.

Shifting his position, stealing to the right of the deadfall, Addington edges ever close to the river, the insistent rub of the current on the shore. He looks up at the twirling yellow leaves. They set him drifting among the tree trunks, aimless as the bits of gold swirling down all around him. The beauty of it is almost too much to endure. A leaf alighting on his shoulder sticks to his sweat. He brushes it away, mesmerized, watches it join the others already heaped on the earth.

Addington lifts his eyes and there is the grizzly. Powerful haunches, long hair like the quills of a porcupine that tremble as the bear rises from the carcass to stand on its hind legs with a startled "Whuff!"

Addington takes two decisive steps to the right to present himself with a lung shot. The bear swings its dished face, its bloody muzzle towards him. Addington draws the bow, feels the fletching touch his cheek, looses the arrow. It hisses, gives a sharp click as it nicks a twig and deflects deep into the shoulder of the grizzly.

The bear grunts with surprise, bites at the shaft. It snaps in the grizzly's jaws. Addington draws a second arrow and nocks it.

The grizzly charges, a roaring, quivering, rolling wave of fur and muscle. Addington's head fills with the storm, the crackle of breaking branches, the yellow leaves spiralling down in a whirlwind. He fires blindly into the golden tornado.

And the bear rears, saliva drizzling from its jaws, red mouth yawning. For an instant, the memory of a small mouth, gasping, panting for air flickers in Addington's mind. The image expands in an explosion of pain as something bats his head, rakes his scalp. He turns, stumbles for the river, steps into air, plummets down the slope. A flap of bloody skin dangles in his eyes. He leaps into the water.

From the rise, Potts sees Addington naked, white as a fish belly, spring off the riverbank and into the shallows. He wades a few yards, water splashing and foaming about his thighs before the bear overtakes him in a swell of boiling water and swats him off his feet. Addington lurches up, stabbing at the grizzly with an arrow in his fist. Another slap bowls him over. The bear's mouth closes on the nape of the Captain's neck, shakes him. He flops limp in the jaws, legs thrashing back and forth like a trout's tail. The grizzly releases his hold; leaves Addington floating face downward in the river, motionless.

Even from a hundred yards, Potts can see the pink stain spreading from the body as the bear rises, pounces on the man's back with his front paws, striking it so hard the body disappears under the water. The corpse squirts up. The bear pummels it furiously. Each time the mangled body bobs to the surface the grizzly batters more red out of it, turns it to pulp with his claws.

Potts's hand finds his quirt; he raises it high above his head. The bear smashes the body one more time. As he does, Potts flashes the quirt down. This time the red water closes over the Captain. It is finished.

25

LUCY It took three weeks before Charles and me found a way out of Fort Edmonton. Then some men who been prospecting gold on the North Saskatchewan had their fill of chilblained hands, leg cramps, and pans without a fleck of colour in them and agreed we could travel back to Fort Benton in their company. Without wagons to slow us up, we arrived right smart three days ago by saddle horse and riding mule.

Ayto was already here from Fort Whoop-Up with Barker and Grunewald and the wagons. He had the worst news for Charles. His brother was dead, killed in "a hunting mishap." Ayto blamed Mr. Potts, said the half-breed proved himself a coward during the bear attack that destroyed Charles's brother, and he was too ashamed to show his pusillanimous face in Benton. Jerry Potts was still at Fort Whoop-Up, "sunk in debauchery to the point of insensibility," according to Ayto. He went on and put himself in a good light, assuring Charles that he had seen to it that the Captain was buried with fitting dignity and solemnity. Right after he finished praising his own good conduct, Ayto asked for money to get him to Helena, where he says he'll look for work. Charles gave it to him. You ask me, it was a small price to pay for a view of that man's back going down the road.

All this misfortune has most naturally thrown Charles into a state of sorrow and confoundment. I have to coax him to take the smallest morsel of food. He says his brain aches from worry and sleepless nights.

Now word has come to Fort Benton that low water on the Upper Missouri means the end of steamboat traffic for the season. If Charles wants to get back to England before winter sets in, he'll have to make his way overland down to St. Louis. Still, he takes no steps to get himself there. No matter how I dread our parting, I thought it only right to make mention of the situation. "Time is passing, Charles," I said. "Oughtn't you to speak to somebody about taking you to St. Louis?"

"I speak to no one but you," was what he said. Then he added, "Let time pass. I care nothing for minutes, hours, or days." The look of despair he wore stopped my mouth. I left it there.

I know Charles fears to face his father. He says the old man will charge him with Addington's death, and will never forgive him for failing to find Simon. The more I have tried to make my Charles see these are foolish thoughts, the angrier he becomes, because, in his heart, Charles does believe the blame is his. Yesterday, contradiction made him roar like a madman. I never believed he could fling such hot and furious words at me.

"Do not speak of my situation!" he shouted. "You understand nothing of my father, the hold he has on me, the power he exerts over me! You cannot comprehend how he would have me grope about in his shadow! So do not speak of it!"

I knew how upset he has been, but pride oftentimes gets the better of me. It came as a shock to be lashed that way by sweet Charles when what I sought to do was help him best as ever I could. My feelings were sore wounded, and, before I lost hold of my own tongue, I marched off to my room here in the Overland Hotel. But then I thought of how he had rented me this room to keep me near him, to keep me from going back to that broken-down wagon with its sad memories. Charles had struck out because he was most frightened and bewildered. Hadn't I been just the same after Madge died? Full of bitterness and spite? Only kindness opened my heart. Charles's kindness.

And, thinking of kindness turned my mind to Custis Straw – a man who once tried to comfort my tribulation, who brought justice to my sister's murderers. He went sick so sudden I never had a chance but to mumble a few words to him. I saw it was time to clean my own slate of rudeness and debt.

My mind so set, I brushed one of my old dresses and made myself respectable and tidy. Leaving my room, I chanced on Charles in the passageway. His sketchbook was under his arm. He asked, "Are you going out, Lucy?" I told him I was off to pay a visit to Custis Straw to see how his recovery was coming along.

"Yes," he said, "I must do the same. Soon." He dropped his eyes to his shirt front and said, "I am most dreadfully sorry for how I just spoke to you."

I told him all was forgiven. Lingering, he looked up and down the corridor. "Well, I will not detain you any longer," he finally declared, and hurried away. Only then did I realize that he had been waiting for me to offer to keep him company while he drew. I was sorry and troubled for not understanding him. But it was too late, he was already gone.

If Custis Straw was back on his feet, I figured to find him in the Stubhorn. When I went in the door, there were four or five customers at the bar, Dooley serving up drinks to them. I hailed him. At once, I noted Dooley wasn't pleased to see me. He held himself poker-stiff and was grudging in his manner. I asked how Straw was making out.

"He's inching along. Improvement is mighty slow. He's up and about some since last week. But Custis ain't himself."

"Is he in his room upstairs? I'd like a word with him."

Rubbing his chin, Dooley made a study of the ceiling. "Don't take this wrong, Mrs. Stoveall, but I don't reckon a visit from you is a good idea. It might set him back in his present condition. Dr. Bengough says he needs his rest and quiet."

Right then, I saw Dooley's eyes do a nervous, hitchy jump. When I glanced back over my shoulder, there was Straw making for a table by the window. Dooley's description hadn't done justice to his miserable state. Nothing's so pitiful as a big man wasted, and Straw was so shrunk up he looked like somebody had dressed a monkey in his clothes. An invalid's shuffle is how he moved, dragging his boots over the floorboards, not looking to right nor left, simply making for that table as if it was his safe haven in life.

Dooley reached down under the counter and hauled up a bottle of whisky and a loaf of bread wrapped in a cloth. "You go out the back way, Mrs. Stoveall. Custis don't need to see you," he hissed at me, going round the bar. I watched him deliver the victuals and drink to the table. When he did, I saw how he situated himself so as to block Straw from catching sight of me.

I wasn't about to take orders from some trumped-up, high-handed Irishman, so I walked directly over. Straw's face was lined, haggard, grey. A bit of colour stole into it about the time he caught sight of me.

"Hello, Custis," I said. "How you been keeping?"

Uneasy, Dooley tarried there for a second, switching his eyes back and forth from the one to the other of us. Free and easy, Straw said, "Tolerable, Mrs. Stoveall. Take a chair." Dooley had no choice then but to hie himself off.

Straw unwrapped the bread bundle and broke off a piece. Crumbs scattered on the tabletop, the loaf was that dry and stale.

I remarked, "That's sorry-looking bread Dooley serves. You want, I can bake you a decent loaf."

Straw took a salt shaker out of his coat pocket and sprinkled his chunk of dry bread, smiling to himself. "Dr. Bengough's given instructions I'm to be kept off rich food. Aloysius watches my diet like a hawk. So I eat my bread garnished with the sweat of my brow – so to speak." He flourished the salt shaker at me, bit into the bread. Flakes of it snowed on his black frock coat.

"What does the doctor say ails you, Custis?"

"Dr. Bengough doesn't rightly know, but a medical man is loath to confess ignorance. He hops from one diagnosis to the other like a flea from dog to dog. Brain fever, beaver fever, Rocky Mountain fever, typhoid, cholera, enteric complaint, malaria. Take your pick. I told him to autopsy my corpse. In the interests of science, to put his mind at rest."

"You ought not to talk that way."

"No? Aloysius says the same." Straw slid the whisky bottle towards me. "Pour yourself a drink, Mrs. Stoveall, if I'm not cheery and gay enough for you."

I'd rubbed his fur the wrong way. That was the second time I'd managed to do that in one day. Still, he had no business being so saucy and I can give it back as good as I get. "No lady sits drinking in a saloon," I snapped.

"Why that's a nice observation, Mrs. Stoveall. I ought to be flattered you put your spotless reputation at risk by paying a visit to the Stubhorn. All on account of me."

Heat rose in my face. "I take it you're making mention of me and Charles. I am well rebuked."

"Charles Gaunt and you are no affair of mine, Mrs. Stoveall."

Straw's hand had a tremor so lively he could scarcely pour the whisky into his jigger. I took the bottle from him and filled the glass level to the lip, and pointed at it. "You hope that poison's going to cure you?"

"Let's just say it helps keep me a restful patient. Dr. Bengough weaned me off the laudanum. Now it falls to me to medicate myself."

"Whisky'll kill you more like, the awful state you're in."

"Why, do I hear regret in your voice, Mrs. Stoveall? I reckoned to leave an unmourned corpse."

Remembering my mission, I took a firm grip on my temper, said as quietly as I could, "I came but for one reason, Custis, and that is to thank you for helping me twice. I have been troubled and bitter-tongued and I never gave you proper gratitude. I ask forgiveness for that now."

"You don't owe me any repentance," was all he said.

I said, "I do repent. I thank you most for settling with the Kelsos."

Straw put a finger inside his loose collar and scratched his neck. I saw how mention of his kin disturbed him. "I don't care to speak of what happened up there. It was necessity. But I'm not proud of it."

"It took courage, I congratulate you on it."

"I don't care to be congratulated for shedding blood, Mrs. Stoveall."

I couldn't say a solitary thing right that day. I stood and held my hand out to him. He grasped it gently, just like he was holding a tiny bird. "It's the past," he said. "Let us agree to forget it."

I nodded to him and left the saloon. But I told myself, Let Custis Straw forget it, I'm not about to.

When I got back to the hotel, Charles was still out. All at once I felt melancholy, plumb worn to a nub. I laid down on the bed and, in a wink, I was asleep.

I dreamed myself running through a mighty field of corn, stalks so high they clipped the sky from sight like treetops do. Behind me, I could hear a dog baying. The blood-thirsty belling made me feel ever so afraid, like a small hunted thing.

I'm desperate-lost in the rattling leaves, a stand of corn tall and dark. The dog can't be put off my scent no matter how I twist and double; his cry is a string tied to my heels, and I drag him along with me no matter which direction I turn.

Then, of a sudden, I come floundering out of the corn patch and into the bright light of full day.

The dog is crouched there, waiting for me, a red bone hound with a knowing look and a long-toothed grin. I can't move nor cry out. Step by step he sidles up on me until he's at my feet. His head drops. I hear him commence to lick the ground.

The sound he makes keeps me from looking down. It's a sloppy, gobbling, greedy noise that sets me to shivering. On and on it goes, until I can't stand it a second more and I have to know what he's lapping.

That's when I see the dark blood of my monthly raining down on the dirt, spattering in the dust. I feel the hot, sticky surge of it out of my body. I can't bring myself to take a step. I got to stand there and watch until the hound eats his fill, until he finally slouches off, stomach sagging under his bony ribs, so full of me his belly nigh brushes the ground.

I woke up crying Charles's name. I wanted to tell someone my dream. But there was nobody to tell it to but four walls. As I lay there, all in a sweaty panic, I came to see I would never speak a word of it to Charles.

Whatever his dreams, they are nothing like that. A fine, well-brought-up gentleman doesn't dream a red bone hound with a taste for woman's blood.

I understood how the signposts of each of our solitary roads can hardly be read by the other because they are so unlike. Sometimes Charles and me can scarce make out each other's speech. Him with his high-flown turns of phrase and his high-stepping words, me with my homely country talk, all knots to him that he can hardly pick apart.

I always reckoned touch was our best true speech, but now I worry I misjudged even that, mistook gentle pity for love.

There's a meaning to the red bone hound, but Charles wouldn't grant it, seeing as how he has no faith in second sight. Truth be known, I can't put the meaning to it in words, but deep down I feel it, in the very pit of my womb.

CUSTIS   If Lucy knew Joel Kelso was back in Fort Benton, she wouldn't be talking so sweet to me, there would be no apologies for Custis Straw then. She'd hold that against me all the way to my grave. Why that brainless boy chose to come back here is beyond me. Probably the thought of being on his own in Blackfoot country scared him back here despite my warnings. Now he seems to have hooked up with that worthless Danny Rand and is just as much under his thumb as he ever was under his brother's. Joel is deprived of a mind of his own.

Danny Rand's uncle, the farrier Tolbert Hewitt, has brought a warning to Aloysius to pass on to me. He said the young fellows have been bandying threats about what they intend to do to me, and I ought to keep clear of them. I'd be more than happy to take Hewitt's advice except for Lucy Stoveall. With Joel Kelso taking up residence in Fort Benton, that's gunpowder and fire in the same room. I fear she might put herself in jeopardy again.

A fine day and a fine dinner at the Overland. Fried liver and bacon, pan potatoes, mashed turnips, soda crackers, corn pudding. If he knew, old Bengough would rant and rave, but let him, this might be my last supper.

I step out gingerly into Front Street. Late September, sunlight shiny and clear as a new washed windowpane. Best weather offered in these parts, bothersome flies and mosquitoes gone, air with the mellow, smoky tang of good whisky to it, a touch of warmth hiding there but no more. I could stand here all day if I had the strength, take pleasure in watching others work while I idle, but I have my own job to do this afternoon, business up the road.

I slip sideways through the door of the smithy. Hewitt's been hot-shoeing mules, the place stinks like burned fingernail clippings. No sign of the farrier about. Joel's forking up muleshit and Danny Rand's whetting a clasp knife on the uppers of his boots.

"Afternoon, gentlemen," I say. Joel startles like he's been saluted by a ghost. Rand looks up, slowly closes the clasp knife and pockets it.

"Joel, I told you to stay clear of Fort Benton. Lucy Stoveall's back in town. I don't want the two of you crossing paths. You better remove yourself from town and do it fast."

"Tell him to kiss your arse, Joel," says Rand, hand moving to his jacket pocket. Joel's holding the fork with the tines straight out at me as if to fend off a charge.

The short walk from the Overland Hotel has caused my legs to start trembling like a newborn colt's. Rand has brought his pistol out, aimed it at my chest. That's the second time that boy has directed his topbreak towards my person. The banked fire of the forge throbs hot and red on his face.

"Every occasion we meet, you've got to wave a gun at me. Put that away, Rand."

"I don't know why I would. There ain't no Dooley with a twelve gauge hereabouts this time."

"You watch him!" Joel cries. "Watch him or he'll do you like he done Tite!"

"Joel, one last thing and then I'm finished with you. There's something I want you to take a look at." As I reach into my jacket pocket, I hear Rand cock the revolver, but I don't stay my hand, just ease it on to the belt and toss it over to Joel. He jumps like I threw him a snake, but he catches it. The belt dangles from his fist.

"First, you told me Titus had a belt like I described. Then you said he didn't. Which is it?"

Joel's turning it over in his hands, puzzlement written large on his face. "I ain't never seen this before," he says. "Titus didn't own no belt like this."

There's a blow. No doubt he's speaking the truth.

My watery bowels spasm. "I got to sit, boys. I been sick for a time." I move to Hewitt's anvil, straddle it, lower myself down careful, not trusting my treacherous guts.

Rand passes the topbreak pistol to Joel, jerks the belt from his hands. "Straw delivered himself into your hands. Let him abide the consequences."

I hear a bird, a rat, some small thing rustle in the rafters. Joel says not a word.

"All I been hearing from you lately is –" Rand screws his voice into a whine, mimicking Joel, " 'He kilt Tite. Shot him like a dog. Straw's going to pay. See if he don't.' " Rand pauses. "So make him pay."

"Now?"

The small thing up in the rafters has gone still. I take out my pocket watch, flick the lid, check the time. "Let's say you'll be gone in an hour, Joel. Go to Bozeman, Virginia City, Helena. Better still, go back to your mamma in Kansas. Because if you don't, I'll have to arm myself and chase you off."

"Do it," says Rand to Joel. "Shoot the bastard."

I keep my eyes on the watch. The minute hand jumps. I start to wind the stem. Stop myself just short of popping the spring. "That's all I have to say." I get to my feet. The two of them are between me and the door. I start towards it. Neither of them move. I step by Rand's shoulder and something snares me by the throat, snatches my boots from the floor, drops me hard on my back in the muleshit. Rand is dragging me across the floor, shouting, "Cocksucker! Cocksucker!" I realize that the belt that choked Madge Dray is around my throat.

My guts cramp, betray me. An almighty stench bursts out of me. The belt slackens, and I flop over on my stomach. Rand steps back. He laughs, whoops. "I scared the shit clean out of Straw!"

I'm crawling, legs weak as water. Can't raise myself, can't stand like a man.

"Custis Straw, so afraid of Danny Rand it ran drizzly shit right out of him!"

I hear Joel say, "Let's go to Helena, Danny."

"Why, you blamed coward. You're afraid of that woman."

"Can't fight a woman," says Joel meekly. "Turns everybody against you."

"Well, put your tail between your legs and go to Helena. I ain't running. What Straw done – dirtying himself – that'll buy me a week of drinks in this town. I intend to spread that about."

"I've been sick!" I shout. "It's my ailment!"

Joel cracks the door of the livery and is gone. When the daylight hits me, I begin to sob.

"Hey, Kelso!" I hear Rand yell. "Hold up there! You taken my topbreak! Goddamn it, Kelso! Stop, I say!" Looking up, I see Danny Rand hustling out of the livery at a dogtrot.

I yank the belt off my neck, shove it in my pocket. Crawl to a stanchion, pull myself up, hide my face in the splintery wood. I'm soaked in shit and blood and shame. I hug that stanchion for a long time, breathing my foulness. Then when my legs steady, I make my escape to Robert E. Lee's laundry and bathhouse.

I never thought to let myself be touched in such a condition. But when the Chinaman sees me stripped trying to wipe my legs with a cloth, losing my balance, nearly toppling over, he takes the cloth from me and swabs me down gentle, clucking over my scrawny frame, saying how I've shrunk. He launders my drawers while I sit in the big tub, weeping.

He brushes the mule shit from my coat. He keeps boiling hot water coming all afternoon because I don't want to get out, only soak away the hours, watch the walls drip with steam, think of Danny Rand going up and down every saloon on Front Street, men howling with laughter because of my disgrace. Everybody pleased to see Custis Straw humbled because of how I've walked among them, proud and full of airs. As the Bible says, "In the mouth of the foolish *is* a rod of pride."

Come early evening, I finally hoist myself out the tub and towel down. Robert E. Lee has a store of powerful, cheap scent on hand for the boys to douse themselves with after they've had a scrub and are ready to sally out on a visit to the whores. I sprinkle myself with it too. Doesn't help, the reek still clings to me.

When I go to put on my coat, I feel the belt in my jacket pocket. I take it out. I've lost so much weight that when I put it around my waist, the tongue fits in the punch hole perfectly. A bad conscience, the guilt of all the dead I left behind me, had to attach itself to something. I always felt that I owned the belt, or it owned me.

Out in the dusk, I finally fathom how, for years, my spirit has wanted to die. But my body wouldn't let it. It held on hard to life in that Washington Hospital. It seems to hold on hard still.

It must have been the same with Old Adam after he was driven from the Garden of Eden. Surely his spirit sickened, begged for death. But his body had found its rightful place, needed the hard old world. Needed to lift the rocks and pull the thistles. Until it could do no more, gave out, and loosed the spirit.

Now I've got to journey back up Front Street where surely Danny Rand has spread news of my shame by now. My body has to put one foot in front of the other, haul my spirit past the faces in the lighted windows, the gapers in the street, the whispers.

26

October arrives and finds Jerry Potts still tarrying at Fort Whoop-Up. After the passing of Falling-Leaves Moon, naked trees shiver in the river bottoms. Over the twenty miles between Fort Kipp and Fort Whoop-Up, the Confederacy of the Blackfoot are camped, Northern Blackfoot, Bloods, and Montana Peigans who have decided to winter in the Queen's country. The Peigans were taught a hard lesson last year when Major Baker fell on Heavy Runner's band and left behind many dead women and children in the snow of the Marias. But in the heart of Blackfoot territory they feel secure from the American seizers. Winter is a time for visiting with friends, for feasting, for smoking the pipe, for laughing and games, for old men to recount brave deeds.

Potts and the Scots half-breed brothers, Alex and Charles McKay, known to the Blackfoot as Unborn Calf and The Bear, ride out to hunt each day from the fort. Everywhere the signs point to the onset of winter. The hair of the buffalo thickens and grows shaggy, the tawny prairie grass tosses in a cold, keening wind, flakes of snow appear suddenly out of nowhere. When the ponies drop their dung, steam hovers above it, just as clouds of midges do in summer. Mornings, the water bucket wears a skin of ice and the metal dipper stings Potts's lips, makes his teeth ache when he drinks from it.

At the beginning of the last week of October, a ferocious squall sweeps down from the Backbone of the World, the Rocky Mountains, and sprays the prairies with a discharge of sleet, short and sharp as a blast of bird shot from a fowling piece. Wrapped in his blankets, Potts listens to it rattle on the roof of the bunkhouse, then stop as suddenly as it began. But the sleet does not vanish like the clamour it made above his head; it lies on the ground, a light dusting of ice. Potts wraps his head in his arms and dozes fitfully.

Shortly before dawn, there is a racket in the Blackfoot camp that lies several hundred yards outside the walls of Fort Whoop-Up. Dogs bark and howl, men shout angrily, women wail. The uproar wakens the McKays too.

Potts rolls out of bed, throws on his clothes and gun belt, grabs his Henry, stuffs several boxes of cartridges into his pockets. The McKays follow suit and the three men hurry out of the bunkhouse into the darkness. Lights flicker in the buildings; traders rush about, their voices loud and anxious, lanterns toss wildly in their hands, enormous shadows slither over the palisades.

The harness-maker sprints across the yard; Potts catches him by the arm, pulls him up short. "What is it?" he yells into the frightened face.

"Christ, don't ask me! But it's devilment! Count on it!" The harness-maker tears himself out of Potts's clutch and hustles to the wall where the silhouettes of armed men can be seen, stark against the starry sky.

Potts turns to the McKays. "Let us go into the camp and see what this is about."

But the jittery guard on the fort gate doesn't want to open it to let the half-breeds pass. Indians may pour through and massacre everyone inside, he says. When Potts, exasperated, unsheathes his skinning knife and threatens to cut the guard's nose off, the man reluctantly gives way, permits them to slip out.

The Blackfoot village is seething. Word has come that a great war party of Cree and Assiniboine have hit a small encampment of Bloods on the lower Belly. While the Bloods slept, the attackers slit their lodge skins, crept into the teepees, and stabbed them to death as they lay in their robes. The brother of Chief Red Crow and many others have been killed. Only one young boy managed to escape and raise the alarm with the Many Tumours and All Short People bands. At this moment, they are holding eight hundred Cree and Assiniboine at bay but cannot do so for long. Gallopers have been sent to the Piegan camps, but they are ten miles off. If help does not come to the Bloods soon, they will be overwhelmed.

The Cree and Assiniboine chiefs Little Pine, Big Bear, Piapot, and Little Mountain, learning of how the white scabs has weakened the Blackfoot, are determined to wipe them from the face of the earth. Even worse, the famous warriors, Yellow Hair and Curly Hair, have been seen riding with them. There is no mistaking the long blond hair, the blue eyes, the fair skins of the sons of the Hudson Bay man, Hugh Sutherland. The Blackfoot know that as much as Yellow Hair and his brother are the spitting images of their white father, their hearts are as one with the people of their Cree mother.

Potts has often heard stories about the Sutherland braves. The one that sticks in his mind is how Yellow Hair answered the Scotchman trader who scolded him, telling him he would be better off between the shafts of a plough than dressed in war clothes. Yellow Hair had said, "I have never been taught anything but fighting. I suppose I have relatives beyond the Big Water who would be sorry to see me leading this kind of life, but how can I help it?" Potts understands his reply.

All about, hasty preparations for the battle are under way. Boys run to lasso their fathers' swiftest ponies. Weapons are broken out, men paint their faces, don eagle-feather bonnets and magical one-horn headdresses, reverently fondle medicine bundles, sing to shields that have the power to turn aside bullets. By twos and threes the warriors ride off as soon as their mounts are saddled. There can be no waiting for laggards when the fight hangs in the balance.

Potts and the McKays exchange looks. "We are as much Blackfoot as the Sutherlands are Cree," Potts declares. "I think this is our fight too."

"Yes," agrees Unborn Calf.

The Bear is pleased. "Yellow Hair claims he has never been taught anything but fighting. Let us see if he has been taught well."

But going to collect their horses from the stables inside Fort Whoop-Up, they find the gate shut to them. No matter how hard they shout and threaten, it stays barred. There is nothing to do but to return to the Blackfoot camp and ask that someone lend them war ponies. More precious time is lost. The last of the Blackfoot warriors have stampeded off into the night, yelling encouragement to one another.

Potts and the McKays finally set out on the trail of the war party, following a track stamped as clear in the sleet as muddy footprints on a bedsheet. They ride up one of the countless coulees that slash the valley of the Belly, deep notches overhung by towering, crumbling banks fantastically weathered and scarred by wind and rain.

A roof-pitch climb up treacherous ground is hard going. At times the horses balk, refuse to take another step, and their riders must spring off their backs, take the reins and lead them. The scrambling mustangs send small, slippery avalanches of dirt and gravel down the slope.

At last, horses and riders stumble up on to the plain. The morning wind greets the half-breeds with the muted sound of distant battle, the flat crack of repeaters, the dull thump of Hudson Bay muskets, faint cries. Laying quirts to their lathered mounts, they whip them into a final, frantic gallop just as Sun's forehead flares above the horizon, staining the chalk-white plain the deep red of heart's blood.

Potts and the McKays reach high ground overlooking the battle just as Mountain Chief and his men are readying themselves to join the fray. Before them, a thousand Blackfoot, Cree, and Assiniboine are engaged in a running skirmish that sprawls over a mile of prairie. The bodies of men and horses dot the whiteness, marking the ebb and flow of the engagement. The cold morning pops with gunfire, rings with war whoops as riders clash in single combat. Those warriors who are afoot loose arrows, parry lance thrusts with parfleche shields, batter one another with stone war clubs, swing empty muskets into the faces of attackers. Some break and flee, are chased down and shot, hacked, stabbed.

Potts jostles his pony to the side of Mountain Chief and his son Big Brave. Big Brave is in a trance-like state. Slowly he lifts and lowers his medicine shield to the rise and fall of his death chant. Over and over he sonorously sings, "My body will be lying on the plains. My body will be lying on the plains." His face is blackened with charcoal; his eye sockets are circled with vermilion. A beaded horse mask of identical colour and design hides his pony's face. The eyes of the horse flash wildly within the vermilion rings. Potts senses the power rising from man and horse; the heat of strong war medicine. Laying his hand on the cat skin over his heart, he asks it to help him today, to bless him with courage and cunning.

Mountain Chief turns to Potts, indicates the hundreds of warriors darting and shifting about on the plain, the bodies strewn on the ground, the horses trotting aimlessly with empty saddles on their backs. "I did not think I would live so long to see such a fight," says Mountain Chief.

Potts does not answer. Big Brave's chanting drums in his ear. He has spotted several dozen Cree who have learned a lesson from their cousins, the Métis. The Cree have dug a ring of rifle pits in the sod against which Piegan riders launch brave but fruitless sorties that are turned aside with withering volleys of musket fire.

Mountain Chief flicks his forefinger at the Cree horsemen sweeping back and forth in fluid attack and counterattack. "Which fat Cree cow do you choose to run, Bear Child?"

Potts shakes his head, thrusts his finger to the men in the shallow foxholes methodically loading and firing. "No!" he shouts. "We must go down against those fighters there! All together as one! We must smash into them hard, make them run."

Big Brave's song breaks off. "Yes!" he cries. "Do as Bear Child says! Listen to Bear Child!"

Potts trots his pony up the line of silent warriors, their bonnet feathers twitching in the wind. "No one must try to count first coup. We must act for the good of all. Any man who thinks only of his own advantage in the buffalo hunt is punished, his lodge is cut to pieces, and scorn heaped on his head. We must hunt the Crees as we do the buffalo, together, no man ahead of the rest. Do you understand?"

Agreement rumbles through the line of Blackfoot. Potts turns his horse, draws his revolver. "Now let us go down! Let us make the Cree pay for killing the brother of Red Crow, for killing our women and children! Make this a day to be painted in the winter count!"

They charge in a predatory wave, singing and shouting battle cries. A score of Cree turn to face the clatter of hooves on frozen ground, the wild rush of horsemen bearing down fast on them. The muskets of the Cree crash, a single clap of noise, of rolling smoke. Potts sees Ugly Man go over the head of his gut-shot roan. Two ponies bolt madly ahead of the Blackfoot, running flat out, riders thrown or shot from their backs.

Mountain Chief's men burst among the Cree fighters. One of them tackles Potts's leg, yanking desperately to pull him from his pony. Potts bangs the part in the Cree's hair so hard with his pistol butt that the grip cracks in his hand. The Cree falls beneath the feet of his horse. Potts jerks one rein, twisting the pony clear, and fires twice into the man reeling in a rifle pit.

Mountain Chief is shouting to tell his men that the Cree have broken and are fleeing their crude emplacements. Afoot or mounted, they dash for a nearby coulee. A squat, stocky Cree runs by Potts; Potts leans backward in the saddle and snaps a shot over the rump of his pony. The impact of the bullet flings the Cree's arms into the air, hurtles him so hard to the earth that the sleet squirts and scatters.

Mountain Chief, hanging on to his terrified, bucking pony, stubbornly clutches the long hair of a Cree. The Cree goes under the pony's belly, snarling its legs. Mountain Chief releases his hold, fights to bring his horse under control, then rides the stunned Cree down, striking him again and again with his coup stick.

Potts catches a flick of colour amid the black-haired Cree headed for the ravine, a head as bright as a September poplar leaf. A tall golden-haired man is covering the retreat. On foot, he calmly backs towards the coulee, keeping up a steady fire with a Many Shots rifle, holding the Blackfoot off as his friends race for shelter.

Potts screams to the Blackfoot, "Cut them down before they reach the coulee! Do not let them get to the coulee!" But Mountain Chief's men have been joined by mounted Peigans and Blackfoot who hold only one thought in their minds, rub out every enemy they can lay hands upon. Potts cannot turn them aside from the slaughter. Blood mingles with sleet, turning the ground slippery with a pink slush.

More Cree and Assiniboine are reaching the safety of the gully as the Blackfoot round up Cree horses, gather captured weapons, brandish scalps. Horses snort their terror, nostrils filled with the smell of man-blood.

Potts had thought Ugly Man was killed in the charge, but he is limping about, waving a revolver he captured from a Cree. "I will kill Crees with their own gun!" he shouts. "I will make them feel their weapons as our people have!"

Potts understands what a bad mistake the Blackfoot have made in letting the foe slip through their fingers. Almost all the Cree and Assiniboine horseman have taken cover in the coulee. Potts sees Curly Hair is now beside his brother, protecting the retreat of the last riders chased by the Blackfoot. The Sutherlands' blond hair flies in the wind as they aim and fire. The lower halves of their faces are painted bright blue, a marking that is clear even at a distance. Potts had never thought he would live to see yellow-haired men with paint on their white skins.

"Come with me!" Potts shouts. "Come with me to the coulee that runs beside the one the Crees hide in!" He trots his pony among the Blackfoot, feverishly gesturing, striking some with his quirt to catch their attention. The younger warriors heed him. "Go with Bear Child! Follow Bear Child!" They leap up on their horses as Potts wheels his pony and gallops away, hanging off his pony's side, snapping revolver shots at the Sutherland boys as they slip down into the gulch.

Now everyone pelts after Bear Child, the warriors of the Blood, the Piegan, the North Blackfoot, all desperate to get at the Cree sheltering in the gully. Mountain Chief, whose horse was shot out from under him in the last minutes of the fight, rides behind Unborn Calf, arms wrapped tight around his waist, bouncing up and down on the hindquarters of McKay's pony. Big Brave races his grey horse alongside them to shield his father and the half-breed from the Cree muskets spitting balls at them from the coulee. He taunts the enemy, flourishes a scalp above his head. Today, in his first big fight, the son of Mountain Chief has already sent three Cree to their deaths.

Led by Potts, the Blackfoot spill down into the gorge, a throng of hundreds of excited men and horses, all thrashing about in confusion. Potts dismounts, starts climbing the side of the coulee, grasping the tough juniper bushes, jabbing a purchase in the soft face of the incline with his moccasined-toes, calling out to the others to follow him. In moments, scores of men are scaling the slope, squirming their way to the top. A few Cree shoot down at them, but are forced back from their exposed position by the fire of the Blackfoot guarding the horses in the bottom of the coulee.

The two gulches wind along cheek by jowl. In places, as little as ten yards separate them. The sides of the coulees act as natural ramparts along which the Cree and Blackfoot distribute themselves, firing whenever an enemy's head bobs into sight. The roar of musketry is a solid wall of sound, rifle smoke forms an impenetrable cloud along the narrow strip separating the combatants. The engagement has become a battle fought in a blinding fog.

Here and there, warriors rush each other's positions, heave boulders down on heads, empty their guns into enemies who are briefly visible in the drifting pall, grapple with ghosts suddenly become flesh. In the crooks of the gulches, isolated pockets of Cree and Blackfoot fight hand to hand. Trapped men turn badger, dig the earth furiously with knives and hatchets, scrape dirt with their fingers in an attempt to provide themselves with a scrap of cover.

The battle teeters back and forth, one side or the other winning isolated victories. Calf Shirt staggers over to Potts and drops down beside him. An arrow has pierced his wrist. "You are wounded," Potts shouts above the din. "I must draw that arrow for you."

Calf Shirt pants in agony, but violently shakes his head. He pulls Potts down so he can speak directly into his ear. "My father painted my face this morning. He told me that he was given a vision that told him I must not pull any arrow from my flesh as long as this fight lasts. If I did as he said, the arrow would be my friend and help me. There were two Cree around that bend that turns to the east; everyone warned me off them because they had already killed several of us." Calf Shirt lifts a broad, double-edge knife with his good hand, twisting the blade. "But I was certain this knife from my bear medicine bundle would overcome them. I armed myself with it and attacked. One of the Cree shot me with an arrow, but I did not let the pain stop me. I seized his bow with my wounded hand and snapped it like a twig. His arrow was a gift that made me strong. I drove my bear knife into him again. The other Cree became afraid of my power and ran, but I overtook him and killed him too. So you see, the arrow must not be drawn from my body until this day's work is completed."

"I understand," says Potts.

Calf Shirt sighs contentedly, closes his eyes. "Let me rest here for a few moments and feel this arrow. When it rouses my anger I will go back and give some other raider a taste of my bear knife."

Potts leaves Calf Shirt, runs stooped along the lip of the ridge, firing his pistols whenever he catches a glimpse of a Cree. When his revolvers empty, he dives back into the coulee, and from there he spies a low butte looking down on the Cree position.

Suddenly, just above him, Potts hears the sound of singing. His eyes shoot upward. An old Cree looms out of the smoke above him, grey hair fanned on his shoulders. His eyes are closed, his face is lifted to the sky, his lips are moving. Potts can just make out the refrain. "I am old. Hear that I am ready to die. Take me now."

Potts leaves the Cree with his old man's wish, his old man's courage, and retraces his steps. Hurrying through the ravine, he finds the Montana Peigans, many of whom carry repeaters, and shouts into their ears what they must do. As they steal up the ravine, he sends the McKay brothers after them, and then collects the young men, tells them to mount up and wait for his signal.

Shortly, the McKays and the Peigans open up a terrific assault from the heights that Potts directed them to. The Cree and Assiniboine are unnerved by this sudden onslaught from an unexpected quarter. The bullets of the Many Shots rip into them, drive them back down the narrow confines of the gulch. Disorder spreads, a mob of panicked warriors cascades down the coulee, a swift-running river of Cree, a spate of heaving heads.

Potts looses his horsemen after them. The time has finally arrived to run the cows just as in the buffalo hunt.

The Blackfoot pursue them hard, killing everyone they overtake, harrying them onward as the Cree flee down the slope of the coulee. They push the Cree braves like their fathers did the Big Hairys in the old days, driving them over a thirty-foot drop to the river. As their enemies tumble over the brink, the most impetuous of the Blackfoot warriors leap their horses over the cliff after them. Ponies break legs, topple, roll, squeal with pain. The air curdles with the screams of the dying.

Potts reins in his pony. The Cree who have made it to the Belly are wading into the freezing water, churning it into foam. They are packed so tight a man could close his eyes, fire, and be sure of killing himself one. Potts yanks the Henry out of his scabbard. "Shoot the Cree in the water! Do not let them cross!" he shouts, and bodies begin to drop, the dead and wounded Cree spinning downstream in the current. The brown water of the Belly colours, shows threads of scarlet, then coiled ropes of red.

On the east side of the river, numb, exhausted Cree who have fought their way across the river drag themselves up the muddy bank. Already, Blackfoot are fording the Belly in pursuit. Potts spots the Sutherlands halting the fleeing Cree, turning them back to make a stand. He heels his pony down the steep bank and into the high river grass, eager to face Yellow Hair and his brother.

Suddenly, the dead and frozen grass crackles as a Cree flushes from hiding. A musket jabs up into Potts's face, blinds him with its flash, stuns him with its explosion, bowls him off the pony's back. For a moment, he gropes the ground on all fours, surrounded by bright, winking lights before he is submerged in a roaring, turbulent darkness.

Bit by bit, the sound of battle tugs him back into consciousness. Groggily, Potts registers astonishment to find himself alive. He gathers his legs under him, hoists himself upright. The Cree who shot at him is nowhere to be seen. Potts notices his pony unconcernedly grazing the grass a few yards off. He turns his eyes to where the fight continues on the eastern river flats, but everything that is distant is hard to make out. He blinks his eyes, but the murk and blur does not clear.

When he rides his pony into the river, the frigid water gnaws his legs; his stones flinch up into his body. But soon they are across, splashing up the embankment, steam bursting from their bodies. Potts looks to the north where he first saw the Sutherlands rallying their men. The shock of the cold water seems to have returned his sight to him. He sees dead men scattered everywhere, some of the Cree lie in heaps where they dropped down one on top of the other. Near a small grove of cottonwoods, the Blackfoot have trapped the last of the warriors, the Sutherland boys.

When Potts rides up, Yellow Hair and his brother are surrounded by taunting Blackfoot who shake their weapons at them threateningly, show the Sutherlands the scalps they have taken from their Cree friends. The brothers sit back to back in a puddle of blood, unable to stand. Both men's legs are useless, broken by bullets. Their carbines are empty, but they have drawn their knives, prepared to fight to the death, to sell their lives dear. Potts swings down from his pony, hurries up to the ring circling them.

The river crossing has melted some of the paint from the brothers' faces, and it runs in thin blue rivulets down their throats. The paint is the colour of their eyes, a hard, glaring sky-blue. Blackfoot prowl around them just out of the reach of their knives, laughing and making sudden, teasing feints. The bravest dash in and strike at them with coup sticks. One young warrior has already been wounded mocking the Sutherlands, he presses a bit of cloth to his forearm to staunch the blood one of them has slashed out of him with his knife.

The Sutherland boys hurl the insults of the Blackfoot back at them. They sneer and beckon their tormentors to come closer, invite them to taste the edge of their knives.

"Enough," Potts calls out. "Finish them."

The young men step back, surprised by Bear Child's command. They finger their weapons in disappointment. The Sutherlands can read the gestures of the Blackfoot, their faces, and they know that in moments they will die. In a high, piping voice of defiance, Curly Hair begins to sing his death chant in Cree. In a low, sombre voice swelling deep from his broad chest, Yellow Hair launches into a different song.

The strangeness of an English death chant fills the Blackfoot with amazement, holds them still.

"Praise God, from whom all blessings flow;
Praise him, all creatures here below;
Praise him above, ye heavenly host;
Praise Father, Son, and Holy Ghost. Amen."

The autumn sunshine bleaches the pale skin of the Sutherlands even whiter, licks the butter of their waist-long hair. They wait, their knives held ready. The ring closes on them, the Blackfoot rush at the cold flash of the Sutherlands' blades. Rifle butts, stone hammers crash down on blond heads, over and over. Potts has no wish to strike them, he only stands and watches what must be done. When the Blackfoot warriors step back, the brothers lie crumpled, their limbs tangled in a final embrace.

After that, there are only the remnants of the invaders to mop up. Ten Cree in a clump of poplar, their musket powder wet from the crossing, one revolver among them, are quickly dispatched. The rest who have made it into brush coverts to the north are allowed to escape. Everyone is tired from the long day's fighting, the Blackfoot dead and wounded must be brought home. Calf Skin's wrist has swollen bigger than his biceps and turned black. Nevertheless, he will not allow anyone to remove the arrow. Strapped to a travois, he is dragged back to his father's lodge.

Potts and the McKays return to the Blood camp near Fort Whoop-Up. All the people honour Bear Child's bravery, the cunning he used in turning the tide of battle in his people's favour. They touch the thirteen scalps hanging from his belt. The children stare at the ear that the Cree warrior scorched with the muzzle flame of his musket, at the specks of black powder embedded in Potts's cheek by the blast. Everyone praises the power of his cat medicine, which protected him even with a musket pushed into his face.

All night long the Bloods sing and dance in celebration of a victory that rubbed out three hundred Cree, but Potts refuses to join them. He hides himself away from his people in Fort Whoop-Up just as Mary hid herself from him the night the Blackfoot destroyed the Crow in Montana. Sitting silent on his bunk, absent-mindedly stroking his raw, burned ear, he thinks of the Sutherlands, half-breeds like himself, singing their two sides, the Cree and the Scottish, as they prepared to meet death.

The next morning, Potts rises early. A soft, bleary snowfall wraps the world in white as he rides to the place where the Sutherlands died. Their pale bodies, stripped by the Blackfoot, are hard to find in the snow. Finally he discovers them, wearing caps of gore instead of long yellow hair.

He works all morning, one by one lifting and carrying heavy stones to pile on the naked bodies of the brothers. In the cold, his fingers become claws, his nails break and bleed prying boulders from the frozen mud. He wishes to honour the Sutherlands who, fair enough to pass as white men, chose to give their lives for their Cree brothers. He wonders if the Scottish raiders his Almost Father Dawson spoke of, the ones who swept down from the high country into the land of the English, left the world with Yellow Hair's song on their lips.

A little past noon his cairn is completed. Even though the Sutherlands were enemies, no Blackfoot will pass it without tucking a pinch of tobacco or a strip of red cloth into its cracks and crannies to honour their courage.

Potts stares off into the screen of snow. Right now, the Crow will be gathering in the basin of the Powder and Bighorn rivers to make winter camp.

Yesterday, he might have died. If the Cree's muzzle had moved a finger breadth to the right, his brains would have been smashed by a musket ball like his own father's were so may years ago. Mitchell would be orphaned as he himself had been.

Potts starts to shake. He is starved for the sight of his boy; his spirit is hungry to press his son close to him. There are no more excuses. The time has come to ride south, to beg forgiveness from his Crow family.

27

ALOYSIUS Custis pulled out of town with Charles Gaunt yesterday. Custis is some better, but I don't judge him fit to travel. I told him this, but you might as well reason with a keg of nails.

All because four days ago a hide hunter by name of Cornelius Kopp rode into Fort Benton from the Basin Country carrying a message to Custis from Jerry Potts that a young, blond white man was living with the Crow down there. According to Kopp, Jerry Potts is camped on the outskirts of a big Crow village, working on his father-in-law to help patch things up between him and his wife, Mary. Strikes me that's a risky business for Potts. Seeing as he has such a mighty reputation as a Crow killer, you'd reckon some young Crow buck would be determined to lift his hair. But Kopp says even though Potts ain't welcome, the Crow don't meddle with him. Maybe his foolhardy bravery won their respect and they've decided it would be bad medicine to touch him.

The particulars the half-breed sent was few. Didn't have no name for the white man but the one the Indians call him by, Born of a Horse. The little Custis learned from Kopp, he passed on directly to Charles Gaunt. That got the Englishman all het up, out of his doldrums. For two days he pitched around town pestering people, offering the moon to anybody who would guide him down to whatever Potts has found. But he didn't get no takers. Ever since Barker and Grunewald got back to Benton, they been running down Englishmen as travelling companions and the Gaunts in particular.

I seen Gaunt do it, right here in my bar, plead with Custis to take him south. He said there was nobody else he could turn to, that he needed to know who the fellow with the Crow was. If Straw wouldn't take him, he had no choice but to try and make it there on his own.

It took some time for Custis to reply. I wondered if he weren't weighing Gaunt's chances of surviving winter travel on his own. I would have been sorely tempted to let him go if I wanted Lucy Stoveall all to my own.

Thing is, Custis melts under begging, and Gaunt begged him mighty insistent. Still, Custis sat staring out the window of the saloon without replying a word. Second week of November, but the day was warm and bright, last gasp of fine weather. Finally, Custis lifted his glass and drained it. "Travel is hazardous this time of year," he said. "Weather is sudden and changeable. Temperature can drop forty degrees in the blink of an eye. Buy us a small tent. Get yourself some warm clothes. We leave tomorrow."

CHARLES   Mr. Straw is proving to be a trial. Ungenerous and unkind of me to think it, given the assistance he is providing me, but nevertheless true. What exasperates me so is that Straw does not understand that I cannot fall victim to unfounded optimism. And yet, I carry a pouch of twenty-dollar gold coins, ransom for the brother I dare not allow myself to believe I will find.

All I ask is to ride along and nurse my thoughts.

Straw seems to interpret my silence as brooding, and attempts to lighten my spirits by emphasizing the Crow's cordiality towards white men, continually blathering on about his horse-buying days with these Indians. Announcing that in all his dealings with them they proved to be upright, dependable, and honest. Telling me that the relations of the Crow with white men have never been marked by the hostility which the Blackfoot and the Sioux feel towards us. If the young white man is Simon, he assures me, I can be certain no harm has befallen him.

I have not retorted that if what Straw says is true, if my brother has been rescued by a people Straw maintains are such good friends of the white race, then why has Simon not been returned safe and sound to civilization?

What's more, Straw's garrulous encomiums on the character of the Crow are liberally sprinkled with asides on their customs, a topic I find it impossible to turn my attention to. Does he think that it will fend off my anxiety to know that these savages are besotted horse lovers who dress their ponies in showy feather bonnets? Or that the men are particularly proud of the length of their hair? Straw even insisted on relating an interminable story about one ancient Crow worthy whose mane measured ten feet and which was kept rolled up in a package that he carried under his arm like a man returning home from a shop with a purchase. On and on, doing nothing to quell my mounting trepidation, only compounding it with irritation.

But after three days of pointless chatter, as the evening light dwindles and the sky fills with a flutter of wet snow, Straw at last says something that gains my interest, announcing off-handedly that he is convinced tomorrow we shall at last locate the Crow village. It is all I can do not to argue that we must continue on in the falling darkness. How swiftly my stoicism evaporates in the heat of my impatience to know the identity of the white man.

A campsite is selected amid a stand of pines, we halter our horses, erect our small tent, start a fire, glumly chew our hardtack and dried meat in a haze of snow. Straw and I scarcely exchange a word. While he sits gazing at the fire completely abstracted and silent for the first time today, the fitful, quavering firelight reveals a man far different from the one I met many months ago, that large, imposing, fleshy fellow. Illness has worked a terrible change in him; his vigour is extinguished. Custis Straw is a mere sketch of what he once was. If a rich, voluptuous painting could be stripped and the drawing which underpins it revealed – there you would have a metaphor for Straw. A sharp blade of nose overhangs a sunken face; the eye sockets are caverns; every plane of his countenance speaks of the underlying skull.

Our cold supper eaten, we silently crawl into our tent, wrap ourselves in our blankets. Straw has cunningly positioned the fire before a large boulder so as to reflect heat and light into our shelter. The pine boughs cut to make our beds fill the interior with a clean, sharp, spicy scent. Through the opening I watch fat flakes of snow wafting down, bouncing in the updraft of the fire until they dissolve in its heat and disappear. My feelings towards Straw soften. I would like to be able to express my genuine thanks to him, but each attempt I have made before has been dismissed with a shrug, as if he believes that to accept my gratitude would lessen himself in his own eyes. What surely lies behind this, and between us, is Lucy.

I'm not proud to think that when she insisted on paying a visit to Straw's sickroom I felt the smallest nudge of jealousy, remembering how she had once hinted to me that Straw was enamoured of her. At the same time I recalled how, after his beating at the hands of Addington, Straw had questioned me with undisguised hostility about Lucy's and my relationship. Following so hard upon the first sharp words I had ever thrown at her, the thought of Lucy taking herself off to him did not sit easily with me.

The unworthiness of this response and the kindness of this man lying with blankets clutched tightly under his chin like a little boy shame me. The firelight flickers on his eyes, vitrified by thought.

I say, "Mr. Straw, you are very quiet tonight. Does something trouble you?"

"Just thinking."

"I see."

Meditatively, he lifts a flask of whisky from under his bed coverings, uncorks it, props himself on an elbow to pass it over. I take a mouthful and hand it back. Straw says, "I've been considering Moses. Not Jerry Potts, mind, but the grand original, the one and only Bible Moses."

How very peculiar, how very like Straw. But at least we are speaking, at least we are being companionable. Straw ponders a moment. "Think of all that old Moses did for God, of how good a servant he was. Why, Moses freed God's people, he passed on Jehovah's messages like a damn telegram boy, he trooped those Hebrews over deserts, put up with their grumbling and grousing, their endless moaning and pissing. He did his very best to act about as well as a man can behave and yet he never got his just recompense." Straw pauses. "Doesn't that seem a hard, unfair reward for a faithful servant?"

Baffled as I am, the only polite response is to plead ignorance. "I have no opinion, Mr. Straw. Bible scholarship is my brother Simon's department."

"It's a puzzler," says Straw. "Moses transported all those Jews to the doorstep of the Promised Land and no sooner did he deliver them to the threshold than God says to Moses, 'Tough titty, but you aren't going to cross over the River Jordan. You're going to die right here, a few steps short of the Promised Land, all of it in plain view.'

"And that throws me. The Bible says Moses did something against God. For the life of me I can't detect what it was. Jehovah says Moses didn't believe in Him, but if Moses wasn't faithful, then who ever could be? Where exactly did old Moses go wrong?"

Warily, I agree. "Indeed."

"So Jehovah lets Moses go up to Pisgah and see across the river to the land he's been hankering for all those long years, lets him look at it, but he doesn't let him cross Jordan. And old Moses dies there without a murmur of complaint; the Hebrews plant him on the wrong side of the river, and everybody goes on about his business in the land of milk and honey."

He falls silent. In the mournful quiet, my sympathy rises for this very odd individual.

"What can it mean – show a man the Promised Land, then don't let him set foot in it?"

"I have no idea. But why do you dwell on this, Mr. Straw?"

"It's an itchy spot in my brain. One thing I'll say is this. If ever I caught sight of the Promised Land, I'd make my way over to it, or die trying. I wouldn't accept it like Moses, go down without a fight." He pauses. "Only I'm never going to see the Promised Land, Gaunt. It's not for me to look on. But it's in your view right now. So don't hesitate, don't make Moses' mistake. Don't listen to any voice but your own sweet wishing. If you want Lucy Stoveall, cross over. Don't keep her waiting on the other side of the bank." That said, he rolls over on his side, turns his face to the wall of the tent.

I am rendered speechless with astonishment. Surely, he will not leave it at that. But almost instantly, the sound of even, calm breathing fills our tent. Having lifted that weight from his shoulders, Straw is deeply, soundly asleep. In the quiet, I feel his dark burden shift, settle on me, souring my anticipation of tomorrow with a restive foreboding.

All night the wet snow falls, sticks to the tent; the canvas roof sags above me.

CUSTIS   Until an hour ago I was doubtful I could deliver on my promise to Gaunt we would find the Crow today. Then, late in the afternoon, we spotted a flat down by the edge of the Bighorn River, snow trampled and splashed with horse piss, piles of dung everywhere, sure evidence of a big herd. We pushed on hard, trusty old Dan scarcely keeping up with Gaunt's horse as he urged him on through the grey light. Now it's before us, a large Crow village, the flames of campfires bouncing amid the pine thickets, the yap of dogs, the happy voices of children at play in the last hour of light. About three hundred yards off, teepees, women stooped over cooking pots, Crow warriors strolling about draped in their blankets and buffalo robes. A boy posted as sentry on the outskirts of the village blows a bone whistle, shouts a warning. I check Gaunt's eagerness, tell him to ease in on the encampment slow and steady, keep his horse to a walk so they don't take us for a threat. A dozen warriors come out to meet us, carbines cradled in their arms, heads swinging from side to side, alert for treachery, on the lookout for raiders concealed in the trees.

I halt, call out my name and my business in pidgin Crow. A familiar voice answers. No mistaking the harsh croak of Pretty Flag, whose throat was stabbed in a fight with the Sioux twenty years ago. Once Pretty Flag gives the all clear, a crowd drifts out from the camp to survey us, among them old friends from my horse-trading days with the Crow, Rotten Tail, Young Badger, Hard Shield, who all press round to reach up and shake my hand. Rotten Tail wants me to come and talk old times with him, Young Badger tempts me with a feast of marrow bones, Hard Shield offers a bed in his lodge.

The Englishman has collected himself a horde of wide-eyed women and children. One little tyke, hardly taller than Gaunt's stirrups, is so taken with his high-topped, shiny boots he strokes them as he would a dog. Another boy stares up at him and shouts questions in Crow. A woman pats his fat horse, murmuring her admiration, only adding to Gaunt's bewilderment.

"Custis, where is Potts?" he calls to me. "Who can we ask about Simon?" His voice is eager, but his eyes are scared. I reckon he's put himself in his brother's shoes, is imagining him lost and marooned in all this strangeness.

I can't answer precisely to Potts's whereabouts, but I do know who to ask about the white man. It's bad form to cut short Indian courtesies, but Gaunt is strung so tight that I turn to Pretty Flag, state the reason for our visit in English because he speaks it better than I talk Crow. "Old friend, excuse my hurry, but we have ridden hard down from Many Houses on the Missouri. We have come because word reached us that a white man is living among the Crow." I gesture to Gaunt. "This man thinks he may be his brother. Is there such a man in the lodges of the Crow? A man called Gaunt?"

In the dimming light I see Pretty Flag's face harden. Even Gaunt can't have missed the sudden change. I throw a glance at the others who understand a little English – Young Badger, Hard Shield, Rotten Tail. Some of their friendliness has blown away, a chill has crept into them at mention of the white man. "There is a Hairy Face here," Pretty Flag answers with grave deliberation. "I do not know what the white men call him. The *bote* has named him Born of a Horse."

I can't read for certain what's going on, but whoever he is, the white man hasn't any friends here. "This man with me is very worried. He will not rest until he knows if this Born of a Horse is his brother. Can you take us to him?"

Pretty Flag shifts his moccasins in the snow, rasps out a question. "Has he come to take his brother away?"

Gaunt bursts out, "Yes, yes! I have brought money! I will pay you anything if you release him!"

"Hold your tongue," I snap.

But Pretty Flag hasn't taken offence. "I am glad you have come. The *bote* makes too much of this Born of a Horse. It is not good that she keeps him in her lodge. We will take you to him, take you to the Lodge of the Sun." With that, the old man turns to his people, shouts to them to lead us to the lodge of the *bote*.

Gaunt can't stop champing at the bit. "Do you think they will surrender him? Do you think my brother has been harmed?"

"Oh, they'll surrender him all right. It appears they don't want any part of him. Something to do with the *bote*, the Holy Being."

"Holy Being? What do you mean?"

I have no explanation, at least not one I'm ready to give him at present. It wouldn't be wise to tell him that if the white man is living with a *bote*, who are great healers, that could mean he's sick or injured. Gaunt is already wan with concern. So all I say is, "Just rest easy for the time being. Take it as it comes."

To my surprise, Gaunt heeds my advice. Simply sits on his horse, chewing his lips, watching as, one by one, the Crow light torches. In the last few minutes, the sun has dipped below the horizon. The pop of pine resin catching fire unsettles the night, flame blows about in the wind, whipping the blackness as thirty or forty warriors mount their ponies.

The Indians lead us off through the snowy pines, Gaunt and I in the rear, side by side, the torches streaming sparks and smoke as we file by Crow lodges. Whole households come out to take a gander. They remain stock-still, watch us in heavy silence, the women wrapped in blankets, heads hooded, black eyes gleaming. Then one young brave slips forward, puts his hands to his hips, pouts and leers at Gaunt like a streetwalker, wriggles lasciviously.

"My God!" exclaims Gaunt. "What is that?"

The young man trots alongside Gaunt's horse. There's no time to explain he was mimicking the *bote* or to explain why. "Don't look at him," I order Gaunt. "Don't give him a thought."

But he's not easy for Gaunt to ignore, so close by his stirrup leather. The young man starts to shout angrily, something about giving back the *bote* to his people. My Crow isn't good enough to make it all out. The Indian grabs a handful of snow, flings it at Gaunt, showers him in white, makes him flinch like he was hit by a stone.

"Easy, easy," I mutter to him under my breath.

Suddenly, Pretty Flag barks words that stop Gaunt's molester dead in his tracks. Pretty Flag urges the Crow into a lope, to put distance between us and the nuisance. With a shaky hand, Gaunt wipes wet snow from his face and heels his horse after the cavalcade. I stop to see if the saucy young buck is still following. He isn't, but he's drilling Gaunt's back with a menacing stare.

As I turn Dan to catch the procession, I see Gaunt twenty yards ahead, chasing the torches. Without a sound, a rider slides his pony out of the trees; sitting silent as a spook he blocks my path. My mouth goes parched, a shiver crawls down my spine.

I call out in Crow, "What do you want?"

The answer comes in English, in a voice I recognize.

"Goddamn it, Potts, you gave me a start." I push my horse up beside him. Potts swings his pony's head and we set off after Gaunt and the torches running like a ribbon of fire through the woods. Pretty Flag has eased the pace now the young Crow has been left behind.

"How come we didn't see you at the village?" I ask Potts.

He stabs a thumb northward. "I'm holed up a couple of miles outside the Crow camp. On a rise. I saw all the lights from there. Came down to see what was going on. Then I spotted you."

"I don't like the feel of this. The Crow aren't happy about the white man."

"Mary's father says they fear he is stealing the *bote*'s power. He says some are afraid there will be no Holy Being to cut the sacred pole for the Sun Dance this summer. No one to say, 'May all our enemies fall like him,' when the tree comes down."

"You've seen the white man?"

"No, he keeps to the lodge of the *bote*. My father-in-law tells me a jealous warrior hit the white man because the *bote* will not lie with any of the warriors since he came. This made the *bote* very angry and she beat the jealous man with a stick so hard that his own wife could not recognize him. I have seen the *bote*. She is large and very strong." He ponders a moment. "My father-in-law believes the white man has made her Christian, taught her it is a sin to lie with many men." Potts smiles.

We are gaining on Gaunt. I call out to him. He reins in his horse, twists round in the saddle. Recognizing Potts, he rushes questions at him in one quaky breath. "Is it my brother? Is the white man Simon?"

"I do not know. But soon you will find out. The Lodge of the Sun is not much farther. Just beyond the edge of the village."

Gaunt's mouth tenses, but he leaves it at that. We ride on at the end of the train of Crow, orange and yellow daubs of light splashing the snow, boughs brushing our shoulders and shining greasy green in the flickering light.

A big clearing in the timber opens before us. The Crow are pressing into it, forming an arc before the biggest Indian lodge I've ever laid eyes on. The three of us shoulder our horses in beside Pretty Flag, whose eyes swivel to Potts, grip him in a coal-black stare. All around me, I hear the hostile murmur of Crow warriors. But Potts shows no sign of fear, simply sits with his hands folded on the pommel of his saddle.

"He is my friend," I say quickly to Pretty Flag, to explain Potts's presence. "He sent word to us of the white man."

Pretty Flag nods thoughtfully. "Potts is nothing to us. He begs his father-in-law for his daughter. Cries and pulls at his leg like a child."

The words don't get a rise out of Potts. He keeps his eyes fixed on the huge lodge gleaming in the light of the torches, glowing like old ivory piano keys. The Crow don't build lodges of more than eighteen skins since such a show of pride is an offence to the spirits. This one is at least twenty-five skins, and they're covered with pictures of buffalo, elk, deer, mountain sheep, horses, all painted in red, blue, yellow, black. Over the entrance a mighty sunburst of dyed porcupine quills is rising. A Holy Being's vision brought home to the real world in bone-coloured hide, bright trader pigments, the finest of quillwork.

There is no sound but the snuffle of horses, the stamp of hooves, the creak of wooden saddle trees. Then Pretty Flag draws himself up on his pony and yells for Born of a Horse to come out, there are white men who want to speak to him. His cry is taken up by the rest of the warriors, a quarrelsome, furious shout. The door flap of the Lodge of the Sun gives a twitch and the uproar dies. We all wait. Beside me, I hear the sharp suck of Gaunt's breath.

The flap is thrown back, a figure passes through the doorway, straightens slowly to full height in the glare of the pine knots. The *bote* is tall, raw-boned, dressed like the Queen of Sheba in all her glory. She wears a red blouse hung with rows of abalone shell, a white doe-skin skirt, leggings so encrusted with brilliant beadwork they must be stiff as tin stovepipes. Her arms are circled from wrist to elbows with copper bracelets that make a jangled music as she sways gracefully towards us. Her hair is long, a clean part down the middle, a stripe of red paint on the scalp. Her nose is fierce, the nostrils flared, the mouth full-lipped.

The *bote*'s dark, hot eyes move over the Crow warriors, picking out each of them, noting them. Then her eyes fall on Gaunt, Potts, and me. She sends us a haughty look.

She begins to speak in a girlish voice too small and sweet for the body, a slight pause between each word for emphasis that allows me to follow most of what she's saying. She chastises the warriors for their shouting, tells them they bellow like bulls in rut. I glance at Charles Gaunt. The sight of the *bote*, the size of her, her way of speaking has turned him into a pillar of staring salt.

Many of the Crow hang their heads while she dresses them down. But Pretty Flag isn't a man to tug a forelock. When the *bote* is done scolding them, Pretty Flag's scarred throat grinds out a handful of words. He says they shouted to make Born of a Horse hear. He says Born of a Horse does not hear anyone but her.

Angrily, the *bote* orders them to go. Potts, Gaunt, and I can stay. The Crow begin to slip off. The warriors' guttural mumble of disappointment, the snort of ponies, the muffled trampling of hooves in snow, wanes away. The torches flit through the trees, disappear. We are alone with the *bote*.

Gaunt bucks up his nerve, says loudly to Potts, "I want you to ask this woman if my brother is in the lodge."

Before Potts can utter a word, the *bote* answers Gaunt. "I am called Talks Different. I know a little English. Born of a Horse teaches me. We say the Our Father prayer together."

Gaunt's face jumps, then slides to another place, sheer relief. "It *is* Simon," he gasps and piles off his horse. "It can be no one else." The news has so unmanned him he stumbles like a drunk as he heads for the lodge. The *bote* flicks out a hand, plucks his sleeve, and stops him with her touch. Like a grand lady turning some interloper away from the door of the big house.

"Please allow me to see my brother," Gaunt says. It is the next thing to a sob.

Potts and I are dismounting carefully, no sudden moves. Gaunt and the *bote* have locked eyes. You can almost see Gaunt's spine stiffen with the strain of holding her gaze. But you've got to give him this, it's clear he's made up his mind not to be turned away. Slowly, he pulls his arm free from the *bote*'s grip, never taking his eyes from hers. "I *will* see him," he repeats, voice louder, steadier. And to my surprise, the *bote* turns on her heel, leads Gaunt to the lodge door. They dip their shoulders, pass through.

Leaving Potts to hold the horses, I follow and find the two of them planted by a small fire under the smoke hole. The little blaze can't light but a bit of the almighty big teepee; the farthest reaches are dark with shadow. I watch Gaunt, who is peering hard into the dimness while the *bote* fondly watches a small Indian boy playing at their feet. He's sweeping the packed-earth floor with a goose wing, swirling patterns in the dust with the feathers.

From the shadows someone declares, "So you've come." The child's head shoots up, he lifts himself from the dirt and patters off, laughing, full of life, headed for the voice. Gaunt's recognized it too. A man in a trance, he picks a burning stick from the fire to light his way, walks uncertainly towards the darkness. I follow behind the *bote*.

Gaunt's brand licks shifting shapes out of the shadows, the little boy crawling up onto the lap of a man hooded in a blanket, the man pressing his cheek to the top of the child's head. Gaunt is directly above them, sprinkling sparks from the stick. The child commences to whimper. He's afraid of the stranger. The *bote*'s man clutches the child to his chest, slowly rocks him from side to side, crooning over and over, "Little bird. Little bird. Little bird. Do not be afraid."

Gaunt whispers, "My God, Simon, you are alive."

Simon lifts his eyes from the child. The blanket slips to his shoulders and reveals long blond hair, a beard of flaxen curls, corn-flower blue eyes. The *bote* suddenly steps to Gaunt's side, bracelets chiming. "I am the one who saved him. Named him. He is mine," she says with quiet authority, the confidence of a queen.

Gaunt doesn't seem to hear her; he's too busy wrestling with the sight of his brother. "You are so changed," he says. "So changed. I recognized your voice at once, but to find you like this –" He sinks to his knees, throws aside his flame, fumbles his brother's hands into his.

Simon smiles, a burst of white teeth and fond affection. "It is good to see you, Charles. You are right. Yes, I am changed. As you can see." Looking about the tent, he remarks softly, " 'It is sown a natural body; it is raised a spiritual body.' "

The oddity of this doesn't seem to strike Charles Gaunt. He's too busy pelting on. "We'll soon get you home. How glad Father will be. How he misses you. How I missed you, Simon. And to find you now, when I had come to the end of hope –"

Simon is bent on something else. Suddenly he says, "Where is Addington? Surely, you haven't left him alone in the Crow camp? You know how impulsive and headstrong he is. I don't want him making trouble here. It would be very dangerous."

At Addington's name, Gaunt's face momentarily collapses. But he recovers, gathers himself for what he must say. "I don't know how to tell you, Simon. Addington and I had words some months past. It led . . . led to a breach. Each of us went our own way." He pauses. "No, perhaps the truth is I . . . I deserted him. Addington was hunting a bear – you know his reckless schemes." A final rush of breath. "And he was killed. Addington is dead, Simon."

Simon goes still, sets the child gently on the ground. Talks Different sweeps the boy up, cradles him against the red blouse. Simon struggles out of the backrest, awkward, slow as an old man, lays a hand on his brother's shoulder, lifts him to his feet, embraces him. Above Gaunt's shoulder Simon's face floats, calm, quiet. He strokes the back of his brother's coat, a soothing, fatherly motion, as if one son in need of comfort has taken the place of another in his arms. He murmurs in Gaunt's ear, "This dreadful, sad news about our brother. How sorry I am to hear it. All summer I waited for the two of you to arrive."

Startled, Gaunt jerks back. "If you had word we sought you, why did you not send us a message?"

"No, Charles, not word as you mean it – word came to me in a dream. Living among the Crow, like Joseph in the land of the Egyptians, I dream many dreams. But let us move closer to the fire. My feet are cold, they're always cold now. If you and your friend will lend me your shoulders –"

I step up, make myself known to him. "Custis Straw."

"Simon Gaunt, but of course you are aware of that," he says with a wry smile. We shake hands, all very correct. Then Simon leans on our shoulders and we move towards the fire supporting his slew-footed, teetery walk, the *bote* leading us, goose and her goslings. His brother's first few lurching steps seemed to have stunned Charles Gaunt into silence. After several moments, he blurts out, "Look at you, Simon! What have these savages done to you!"

"Nothing except save my life. Or rather Talks Different did," says Simon, nodding warmly in the direction of the *bote*. "You see, the Reverend Witherspoon led us into a blizzard. Six of my toes went black with gangrene from the frost. They needed to be amputated. Talks Different performed the surgery. She is a wonderful healer."

Heartened by Simon's praise, the *bote* breaks into a pleased smile, fingers the abalone shells on her blouse.

Gaunt is livid. "I tried. I tried to warn you about Witherspoon. But you wouldn't listen."

"It was Witherspoon who brought me here from England," Simon says gently. "The hand of God is a hidden hand."

The *bote* spreads robes by the fire and we seat ourselves on them. Gaunt on one side of his brother, the *bote* on the other, the little boy nestled in her lap. She fusses with Simon, arranging the blanket over his shoulders. Gaunt turns his eyes away from this display. Across from the three of them, I toss pieces of wood in the fire, feeding the ragged flames as Simon stretches his moccasins out to the blaze and begins to speak.

"Nine months ago, I dreamed of two starving horses. One a grey nag covered in sores, the other a blind horse. It had glass buttons for eyes. They came to the Lodge of the Sun. The whole world was a desert, nothing but dust, not a scrap of grass to be had. In their hunger, they began to eat the hide off our lodge poles, mouths dripping blood. I did not have the strength to drive them off, to send them away. All I could do was weep and beg them to stop." Simon hesitates, then says, "I did not understand its meaning until Talks Different interpreted it for me. The grey horse was Addington, the one with the button eyes was you. She said my brothers were coming to take me back to England." There is a long pause, Simon's last sentence hangs in the air. Gaunt leans towards Simon eagerly. "You see, Charles, I am sorry to disappoint you, but I will remain here." He nods at Talks Different and the boy.

Charles Gaunt drops his head in the palm of one hand. After a considerable interval, he asks in a hushed voice, "Where is the child's father?"

The *bote* suddenly shifts on her robe; the copper bracelets clink angrily.

Simon answers, "I am his father."

Gaunt keeps his eyes on the ground. "The boy is too old to be your child, Simon. He belongs to that woman."

"To us both."

I clear my throat. Gaunt looks up at me, hopeful I'm rallying to his banner. "I reckon what your brother means to say is the boy is adopted."

" 'Suffer the little children to come on to me,' " says Simon. "The

352

botes are paragons of charity. Six months ago both his parents died – of consumption. Now he is our child. His name is Red Calf."

Gaunt sits picking his words over. I guess that he's shucking some, taking up others. When he starts to talk, he does so with full deliberation, full care. "Simon, this is so much like you. I understand what you say, understand it is prompted by Christian idealism. Your large-heartedness does you credit. But your sense of duty, of responsibility, is misplaced."

The *bote* leans against Simon, rubs her cheek on his shoulder like a cat. Dotingly, he touches her hair. Then the *bote* straightens up. She's staked public claim to her man. It's out in the open now, the gist of it, if not all the particulars. This much anyway, a declaration of love.

Gaunt's taken it in, and it's frozen him. When he finally finds his voice, it is so low, so faint he can hardly be heard above the crackle of the fire. "And what do you expect me to tell Father?"

"That I am lost, dead. He would have no argument with either description if the facts were known to him. But as you see, I am neither. I'm sorry, Charles."

I reckon there's a moment when a man knows everything is lost, his flesh and bones sense it before his mind does. That's Charles Gaunt right now.

The *bote* gives him a final push. "You will not eat our lodge. You go now."

I get to my feet, cross to Gaunt, hoist him to his feet. He doesn't resist or fuss. He's too shaken.

"Charles," Simon calls after us, but I keep Gaunt on the move. Hand on his elbow, I direct him out of the Lodge of the Sun to faithful Potts waiting slouched in the night.

Potts offers us an invitation to camp with him. Riding single file through the trees, not a word is said. I best sleep in Potts's shelter tonight, let Gaunt have the tent to himself. His grief requires privacy, and I need to consider how I'm going to tell him whatever more I decide he needs to know.

I never did give that question my full consideration because once we got the tent pitched and Gaunt crawled into it, Potts and I broke into my store of whisky. The thing is, drinking with Potts, if you pull the cork on a bottle there's no stopping until you follow your face clean to the bottom. And if you're fool enough to pull the cork on the second one, the same rule applies.

We made a sorry sight the next morning, the two of us trying to set a fire in the wet snow, still half-drunk, bilious and shivering like shaved dogs. That's how Gaunt found us, but he didn't seem to note our condition, how our nerves were all raw and scraped and our moods tetchy. He was too full of crackpot schemes he'd lain awake all night dreaming up. The first being that the three of us ought to kidnap his brother and shanghai him off to Fort Benton with us. I told him straight out I was having no part of that. He wanted to know why.

"Because I've got no interest in tangling with the Crow. And what's more, I don't hold with press-ganging a man into something he doesn't want." It struck me that godforsaken, chilly morning that the Englishman treated everybody as if he were the lord of the earth and the rest of us his damn servants. If he wanted to go down to the Crow country, I was expected to jump and do his bidding. Who put up the tent every night? And who happened to be freezing their arses trying to start him his breakfast fire with sopping wood?

It took him aback, me being short with him. He said, "Very well. Then I have another proposal I shall put to Simon. If he won't give this woman up, it's impossible for him to return to England. But I think I can persuade him to take the boy and her to Fort Benton to live."

Just like that. Take her and the boy to Fort Benton to live. It riled me how he believed things ought to fall into place just because he wanted them to. He wooed Lucy Stoveall and got his way with her quick enough. But this wasn't going to be as easy for him as Lucy had been.

"Give it up, Gaunt. They won't go to Fort Benton."

"Who are you to say what is and what isn't going to happen? I saw several instances of Indian women and white men living together in Fort Benton. I grant you I am not pleased at the prospect, but better that than my brother living the way he is now. Exiled from his own people."

I lost my temper then. I asked did he want his brother to end up like Private Noonan? Gaunt wanted to know who Private Noonan was, and what did he have to do with Simon?

So I started to tell him.

"Private Noonan was the husband of a regimental laundress at Fort Lincoln. Mrs. Noonan had been married before – to another soldier – but he had died and left her a widow. Private Noonan and her were small people, just a lowly private and a shirt-scrubber. Anyway, when he was off on manoeuvres, his wife fell ill. On her deathbed she begged the ladies of the fort that when she expired she wanted to be buried in the clothes she wore, under no circumstances should they wash her body. She claimed her sense of modesty and pro-priety could not bear the thought of it. Well, Mrs. Noonan died before her husband got back to the fort and the ladies didn't respect her wishes. They stripped Mrs. Noonan and they got a terrible shock. Mrs. Noonan was a man. Shortly after, Private Noonan shot himself in the stables. He couldn't take the bullyragging from the rest of the soldiers. Do you want that for your brother?"

Gaunt took it hard. Maybe it was seeing him knocked down a peg, lose that smug English air that made me understand what I'd done, the cruelty of it. I tried to talk him through this business, enlisting Potts's help whenever I could. I told Gaunt about the first time a French beaver man pointed out a *bote* to me among the Gros Ventre up in the Sweetgrass Hills. The trapper called her a *berdache*, the name the French had given them, but every Indian tribe has their own word for such persons. *Bote* in Crow, *wintke* in Sioux, *he man eh* in Cheyenne. If you translate them into English, they come out roughly the same, Two Spirit, I told Gaunt. I said that an old Crow man once informed me that it's the mystery of two spirits in one body that makes a *bote* holy, a creature both male and female, yet more than either. It gives them extraordinary spirit power. The old man had said that generally the female spirit shows itself early. A little boy wishes

355

to keep company with the women, to sew and to bead, he begs his parents to dress him as a girl. Not to do as the child wishes would be wrong because he is born on a path, and it would be evil, a crime against nature to make him deny his spirit.

Then Potts stepped in. He said his wife had told him of a Crow warrior who in middle-age was spoken to by the *bote* spirit in a dream. The man struggled against his vision for a long time. Everything went wrong for him because he did not obey it. But the real nature is always stronger than the body, and finally the warrior accepted his path, put aside his weapons, and became a woman. Potts said that any man who took a Two Spirit for a wife was blessed. Everybody knew the Two Spirits were builders of mighty lodges, healers of the sick, graceful dancers, fine beadworkers. They brought good fortune to everyone they favoured. Potts said that an Assiniboine had once passed on to him a rumour that the great Sioux war chief Crazy Horse had several *wintke* wives and the prophet Sitting Bull had one too. The Sioux assumed that the power these men held owed something to their Two Spirit wives. A Sioux warrior would give many rich presents to a *wintke* just to have her give a name to his baby.

Gaunt listened, but I'm not sure he heard. When Potts and I were done, he got to his feet and walked away from us. He was a long time getting back. When he did, he struck me as being even more determined to save his brother from the *bote*, now he knew how matters stood between her and Simon.

In the past few days, Gaunt returned again and again to the Lodge of the Sun, trying to persuade his brother to come back to England with him. I feared the *bote* might lose patience and hand him a drubbing, but Gaunt says she seems to get pleasure out of hearing Simon refuse him.

With the writing plain on the wall, Charles Gaunt is acting as a man is liable to do when everything he wants is thwarted. Now he's throwing all his energy into doing what he can do to avoid facing what is outside of his power to accomplish. It prods him to wild, hasty decisions. Yesterday, he talked Potts into guiding him down to St. Louis. Later, he handed me two letters, one addressed to the I. G.

Baker firm, the other to Lucy Stoveall, impressing on me how important it is that I place it *directly* into her hands.

This morning, Gaunt headed off in the direction of the Lodge of the Sun. When he came back so downcast, I picked up my Henry and pretended to go off to hunt, just to give him a little time alone to swallow one more sore defeat.

The weather has taken a turn for the worse. A sharp spell of cold settling in from the north, winter baring its teeth. Gaunt suggested we take a tramp to stir up our blood, work a little warmth into our bones. I followed his lead and he walked us into the Crow camp. He was mighty pensive as we wandered through it. Most of the Crow men were gone, likely off on a buffalo hunt. The women were fleshing bighorn sheep hides and butchering deer. Old codgers were bundled up in their robes, nodding their grey heads in agreement to whatever their companions had to say. All of them ignored us. We didn't exist.

We wandered amid the white-blanketed pines in a thick silence, Gaunt kicking at the crusty snow with his boots. After a bit, he said to me, "I believe my brother has not long to live."

"Your brother looked fit enough to me. Aside from his feet."

"I said to Simon that he cannot bet on his circumstances staying as they are now. In ten years, the old life of the Crow will be gone. Settlers, civilization will put an end to it. Do you know what his answer was? That is why he chooses to stay. The brevity of the life he is leading makes it all the more precious to him."

I kept quiet. We came upon moccasin tracks. Gaunt began to set his feet in the prints in the snow. It seemed to help him think, occupying himself in that fashion. Soon, the Indian's trail disappeared into a thicket. Gaunt stopped, as if he was considering following the trail wherever it led. There was frost in his eyebrows; the white fog of his breath marked the quick-time of his breathing.

"Mr. Potts presented me with Addington's personal effects after I returned from my visit to Simon. Pocket watch, ring, even the clothing. He refused to surrender it to Ayto's keeping." Gaunt's brow furrowed. "There was no blood on the clothes, not a tear or rip. Very strange considering how he died, don't you think?"

"What do you mean?"

"Ayto said he saw the body before it was buried. It was mauled beyond recognition." Hands stuffed in his coat pockets, Gaunt began to shiver. "It was very scrupulous of Mr. Potts to safeguard those articles until he could return them to me."

"Yes."

He took out a handkerchief and blew his nose. "But the one particular article my father would have wished as a keepsake, because Addington was so attached to it, was missing. Very odd. But perhaps Potts judged it worthless and discarded it. I did not wish to offend him by asking after the item." He paused before musing, "Then again, did Addington forget to bring it from England?"

It was plain to me Charles Gaunt was thinking aloud, moving hand over hand down some treacherous wall, touching Addington's death, touching Simon's choosing the *bote* over him. Trying to feel his way to a place where he could sum it all up, make sense of it.

"Addington believed the item brought him luck. Superstition – believing in something that isn't there. Simon is no different. You know, when he was a boy he used to fondle buttons. He acted as if there was life in them. Gave every evidence that he felt this life. It is a disease of the Gaunts – superstition. I'm the only one untouched by it."

Gaunt began to walk once more. Minutes passed. "As a child, Addington adored our gamekeeper, old Caitlin. Tagged along at his heels wherever he went like a faithful terrier. When the time came for Addington to be sent away to school, he begged the gamekeeper for a memento, something to take away with him to remember the old man by. Do you know what he gave him? His belt. He took it off and said, 'There you go, young master. If I know ye, like as not ye'll be in and out of trouble at that school. When time comes to tan your arse, ask them to use this on you. That'll recall your old friend Caitlin well enough, bring him to mind. My own boys certain do remember me by it.'" Gaunt laughed. There was no pleasure, no trace of mirth in the sound. "When Addington came to manhood, he wore Caitlin's belt on sporting occasions, riding to hounds, shooting. Quite incongruous since my brother was a bit of a dandy among the sporting set. To wear the belt of a servant hardly seemed proper. But Addington believed it brought him success in the field."

We walked on. Twilight was falling, everything growing dark.

"What did this belt look like?"

Gaunt's brow furrowed. "A sort of workman's belt, wide, thick, black leather. I don't remember exactly. You see, what intrigued me about it was what it meant to Addington. The idea of it. That's why I'm sure he would not have gone hunting for the bear without it."

So there it is. I'll never know because I got rid of that belt. Chopped it to pieces. Burned them the day after I'd seen Joel Kelso's face in the livery stable and knew that the belt had never belonged to Titus. I told myself the time had come to stop fingering Madge Dray's death, turning it over and over in my hands, carrying it around in my pocket.

But if it was the Captain's belt, would he have left his luck on a young girl's neck? I could ask Gaunt whether he remembers studs. But I won't. Because, God willing, here's where I make an end to it.

❖ ❖ ❖

For weeks, Potts has walked in circles around what stakes him fast – Mary and Mitchell. Now it seems he must cut the tether. His father-in-law, who has been carrying Potts's messages to where Mary is camped many miles away on the Powder River, says no more parley. She will not come to speak to Potts. And she warns him if he shows his face at the door of her new husband's lodge, there will be trouble, bloodshed.

What Mary does not know is that he has already paid a visit to see Mitchell, tucked himself away in a clump of brush outside the Crow camp, hunkered there for hours on the slim chance he might catch a glimpse of his boy.

He had recognized Mitchell the moment he laid eyes on him. His son, plump, bow-legged as his father, arms squeezing a ball of squirming, yelping fur, a protesting pup. As soon as he saw that, he threw his eyes about, looking for the mother dog. She couldn't be far off. If the bitch spotted his son manhandling one of her litter, she might sink her teeth in him.

The three-year-old-boy reeled and staggered under the weight of the pup, fighting to curb its frantic efforts to escape. Finally, the struggle became too much and he dropped down on his buttocks a short way from Potts's hiding place. Holding the pup trapped between his fat knees, Mitchell vigorously scratched the belly of the wriggling dog, bent his head to scold it in Crow.

Out of the corner of his eye, Potts saw a skinny bitch lope up a nearby ridge, stop, then begin to sidle down it, pendulous teats swinging, lips curled, fangs exposed. The sight of her brought him into the open to put himself between her and his son. His sudden appearance snapped Mitchell's face up, loosened his grip on the pup. It squirted out of his lap, waddled eagerly to its mother's side. Mitchell slowly pushing himself to his feet, gaping at him, Potts unable to bring himself to move despite the danger of being discovered so near his wife's camp. The boy's eyes widening, his mouth puckering tighter. Father and son locked face to face, frozen in the ice of an unexpected encounter.

Then Mitchell turned and ran.

Two steps and Potts overtook him, swept his son up in his arms, felt the fierce churning of the stocky legs battering his hips, heard the boy's scream of warning. "Enemy!" Potts clamped a hand to his mouth, choking off Mitchell's cry.

If anyone heard, they paid no heed, thought it only a shout in a boys' game of war. Potts hugged the little body hard, hand covering everything of the tiny face but the black eyes, pools of terror. There was no recognition in those eyes; they did not remember him, were blank of everything but the tightening coil of panic. The body did not know him. Potts could feel the cold of Mitchell's flesh clean through his son's buckskin jacket. The chilly stiffness of a dead child.

Seconds passed. Slowly, Potts set Mitchell on his feet, held him firmly by one shoulder. He gestured to a stick lying on the ground. "Count coup."

Mitchell looked up in amazement. The enemy was ordering him to humiliate him in battle. The little boy did as he was told, slowly reached down, grasped the stick. "Count coup," Potts demanded. The boy hesitated, then struck his father twice on the thigh, so fiercely the rotten stick snapped.

"Now I will run from you," said Potts. "I will run because the bravery and power of a Crow warrior makes me afraid."

And he did, springing through the clutching bushes to where his pony waited.

Now he and the Englishman are about to ride to where boats still raise smoke and beat the water wild with their paddles, down to St. Louis, the city Potts's two Almost Fathers, Harvey and Dawson, had fled to, orphaning him those many years ago. Maybe he would find them still there, mad Harvey drinking and fighting, Dawson worrying about business and counting money. It would be good to see his Almost Fathers again, to tell them what he had become. A man with a hundred horses, a man who bore the honour name Bear Child.

Many years ago, his mother, Crooked Back, had dreamed he would be the child of three fathers. Not Kanai, not white, but a being made strong and strange by mixed blood and mixed influences. Andrew Potts, whose face he could not remember, had given him white man's blood. Harvey had roared in his cups, sworn and beat him, teaching him with every blow the lesson that it was a far better thing to be feared than to be afraid. Then came his last father, Dawson, who tried to prod the white mind in him, teaching him to sign his name, to add and subtract, telling him stories of his Scots ancestors across the Big Water, the wild, free raiders who danced their victories over a holy cross of swords laid on the ground.

His own father had died when Jerry was a baby. To his son, Mitchell, he was now dead. But perhaps to be shaped by many hands was a fortunate thing, far better than to be shaped by a single hand. A bundle of sticks does not break as easily as one stick. For Mitchell's sake, he prayed his son would become such a bundle. Whatever Jerry Potts could give him had already been given.

28

LUCY Expecting a blow doesn't make it easier to bear. Abner Stoveall taught me that. You wait for it to land, your shoulders scrunch up, your back goes hard as a plank, every muscle pulls tight, the pain lies in wait under your skin, ready to shriek. So when it lands, maybe it hurts all the more because you're prepared for its coming.

I saw for the longest time how it was going to fall out with Charles and me. Even when he took no steps to travel down to St. Louis with the season growing late, cold weather threatening, I didn't allow myself to hope he meant to stay here in the Overland with me for the winter. In my heart, I knew sooner or later Charles would leave off from me and go back to Old England. These good days are but for a little bit, I told myself. Be satisfied. Sweetness goes; it's not for forever, it won't last. I knew it well, that one day for his sake I'd have to renounce him.

Yesterday, when I heard those heavy boots in the hall outside my door, I felt that it was Custis Straw come back to me, not Charles. Once a heavy man, you don't lose the tread, you set your feet solid. It's your way of walking through the world. His knock at the door made me guess the news he was bringing wasn't good. A mousy little rap, Excuse me, please. I got something hard to tell, it said.

Straw came in wearing snow on his shoulders. It didn't even have time to melt, he came up the stairs of the Overland that quick. I was setting on the bed, didn't even blink, waiting for the blow to land. Straw had about as much colour as the envelope in his hand. He laid the letter on the table and said, "Charles asked me to give you this."

I pinched the bridge of my nose to dam the tears back. I don't believe he saw. I said, "I thank you kindly, Custis."

He shifted his feet and a little snow melted, dripped to the floorboards. Then he said, "Well, I'll leave you then."

"I'd be grateful," was all I could manage. Grateful I was when he closed the door behind him so quiet and gentle, like I was a sleeping baby. I stared at the letter for the longest time before I dared to open it.

Charles writes a fine hand, as pretty as he paints, but I had to con out the meaning of a good many of the words.

November 20, 1871

Dearest Lucy,

My brother Simon is found. To make a long tale short, he refuses to return to England. He has formed a preposterous liaison with an Indian person, so unseemly I shall pass over it without further comment. Despite all my best efforts to persuade him to repudiate this attachment, he stubbornly refuses. To place it in the most generous light, I can only surmise that to do so strikes him as dishonourable.

So I am brought to a point I would dearly prefer to avoid, if avoiding it did not brand me a coward. You have certainly noted my uneasiness of mind these past weeks. One day deciding to return to Father to inform him of Addington's death and my failure to learn anything of Simon – the next shrinking from the task, fearing the consequences – my father's rage and his certain disappointment in me and my poor efforts. I procrastinated, hoping procrastination would save me. I admit to having hoped that one morning I would awake and find myself cut off from England by ice and snow, that I would be excused for a term from performing what I so dreaded.

Dear Lucy, I see now that I can no longer shirk my responsibilities. I must go to Father to report what has transpired, the death of one son and the refusal of another to return to his family. I owe Father at least this much consideration.

I write to you with every confidence that you will accept the justice of my decision to make an immediate departure for England. Simply put, I cannot bear to keep my distressing knowledge to myself any longer. The burden of silence weighs too heavily upon me.

So tomorrow, I start for St. Louis in the company of Mr. Potts, who has graciously agreed to take me there. I am certain that I may depend on that good and reliable man to see me well and safely on my way. From St. Louis I shall take the train to New York, or if it is more expeditious, board a packet to New Orleans and obtain passage to England from there.

I proceed in this manner because it is my fear that if I were to return to Fort Benton to make my goodbye of you, all my resolve and feeble courage would dissolve in your presence, and render me helpless to fulfil my clear obligation to my father.

But be assured our separation is only temporary. I will be back in Fort Benton to collect you in the spring at the earliest date possible. I implore you to wait for me there. I have written a letter to I. G. Baker asking them to store all of my effects and Addington's. I have also ordered them to place all funds of mine in their hands at your disposal. You shall have no concern in that regard.

In the past few days I have thought of nothing but our future. Now I open my mind to you. Your husband is dead. Madge is dead. You are alone in the world, and I ask you to lean upon me. Despite my obvious failure to do what Father has asked, I will convince him to settle an allowance on me sufficient for us to take up residence abroad. The two of us could settle very comfortably in Italy, where we would be exempt from society's scrutiny. England presents too many impediments to our happiness and, frankly, Father would not countenance our residing there under the eyes of his friends and associates. His notions of propriety are very strict. If he refuses my entreaty – and I warn you Father is a tyrannical and headstrong man – we must live on whatever I can earn by my brush, or by giving English lessons.

I know this letter must smell of musty, pragmatic concerns. But seeing my way through to honourably discharge my commitments has been my salvation of late. One shock has followed another in such rapid succession that only by concentrating my mind on matters of business have I been able to shore it up when it threatens to crumble.

Addington's death was a greater blow to me than I first admitted to myself. I believed I was correct to break with him at Fort Edmonton after his despicable behaviour towards you. Now I confess that Addington was very ill in body and mind when he committed his assault on your person. Lately I ask myself, Could not a little brotherly care and solicitude have preserved his life? In dark moments, I have been forced to ask myself whether in the deepest recesses of my mind I did not wish for Addington's death. Often I am beset by a picture of my brother's ripped and torn body, a feeling that he was destroyed by my wish, disguised as a ravening bear.

And now my beloved twin has turned his back on Father and me, and I wonder if I have not had some hand in that too.

But enough of such despairing thoughts. Let me turn to happier ones. I promise to write as often as possible and beg you to do the same. In fact, write to me as soon as you receive this, write your thoughts on all these things so that when I arrive in England some part of you will be there to welcome me. You shall find the address of Father's residence below my signature.

Our pending separation saddens me deeply; it is a step I would not take if I could see my way to any other. Dearest Lucy, understand this is for the best. A few months is not so very long, a few months is nothing. Our real life begins in a little while.

Please keep my paintings secure with you in the Overland. I trust them to no other hands but yours.

Your loving Charles

It took me a good while to spell out all the words, work them through to sense. But when I did, I could read plain between the lines of that clear hand. He's a deep well of pain and confusion, more than I reckoned. My heart breaks for him. I know something else. Every word Charles wrote he thinks he believes because he's got to blind himself. But I can see the truth of it. I have no other choice but to look on it steady.

In so many words, he said his brother threw himself away on an Indian woman. Charles's circumstances are no different. He can't raise me up, but I can damn sure pull him down. I won't do it.

A fact is a hard grindstone to rub your nose on, but I've done it all my life. Yoked to me, an ignorant country woman, he'd have a bitter time of it. I'd be a shame to him. He would wear down over time. It's the nature of whatever is soft and fine to be done so.

Once he gets among his own kind, things will look a good deal different. I'll seem wondrous strange to him from distant England. They say absence makes the heart grow fonder, but I don't have faith in that. If it were true, we'd love the dead more than the living.

I don't fault him for what I know is going to happen. How could I? I'm in Charles's debt. After Madge was taken from me, I thought my heart was forever shut, but he unbarred it. Never mind I'm alone again, one bird on a bough in a cold wind.

Last night, I rubbed his letter on my breasts as if I could feel his hands in his words. I licked it as if I might taste his skin. I lapped the paper like a cat laps cream, or like the red bone hound in my dream licked my blood from the ground.

My moon blood has stopped its flow. Call me a fool, but I'm glad of my condition.

29

CHARLES It has been four months now since I received Jerry Potts's obituary and Custis Straw's summons to North America. Memory is a restless spirit and Straw's message has roused it. In solitary moments, I harken back to that arduous journey across the plains undertaken more than two decades ago, an ordeal the consequences of which I could not have foreseen. That journey blew my life off-course and made of Simon, Addington, Father, and Lucy ever present shades of regret.

How clearly I recall coming down the gangplank of that New Orleans cotton boat on a December day to be greeted by the same grimy Liverpudlian smoke and clamour that had waved me off nine months before. I had not warned Father of my coming. I found myself a room in a commercial travellers' hotel, sent Father a telegram that contained no other information than that he should expect me the following day on the seven-fifteen evening train. Exhausted from my journey, dreading to face the morrow, I collapsed fully clothed on my bed and slept the sleep of the dead.

The next day, as the railway coach rolled through the mist-swathed English countryside, I was brought to the brink of tears by the familiar sights – stark winter hedgerows, cottages, flocks of black-faced sheep; dark, low-slung clouds suddenly rent by coruscated shafts of winter sunlight. When we were children, Simon swore to me that angels rode upon such glittering beams down from heaven to earth, and back from earth to heaven.

Our last meeting filled my thoughts. My final appeal to Simon had reached an impasse; he would not relent. Seeing my distress, he had done as he had so often done before, clasped a hand to the back of my neck, drew me near, laid his forehead on mine as if he could penetrate my thoughts with his, make our minds one. When our brows touched, I began to weep. If Addington could not survive this savage land, what chance had gentle, guileless Simon? Already the frontier had reduced him to a hobbling cripple. Disease, starvation, or a band of Blackfoot raiders would sooner or later snuff out his life.

"It is not too late to change your mind," I implored him. "Come home with me. I swear that neither Father nor anyone else shall ever hear a word of this. Our secret and our secret alone. Kept just as when we were boys."

"We are not boys any longer, Charles. We are men. Each of us has our path to travel. To turn from it invites nothing but misery." And with that, he took me in his arms one last time, released me, and limped back to the Lodge of the Sun, released me to carry my bitter news back home.

By the time my train drew into our local station, winter dark had obliterated from sight all comforting English scenes. I was surprised to find there was no vehicle on hand to collect me. I might have hired a dogcart in the village to transport myself and my bags to Sythe Grange, but decided the two-mile walk would give me time to organize my thoughts. All day I had pushed out of mind the harrowing prospect of delivering my news to Father. Now I felt like a solicitor entering court on an important case bereft of a brief, or even hastily scribbled notes.

I left my bags in the care of the station master, buttoned my overcoat, turned up my collar, and set out. Remembering how Addington had described Father's mental state to me in Fort Benton, I uneasily wondered if what my brother had said were true. Was that the explanation for no one meeting my train?

A mile on, it began to rain. Large drops plinked on my hat, then slowly gathered into a deluge. Slogging along the muddy lane, I grew more and more dispirited and anxious. When I finally reached the wrought-iron gates of Sythe Grange, I found them hanging open on their hinges. Beyond the gates rose the formidable silhouette of the house, lower floors unaccountably black at such an early hour. The only lights showing were those of the servants' quarters just below the roof.

I had never seen my father's house in such a queer condition. An eel of panic slithered in my gut, propelling me quickly up the gravel path, heart lurching in my chest, boots spraying pebbles. Suddenly, against the sky, I spotted the broken branch of a tree dangling from a shred of bark like a hanged man. I halted, wiped a mingling of rain and sweat from my brow. Father was a martinet when it came to the upkeep of the grounds. Why had the damaged limb not been pruned? Uneasily, I cast my eyes about me and discovered other signs of neglect. At my very feet, weeds blackened by frost stood in the carriage path. They were dead now, but had evidently flourished there in season. Looking up, I spied a jostling mass, milling near the French doors which gave out on to the garden. To escape the rain, Father's deer had huddled close to the walls and were trampling his precious shrubs.

I ran the last hundred yards to the house, threw myself at the door, wielded the knocker like a hammer. No one answered. I called out, banged away insistently. At last, I caught the glimmer of a lamp in a window and, moments later, heard the lock turn. Moorman flung open the door.

Startled, the butler retreated several steps. Clearly my arrival was a shock to him. Giving him not a second to recover his composure, I demanded, "Why do I find the house locked and dark, Moorman? The grounds in such a deplorable state?"

Moorman was shielding his breath with a trembling hand, but I had already caught a whiff of it, ripe with Father's port and cheroots.

"Ah, sir," the old rogue replied, playing for time, "welcome home! But you're soaked clean through! Allow me to remove your coat before you take a chill. Let me light you a good fire, sir!" This was confirmation Moorman was three sheets to the wind. Under no other circumstances would he have volunteered to lay a fire, to perform a housemaid's task, to have so forgotten the dignity of his station.

As levelly as I could, I said, "Answers first. Then a fire."

That sobered him. He drew himself up like a guardsman on parade.

"I sent a telegram. Did you not receive it?"

"Perhaps, sir," he answered shiftily.

"Was it not read?"

"It is not my place to read messages addressed to my master, sir."

"So Father decided no conveyance was to be sent to collect me."

"Mr. Gaunt has been indisposed since September. You will find him not quite himself."

"Father is ill?"

"Mr. Gaunt has descended into an unhappy mental state. The cause of it a cerebral haemorrhage. He no longer has any interest in the mail, in newspapers, in the outside world. He will not permit visitors to be admitted to the house, and he has even gone so far as to ban Dr. Greene from the Grange."

I cut Moorman short. "Where is my father?"

"In the library, sir. It is the spot he finds most congenial these days."

I ordered Moorman to light the way. As we climbed the stairs, my legs trembled so that I had to cling to the banister. Moorman was doing his best to exonerate himself for the state of affairs in which I found Sythe Grange. "It has been a most difficult time, sir. The servants did not receive their six months' pay. This occasioned discontent and some desertions. Two of the maids left for employment in the mills – you can be sure I gave them no characters – and Meadows the footman has left us. The gardeners have downed tools and refuse to work until their wages are paid. Walker was lured away a month ago by Lord Tryan's estate manager. I have come near the end of my wits. The butcher and the grocer extended credit – but Mr. Gaunt has been deaf to all my appeals to settle accounts. The shopkeepers continually threaten not to deliver any more goods. We have been doing our best, sir, living hand to mouth as it were, awaiting the return of yourself and your brother –"

"Addington has not returned. He fell victim to a terrible accident in America. I regret to inform you he is dead." When I spoke these words, I heard them as if I were outside myself, as if they were merely an involuntary rehearsal for what I was to say to Father in a few moments.

Moorman halted at the top of the stairs. "Mr. Addington dead?"

"Yes." There was a catch in my throat. "And nothing learned of Simon." I paused. Moorman peered at me, bewildered by my bluntness. "I think that is enough said for the moment."

"As you wish, sir."

We moved down the corridor and came to the library. Moorman hesitated. "I warn you, sir, you will find your father very changed," he whispered, swung open the door, and ushered me in. The library had always been my favourite room in the house, but now, swathed in shadow, heavy with an awful silence, it came close to completely unnerving me. At the farthest end of the library, before the tall windows overlooking an unkempt lawn, I could discern my father huddled in a chair. With the exception of the lamp which Moorman carried, there was no source of illumination in the room. Father had been seated in utter darkness.

As we approached the old gentleman, Moorman's lamp threw a twitchy shimmer over thousands of volumes which had once been Simon's and my delight. That night, however, those towering shelves induced claustrophobia, made me feel I was venturing into a chasm from which there was no escape, which was relentlessly funnelling me towards judgment.

Our light danced nearer and nearer to the hunched figure, but Father did not react to it; he simply remained inexplicably still in what I presently made out to be a Bath chair. At first I thought him asleep, but then I saw that his whole being was concentrated on the window and the nebulous vision of infinite night it framed. I came round the chair to face him, partially blocking his view, but this did not distract his mesmerized stare, or bring him to acknowledge me.

"Father," I said, "it is Charles." His tongue passed over his lips, but this was his only response. I motioned to Moorman to place the lamp on the desk and quietly requested him to leave us, which he no doubt did gratefully. There was only myself and the ruin in the Bath chair. The damage inflicted by the stroke appeared to have been restricted to the left side of his body. That corner of my father's mouth sagged in a disturbing leer, as if he had been smitten in the midst of a senile, lecherous reverie. The left eyelid dangled helpless as a broken shutter. Crumbs littered the rug which lay over his knees, stains spotted his linen, his hair and whiskers needed trimming. He stank of urine. Moorman would have plenty to answer for tomorrow.

I followed my father's gaze, but all I could see was a window awash in rain, wavering shapes carved by ripples on the pane.

The fingers of his sound hand were scratching at the arm of the chair in great agitation. I laid my hand on his, trying to make him stop, but the icy fingers continued to flex themselves under my palm. "Father," I said, "do you know me?"

I thought I saw him nod, but could not be certain.

"Can you speak, Father? If you can speak, please do."

With a spark of his old irritability, Father snatched his hand from under mine, lifted a finger, and imperiously stabbed it at the rainy, blowing blackness. "Them," he moaned. Then loudly, insistently he cried, "Them! Them!"

I moved closer to the window. Abruptly and inexplicably the rain ceased and the streams coursing down the glass faltered, allowing me to pick out a file of deer trooping back to the copses.

"Do you wish to see your deer?" I asked, stepping behind his chair and preparing to push it nearer the window. As I did, Father recoiled, violently writhing in the chair like a man thrust into the flames of a bonfire.

I bent over his shoulder, down into the sour smell which rose from his unwashed body. "No? You do not wish to be closer to the window?"

"No! No! They watch me!" he cried. The pronoun pierced me like a sword thrust. Suddenly it came to me what Father had been seeking

372

in the ill-defined shapes drawn by the rain. A glimpse of the unseen presences Addington had mentioned to me in Fort Benton. Faceless enemies who circle weakness, lurk in doorways, mutter threats in the night. As real to Father as age, decay, and confinement in a Bath chair.

I backed him away from the window.

There was much for me to do, debts to be paid, servants to hire to fill the places left vacant by those who had left our employ, discipline to be restored among those who had stayed. The next morning, I had Moorman up on the carpet. I roared at him in the best Gaunt style, but did what my father would never have done under the circumstances. I let him keep his job.

Christmas came and went, a dismal holiday. Father was my chief preoccupation. I engaged a nurse and consulted frequently with Dr. Greene about his care. It was evident Father was beyond comprehending anything I could tell him of Simon or Addington. Never once did he remark on the absence of his children; it seemed he recollected nothing of the events which had taken us all to America. He seldom spoke and when he did his utterances were disconnected and nonsensical. Dr. Greene's opinion was that he would never recover his faculties and that more apoplectic attacks would inevitably follow. It was only a matter of time before they would culminate in his demise.

While I was spared informing Father of the fates of his two sons, the inquiries of neighbours about my brothers had to be dealt with. I could speak frankly of Addington's death, but Simon was a different matter. I said nothing beyond that he had not been found. I still nurtured the hope that the discomfort of Simon's existence, the filth, the company of the savage and barbarous Crow might bring him to his senses. It was impossible to believe he could play renegade forever, and I was determined that when he returned to Sythe Grange, to me, there should be no scandal, no blot upon his name.

At every turn, I came upon some reminder of Simon and the joy we once knew together. One day, searching the library for some volume to help me forget for an hour or two my troubles, I chanced upon *Robinson Crusoe*. It had been Simon's favourite book. When I opened it I saw one of my drawings on the margin of a page, a childish attempt at illustration. Simon had, as it were, dictated this sketch to me from the detailed picture he had formed in his mind of Crusoe and Friday, correcting or applauding every stroke of my pencil.

Clenching the book in my hands, I wondered if even then Simon fantasized a life in some barren waste, an existence shared with a primitive incapable of pronouncing judgment on his oddities.

I spent much time with Father, trundling him around the estate in his chair so he could have the benefit of fresh air, calling to his notice the peacefully grazing deer, the rooks' nests in the trees, wheeling him to the stables to pat the horses. Nevertheless, I sensed he was never completely at ease out of doors. His obsession that he was being watched did not abate. But I did discover that the conservatory provided him a measure of contentment. There the two of us would sit, Father fondling the petals of flowers, stroking glossy leaves with an expression of awe on his face so very much like Simon's own reverence for buttons and other commonplace things.

Weeks had passed without any word from Lucy. I consoled myself with the thought that this was to be expected, winter on the frontier would make an unreliable post even more so. But as day succeeded day and still no letter arrived, my unhappiness intensified. Each morning I wrote to her, told her of my struggle to ease Father's mind, of my dejection, of my loneliness in a house which held many servants, but no one in whom I could confide. If only she were here to support me with her common sense, womanly strength, perseverance, goodness, and affection, I said, spilling words onto the page.

January came and went and suspicion began to raise its head. Had Custis Straw withheld the letter I had given him to deliver to her? Had a penniless Lucy, believing herself abandoned by me, decamped from Fort Benton? Perhaps sought Custis Straw's protection?

I spent sleepless nights invoking her presence; her forthright, unabashed laughter; the touch of her capable, strong hands; in recollecting those disturbing, lovely brown eyes which had plumbed me with unladylike directness; in imagining her warm white body curled against mine. Thank God, never again, in all the years which have passed, have I felt the panic of the interminable hours of those nights, a conviction that I was cursed, that everyone I loved – Simon, Lucy – had deserted me.

In the last week of February my worst fears were confirmed. A letter arrived dated the 16th of December. It came from the firm of I. G. Baker and informed me that my journals, sketches, and water-colours had been delivered into their custody by Mrs. Lucy Stoveall to be held with other property of Addington's and mine in their keeping. They awaited my instructions as to the disposal of these articles as well as the balance of monies in my account.

The import of this was clear. Nevertheless, half-crazed, I took the humiliating step of appealing to Aloysius Dooley for any information he had of Lucy, or the reasons behind her actions. The Irishman's answer reached me on the 30th of May. For twenty years I have kept his letter.

April 30, 1872
   Dear Mr. Charles,
Thanks for asking I'm pretty fare. I best get strait to it. Custis and Lucy got married the week before Christmass. The wedding was pretty tolerable. I was best man. They was married by that dam blackgard Justis Daniels seeing as no preest or proper preecher was on hand. The Justis didint want to oblige him but Straw offered him a hundret dollars so Daniels done it. Straw reckont it a vicktory to be married by his old enemy and crowed like a rooster over it. I no this to be a bad shock to you Mr Charles but nyther Lucy nor Custis is to be understood by man nor beast. They are a flitey pare of cuckoos. Rite after New Years they left in tur-rible weather for San Fransisko. Straw sold up all his wurldly goods to take her there on a womans wim. Like as not this is no comfort to you Mr Charles but it ain't our part to try to see into the mind of a man like Custis Straw. He got no bisness getting marryed his time of life I told him so – he just laffed. He is a charackter and I miss his hijinks and capers stirring up trubble

round these parts. I wisht he didint do what he done but the milk is spilt and no use crying over it. Hope you are hale and harty. Nothing more here.

Yours truly,
Aloysius Donald Dooley

Upon receiving this, all sense of dignity crumbled. I hatched desperate, hare-brained schemes. I would go to San Francisco immediately, track down the pair of them, charge Straw with his perfidy. Surely, once apprised of his baseness, Lucy would leave him.

I mulled over my injuries, made feverish plans for a hasty departure. This was exactly what I was doing as I sat one afternoon with Father. Suddenly, his cheek began to twitch as if an insect were scurrying across its withered waste. The teacup dropped from his hand with an alarming clatter, his shoulders sagged, and Father slumped forward onto the Turkey carpet, senseless. All that pride, strength, indomitable will obliterated in an instant, wiped from the earth before I could spring from my chair. I knelt beside him, fumbling for a pulse. There was none. I stood then, and looked down at him, searching the author of my being for something of myself. In a face already turning bloodless and grey, I could detect signs of Addington's reckless bravery, Simon's stubborn resolve, but not a trace of Charles Gaunt. So it fell to the weakest of his children to close his eyes.

It was Father's death, the making of arrangements for his funeral, which brought me to my senses, wrenched me out of the absurdity of my plans. Even if I were to locate Lucy and Straw in San Francisco, a highly doubtful proposition, what would that accomplish except my own degradation? The spurned lover making himself ridiculous. Lucy was indisputably married. As Dooley had said, the milk was spilt, crying over it was pointless.

Still, I bore the mark of my betrayal at the hands of Lucy Stoveall, a martyr's cast widely interpreted as filial piety by the local worthies who assembled for Henry Gaunt's interment. My solemn air was much approved by the respectable. And the dogged melancholy which settled on me in the weeks following the funeral attracted several young ladies eager to proffer sympathy and provide solace of an uplifting sort. Miss Venables came to play Liszt on my piano and commiserate with me on "three family tragedies coming so close in succession." Miss Curtin brought a jar of black currant jam concocted by her own pretty hands and had the effrontery to ask me to pray with her. The flutter in nearby dovecotes was too much to bear. What were these silly young girls compared to Lucy Stoveall? I took wing to Italy.

I left Sythe Grange fully staffed with a firm warning to Moorman that he might expect me back, unannounced, at any moment. There was to be no more repetition of negligence. I was determined that if Simon should return in my absence everything would be trim, tidy, and welcoming.

My last act before setting off was to unlock the room where I had begun Father's mural. It was the first time I had entered it since my return. Everything was as I had left it fourteen months before, candles with blackened wicks anchored in their drippings, worktables spread with sketches and cartoons, the figures of a few servants painted on the walls. I was sure now Father had kept his word to me and had not inspected these precincts while I was gone, nothing seemed to have been disturbed.

I wandered about touching tubes of paint, here and there examining a sketch. My hand fell on the drawing of Addington that I had copied from a photograph. I remembered altering the image, giving my brother a fixed and brutal aspect. How certain I had been then that it was my prerogative to depict Henry Gaunt as an absurd Jove, Addington as a ridiculous Emperor, ruler of nothing but a pack of servants. I had intended to condemn them both to peel from the walls flake by flake of paint, to disintegrate bit by bit. What a puerile, child-like rebellion in the face of the sorrow and suffering of the past months.

I ordered it whitewashed over.

It was high summer when I arrived in Italy. The country was full of blaring sunshine. I felt that everywhere I went my misery was exposed by the ferocious light and was evident to all. The unaffected grace of some woman crossing a sun-burnished piazza, or the hands of a peasant's wife dextrously laying out produce in a market stall would recall the unaffected earthiness of Lucy Stoveall and stab me with longing. A mere glimpse of a Bellini, a Tintoretto, a Raphael, a Titian, a Da Vinci brought home to me my worthlessness as an artist. I strode the cobbled streets of dusty hillside villages at a frantic pace, trying to outdistance my thoughts. I crept into tiny churches never frequented by tourists and, despite my unbelief, prayed to painted saints for Simon's preservation.

I could not mend my heart so I grew a protective shell, a carapace to shield it from further injury. Thus began the ossification of Charles Gaunt. I made myself a solitude. Those querulous British sightseers I encountered in *pensiones* and *trattoria* who wished to share with a countryman complaints about venal guides and foreign food were cut with a sharp tongue, or frozen with my icy manner.

I spent three years in Italy. I began to read poetry again, Simon's favourite poets. Particularly in Blake, I found something I had not earlier recognized. These were not happy years, but I could not imagine my life any more satisfactory for being in another location. Certainly not in Sythe Grange or the house in Grosvenor Square, both filled with memories. But at last, some obscure sense of duty returned me to England, where I divided my time between the estate and London. People found me changed. The distant manner and acid tongue I had cultivated abroad served me as well at home as it had in Italy. They were a defence against friendship, setting the bounds at mere acquaintanceship.

The passing years worked other changes. Gradually, Charles Gaunt became Charlie Gaunt, who, in time, became good old Charlie Gaunt, a man in the middle years of life who was spoken of as already ancient, a queer duck, wealthy enough not to need to paint but odd enough to want to do it. Because once back in England I did resume painting, not with any conviction, but to establish myself as someone a cut above the commonplace. I had a particular terror of the commonplace.

My pain dulled with time, slowly replaced by the numbness which overtakes even the best of actors when they are required to play a role too long. I read and I painted. In my self-despising moments, I would often think of Simon, who had despised no one, not even me, who so richly deserved it. I heard nothing of him. Each year I performed a ritual, wrote to I. G. Baker to inquire whether anything was known of my brother. The reply was always the same. No. Eventually, my letters went unanswered.

So I live in my imagination, that is where my life has taken thirsty root. Perhaps there I can resurrect Simon as I did Lucy. In my mind, I transported her to piazzas brimming with light, set her to stand by the silken sheen of the setting sun on a Venetian lagoon. There she grew finer and finer. Ever more wise, ever more loving. I imagined her in the gowns I had admired on certain women, strolling with a dainty parasol upon her shoulder, speaking Italian like a native. An illusion so cheering I came to write it – poems dedicated to what might have been. In my verse, Lucy still hovers beyond my reach, but there I can gaze upon her as nowhere else. It brings a tiny leap of life, a small stirring in the depths of my dusty heart.

So Straw's note remains hidden away in a drawer, out of sight. I cannot bring myself to acknowledge it. Twenty-five years ago, Custis Straw dealt me a blow I have never forgotten. Even now, it seems I fear to risk another at his hand.

30

Thomas Harkness anxiously surveyed the lobby of the hotel for his quarry. Since Harkness had arrived in London ten days ago, he had written two letters and sent one telegram attempting to negotiate an interview with the poet. At last, Charles Gaunt had reluctantly agreed – if they met in a hotel. He clung to his privacy, would not have his home in Grosvenor Square invaded by a journalist. Now Harkness feared that at the last moment the chary poet had been visited by second thoughts and had reneged on their agreement. But then, near a potted fern, he spied a distinguished-looking individual seated, hair greying at the temples, nose aquiline. There was something about the cut of the suit that struck Harkness as indefinably artistic. Giving his shoulders a nervous hitch, the reporter approached.

"Mr. Gaunt? Mr. Charles Gaunt?"

"Yes."

"Thomas Harkness."

They shook hands and Gaunt gestured to a chair where Harkness settled himself, retrieved a notebook from the satchel he carried, and propped it on his knees. "Thank you for your willingness to give me a few moments of your time, Mr. Gaunt. Our readers do appreciate a glimpse of the larger world that accomplished gentlemen like yourself can provide."

Charles Gaunt smiled in a way that expressed his doubt about his accomplishment or that there was anything he could provide, and offered Harkness a Turkish cigarette from a silver case. The two men lit up and blew savoury smoke at the ceiling. Gaunt said, "I am curious about one thing, Mr. Harkness. Does a newspaper in . . . in *Calgary*, is it? Remind me, that is the place?"

"Yes, yes, Calgary," Harkness confirmed.

"Does a newspaper in Calgary maintain a correspondent in London?"

Harkness bobbed his head sheepishly. "No. My new bride and I are honeymooning in Europe – our first time abroad – and the expenses are rather heavy, so I occasionally send dispatches back home to make something extra. Chiefly to Calgary, but sometimes Montreal or Toronto. Depending on public interest in the topic." Gaunt said nothing, simply tapped his cigarette in the ashtray. Harkness continued. "I believe that our little out-of-the-way place ought to learn something about Charles Gaunt the poet."

"Not the poet. A single volume hardly earns me the right to the title poet."

"But *The Spanish Steps* – several of the most noteworthy critics deem it something special."

Gaunt avoided comment on the taste of critics. "I had not thought *The Spanish Steps* had travelled so far, all the way to Calgary, the North-West Territories, Canada," was all he said. Harkness wondered if Gaunt was intending irony when he stated the address in such detail.

"The fame of the newer authors of the British Isles does take time to reach us. But I correspond regularly with friends in Montreal, fellow graduates of McGill . . ." Harkness's confidence dipped when he realized the name of his alma mater meant nothing to the Englishman. "At any rate," he said, hastening on, "one of my old classmates spoke very highly of your poems – went so far as to send me a copy of *The Spanish Steps*. I found it remarkable."

"This is all very flattering, very gratifying," murmured Gaunt.

To the reporter, Charles Gaunt did not look gratified at all. His gaze wandered about the lobby as he spoke, noting the comings and goings of the hotel's residents, an elderly porter's struggle to wrestle a steamer trunk into submission. "Readers would be very interested to know something of the life of a London man of letters," Harkness said. "Do you move much in literary circles?"

A shadow of a smile appeared on Gaunt's lips. "No, certainly not. I live a very shy, retiring life. An old bachelor's existence."

"Who among the Greats were your friends?"

"Greats?"

"Perhaps you were acquainted with Lord Alfred Tennyson?" Harkness inquired hopefully.

"Alas, our paths never crossed."

"Given the strong link with Italy in your work . . . perhaps you knew Mr. Robert Browning?"

"Regrettably, I never had the pleasure of Mr. Browning's acquaintance."

"Hardy?"

"No. No Hardy. Sorry."

Gaunt registered the reporter's disappointment. Really, he ought to give the poor fellow something. "Those poets I knew, or know – and I caution you my knowledge of them is very slight – were those connected in some way with the world of painting. William Morris, both Rossettis, Dante and Christina –"

The young man could not curb his enthusiasm. "You know Miss Rossetti!"

"A little," Gaunt admitted grudgingly. "She is even more private than myself. Her interests now are chiefly religious."

Gaunt was startled to hear Harkness launch into a recitation from Miss Christina's work. " 'My heart is like a singing bird / Whose nest is in a watered shoot: / My heart is like an apple tree / Whose boughs are bent with thickset fruit.' " The fellow suddenly arrested his declamation. Clearly abashed by how he had spontaneously combusted, he scrambled back to a more suitable, proper journalistic detachment. "Mr. Gaunt, you say you know those poets who have some connection with the world of painting – does that mean you are a connoisseur of fine art? Perhaps a collector?"

Gaunt was amused. "No. Painting has been my profession for the last twenty years – principally portraits."

"A man of many talents, many parts," Harkness said, embarrassed by his ignorance. "And what brought you to poetry, Mr. Gaunt? Caused you to change horses, as it were?"

To the young man, Gaunt's self-possession appeared to waver. The poet won a little time to compose himself by stubbing out his cigarette with great thoroughness. "A difficult question, Mr. Harkness. As clearly you are yourself, I have been a lover of poetry. One day I thought I would try my hand at some verse – only for my own amusement, you know. Later, I showed my poems to a friend who I thought was qualified to give an honest opinion, a gentleman in the publishing trade. Against my better judgment, I was persuaded to allow his firm to print them."

"But what pushed you to write at this time? There must have been some remarkable inspiration that turned you from pictures to words. What was it?"

Gaunt studied Harkness's face. Was that a glint of cunning in the young man's eye? What was he attempting to draw out of him? Steadily, he said, "Let us say I found a subject not amenable to expression in portraiture."

"The woman with 'the hair burnished red' who haunts you in Italy, you mean. Your own Beatrice. Why could she not be painted just as easily as written? Seated under an olive tree, say?"

"Because she is imagined," said Gaunt curtly. "There is no model who might have sat for me. My poems have nothing to do with an existing person."

"But surely –"

Gaunt cut him off. "That is all I have to say on the matter."

Harkness contemplated pressing the question. For the briefest of moments, Charles Gaunt looked like prey pursued. Harkness immediately apologized. "I am sorry. Of course, I should not be so forward."

Gaunt, seeking breathing space, remarked, "Lately, one sees a good deal in the British press of your part of the world. Advertisements for settlers, much talk of boundless opportunity."

"One could say Western Canada changes by the hour," Harkness said with fervour. "Towns and cities arise almost overnight. Why,

Winnipeg, in the province of Manitoba, already has a population of several hundred thousand and is a bustling rail centre. There are those who say that in a decade it shall surpass Chicago. And Calgary, only a short time ago, it was nothing but a whisky post on the Bow River, and now it is the coming place. Hotels, businesses, it boils with activity." He paused. "You might pay us a visit. The better class of citizen is very eager to attend lectures on literary topics. We do not wish to moulder in a cultural wasteland. You should give it your consideration."

Harkness was studying his reaction to the proposal. Being watched so closely disconcerted Gaunt. He decided to surprise the reporter. "I think not," he said. "It would be disappointing for me to see those wild prairies I visited as a young man so changed."

Harkness let the remark pass without comment. All he said was, "Perhaps you shall reconsider. You might find it pleasant to revisit old memories and old acquaintances."

Gaunt found it very strange that the reporter expressed no surprise that he, Gaunt, had once visited the West. It would be best to find out exactly what he knew of his personal history and how he knew it. "No," Charles Gaunt said, "I prefer not to. Besides, who would be left from the old days? Only several months ago I was informed of the death of a former acquaintance. It was a sad moment, to learn of the demise of Jerry Potts. I had not seen him for twenty-five years, but one still feels the loss."

"Consumption and drink did him in, poor fellow," said Harkness. "But perhaps it was for the best. He had outlived his day."

"A rather harsh judgment," said Gaunt, disguising his astonishment that the young man recognized Jerry Potts's name.

"No, no," said Harkness, hurrying to correct himself. "I did not express myself well. I do not mean to dismiss him. I have the greatest sympathy for Mr. Potts and, in fact, regard him as a tragic figure. A man who had a hand in every step that brought the citizens of the North-West to our present state of peace and prosperity but who himself received no share of it. He was, unwittingly, a tool in the destruction of the world he loved."

"I know nothing of his later life," Gaunt confessed.

Harkness did. Eagerly, he related Potts's apparently famous rescue of the North-West Mounted Police force. He described the red column coming to the end of their long march West, the representatives of Canada and the Empire on the verge of starvation, demoralized and on their last legs until Potts led them to food, water, and secured them a safe haven in which to regroup. Shortly after that episode, Potts had guided the police to Fort Whoop-Up, helping to destroy the American liquor trade and perhaps in so doing, saving the North-West from falling into Yankee hands.

Harkness painted a heroic storybook picture. He claimed Potts had been not only a guide to the lawmen, but also their teacher. He spoke of his work as a translator during treaty negotiations between the government of the Dominion of Canada and the Blackfoot. The reporter said that Potts had exerted influence with the Blackfoot nation in all their dealings with the whites, and had actually had a hand in persuading his war-like people not to join forces with the Cree and Métis when they rose up in revolt against the federal government eleven short years ago. Harkness went on to speculate that if an alliance had been forged between the plains tribes, who could say what the outcome of the rebellion would have been, or how much blood would have been expended in an endless, brutal repetition of the American Indian wars?

Gaunt perceived that the young man was riding a private hobby horse; he glowed as he spoke. Very earnestly, Harkness declared the fascination Potts held for him. He saw the half-breed scout as a perfectly equipped factotum for a crucial transition in history. Master of Indian tongues, mental geographer of an unmapped land, Potts also had strong links to white society, all this making him an invaluable bridge between two worlds. Yet once civilization had been established in the wilds, and railroads, banks, and schools had been established, Potts was dispensable. Rather grandiosely, Harkness said, "To me, Potts is a mythical being – avatar of the old *and* the new."

Gaunt felt he had been audience for both a history lesson and a eulogy. Still, he was grateful to know these things. Quietly, he said,

"News of the rebellion did, of course, reach London. It was not perceived as being of great moment. The newspapers here had nothing to say of Jerry Potts, as far as I can recall."

"Well, now that he is dead, Potts has gained a certain fame in our part of the world. We can forget our guilt in using him. Acknowledge a debt which is safely beyond reach of paying."

"You are very philosophical," remarked Gaunt.

Harkness realized he had been commanding the bully pulpit. With a deprecating smile, he tried to excuse himself. "Let us say that the editorials I am not permitted to write must find an outlet. Even if that outlet is an unsuspecting stranger. My views on Potts are informed by my father-in-law's long friendship with him. In latter years they shared many a bottle reviewing their salad days." Harkness saw the austere figure before him smile knowingly. Perhaps a pleasant memory of Potts in his cups had been awakened. "You see, when Potts was alive, I never heard anyone speak of him as if he were anything but a child – or an amusing mascot for the Mounted Police. I find it hypocritical, an insult to his true stature."

"Yes," said Gaunt, "Mr. Potts was a man of remarkable qualities. However, I confess I came to realize the full extent of them only upon reflection, after we parted. He was of great service to me once and I, like your countrymen, did not give him my thanks when I should have."

The conversation fell into a pensive lull. The two men turned their attention to the gentlemen and ladies who were coming down the hotel stairs prepared for a night out on the town. Dinner jackets and splendid gowns were much in evidence.

Gaunt startled Harkness out of his reverie. "There is more to this than a simple interview, Mr. Harkness. Isn't there?" Gaunt saw he had struck home. The reporter grew red and flustered. "I thought so. What is behind this exactly?" He offered another cigarette to Harkness to give the reporter an opportunity to collect himself. Harkness took the cigarette but did not light it, simply flicked it rapidly against the back of his hand.

"You are right," he said at last. "Although I wish to make it clear that I would have been delighted to meet you for no other reason than to express the esteem in which I hold your book."

"Go on," said Gaunt. He suspected the young man had poetry he wished to show him.

"I come as an emissary. With a message."

"A message from whom?"

"Mr. Custis Straw."

Consternation sprang into Gaunt's face, swiftly followed by a look of profound distaste. "I desire no communication with Mr. Straw," he said stiffly.

Having come this far, Harkness would not swerve from his purpose. "There are several things he wished you to know. The first was that he did not betray your trust. Your letter to Lucy Stoveall was delivered. He did his duty by you."

"It is impertinent of you to raise such matters. Even more impertinent of you to seek me out under false pretences," said Gaunt furiously.

"Mr. Gaunt, I have the greatest respect for you. But on balance, I owe my father-in-law even more consideration."

"Father-in-law, is it?" Gaunt began to rise from his chair.

Harkness was not prepared to yield until he had his say. "And Custis Straw wished you to understand he did nothing to come between you and Lucy Stoveall. It was she who proposed marriage to him when she found herself with child."

Charles Gaunt was on his feet, but he was not moving.

Quietly, Harkness said, "Mr. Straw would have preferred to put this in your hands himself. But he died several months ago." Harkness rummaged in his satchel, produced a rectangle wrapped in white tissue paper. "He particularly wished you to have this."

Gaunt accepted the article and dropped back down in his chair like a man exhausted. He removed the paper wrapping, revealing a photograph in a silver frame, a picture of a young woman somehow familiar to him. Then he recollected the daguerreotype Lucy Stoveall had proudly showed him so many years ago. He was looking at her murdered sister, Madge. Yet something about the picture perplexed him, something he could not quite put his finger on. He held it up to Harkness. "Who is this young woman?"

"It is my wife, Marjorie. Her mother named her after a beloved sister."

Charles saw what had thrown him. A puffed-sleeve blouse, high-necked collar. Clothes of very recent fashion.

The reporter said, "Mrs. Straw maintains that Marjorie is the spitting image of her Aunt Madge."

"She is very beautiful," Gaunt softly said, riveted by the image.

"Yes. Of course, I agree."

Gaunt sat with the picture gripped in his hands. Harkness was afraid the metal frame might buckle, the glass crack. "I am sorry to have imposed on you, but Mr. Straw exacted a promise from me in his final days. I could not refuse him. He died of cancer. My father-in-law met a very painful end with the utmost dignity and resolve."

"I am very sorry to hear it," said Gaunt.

"He thought you must know."

"Why now?" said Gaunt, so softly Harkness had to strain to hear him.

"From what I can gather Mr. Straw always felt you should be informed. Mrs. Straw was against it. You see, Marjorie worshipped the ground her father walked on. They were very close. She was the apple of his eye, the light of his life. Mrs. Straw believed it better if certain matters not be aired that might imperil their loving relationship."

"And why has she reversed her stance?"

"She has not. This is entirely Mr. Straw's doing. He was very distressed you did not answer his message. He feared the truth would die with him. One day he took me aside and divulged it. Custis Straw was a man of honour. He believed you had a right to know. Knowing of our plans to honeymoon in England, he said I must meet with you."

"And your wife . . . Marjorie, did he speak to her?"

The reporter shook his head. "No. My father-in-law was a very old-fashioned man. He thought this a matter to be dealt with gentleman to gentleman. He wished me to weigh how you received the news – and go from there."

"And where do we go? From here."

"I see the justice of both Mr. and Mrs. Straw's positions. And my wife took her father's death very hard. I believe now is not the time to confuse her grief with such a revelation. And I have Marjorie's mother to consider. For her the subject remains closed."

"I would like to see my daughter," said Gaunt.

The young man gave no reply for a time. His fingers toyed with the crease of his trousers. At last, he said, "We pay a visit to St. Paul's Cathedral tomorrow. Between one and two o'clock. If you were there, on the steps, watching the visitors come and go, I would have no objection. But I ask you to promise that you shall not reveal yourself or your relationship to my wife."

"I shall do as you wish. I give you my word."

Harkness dropped his eyes to the carpet. "Someday, no doubt, all this will be known to Marjorie. Perhaps her mother will relent in her opposition."

"She is well, Mrs. Straw?"

"Yes, very well, very busy. After a stay in California, Straw established a ranch outside of Calgary at a propitious time, just before the influx of settlers. He prospered selling horses and cattle to them, roamed about the countryside like a vagabond making trades and deals. He had a gift, money seemed to drop in his lap. But it was Mrs. Straw who really built up the ranch, saw to the day-to-day running of it. The neighbours used to say that when it came to work, Custis Straw was not half the man his wife was. She has always led the hired hands by the example of her energy. Each morning, she is first out of bed and each night last into it."

"I am not surprised to hear her character is unchanged. To me, she seemed a force of nature."

"You might pay a visit," said Harkness. "Mr. Straw was relying on your presence to change his wife's mind on the question of Marjorie. It is why he wrote you. He said if she were to see you again things would come right."

Gaunt restlessly turned over the photograph. "If you would excuse me –" he began.

"Of course," said the reporter, leaping to his feet, ready to oblige.

Gaunt glanced up at Harkness. "You write poetry of your own, do you not?"

The young man coloured. "I am discovered. How did you know?"

"Because you demonstrate such zeal for it." Then he added, "And you are young." Gaunt hesitated. "When you asked why I chose to write my heroine rather than to paint her, I did not give you a truthful answer. The reason is this. Never once did I paint a picture prompted by desire or love. The praise my verse has won is not due to its excellence as poetry, but rather because of the genuine passion it so awkwardly expresses. The reviewers have never realized that. Follow your passion, Mr. Harkness, when you put pen to paper."

"I shall remember."

The two men shook hands and parted. Gaunt's gaze followed Thomas Harkness until he had passed through the lobby doors. Then he carefully rewrapped the photograph of his daughter in its paper, tucked it under his arm, and left the hotel. There were hansom cabs waiting for fares outside, but he did not engage one. He wished to walk. Night had fallen while he and Harkness sat in the brilliantly lit lobby. He thought of how Harkness had said Potts was never given his due. Now it appeared that he had never given Custis Straw the credit that was his.

Nostalgic for stars, Charles glanced up to the heavens, but the coal smoke of London and an overcast sky let not so much as a glint of light reach him. He strolled on, trying to remember the prairie stars, their subtle, sidereal motions, the drift of constellations, the little fiery cogs comprising a vast, intricate, indifferent chronometer of earthly life. He had requested to see his daughter, but would he go? He was not certain. But if he chose to, tomorrow he would see a child of his own body climbing the steps of St. Paul's Cathedral.

It made him think of the final poem of his book, the one that had provided him with its title. The one in which the woman who had haunted the other poems – appearing in hillside towns, in vineyards and olive groves, by a shimmering canal in Venice, gliding through the sepia light of a church in Florence, crossing a sun-spattered piazza in Naples – makes a last, visionary appearance in Rome, poised on the top of the Spanish Steps before the Trinita dei Monti, fiery-headed, sloe-eyed. And the poet stands peering up at her, hand shielding his gaze from the piercing sunshine.

It seemed that Custis Straw was urging him to cross over one more time.

Gaunt imagined a different ending for his book. The man at the foot of the stairs takes one step, then a second, then a third. He lacks the courage to look up during his slow ascent, afraid to see that once again she has disappeared. But still, is it not better to make the climb, whatever the outcome? And what if, on gaining the top, he lifts his eyes and finds her still standing there, waiting, despite how very long it has taken him to reach her?

Under a gaslight he paused to check his pocket watch. The hour was later than he thought. Charles Gaunt walked on quickly to his house in Grosvenor Square.

ACKNOWLEDGEMENTS

The works I relied on in researching this novel are too many to list, but I would like to note a number of them. George Bird Grinnell's *Blackfoot Lodge Tales: The Story of a Prairie People* (University of Nebraska Press, 1962); Marjorie Wilkins Campbell's *The Saskatchewan* (Clarke, Irwin & Company, 1982); Walter L. Williams's *The Spirit and the Flesh: Sexual Diversity in American Indian Culture* (Beacon Press, 1992); James M. McPherson's *For Cause and Comrades: Why Men Fought in the Civil War* (Oxford University Press, 1997); Philip S. Long's *Jerry Potts: Scout, Frontiersman and Hero* (Bonanza Books, 1974); Ronald Pearsall's *The Worm in the Bud: The World of Victorian Sexuality* (Penguin Books, 1983); William Gaunt's *The Pre-Raphaelite Tragedy* (Cardinal, 1975); *The Last Great Indian Battle*, Occasional Paper no. 30, Lethbridge Historical Society, 1997. As well, I would like to make mention of two articles, Hugh A. Dempsey's "Jerry Potts: Plainsman" in *Montana: The Magazine of Western History*, Autumn 1967, and Gord Tolton's "Battle on the Belly River" in *True West*, September 2000.

I also wish to acknowledge the generous, unstinting assistance of Richard Shockely, Doran Degenstein, Malcolm Greenshields, and Gord Tolton of the Fort Whoop-Up Interpretive Society, and, above all, my late brother-in-law, Norman Nagel, who taught me so much about Chesterfield House and showed me so many wonderful historical sites.

I thank my editor, Ellen Seligman, and my agent, Dean Cooke, for their invaluable advice and assistance.

New Paperback Editions

"Vanderhaeghe's frontier trilogy . . .
is a rumination on the birth of the nation itself."
– *Toronto Star*

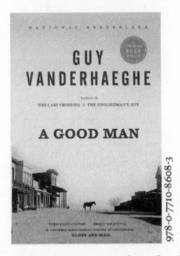

"A towering achievement worthy of celebration."
– *Globe and Mail*

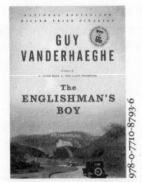

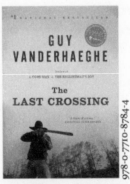

Winner of the Governor
General's Award

A Canada Reads winner

GUY VANDERHAEGHE's most recent highly acclaimed novels are *A Good Man* (2011), *The Last Crossing* (2002), and *The Englishman's Boy* (1996), which have come to be thought of as his frontier trilogy. His previous fiction is *Things As They Are* (1992), *Homesick* (1989), *My Present Age* (1984), *The Trouble With Heroes* (1983), and *Man Descending* (1982). Among the many prizes and honours Vanderhaeghe has received are the Canada Reads award, the Governor General's Award (twice), the Writers' Trust Timothy Findley Award, multiple Saskatchewan Book Awards, and the Harbourfront Festival Prize. He has been a finalist for The Giller Prize, the International IMPAC Dublin Literary Award, and the Regional Commonwealth Writers' Prize. *The Englishman's Boy* appeared on CBC as a television mini-series. Guy Vanderhaeghe lives in Saskatchewan.